THE ORPHAN GIRL

CHRISSIE WALSH

An Aria Book

ALSO BY CHRISSIE WALSH

The Girl from the Mill

The Child from the Ash Pits

The Collier's Wife

First published in the UK in 2021 by Head of Zeus Ltd
This paperback edition first published in 2022 by Head of Zeus Ltd,
part of Bloomsbury Publishing Plc

9 7 5 3 1 2 4 6 8

A CIP catalogue record for this book is available from the British Library.

ISBN (PB): 9781801105606
ISBN (E): 9781801105583

Cover design © Leah Jacobs-Gordon

Head of Zeus
5–8 Hardwick Street
London EC1R 4RG
www.headofzeus.com

Printed and bound by CPI Group (UK) Ltd, Croydon, CR0 4YY

'And ever has it been known that love knows no depth until the hour of separation.'

KAHLIL GIBRAN

For my son, Charles

ONE

KNARESBOROUGH FAIR, WEST YORKSHIRE, 1897

In the half-light of flaming torches and flickering shadows Fennix Simmonite pushed his way through the jostling crowds, his feet unsteady and his head spinning. The hurdy-gurdy's raucous blare drummed in his ears and the sharp tang of frying onions curdled his guts. Still, it had been a good day. At the horse fair he'd flashed a sturdy, piebald cob and sold her at a grand price. Then, he'd celebrated in the beer tent.

Now, as he skirted the whirling cocks and hens, he felt the urgent need to piss. Staggering between the stalls and sideshows then ducking into a dark, narrow passage behind the candyfloss stand, he undid his flies. Hot piss squirted into the grass, its acrid stink vying with the sweet smell of the sticky confectionary. Buttoning up, he sighed his relief. God, but he'd needed that!

Somewhat sobered, he tugged at the points of his leather waistcoat and then, setting his billycock hat square on his head, he blundered back the way he had come – only to meet slap-bang with a woman running towards him. Unbalanced,

Fennix shot out his arms, his hands burrowing under her heavy, woollen cloak. When he tried to release her she held him fast.

'Help me! Help me! Don't let them find me,' she gasped.

Fennix felt the heat from her body against his own and her flowing red locks tickling his cheek. Even though she was distressed he could see she was a beauty, and he knew by the way she spoke and the feel of fine silk under his fingers that she was no village lass or gypsy girl. Quickly, he withdrew his arms.

'Please, take me to safety,' she sobbed, clutching at his waistcoat.

'Why?' he said stupidly. 'What are you afeared of?'

'Two men... trying to find me.'

'What men? Where?'

'They're out there now, searching for me. You mustn't let them take me.'

Her words came out in great gulps and sobs.

Befuddled, but full of Dutch courage and feeling rather heroic, Fennix grasped her by the hand. 'Come along of me; I'll not let them harm ye,' he said boldly, swaggering along the dark passage with the woman stumbling in his wake. As they came to the end of it, Fennix was about to blunder out into the open when she pulled him to an abrupt halt. Peering from behind the candyfloss stand, she scanned the crowd.

'Over there – that's them,' she whispered.

Fennix stuck out his head and looked to where she pointed. He saw two burly fellows, their eyes ranging the fair field but, fortunately, not in their direction. He gripped her hand all the tighter, and trailing her behind him he staggered towards the safety of the sprawling gypsy encampment. The woman hung heavily on his arm, her breathing laboured and her daintily shod feet struggling with the rough terrain as he pulled her along. Every now and then, Fennix risked looking back to make sure they were not being followed.

Soon, they were clear of the bright lights of the fair and hidden in the shadows of the encampment. By now, Fennix was puffing like a grampus and he slowed his pace. The woman gasped her relief, her body sagging against his as they threaded their way through the maze of wagons. Fennix looked back yet again, and certain that they were not being pursued he halted, roughly extricating his arm from the woman's grasp as he turned to face her. Released too suddenly, she wobbled unsteadily as she returned his gaze. Anxious green eyes, wide with fear, questioned Fennix's bleary stare. She saw the doubt in his own and hissed, 'What now?'

Fennix gave a defeated shrug, and then walked a few more paces to a brightly painted vardo with a green bow top. He placed one booted foot on the step, and crooking his finger he beckoned the woman to follow him. Then, giving her what he hoped was a stern look, he placed two fingers of one hand against his lips and with the other hand he opened the vardo's door.

'No noise now,' he whispered. 'Don't waken the child.'

The woman blinked her reply. Hastily, he bundled her inside and closed the door behind him. As she looked about her at the neat and tidy little home, Fennix looked at her. In the dim light of the one lamp he had left burning he could see that he had brought home a fine lady. Dishevelled she may be, he thought, but there was no denying her grand bearing and the cut of her fine cloak; fine, dark blue wool on the outside and its lining a velvet of a paler blue. She saw him looking at her and pulled the cloak closely round her body.

'Sit ye down and rest yourself,' he said, pointing to a narrow cot that was built into the vardo's wall. She sank down on it and Fennix moved further into the wagon. What in hell's name was he to do with her? he wondered, as he lifted two cups from a shelf above the stove and a bottle from the locker beside it. The amber liquid slopped on to the top of the locker as he filled the cups. 'Here,' he said, holding out a cup, 'take a sup of this; t'will calm ye.'

She drank greedily, and having emptied the cup she managed a wan smile.

'Thank you,' she said. Fennix nodded, uncertain what to do next. Before he could order his addled brain, she said, 'I apologise for placing you in this awkward situation but I had no one else to turn to; I could not let those men return me to my husband for fear he might kill me.'

Fennix almost choked on his rum, a shiver running down his spine as he stuttered, 'Husband? Kill ye? Why, what have ye done?' He refilled his cup and drank deeply. What had he let himself in for? What if the men should find her with him? Gorjers didn't take kindly to gypsies; and he had the child to think of.

She swept her mane of red hair back from her face, exposing her slender white neck and the cloak's padded collar. It was embroidered with gold thread and fastened with a gilded clasp. Fennix wondered at the cost of such a cloak.

The woman gave a ragged sigh. 'Some while ago I made a foolish error of judgement, and now I find myself faced with a dreadful predicament; one that will soon be resolved if only I can distance myself from Knaresborough for a short while.' She gazed off into space, lost in her own thoughts as she fingered the gold, heart-shaped locket that nestled in the hollow of her throat.

Fennix felt the urge to lie down, the woman's curious way of talking filling him with confusion and the drink making his head swim. 'Rest ye there awhile,' he mumbled, tottering deeper into the vardo. Slumping into a cot against the end wall, he sank into oblivion.

* * *

Eli Simmonite listened to his only son, a mixture of incredulity and disgust written plain on his leathery face. Fennix had burst into Eli's vardo at first light. The old man was annoyed at being wakened so abruptly and even more annoyed by what he had just heard.

'Where be she now?'

'In the wagon, sleeping.' Fennix hung his head in embarrassment.

Eli swung his feet to the floor and came upright. 'Get rid of her. Now!' he growled, pushing Fennix towards the door. 'Go, ye stupid dinlow; send her packing before they come here looking for her.'

Fennix stumbled out of the wagon. Eli dressed quickly, fuming at what his son had told him. Fennix was foolish, always had been. Why was it that he'd been blessed with only the one son, and he a stupid idiot? He cursed under his breath. The lad was thirty years of age, and yet Eli was still committed to looking out for him. He shook his head, exasperated, but he knew as he did so that it was up to him to him to rectify Fennix's foolishness. Eli loved him.

The woman was awake and drinking coffee when Eli stepped inside Fennix's vardo. He eyed her suspiciously, noting her fine woollen cloak and the elegant way she held the cup. Confidently, she met his gaze and before he could speak she said, 'You wouldn't send a woman to her death, would you?' Although she sounded overly confident there was something about the way she clutched her abdomen that made Eli think she was in pain.

Taken aback by her arrogant tone and forthright manner, Eli was tempted to fling her out of the wagon and send her packing. Instead he spoke to Fennix.

'Get the horses. We're leaving. They'll not find her here if we put a few miles between them and us before we see her off.' He turned to leave. 'I'll let the others know we're going.' He stumped down the steps, his back rigid.

Eli rapped on the side of the vardo alongside his own, and without waiting for an answer he did the same at the next wagon. Clem Boswell stuck his head out over the half-leaf door of the first vardo and seconds later Bosco Doe stepped out of his. They both looked curiously at the head of their clan.

'What is it, Eli?' called Clem.

'Something untoward has come up. Me an' Fennix be leaving now. We'll meet with ye at Appleby.'

Clem and Bosco exchanged puzzled glances. 'But the fair still has two days to run,' said Bosco.

Eli shrugged. 'That be so, but we're leaving now.'

Charity Doe, Bosco's wife, came to her doorway. 'Why now, Eli? We allus travels together, have done as long as I remembers.'

'We'll be with ye at Appleby,' replied Eli, his tone brooking no further questions. He hurried back to his vardo. It angered him to leave his little clan behind. They had travelled the roads together for years, the clan getting smaller year on year. Times were changing; soon there would be no gypsies.

* * *

Milo wakened to the rattle of horse's harness and the jolt of the vardo as his father hitched the horses into the shafts. Where were they going? he wondered.

And why? The fair had still two days to run, and although Dadda had sold the horses Pappa still had lots of pegs and wooden spoons to sell. He turned over in his cot that was tucked into a small space at the far end of the vardo and then he saw the woman. She was standing by the stove, a cup of coffee in her hand, and the long cloak she wore hung loose over a dress the colour of a summer sky.

For one split second Milo wondered if it was his mamma come back from heaven. He had no memory of what his mother had looked like. She had died four years ago giving birth to him, but there had never been a woman in the vardo before now so he could have been forgiven for thinking she was his mother. Milo slipped out of bed.

Quickly, the woman drew her cloak together and smiled at him. 'And who might you be?' she asked.

Milo just stared. Where were Dadda and Pappa? He ran to the door and leapt down the steps, relieved when he saw Fennix and Eli hitching the horses to the vardo. He ran to Fennix, tugging at his sleeve and crying, 'There's a lady...'

'Hush ye now!' hissed Eli, but he had no sooner said it than the woman appeared in the vardo's doorway. 'Get ye back inside,' he urged, glaring at her.

Shocked by the harshness of his request, she did as she was asked. Eli looked round nervously, his heart sinking when he saw that Django Loveridge had spied her. There was no love lost between Eli and Django He was the last person Eli would have trusted to know his business.

'Get a move on,' he yelled to Fennix.

* * *

Mid-afternoon, Eli and Fennix drew their wagons into a lay-by some twelve miles from Knaresborough. The horses were weary, and Eli reckoned that they had put enough distance between themselves and whoever it was the woman feared. He climbed down from the driving seat and beckoned for Fennix to do the same. 'We'll rest here a while and move on again before dusk,' he told him. 'She can make her way to wherever she chooses, but we're taking her no further.'

Fennix nodded dumbly. He scanned the fields on either side of the road, vaguely wondering where the woman would go from here. There were no signs of habitation, save for a barn way off in the distance. 'I'll go and tell her,' he muttered.

Eli unhitched the horses, and seeing the grass in the lay-by was too sparse, he led them to the edge of a nearby field where the grass was long and lush. On his return, he began gathering sticks from the hedgerow to make a fire. He lit his stove only in the depths of winter, although Fennix kept his alight for much of the year for the sake of the child. Eli preferred to cook out in the open, and within no time he had a small fire blazing. Milo joined him, and at his grandfather's instruction he fetched the pan and the coffee pot from inside the vardo. On his return he asked, 'Who's the lady?'

'None o' your business. Forget ye ever seen her,' Eli said, in such a way that Milo knew it was useless to argue. But how can you forget you've seen someone when you have? he wondered as he threw a stick for his grandfather's lurcher to chase.

Inside his vardo, Fennix stared helplessly at the woman as

she pleaded her case. She was lying in the cot under her voluminous cloak and he could not ignore how pale and fraught she looked. A fine sheen of sweat moistened her face, and every now and then she screwed up her features and clamped her lower lip between her teeth. 'You can't abandon me now. Keep me with you for a day or two. Take me to the next big town and then I'll be gone,' she panted, her words coming out in short, sharp gusts.

Sober now, Fennix felt a twinge of irritation. 'Why should we? You're well clear of the men who were after you.' When she gave a loud groan, he turned on his heel and stamped out of the wagon.

'She's not for movin',' he told Eli, and helped himself to coffee from the pot on the fire. 'She's lying in the bed just moanin' an' groanin'.'

'She'll move soon enough when I give her the word.' Eli flipped pancakes on the griddle and watched them browning. Satisfied, he handed one to Milo and then to Fennix, and taking one for himself he went and perched on the shaft of his wagon. His hunger staved, he returned to the fire and was refilling his cup with coffee when a piercing scream from Fennix's vardo had him slopping coffee into the flames. The fire hissed and sputtered. Eli cursed as he tossed aside the pot and cup. Milo let out a yell and jumped to his feet. So did Fennix, and together they followed Eli to the vardo.

Half-in and half-out of the doorway, Eli turned and bawled, 'Keep the boy away; don't let him in!'

Fennix shoved Milo to one side, and telling him to stay outside and not move an inch, he followed Eli inside. 'Christ Almighty,' he cried, slamming the door shut.

The woman's cloak had fallen to the floor, and the skirt of her blue silk dress was up round her shoulders. Her legs were bent at the knees, her heels digging into the pallet and her back arched as her body contorted. A dark wetness stained the sheet under her.

'Help me,' she gasped, her fingers tugging frantically at the laces of her corset.

Eli was the first to move. Fingers fumbling, he undid the laces and dragged the corset from under her. 'Don't just stand there gawping, boy,' grunted Eli, 'get water and towels.'

Fennix blundered over to the stove, grabbed towels from the rail above it and tossed them to Eli. Then he sloshed water from a barrel into a large bowl. Later, he'd throw the bowl away, he told himself. He didn't want that woman's blood contaminating his washing bowl. His guts curdled and sweat blinded him. God, what had he let himself in for by helping her? He'd had no idea she was with child. Cloaked in his own ignorance, he went to assist Eli.

* * *

Milo was throwing soil on the dying fire, just as Pappa had taught him to do, when he heard a baby crying. Startled, he looked round about him but saw nobody. The lurcher heard it too and began to bark. Then Milo realised the cry was coming from inside his vardo. He ran to the door and hammered it with his fists. It stayed closed.

Milo sat on the step, feeling the vardo sway as the people inside moved about. He listened to the baby's pathetic wails and wondered how a baby had got inside his vardo without him knowing. After a while, he hammered on the door again, and this time his dadda opened it. Before his father could stop him Milo shoved past Fennix's legs and shot into the wagon.

The lady was on the bed, a baby with a mop of bright red

hair clutched to her breast. Milo stared. He stuck his thumb between his teeth and bit down hard on it to make sure he wasn't dreaming. Then he waited for someone to explain what was going on. He looked at Eli and then at Fennix. Milo could tell that Pappa was angry, his mouth twisted in a bitter line and his eyes narrow. His dadda looked frightened. The lady looked pale and tired. He crept nearer the bed and peered at the baby. It had a little mouth like a rosebud. He liked that.

'Get ye down there,' Eli said, pointing to Milo's cot. Milo scurried further into the wagon; he didn't like it when Pappa was angry. Then he curled up with his favourite blanket and lay watching and listening.

'What now?' Fennix said, his voice wobbling.

'What now, ye fool? Isn't it enough that ye drink yourself stupid and waste your money without falling in with a woman that has a baby in her belly just waiting to come out. You're a fool, Fennix.' Although Eli kept his voice low, hissing and growling as he berated his son, Milo heard every word.

'I wasn't to know that,' Fennix muttered. 'She begged me to help her, said they'd kill her if they caught her.'

At the word 'kill', Milo shivered. The lady must be bad if somebody wanted to kill her. He wished his dadda had never found her. And what about the baby? His head felt muddled and he just wanted to be back at Knaresborough Fair selling pegs with Pappa or sharing the rides with the Boswell boys.

'That she told ye such should have been enough to bring ye to your senses and leave her be,' Eli continued, shaking his head in despair, 'but no, fool that ye are, ye dragged us all into danger.'

Milo clutched his blanket all the tighter. The lady had put his dadda in danger, but his dadda just stood there with his chin on his chest, looking stupid. The baby began to cry, Eli and Fennix twitching at the sound as though they had forgotten its presence. Milo heard the lady making soothing noises and the baby stopped crying.

'Burn them,' said Eli, 'and then we'll be on our way.' Milo froze. Was Dadda going to burn the lady and the baby? He hid his head under the blanket.

Gingerly, Fennix lifted the bundle of stained sheets and towels beside the door. Eli growled, 'Get a move on. The quicker we're off again, the better. We'll set her and the child down in the next town and be shot of her.' He rubbed his palms together as if to clean them of something nasty and stumped out of the vardo to fetch the horses. Fennix followed him.

Milo's heart leapt; he'd damped the fire. Dadda couldn't burn the baby.

Out in the open, glad to be away from his father's anger and the mewling child, Fennix kicked at the last smouldering embers, stirring them to life. The sun was behind the clouds, rain threatening, and Fennix's spirit diminished along with the heat of the June day. As the rags caught alight he thought about the woman and the baby. Memories of his own dead wife, Milo's mother, flooded back. His beautiful Gloriana had lived but an hour after Milo's birth for all Charity Doe and Sufina Boswell's struggles to save her. It seemed cruel to leave the woman to fend for herself so soon, and the child not an hour old. How would they fare? He stared into the flames, deep in thought.

Inside the vardo, Milo heard the lady moving about but he dared not go and look. Pushing aside his blanket and craning his neck, he peered down the length of the space. The blue cloak lay on the floor. It looked like a pool of dark water.

It moved, swirling upwards until it disappeared from his view.

* * *

Out of Milo's sight, Celia Asquith had shifted the baby from her breast and tucked it carefully between two pillows before reaching down and pulling the cloak onto the bed. With her fingernails she picked at the stitching on the underside of its padded collar. The threads broke easily. Next, she unclasped the chain that held the locket nestled between her breasts. Letting the necklace slip free she weighed it in the palm of her hand, her gaze almost fearful as she stared at it. It was her only valuable possession, and she would need to sell it to support herself and the child in the days ahead. She could not risk the gypsies stealing it or demanding it in payment for their help.

Her fingers trembled as she opened it, tears springing to her eyes as she gazed into the heart-shaped case at the handsome face of her lover. One swift kiss and she clicked the locket shut. Then, prodding and poking with her long middle finger, she inserted the necklace deep inside the collar's padding. It would be safe there. She fell back against the pillow, exhausted, but she could not ignore the urgent need to empty her bladder.

On legs that felt decidedly unsteady Celia climbed out of the cot, swaying woozily as she shook the creases from her dress. It was badly stained and clung damply to her legs. She slipped her feet into her shoes, inwardly cringing at the indignity of having to relieve herself in the bushes outside.

Milo shrank back as she approached him with the baby in her arms. 'Take care of her whilst I go outside,' she said, tucking the baby into the curve of Milo's body and covering them with her cloak. Milo glowed with pleasure and placed a protective arm round the soft, warm bundle. Celia moved towards the vardo's door, peering this way and that before stepping out.

* * *

The rags now ashes, Fennix began to stamp out the fire. He decided he'd stand up to Eli and insist he let the woman stay with them until such time as she could make her own way back to Knaresborough. Lost in thought as to how he might persuade Eli to relent, he was still staring into the dying embers when the woman stepped out of the vardo. Fennix did not see her, but he did hear the thud of hooves and the rattle of a carriage as it clattered to a halt in the lay-by.

He whirled round.

Across the distance, Eli also saw it. He dropped the harness, and shouting at the top of his lungs he began to move as fast as he was able. The dog barked, lunging the length of the rope that tied it to Eli's vardo.

The carriage door flew open. Two burly men armed with cudgels leapt out.

'Where is she? Hand her over,' one of them yelled, bearing down on Fennix.

Fennix froze.

'She's here. I've got her,' shouted the other one, dragging Celia from behind the vardo.

Fennix stared into the face of his aggressor. The cudgel that knocked him senseless split his forehead to the bone, blood pouring into his eyes as he fell.

Eli shouted again and quickened his pace. The men

bundled the woman into the carriage, scrambling in after her as the vehicle moved off.

Eli fell to his knees. Fennix was lying in a pool of blood, his eyes wide open as he stared emptily up into the darkening sky.

* * *

For two long days and longer nights, Eli stayed in the lay-by. He moved Milo and the baby into his own vardo and then placed Fennix's body in his, his heart breaking as he lovingly washed the blood from his son's battered head and laid him out in clean, white sheets. His hands shook, as much out of fear for breaking with tradition as with the devastation he felt. Romany law forbids a family member to touch the body of the deceased. But there were no outsiders to perform the gory task so through eyes blurred with tears, Eli had to do it.

In keeping with his beliefs and his fear of the supernatural, Eli neither washed nor shaved or combed his hair, and although he fed Milo and the baby he ate nothing himself, coffee and brandy the only sustenance that mourning allowed. He was waiting for the Boswells and the Does to meet up with him, as he knew they would. Only then could he bury his son, set fire to Fennix's vardo and burn his possessions.

He fashioned a feeder from a narrow-necked medicine bottle and filled it with a mixture of water and the condensed milk he used in his coffee. The baby's pitiful cries played on his nerves and he felt inept when trying to offer comfort. In his large, gnarled hands her tiny body felt like a bag of broken twigs.

One night, as he rocked her in his arms and paced the

floor, he was reminded of how the lurcher's pups had mewed and whined when they couldn't get close enough to their mother to feel her body heat and breathe in her scent. He wrapped the baby in the blue cloak, the padded collar tucked beneath her tiny chin. Her crying ceased, and she slept through until dawn. After that, he swaddled the little girl in the cloak day and night. Milo watched over her like a cat with kittens.

The Boswells and the Does arrived on the third day, aghast when they found the old man swamped in grief, and with a baby to care for. It was a sorry band of travellers who rode on, not towards Appleby but to Crakehill, the village where Eli had married his wife, Sabina, many years before. To honour his son, Eli was driving the vardo with Fennix's body inside, and Bosco's eldest son, Ansil, drove Eli's. They lined up the vardos alongside the wall of a neglected graveyard.

A dank, grey mist hung over the cluster of cottages and the little church. Clem and Bosco hurried off to find the priest, returning a while later with a roughly made coffin and three strong men bearing spades. Eli led them to a grave and they plunged in their spades, tossing the loamy soil into an ever-increasing pile. Milo stood on the vardo's step and peered over the wall, watching them dig. Inside the vardo the baby whimpered, and in the graveyard the hole grew deeper. A heavy rain broke free from the clouds.

Charity brought Milo a pancake and then took the baby away to feed her. Charity was crying, but Milo couldn't cry even though his throat ached and his chest felt full. He went and stood next to Pappa. Stiff and dry-eyed, Eli was standing under a huge sycamore, oblivious to the raindrops dripping from its branches. Plip, plop, plip, plop, on the crown of

Pappa's bowler hat. Milo couldn't help smiling, and he wondered if the tree was crying for Dadda; his pappa wasn't.

A short time later a wizened priest arrived, his vestments musty with age. Milo watched as Pappa and the other men lifted his father into the long box. The man in the lace-edged dress walked round it, mumbling strange words and waving a pot of sweet-smelling smoke. Then he splashed water over the box and mumbled more words as it was lowered into the hole; the same plot in which Sabina, Eli's wife and Fennix's mother, now rested. Tied to the back of Eli's vardo, the dog howled at the sky.

Eli lifted a handful of soil and tossed it into the hole. Then he bade Milo do the same. As the soil landed with a dull thud, Milo could bear no more. Hating the idea of his father lying under clods of cold, damp earth he ran to the vardo, and flinging himself onto his bed, he let his tears flow.

That none of their larger community was there to mourn his son added to Eli's grief, for it was customary for fellow travellers to come from far and wide when a clan member died. He tottered ahead of the few mourners, doing his best to hold his head high and his back straight as they walked out to the road.

The vardos trundled to the outskirts of the village, and in time-honoured tradition they burned Fennix's vardo. Milo hid his face against Eli's legs as the hungry flames ate his home and all Dadda's possessions. Then they set out for Appleby.

On the journey, Sufina and Charity took turns caring for the baby, but neither did it willingly. The child was bad luck, her presence a constant reminder that her mother had been the cause of Fennix's death. It hurt and angered them that their beloved clan leader seethed with rage or sank into a deep depression every time he looked at her. But nature being what it is, and they being decent women, they tended the child.

Milo was the only one to take any pleasure from her. He soothed her when she cried, tickled her toes and let her pull his hair to make her smile. After a while, her hair as fiery as the setting sun, he called her Rosie.

TWO

WHITLEY, WEST YORKSHIRE, 1901

The horses pulling the vardos clopped off the road and into a copse on the outskirts of Whitley Upper, the lush grass muffling the flinty ring of horseshoes and the scrape of iron-bound wheels as they came to a halt. Three caravans in all, they formed a rough semicircle under the leafy canopy, the piercing rays of the setting sun dappling the canvas bow tops and gleaming on the gaily painted patterns on their front and rear walls. With a green backdrop of ash and oak it resembled a scene from of a Constable painting.

Eli Simmonite rested the reins across his knees, and shifting awkwardly in his seat on the driver's step, he stretched his arms wide to ease his aching bones.

'Get ye down,' he ordered the boy and girl sitting alongside him.

Milo jumped, his supple young limbs, tanned by nine summers, landing him easily on the grass. Spinning on his heel and flicking back the tangle of greasy, black curls that fell over his forehead he reached up to swing four-year-old Rosie down beside him. As soon as her feet touched the ground she scurried up to the front of the shafts, her copper curls a fiery halo caught in the glare of the sun.

'Here we are, Sheba an' Flicker. You can take a nice rest now and eat the lovely grass,' she cried, rubbing the velvety noses of the weary horses. Their heads obligingly drooped as they cropped the grass.

Sceptically, Eli watched as she patted and stroked, jigging from one horse to the other. *That girl leaves neither man nor beast in peace,* he thought. *She always has to be at something, the interfering little hussy.* Shaking his head and sighing heavily, he turned his attention to his grandson.

'Get the cans and away to the Big House for milk, Milo. Let 'em know we're here.' His expression souring, Eli nodded at Rosie and growled, 'And take that one with you.'

Milo leapt up to the driver's step, opened the wagon's door and dodged inside, leaping out seconds later holding enamelled lidded cans in either hand.

'Come on, Rosie, come with me,' he cried, waving the cans aloft.

Rosie's bare brown feet skimmed the grass. Milo handed her one of the spotless containers. Proud to be useful, she hugged the can to her chest.

'Mind ye go to the back door, and watch out for the dogs,' Eli warned, as he gestured towards the house just visible in the parkland across the road from the copse. 'Mind ye ask nicely for the milk and remember to say thank you.'

'I knows how to ask, Pappa,' said Milo, his intelligent dark eyes flashing an understanding belying his years. He called to Rosie who, with the milk can as her partner, was bobbing up and down in a pretty little dance that ended in disaster as she tripped over a tussock of grass.

Eli tsked. 'And take her with you,' he repeated harshly.

Milo strode out, Rosie pumping her short legs to catch up with him and calling, 'Wait for me, Milo.'

Eli kept his rheumy eyes on the children until they vanished from sight and then climbed down from his seat, his knees cracking under him as his feet hit the ground. He shook his head despondently, and the furrows in his weathered face deepened. Today he felt all of his seventy years.

Bosco Doe strolled over to him. 'Shall I send me boys to tell 'em we're here?'

'Already done,' Eli said. 'Milo's away over for milk. He'll tell 'em.'

Bosco looked peeved. His boys had been denied the opportunity to make the all-important announcement, and in order to redress the situation he said, 'Your young'uns are likely to spill it afore it gets this far so I'll send my lads over to make sure we get some.' He gave a cocky nod before walking away.

Frowning, Eli watched him go. Bosco was a braggart, and his sons were bullyboys. And he didn't care for the way Bosco had looked at him. He knew that Bosco was thinking that the time was ripe for Eli to step down so that he could make the decisions. Well, he'd be damned before he let him. Eli unhitched the horses, and thrusting back his shoulders and walking stoutly he led them further into the glade, tethering them to a sturdy ash before going back to the vardo.

Perched on the step, he reached into his pocket for his pipe. He tamped the tobacco and lit it, and as he sucked in its fragrance his annoyance dissipated. *I'm imagining things; Bosco's just being Bosco. I've years left in me yet,* he told himself. *It's that damned red-haired besom has me nerves on edge. Into this and into that, an' the older she gets the more I'm at a loss to know what to do with her. I know what to wi' lads...*

but girls... He sucked feverishly on his pipe, sparks flickering upwards as he tussled with his thoughts.

As though from a greater distance he heard his travelling companions busy making camp, the clanking of pots and the women's chatter and, above it, Clem Boswell's raucous voice. 'Hoy, Eli! I'm just after saying it's a long time since we were this way. Now we're here let's hope there's two good weeks' work for us and the weather stays dry.'

Eli acknowledged Clem's remark with a wave of his pipe, the very thought of picking peas for two weeks punching his gut. He regretted the arrangements that he had made with the farmer last harvest when they were picking his potatoes; but a promise was a promise. He'd avoided pea picking for seven years, but work was scarcer these days and they had to take whatever they could find. Working the fairs brought in some money, but it was the harvesting of fruit and vegetables that kept them solvent throughout the year.

But he was too old to pick peas, he told himself, the work was backbreaking and his fingers were too knobbly to pick fast enough. He dreaded the thought of rising at six the next morning to toil until sundown amongst acres of peas. And whilst he was doing that he had to keep an eye out for that blasted wee girl, stop her wandering off and getting into mischief. He couldn't rely on the women or their daughters to mind her as they often did; they'd be too busy working. Rosie was a hindrance at times like this, but he still felt responsible for her safety.

Clem's wife, Sufina, came waddling across the grass to Eli's vardo. 'Here ye are, Eli, take the dust from your throat; the fire's lit, an' the stew won't be long in coming.' She handed Eli a tin mug filled with steaming coffee. He smiled his thanks, his earlier doubts vanishing. His companions still acknowledged his superiority as head of the clan, even though, right now, he felt akin to useless.

Eli sipped his coffee, the hot enamel mug scalding his lips.

In another mood he might have worked alongside the men and boys gathering sticks for the fire, but this evening he felt no compulsion to do so – and he knew that they would not expect it of him. Instead, he watched Charity and Sufina chop vegetables for the pot, safe in the knowledge that he was still their leader. A warm smile creased his face.

They were on the whole a good bunch, related by blood one way or another. He'd seen their numbers dwindle year on year – seven wagons the last time they'd picked peas here, if he remembered rightly – and in the years before that maybe a dozen or more. The old ways were going, he reflected sadly, the travelling people choosing to settle in the towns where work was plentiful, and the machinery that they were using on the farms these days stealing the jobs that had previously relied on the sweat of a man's labours. His father, and his father before him, had picked peas in this very same place. Musing on this, Eli's thoughts turned to Fennix. It was wrong for his son to be lying in the cold earth when he should be here picking peas alongside him, and his son, Milo. That was the way it should be, and would have been had it not been for the red-haired woman who'd saddled him with her brat of a daughter.

Eli drained his cup, the thought of Rosie making the coffee taste unusually bitter. Such thoughts bothered him. Try as he might, Eli couldn't muster any love for Rosie, whereas his love for Milo felt as natural as breathing and now, thinking about his grandson, his lips curved and his dark, brooding eyes took on a warmer glow.

Milo was a grand lad; far wiser than his father, Fennix,

had ever been, Eli acknowledged. His heart still ached at the loss of his son, and it saddened him to think that the boy had neither father nor mother, but Eli had no qualms about rearing Milo; he considered it a privilege. It was the red-haired chauv and what to do with her that tormented him. She was neither kith nor kin.

* * *

Meanwhile, Milo kept a tight hold of Rosie's hand and a sharp eye out for the dogs as they trotted up a narrow lane that led to the rear of the large, sandstone house that was Whitley Hey. The house looked shabbier than he remembered it, the lawns neglected and the flower beds overgrown.

'Do we know where we're going?' Rosie tugged at Milo's hand.

'Course I do. I picked potatoes here last year an' the year before.'

'Where was I?'

'You were too little. You stayed in the camp with Kizzy Doe to mind you.'

'Where's Kizzy now?'

'She got married and went to live with her husband's family.'

'Is Kizzy the girl who came back to show Charity the baby?'

Milo nodded.

'Where did she get the baby from?'

Milo's forehead puckered as he thought how best to answer Rosie. 'She's its mamma. She grew it herself like Bosco's Labrador grew her pups.'

Rosie's eyes widened. She stopped in her tracks.

'Did my mamma grow me?'

Milo stopped too, quite taken aback by the question. He shuffled his feet, lost for words. Nobody ever talked about Rosie's mamma. Eli forbade it, and although Milo had a vague memory of a red-haired lady giving him Rosie to look after, it was all he had. He also knew that Rosie's blue cloak, the one she couldn't sleep without, had belonged to the lady. As time had gone by, he just assumed that Rosie understood she was like him, a child who had never known its mother and therefore didn't talk about her.

'Stop asking daft questions,' he snapped, and set off walking again.

Rosie ran after him. She wanted answers.

'But did she? Did she grow me in her belly like Bosco's Lab?'

'I suppose so,' Milo mumbled, his ears red with embarrassment. He wished with all his heart that Rosie would just shut up.

'Then where's my mamma now?' she cried, her cheeks blooming with frustration.

Frowning, Milo conjured with his thoughts for several seconds before giving her an answer. 'She's gone to heaven like mine did. The angels took her away.'

Satisfied that he'd found the perfect answer, he relaxed, although deep inside he knew that it was a lie. The red-haired lady had suddenly disappeared, and his father had been killed. He wasn't exactly sure how it had happened, but he knew that Pappa and the clan blamed the lady – and Rosie – for Dadda's death.

'Did your mamma and mine fly up into the sky with the angels?' Rosie asked, waving the milk can aloft and speaking in awed tones.

'Something like that. That's why Pappa has to mind us until we're grown.'

They were almost at the place where the lane turned to the rear of the house.

'I don't need minding, 'cos I'm big enough now, aren't I?' said Rosie, pulling her hand free and skipping ahead only to stop as a pair of black and white collies loped round the corner. 'Come, doggies, come to Rosie,' she cried, tossing the milk can on the grass and trotting towards the dogs.

Heedless of Eli's warning and Milo's anxious cry, she held out her hand invitingly. The dogs raised their hackles and growled, and Rosie would have patted them had not Milo yelled again and Albert Stubbs, the farm manager, appeared behind them. He carried a stout stick. Rosie ran back to Milo.

'You must be one of Eli's lads?' Stubbs said, slapping the stick against his boot.

Rosie gripped Milo's hand tighter. Was he about to whack her like Pappa did whenever she was bad?

'That's right, mister. He said to let you know we were here,' Milo said, retrieving the milk can from the grass.

The man grinned. 'Tell him six o'clock sharp,' he said and, calling the dogs to heel, he strode off down the lane.

Milo was cross. 'Do you not listen? You never pat a dog you don't know,' he said as they rounded the corner and entered the cobbled yard.

Rosie pouted, but her sulks were soon forgotten when she spied a strange iron contraption with a handle in the middle of the yard. 'What's that?' she cried, pulling her hand free and racing across the yard.

'It's a water pump. Leave it be,' Milo snapped, too late to prevent her from vigorously depressing the pump handle. Water gushed onto the cobbles. Rosie laughed, squirting more water before Milo grasped her arm and pulled her towards the house. He rapped on the back door. 'Look biddable, and when they give us the milk remember to say thank you,' he instructed.

Unabashed, Rosie piped, 'Thank you, thank you, thank you,' in a silly voice. Milo gave her a push and a threatening glare.

The back door opened. A young girl in a neat grey dress and crisp white apron and cap stared at them haughtily, her nose rising a full centimetre before she turned and called to someone out of sight: 'The gypsies are here.' Milo narrowed his eyes. Rosie admired the frilly white cap, thinking that she'd like to wear it.

'Right you are, Florrie. Be with you in a minute,' a voice called back.

'Is your name Florrie? Your hat's funny. I'd like one like that.'

The maid's hand flew to her cap as though she thought Rosie might steal it.

Rosie thought she was about to hand it over, and was disappointed when the maid held on to it, saying, 'Mrs Naggs is coming now.'

A buxom woman in a voluminous striped apron bustled to the door, her face wreathed in smiles as she cried, 'Are you here to pick the peas? We've been expecting you.' Clara Naggs gave Milo a closer look. 'Oh, I remember you, though you've grown some since last harvest.' Then she patted Rosie's copper curls. 'My, but you're a pretty one. Is it milk you want?' She reached for the cans.

'Yes, please.' Rosie smiled endearingly at the cook. Milo smiled too, proud that Mrs Naggs had remembered him.

The cans filled, a biscuit to munch and thanks given, Milo

and Rosie trotted out of the yard. Rosie was under strict orders to keep the can upright. Back on the path they saw Bosco's sons, Shadrach and Ansil, coming towards them. Milo groaned. 'Don't let 'em steal our milk,' he warned Rosie as the bullyboys drew nearer. Milo tensed, ready to fight if need be. Rosie pressed her fingers hard on the can's lid in case she had to run.

'Hand it over,' Shadrach ordered, as he drew level with them.

'Aye, save us the bother,' sneered Ansil.

'Fetch your own.' Milo hugged the can to his chest.

'We got biscuits,' Rosie said smugly, and held out a tiny morsel. 'If you ask nicely and remember to say thank you, you might get some.' The Does glanced at one another and then set off running towards the house. Milo burst out laughing.

'Now why didn't I think of that?' He chortled. 'You're as fly as a cuckoo, Rosie Nobody.'

THREE

Pale bands of dawn's yellow light pierced the canopy of ash and oak. They shone down on the bow-topped roof of Eli's vardo and lanced the narrow gaps at either side of the door. Inside the wagon, Eli lay cramped in his bed and listened to the sounds outside: the rattle of pots, the cracking of sticks for the fire, the jingle of harness and Sufina Boswell calling out to Charity Doe. A whiff of wood smoke let him know that the fire was now alight and that soon the coffee would be brewed and the oats boiled.

Slowly and painfully he edged his legs over the side of the bed, scrabbling his feet to find purchase on the floor before sitting upright. Then he sat for a minute or two, willing his aching joints to stop their nagging and his breathing to steady itself. A cold clutch of fear grabbed at his heart. Was it just that he had to go and pick peas making him feel so stiff or was it a sign that he was about to meet his maker? He stretched his arms wide and then got to his feet. No use harbouring such thoughts, he told himself, life had to go on.

'Up with you,' he cried, his voice overly loud in the

enclosed space with Milo and Rosie lying not two feet away from him.

The mound of brightly coloured blankets and a dark blue woollen cloak undulated like a garish sea creature rising to the ocean's surface as a head popped out at either end; one a mass of tangled copper curls and the other black as a raven's wing. Milo grinned, the last vestiges of sleep disappearing instantly as he sprang from the bed. Rosie scowled and burrowed deeper, the cloak's padded collar tucked beneath her chin. She never slept without it.

Eli tutted and then, with surprising alacrity, he yanked the cloak aside. 'Up, ye lazy besom,' he roared, 'and don't try my patience at this hour of day.'

Rosie rolled out of bed, and taking care not to jog elbows or tread on feet in the narrow confines of the wagon, Eli and his wards dressed for the day. Before they left to join the others for a communal breakfast – Eli rarely cooked these days – he made Milo and Rosie make the beds and tidy the living area ready for their return at the end of the day. There was no need to clean out the stove, for Eli only lit it in the depths of winter. Clothes were folded and put away in chests lining the wagon's walls and the dishes and mugs they would use for breakfast taken down from the rack above the little sink.

Out in the copse, the Boswells and the Does sat round the fire. Rosie tucked herself between Doria and Elvira Boswell, Sufina and Clem's daughters. Girls of eleven and nine respectively, they liked to mother Rosie and she revelled in their attention. Milo crouched with the Boswell boys, Rudy and Sep. Rudy was the same age as Milo, and Sep two years younger. When everyone was settled Charity filled their bowls with boiled oats from the huge pot simmering over the fire. Milo and Rosie drank water, but Eli's mug was filled with strong, black coffee. Sufina flipped potato cakes on a griddle and, the porridge eaten, she handed one to each member of the clan. Clem and Eli sat with Bosco and his sons, Shadrach and Ansil. At fifteen and fourteen they considered themselves far too grown-up to sit with the other children.

Bosco got to his feet and clicked his fingers. 'Time we made a move,' he said.

Eli was thinking: *There he goes again, giving the orders.* Even so, Eli stood, as did Clem and the boys. Doria and Elvira took Rosie's hands, leaving Charity and Sufina to clear the breakfast dishes before following on later. Eli strode out manfully but by the time they reached the fields his energy was sapped. Yet, the work had to be done. What with newfangled machinery stealing their livelihood year on year, peas were still one of the crops that had to be picked by hand, and the pay was good.

'Start with this field,' said Albert Stubbs, standing by the gate and waving his stick at row upon row of sprouting peas. To Eli, who had travelled many times to Scarborough and Whitby, the field looked as big as the North Sea. His heart sank. Albert clapped his hand on the large, iron weighing machine and then pointed to the huge pile of sacks next to it. 'Don't be putting any stones or clods of earth in 'em to cheat the weight,' he warned, glaring at the young boys.

'You know us better than that,' growled Eli, annoyed that Albert should think them untrustworthy.

'Aye, I do, Eli. It's just that the last lot o' pickers we had were scallywags.' He slapped Eli's shoulder and beamed. 'It's good to see you back.' Then he turned to the girls. 'Keep your eyes on the pickers, and when you collect a full sack make sure you have an empty one to give 'em. We don't want any time wasting.' Doria and Elvira nodded, but Rosie wasn't listening.

Making a leap for the large iron scales, she landed squarely on the flat plate, crowing delightedly as the scales dipped under her weight and the moving bar at the top clanged noisily. Eli lifted her bodily, dumping her back on the ground and glaring at her. In return, Rosie grinned cheekily. Eli snorted and turned his back.

The men and boys trooped into the field, sacks in hand. Slowly they worked their way down the rows, lifting and shaking the long stalks to loosen the pods. Hands clawed, they stripped the pods from the stalks and when a sack was full they signalled to the girls with a wave of an arm. The girls ran with fresh sacks and then dragged the full ones to the weighing machine for Albert to check their weight. Twice Rosie lost her grip on the sack she was pulling, the peas spilling out behind her. She left them where they lay.

'Pick 'em up,' shouted Albert, his broad, flat face turning purple. Rosie ignored him and took off into the hedge bottom where she found a litter of newly born kittens. Curled up in a writhing ball, they crawled over one another mewing pitifully. Their mother nowhere in sight, Rosie tried feeding them blades of grass and dandelion leaves. When Sufina and Charity arrived with water and bread and apples and cheese, Rosie abandoned the kittens.

Eli sank down by the hedge and balefully watched Rosie stuff her mouth.

***

In an upstairs room overlooking the rear yard of the house, Celeste Threppleton dabbed at a patch of cerulean blue and then flung her paintbrush across the room. 'There, Monsieur Monet! It's ruined,' she cried, grabbing a rag and rubbing furiously at the canvas on her easel. It was late in the afternoon and her painting wasn't going at all well today, the colours refusing to blend and blur in that misty, ethereal quality Monsieur Monet so easily achieved and Celeste so impatiently craved.

Seated in a corner of the room, Hortense Leger calmly adjusted the circular frame on her knee and poked her needle in and out of the canvas stretched across it. Celeste glared at her, the spots on her high cheekbones matching the tapestry's scarlet, cross-shaped stitches.

'It's not fair,' she whined. 'Godfrey says we have to settle our bill before Gadsby's will supply my paints, and now I don't have the right colours, I don't have any decent brushes, and I'm down to my last canvas. How am I meant to create works of art without them?' Hortense remained silent.

It didn't occur to Celeste for one moment that, regardless of paint and brushes, she lacked the necessary skills that had come so naturally to Claude Monet; and Hortense, her cousin, was not about to tell her. She had long since tired of her cousin's obsessions. Snipping scarlet thread from her tapestry, she rethreaded her needle with a length of green. The silence in the studio hung like a shroud.

'Ring-a-ring o' roses, a pocket full of posies.' The bell-like tones floated up from the yard below. Celeste flounced to the open window.

'Titian,' she gasped, 'a Titian cherub in our yard.' She whirled round to face Hortense. 'A portrait! I'll paint a portrait, and Monsieur Monet and his elusive shapes and colours can go hang. Fetch her to me, Hortense. Now!'

Slowly, Hortense set aside her tapestry and approached

the window. A little girl with bright red hair was skipping round and round the water pump in the centre of the yard.

'Come! Come!' Celeste flapped her hands in Hortense's face. 'I want to take a closer look at her.' She dashed from the room, Hortense following at a slower pace, her back rigid and her expression disdainful.

* * *

Down below, Milo waited at the kitchen door for the milk cans to be filled. It was the end of the first week of pea picking and he was looking forward to a well-earned rest, the next day being Sunday. Suddenly, he heard a hubbub coming from the kitchen, a high-pitched voice over-riding that of Clara Naggs, the cook, as it demanded, 'Go and fetch her. Bring her to the drawing room. I want to see her. Now!'

In the next minute, the cook and the maid arrived at the door without the milk cans. Clara looked flustered and the maid bemused.

'Madam wants your sister. You're to bring her inside,' Clara said.

Milo turned. 'Oy, Rosie! Stop that and be quiet.' He turned back to the cook. 'Sorry, Mrs Naggs, I didn't know she was annoying anybody. It won't happen again.'

'Oh, she's not in trouble, lad, it's just that the mistress wants to have a closer look at her.' She gave an embarrassed shrug and whispered, 'She takes these funny notions now and again. It's to do with her being an artist, I suppose.' She didn't add that, personally, she thought her mistress was unhinged, and that she herself objected to having to make do with cheap cuts of meat and being without spices because Madam spent the housekeeping money on paints and canvas.

Rosie skipped up to Milo, keen to hear what the cook was saying, and keener still to get a biscuit.

'Why would the lady want to look at Rosie?' Milo said warily.

Mrs Naggs sighed. 'Like I said, it's summat to do with her painting. Bring her in. It doesn't do to keep Madam waiting.'

Unsure, Milo took Rosie's hand. 'The lady wants to look at you, so you be nice and polite.' Rosie gave him a smile, all teeth.

'Come this way.' Mrs Naggs bustled down the passage to where Hortense waited at the foot of the backstairs. Dressed head to toe in black and with her black hair scraped back from her forehead into a tight chignon, she looked as sleek as a seal.

'You're to come to the drawing room,' she snapped, giving an imperious glare and crooking her finger. She led them upwards to a large hallway, Milo's eyes boggling at the paintings covering the walls, and Rosie wondering if the lady was going to give them biscuits.

Hortense opened the door into a room at the front of the house. A large, long room, its windows looked out onto the garden. The walls were painted a virulent shade of green and a clutter of shabby sofas, chairs and small tables were scattered haphazardly on a faded red and blue carpet. Bureaux either side of a huge fireplace wore a liberal coating of dust, the entire room giving off an air of neglect. Over by the window Celeste was jigging impatiently, her eyes flashing when she saw Rosie.

'Ah, there you are,' she squealed. 'Come closer. Let me look at you.'

Rosie looked at Milo. 'Go on,' he said, giving her a nudge. 'The lady wants to look at you.' He felt uneasy.

'Why?' Rosie scowled. She didn't like the lady's pallid,

bony face or the sharp blue eyes that peered at her from between curtains of tatty, pale hair. She did, however, like the lady's baggy smock. It was splattered with bright colours and reminded her of the clown she had seen at Skipton fair.

Celeste darted forward and clasped Rosie's hand. 'Come, child, let me see you in the light.' She pulled Rosie over to the window turning her this way and that and Rosie, thinking it was a game, soon forgot her misgivings. Complying merrily, she swung to left and right and back again. The strange lady might look ugly but she was fun. Rosie giggled, giving Celeste her best smile.

'Oh wonderful, wonderful, an angelic face surrounded by a halo of fire,' cried Celeste. 'A Titian; a Titian, if ever I saw one.'

Milo thought she must have a cold. He hoped Rosie didn't catch it.

Celeste turned to him. 'I want to paint a portrait of your sister. I want her to come every day and sit for me.'

'She's not my sister,' said Milo, thinking that he was dealing with a madwoman, and unsure what a portrait was.

'Not your sister?' echoed Celeste.

Milo shook his head. 'She's nobody's girl; she don't belong to any of us. Pappa says we just got lumbered with her – but I don't mind.' He winked at Rosie.

For a moment Celeste looked confused. Then, her face brightening she said, 'No matter, just bring her to sit for me.'

'She don't much care for sitting,' Milo said, and then added, 'You'll have to ask Pappa,' but he didn't for one second think that Eli would care what the madwoman did with Rosie. He'd be glad to see the back of her.

'Get Stubbs to arrange it,' Celeste said to Hortense, who

all this time had been standing by the door with a dubious expression on her face.

'Are we going to have biscuits?' Rosie wheedled.

'Oh, you adorable creature,' Celeste gushed. 'Hortense, tell Mrs Naggs to give her biscuits, cake, and whatever she wants,' and then, poking Milo's chest with a long, bony finger she cried, 'And you make sure she comes tomorrow. I can't wait to get started.'

* * *

'Am I going to see the funny lady again?' Rosie delved into the bag of sweet stuff and then crammed a fairy cake into her mouth. She held out the bag to Milo.

'It'll be for Pappa to say,' he replied, extracting a bun.

'What will I do when I'm with the lady? Will we play games?'

'She says she wants you to sit with her.'

Rosie, her cheeks bulging, pulled a face. 'I don't like sitting.'

'I think she wants to paint you when you're sitting still,' Milo said, but he didn't sound too sure.

Rosie's eyes widened. 'What colour will she paint me?' She looked up at Milo, horrified. 'I don't want her to paint me black.'

Milo laughed. 'She's not going to paint you, she's going to paint a picture of you on a piece of paper, you dinlow.'

Rosie looked relieved. 'She can then, if she wants. I don't mind as long as she gives me lots more of these.' She waved the almost empty bag.

* * *

Stubbs came to the campsite later that evening. Eli listened to what he had to say.

'Aye, tell the lady it's fine by me; the besom's no good in the fields so she might as well go and sit in the Big House. An' if she gives your mistress any nonsense tell her she has my permission to skelp her backside.'

FOUR

Milo knocked on the kitchen door at the Big House, and when Florrie answered it he said, 'I've brought her, like the lady said.' He gave Rosie a little shove towards the door and then turned tail and ran to join his grandfather in the pea field.

Florrie led Rosie into the kitchen. 'The boy brung her, Mrs Naggs; shall I go an' tell Miss Hortense?'

Clara waved a floury hand at Rosie. 'Oh, here you are, lovey, just as Madam ordered,' and turning to Florrie she added, 'I didn't think they'd let her come; gypsies are strange folk.' She beckoned to Rosie, saying, 'Come sit yourself here, lovey, an' I'll fix you something to eat. I'll bet you haven't had any breakfast.' Her tone implying that eating at normal times was something gypsies didn't do. Wiping her hands on her apron, Clara went to the stove and spooned a boiled egg from a saucepan. Setting it in a cup on a plate, she sliced off the top.

Rosie had breakfasted on porridge and pancake but she wasn't about to let Mrs Naggs know that. She climbed up on a stool at the table and smiled sweetly.

'Now then, lovey, you tuck into this,' said Mrs Naggs, placing the egg in front of Rosie, along with a spoon and a slice of freshly baked bread, 'and you, Florrie, off you go and let that one upstairs know she's here.' Florrie didn't need Mrs Naggs to tell her she meant Hortense; the young maid had witnessed too many spats between the cook and Madam's companion not to be aware that the disrespect was mutual.

Rosie lifted her spoon and tucked in.

* * *

'Venetian red, I must have Venetian red.'

Celeste's squeals bounced off the studio walls as she scrabbled frantically through the trays on the table. 'Help me, Hortense, help me find it,' she cried, scattering flattened and twisted tubes of paint over the table and down to the floor.

Silently, Hortense handed her a tube of Venetian red. Celeste grasped it and then fiercely embraced Hortense. 'Oh, you are an utter treasure. What would I do without you?' she gushed. Stiff as a ramrod, Hortense waited to be released. As an impoverished first cousin of Celeste's, she paid a high price for the position of companion but it was her only means of having a roof over her head and food in her belly – and being near to Godfrey.

'Go now, and bring her to me the moment she arrives,' cried Celeste, pushing Hortense towards the door. 'I must prepare the canvas.' She darted over to the easel by the window and began smearing white paint onto a canvas, her enthusiastic brushstrokes splattering the floor and windowpanes.

'A Titian, a Titian, I'm going to paint a Titian,' she sang in a tuneless, squeaky voice as she slapped and daubed with gay abandon. Hortense hurried from the studio, as much to escape the ridiculous spectacle as to do as she was asked.

On her way to the backstairs, Hortense met Godfrey Threppleton. He was carrying a sheaf of papers and, as usual, he appeared to be highly distracted. He would have hurried on by had not Hortense blocked his way. He paled and dithered, mumbling, 'Good morning, Hortense, are you well today?'

Hortense's sloe-black eyes gleamed with passion. She closed in on him, purring, 'Well enough, Godfrey. And you? Shall I come to your room later?'

Godfrey trembled, and pathetically flapping the sheaf of papers he muttered, 'I'm rather tied up with Homer and...' Hortense's face twisted and the obsidian slits of her eyes bored into Godfrey's. He quailed visibly, and ducking his head he sidestepped her and hurried along the landing. Outside his study door he paused, and as if to take the heat out of what had just taken place he called back, 'And how is my wife today?'

'As she always is,' Hortense muttered to his departing back. *And I'm the one who has to cater to her whims and entertain her whilst you cocoon yourself in your study writing yet another version of 'The Iliad'*, she thought bitterly. She often wondered if Godfrey did actually write anything at all, for nothing was ever published. Or was such a mighty task as rewriting Homer the perfect excuse for him to avoid dealing with reality?

Hortense had realised a long time ago that Godfrey's need for her was far less than hers for him, and that he had turned to her purely to satisfy his masculine urges; a satisfaction his unstable wife denied him. But still, she lived in hope that once he had succeeded in publishing his writing he would return to London, taking her with him and leaving Celeste behind; after all, a successful writer couldn't afford to be saddled with an insane wife. It made perfect sense to leave her to pursue her crazy notions rather than let her damage his reputation.

What a sad and sorry household we are, she thought, as she stood at the head of the stairs gazing down into the hallway. *Celeste thinks of nobody but herself, Godfrey is obsessed with Homer, and I am caught in a cleft stick. I've nowhere else to go and nothing left to do but wait for him to truly return my affection.* Godfrey no longer loved Celeste; Hortense knew that. There were days when their paths hardly crossed. Apart from the occasional shared evening meal they lived separate lives, Godfrey in his study and Celeste in her studio or in her bedroom: days when Celeste never left her bed, a bed she didn't share with Godfrey.

And is that the only reason he occasionally shares mine, Hortense thought bitterly as she descended the stairs, *or does he care for me enough to take me away from here?* Hortense didn't know, and the longer she waited the more she resented her situation.

* * *

Inside his study, Godfrey flung the sheaf of papers down on his cluttered desk, and flopping into his chair he buried his head in his hands. His palms were moist and his stomach churned. How could he have been so weak and foolish to allow himself to fall into Hortense's clutches? Marry in haste and repent at leisure, he told himself, thinking back to his heady, whirlwind courtship and marriage to Celeste.

How was he to know that his giddy wife would not even

consummate their marriage? That she would become more and more whimsical with each passing year. He had struggled to suppress his sexual urges and was disgusted when he failed, but he was a young man, and he knew that much as he regretted each occasional tryst with Hortense, his resolve would weaken yet again. He picked up his pen and glanced at what he had written earlier. Homer's words taunted him: '*Of all creatures that breathe and move upon the earth, nothing is bred that is weaker than man.*'

* * *

Florrie met Hortense at the top of the backstairs, and by the time they arrived in the kitchen Rosie had scraped the eggshell clean and eaten every crumb of bread.

Hortense frowned. 'I didn't tell you to feed the child, Mrs Naggs.'

'And you didn't tell me not to.' The cook kept her back to Hortense and carried on pouring water into a large pan.

'Come!' Hortense crooked her finger at Rosie. 'Madam is waiting.'

Reluctantly, Rosie followed her. She didn't like this lady. Everything about her was black, her eyes like two sharp chips of coal, her hair as black as night, and the fusty dress that hung about her bony body like the feathers of a dead crow. As they climbed the backstairs Rosie felt her knickers dampening. Milo got mad when she peed herself, but even so, she was sorry he wasn't with her. Squeezing her plump, little thighs together she tottered behind Hortense, into the hallway, up the main staircase and into the studio.

'Come close, let me look at you,' cried Celeste, jigging impatiently on the balls of her feet. Rosie stood her ground.

The crazy lady was wearing the same paint-spattered smock from the day before, her hair in tatters and her cheeks flushed bright pink. Rosie shuffled her feet and let her gaze travel round the room. Strange pictures lined the walls; huge blurry scenes of churches and bridges, bowls of fruit, and people with misshapen arms and legs and heads too big. By the window a big, blank white board was propped on a long-legged stand, and next to it was a small table littered with brushes. What games were they going to play in here? she wondered. Sticking out her bottom lip she rested her puzzled blue-green eyes on Celeste.

Celeste darted across the room, and clasping Rosie's wrist she pulled her over to the big, white board. Then she began turning her this way and that and squealing, 'A Titian! A Titian! A perfect Titian.'

Oh, so we're playing the swinging game again, thought Rosie as she whirled from side to side, but it wasn't as much fun as it had been the day before; and she didn't like the way the lady's spit spattered her cheeks every time she sneezed. At last, Celeste let go of her, her face puckering with disappointment.

'But she won't do,' she whined. 'She's grubby and unkempt. Cherubs are pure and spotless.' Dragging Rosie across the room, and then almost flinging her at Hortense she cried, 'Scrub her until she shines and...' none too gently she lifted a hank of Rosie's hair and let it drop distastefully '...and wash her hair. It must gleam and flow like a river of silk.'

Rosie looked alarmed. Was the funny lady telling the mean one to wash her? Only when she was particularly dirty did Eli charge Sufina or Charity with the task of stripping her and washing away the grime. She looked towards the door, prepared to run.

Too late, Hortense whisked her out of the studio, down a passageway and into a small, tiled room. A long tub stood against the wall and on a dresser there were two large jugs. A thick towel was draped over a wooden stand. Rosie was still planning to make a run for it when Hortense twiddled the silver things at the end of the tub. Water gushed out, and Rosie dropped her guard, surprised.

Hortense swooped, yanking Rosie's rough cotton smock up and over her head. Rosie backed away, her hands clutching her knickers. The mean one wasn't going to see her bare bottom. Hortense was undeterred, Rosie wincing as a sharp slap on her bared legs brought her to heel.

'Stand still and do as you are bid,' said Hortense, her words as sharp as the slap she had just delivered. She saw no reason to be gentle with the child. Her own childhood had been a litany of harsh words and regular beatings. Why should this one be treated differently?

Rosie wanted to run to Milo and Pappa, but then she remembered yesterday's treats and stood scowling as Hortense stripped her bare and lifted her into the tub. Rosie landed on her bottom, flailing about in the tepid water. She had never before been wet all over. Another stinging slap and she allowed Hortense to soap and scrub her. But worse was yet to come.

Hortense filled and then upended a jug, water cascading over Rosie's head. Rosie's scream bounced off the tiled walls. Before she could draw her next breath Hortense began pummelling her head with a bar of soap, Rosie crying out as the lather stung her eyes. She slapped her hands on the water and pumped her legs, water flying in all directions. Hortense dowsed Rosie's head again and again, her eyes glittering with malicious pleasure. Then she hauled her out of the tub and towelled her roughly. Rosie trembled and sobbed. What on earth would happen next?

To her surprise, what followed was pleasant. Hortense sprinkled her with sweet-smelling powder and dusted her down, her long, bony fingers quite gentle. By now, all the fight had gone out of Rosie. Shivering, and feeling extremely vulnerable, Rosie covered her crotch with her hands and allowed Hortense to lead her back to the studio. She couldn't recall a time when she had walked about completely naked, and she didn't like it.

'Come and let me dress you,' cried Celeste, holding out one of her own shifts that she had cut down to size. Eager to cover her nakedness, Rosie let her slip the filmy, white dress over her head, shivering with pleasure at the feel of it. A glance in the long mirror against the wall and she could hardly believe the reflection was hers. She did a little twirl. Things were beginning to look better.

'Oh, the darling, the darling,' Celeste cooed, for Rosie truly looked adorable.

Her clean, plump, sun-kissed limbs glowed, enhancing the beauty of the pretty, white shift, but even so Celeste was not satisfied. She scowled. 'But her hair's too wet; it has to gleam and flow.' The scowl became a manic grin. 'I know what we'll do! We'll play hide-and-seek,' she shrieked.

In and out of rooms on the same floor as the studio they chased and hid and found, Celeste's excited cries rivalling Rosie own, and Rosie's tresses bouncing back to a glorious tangle of gleaming copper with all the dashing about. She was glad she hadn't escaped; this was better than picking peas.

Quite out of breath, they returned to the studio. Up on a table, Rosie lolled against embroidered cushions propped on a soft, blue blanket that Celeste told her was sky. She tried not to fidget as Celeste sketched with swift strokes and then dabbed paint onto the big board that she called 'a canvas'.

'I'm painting your portrait and it's going to be beauoooootiful,' she gushed. Rosie didn't know what a portrait was but she tried to sit still to please the lady as, every now and then, Celeste darted from the easel to pop a sugary titbit into Rosie's mouth.

At last, Celeste set aside her brushes, a scowl on her face. 'My inspiration is quite evading me. I feel quite faint,' she moaned, and then, all agog and in a complete tizzy she cried, 'Let's play hide-and-seek in the garden.'

Rosie leapt off the table.

Hortense, who all the while had been sitting in a corner of the room stitching her tapestry, set it aside and stood. 'The child isn't dressed for outdoors.'

'Pooh!' Celeste scoffed. 'The sun is shining and it's warm as warm. She'll come to no harm.' She paused in her flurry and snapped, 'And don't keep referring to her as the child. She has a name.' Only then did it occur to her that she didn't know what it was. She slapped a hand to her mouth, giggles sputtering through her fingers as she asked, 'What do they call you, child?'

When Rosie answered, Celeste gushed, 'Oh, how sweet. My rosy, red-haired Rosie.' She grabbed Rosie's hands, jigging her round and round and singing in a high, tuneless voice, 'Ring-a-ring o' roses, a pocket full of posies, A-tishoo, A-tishoo...' On the last line she flopped to the floor in an untidy heap, pulling Rosie with her. Rosie giggled and waved her legs in the air and Celeste cried, 'That will be our song. Isn't that fun, Hortense?'

'It's a plague song, but then this latest scheme of yours

and this child may well turn out to be just that. A plague,' Hortense said contemptuously.

Celeste looked about to cry. 'Oh, Hortense, don't be cross with me. I'm having such a jolly time, a Titian to paint and a little playmate to make me happy.' She got to her feet, yanking Rosie up by the hand. 'And happy I will be. Come along, my little Rosie Posie, let us have some fun.' She whisked Rosie out of the studio and they hurtled downstairs. Hortense followed at a slower pace, a look of resignation on her face.

* * *

Milo called to collect Rosie. 'What did you have to do?' he said, taking her hand as they walked across the yard.

'Sit on a table and keep still,' said Rosie.

'All day?' Rosie heard the concern in Milo's voice.

'No, silly! We played hide-and-seek and the mad lady splashed paint on a big, white board. I had to wear a pretty little white frock, and I didn't have my knickers on,' said Rosie, now dressed in her own grubby underwear and smock.

Milo's eyes popped. 'Why?' he asked anxiously.

'I don't know!' piped Rosie, in a voice that suggested he was stupid. 'She gave me cake.'

'Hmm, cake,' Milo said enviously, and stopped feeling sorry for her. He gave her a hard look, about to ask had she still got some hidden in her smock pocket. Instead, he gasped and said, 'You're all cleaned up and your hair's all shiny.'

'That's 'cos the mean one washed me in a big tub. I cried.' Rosie raised big, sad eyes to him, looking for pity.

Milo squeezed her hand. 'Ne'er mind,' he said, 'it makes you look nice. Did you save some cake for me?'

Rosie shook her head. 'But I will when I go again,' she said.

* * *

This then became the pattern of Rosie's days. Sit still; play games; sit still again. Rosie considered that sitting still was a small price to pay for all the fun and games that Celeste concocted, not to mention the supply of sweet treats and not having to go into the fields with all those peas.

FIVE

'We be leaving here day after tomorrow then,' Eli said as they sat round the campfire one week later. Rosie's face fell.

'That be so, there's less than half a field to pick,' Bosco confirmed.

'Can't say I'm not glad to see the back of it,' grunted Eli.

'Is it Appleby we're for next?' said Sufina, circling the group and handing out bowls of thick brown stew.

Milo cheered – he loved the horse fair at Appleby – but Rosie pulled a face. She thought about the long, boring journey on the road, and about Eli who always seemed to be cross with her. Then she thought about Celeste and the sweet treats and the silly games that were so much more fun than having to do the simple chores that Eli insisted on, and then having to suffer the rough edge of his tongue when she did something wrong. Rosie listened to what Pappa was saying and decided she didn't like it.

'Aye, we'll head north for Appleby, stopping off at Ilkley and Skipton for the fairs, then it be back down this way for potato picking,' Eli continued. They all knew this well for they travelled the same routes year on year, but they allowed Eli, as head of the clan, to dictate the when and where of it. That they no longer went to Knaresborough went without saying.

'I don't want to go,' Rosie said, sticking out her bottom lip and scowling at Eli.

'Ye'll go where you're bidden,' growled Eli.

* * *

'The gypsies leave tomorrow.' Standing in the doorway of Celeste's bedroom, Hortense delivered the information with obvious glee. Of all Celeste's foibles, she disapproved of this latest one intensely.

Celeste swung round, half in and half out of her night-dress. 'What! They can't leave. My painting isn't finished.'

Hortense shrugged. 'You'll have to finish it without her.' She didn't add that the portrait of Rosie was a travesty far worse than the discarded Monets.

Celeste tossed her nightdress to the floor. 'Help me dress, and quickly. I have serious business to attend to,' she cried, stamping her feet impatiently. She dressed hastily, screeching childishly, and slapping at Hortense's bent head when she deliberately dawdled over fastening the plackets on a faded blue gown. Out of fashion and frayed at the hem it was proof that just as there was no money to buy paints there was none to refurbish her wardrobe.

Hortense came upright, her hands smoothing the hair that Celeste's sharp fingers had disturbed and then shaking out the creases on her own simple black dress. 'Shall I order your breakfast?' She asked this in the same flat tones she always used, although deep inside she yearned to slap Celeste's petulant face.

'No, no, I must find Godfrey. I have a serious matter to discuss with him.' She hurried from the bedroom, leaving Hortense bitterly surveying the mess she had left behind, and all the while wondering what was so serious that Celeste needed to discuss it with Godfrey.

'Godfrey, darling,' Celeste cried, as she entered his study without knocking.

Startled, Godfrey swung his chair away from his desk and stared at her as though she was some alien creature landed from outer space. He pushed back the hair on his brow with ink-stained fingers, his eyes almost fearful as he waited to hear what she had to say.

Celeste pranced to his side and then plopped onto his knee. Woodenly, he allowed her to stay there. 'Darling,' she gushed, 'I don't wish to disturb you, but I have a favour to ask.' Coquettishly, she twisted a length of her straggly hair round her finger and smiled appealingly.

Utterly bemused, and his mind still struggling with the death of Patroclus and Achilles' revenge, Godfrey let her prattle on, only half-listening.

'I understand the importance of your work—' she gestured to the mound of papers scattered on the desk '—and why it is you have little time to spend with me, so I have thought up a splendid idea to occupy me when I'm not painting and am feeling lonely. I would like a child.'

Godfrey's heart almost stopped. What was this about a child? Did Celeste intend to become a proper wife? Considering her mental state, he didn't wholly welcome the idea. Shocked to the core, he would have tipped her off his knee had she not clung fast. As it was, he sat stunned into silence, his thoughts in turmoil.

'Think of it, my dear: a child in the house to bring us joy, and my work hung in the Academy; a portrait of a Titian-haired cherub that could well be my magnum opus,' Celeste continued, her pale, demonic eyes seeking his, beseechingly. Then, and only then did he realise to whom she was referring.

Godfrey groaned internally, relief combined with concern. It was the brazen, little red-haired minx, the one who made such a racket as she chased the floors above his head. He had complained, but of course Celeste had ignored him.

Made anxious by his silence, Celeste wriggled on his knee. 'So, what do you say?' she urged.

At last Godfrey found his voice. 'You can't take the child into our home and keep her. Her parents wouldn't allow it; and when you tire of her, what then?'

He knew all too well how quickly his whimsical wife shifted her fascinations.

'But she doesn't belong to anyone – the boy said as much,' Celeste cried impatiently. 'She's a gypsy child.' She pressed her fists to her cheeks and pouted, petulantly. 'Gypsies sell their children, so I've heard,' she argued, 'and I'm sure that if we offer them a small sum they'll let me have her.'

This time Godfrey groaned out loud. 'My dear, is it possible it has slipped your mind? *We* don't have any money.'

Godfrey said this wearily. As a second son, and one who had chosen academia rather than business, Godfrey was totally reliant on his older brother, Hildred, for the upkeep of Whitley Hey and all other expenses. That he had, as yet, failed to find a foothold in the publishing world shrouded him in shame. Furthermore, his knees ached under Celeste's weight and he was anxious to return to Troy so that Achilles could kill Hector and ransom his body.

Pushing Celeste off his cramped legs he said, 'If that is what you want, my dear, then go ahead and bargain with them. The offer of a good home should be sufficient without any money having to change hands.' He said it with the certainty that the gypsies would refuse her request.

Celeste squealed her delight, and throwing herself at him she plopped a kiss on the end of his nose and then skittered from the room. Godfrey swung his chair back round and picked up his pen, musing. With a child to entertain his fractious and often hysterical wife, he would be left in peace to conquer Troy.

* * *

'By rights she's not mine to give; she don't belong to me. I just got her by accident, in a manner of speaking. She be the child of a woman who camped along of us then ran off, leaving her behind.'

Eli shuffled his feet uncomfortably on the carpet in the drawing room and twisted his hat in his hands as he gave his sketchy version of how Rosie came to be in his possession. He deliberately didn't mention Fennix's death, and addressed his words to the fireplace rather than to Celeste on the sofa with Rosie, and Hortense and Mrs Naggs standing behind it. He hadn't expected to have an audience of three, and he deliberately avoided meeting their eyes as he spun his words. A sneaky glance at Rosie let him know she was paying him no heed as she fiddled with the cushions on the sofa.

Only when he finished did he cast anxious glances from one face to another, cursing silently at having let Stubbs persuade him to attend Madam in the Big House. But seeing as how he had thought the lady was about to compensate him for allowing Rosie to spend time with her, greed had over-ruled his judgement. Instead, she had made her strange request.

Milo had listened with misgivings and now he hissed, 'No, Pappa, you can't let them have her.' He looked across the room to where Rosie was trying to balance a cushion on the top of her head. He thought: *She looks like an angel dressed in that flimsy, white cotton frock, and she has no idea we are talking about her*.

'Hush, boy,' Celeste snapped.

Rosie giggled and tossed the cushion at him. It fell short. Celeste pushed her off the sofa. 'Mrs Naggs take her for milk and biscuits,' she ordered.

Clara gave Milo a pitying glance as she led Rosie out of the room.

Celeste flapped her hands distractedly. 'So, you have no objection to my keeping her,' she said, fixing Eli with a glare.

Eli looked at Milo for an answer. Milo's eyes were wet with unshed tears.

'No, Pappa; she's our Rosie. You can't give her away.'

Eli's eyes roamed the room. The girl was nothing to him but a dreadful, daily reminder of Fennix's fate, and this strange woman was offering to free him of that and the responsibility of caring for her. How many times had he wished for such a solution? He rubbed his jaw, his palm rasping against the stubble on his chin. These people had money, it was a grand house, and here the girl would be better cared for than on the road.

Celeste, annoyed by Eli's silence, addressed him in a voice brittle with impatience. 'Well, old man, what do you say?' She just wanted the old fool to agree so she could send him and the meddlesome boy on their way.

Eli heaved a sigh and then nodded. 'Aye, take her, for I've no will to rear her.'

Celeste clapped her hands gleefully. 'How fortunate for you then that I am prepared to take her on as my own.' Crowing with delight she jumped up from the couch to shake Eli's hand.

Milo was aghast. He yanked on Eli's coat. 'No, Pappa! No!' he cried, tears streaming down his cheeks. 'She's our Rosie. We can't let her go.'

Eli placed a heavy hand on Milo's shoulder, and gripping it tightly he growled, 'She's not ours, Milo. She's nobody's child.'

* * *

Later that night, as Milo slid his legs under the blankets on his bed in the vardo they didn't collide with Rosie's warm, little body, neither did she turn over and tickle the soles of his feet or tweak his toes. The bed was all his for the first time in more than four years. Rosie was in a bed somewhere in the Big House.

Tears slipped out of the corners of Milo's eyes and he wondered if she also was sleeping alone. He didn't like the thought of her lying in a strange bed, lonely and frightened. Was she missing him as much as he missed her? He listened to Eli's raspy breathing and hated him for what he had done.

* * *

In the Big House, in a soft, wide bed, in a room so large she was afraid of the dark shapes and shadows that loomed in every corner, Rosie cried quiet tears. Why was she sleeping here, she wondered, and why had Shadrach Doe brought her clothes and the blue cloak in a bag to the kitchen door as she was eating her supper? Mrs Naggs had looked very cross. And why had the mean one bundled her into this room and made her undress and get into bed?

Through the gap in the maroon velvet curtains, Rosie watched the stars come out. A big, yellow moon sailed slowly by, as she tried to understand why Milo hadn't come to take her back to the vardo.

SIX

Unceremoniously, Hortense dumped Rosie onto a stool at the end of the kitchen table. 'Give the child her breakfast, Mrs Naggs.' It was the end of Rosie's first week at Whitley Hey, a week filed with fear and confusion as she waited for Milo to come and take her home.

Clara cast a concerned over Rosie who was wearing just her shift and knickers. 'The child's not dressed, Miss Hortense,' she said reprovingly.

'Not necessary,' Hortense replied briskly, and then, her tone with laced with sarcasm she explained, 'We're painting again today and she'll be a cherub as soon as she's fed and washed. I'll be back for her shortly.'

'Painting! Cherubs? Poor little soul,' Clara retorted to Hortense's departing back. She filled a bowl with porridge and then buttered a thick slice of toast. 'There, lovey, get that into you before that one comes back to take you upstairs for more nonsense.' Rosie tucked in; eating was comforting.

'It's a crying shame, that's what it is, using the bairn to

keep her ladyship happy,' Clara grimly told Florrie as she poured Rosie a cup of tea.

'I'd not want her to paint my picture if it's anything like them others she done,' replied Florrie, giving Rosie a pitying glance.

But Rosie paid them no heed; she was too busy scoffing the creamy porridge and biting off chunks of buttery toast. Mrs Naggs's breakfasts were far tastier than Sufina Boswell's thin gruel and burnt oatcakes.

Rosie was downing the last mouthful of her porridge when Hortense returned, and without waiting for her to finish her toast, she pulled Rosie from the stool and whisked her up the backstairs. Balefully, Clara watched them go.

For the past seven days Hortense had been hopeful that Eli, having had second thoughts about the enormity of what he had done, would return filled with regret and beg to reclaim the child. Now, it seemed highly unlikely and as she chivvied Rosie up the stairs to the studio Hortense's resentment deepened with every step she mounted. Silently cursing Celeste, she vented her feelings by giving Rosie's backside a harsh smack. Rosie yelped and climbed faster. Hortense scowled at the little girl's bare chubby legs. Rosie's presence had changed the tenor of the house, and for some strange reason she couldn't quite pinpoint Hortense felt threatened by it. Rosie gambolled along the landing, and as they passed by Godfrey's study door, a glimmer of a smile twitched the corners of Hortense's mouth as she thought fondly of him sitting at his desk, his head bowed over his writing.

* * *

'When am I going home? When is Milo coming to get me?' For the past week, Rosie had asked these questions a dozen times a day, but neither Celeste nor Hortense gave her sensible answers. This morning she repeated them again.

'You are home, darling. You live here now,' trilled Celeste. 'You're my little girl. My little Titian.'

'No, I'm not,' Rosie said sulkily. 'I'm Milo and Pappa's girl.'

'You may as well forget all about them,' Hortense told her harshly. 'He isn't coming back for you. You live here now.'

Rosie's lip wobbled. 'But I don't want to live here. I want to go back to Milo and Pappa.' She stamped her feet and wailed. Hortense snatched at her hand and trailed her to the bathroom. After an awful lot of what Rosie thought was unnecessary washing and brushing, Hortense pulled the cherub dress over her head and trailed her back into the studio.

'Come, little cherub, up on to the table. I'm itching to paint your hair today,' Celeste cooed, waving her paintbrush enticingly. Today she looked particularly deranged, her greasy locks knotted in clumps on the top of her head, and her smock a riot of Venetian red and sky blue smudges.

Rosie screamed. She'd had enough. 'Let me go home,' she roared, her face smudged with snot and tears and as red as her hair.

Celeste screeched back at her, 'I can't paint you when you're looking like that. Cherubs are sweet, not ugly.' She flung the paintbrush across the studio. 'Take her away. I don't want to paint her today.' She ran from the studio wailing.

* * *

On that day, Hortense slapped Rosie's bare bottom so hard that her fingerprints were still visible two days later. Rosie stopped asking to go home, but she didn't forget about Milo.

She missed him dreadfully, and not even the sweet treats could make up for the loss of his company, or her cosy little bed in the vardo and the happy jog-trot of the ponies as they travelled the road in search of new adventures. Now, each day was the same, and what happened next all depended on Celeste's mood.

Up on the table, Rosie lolled amongst the cushions and the flowers, a chubby cherub with porcelain white skin and a waterfall of bright, red hair. The scratchy cushions and the sickly smell of the wilting flowers made her pout disagreeably. 'Oh, darling, that look is just perfect,' Celeste would cry, as she daubed paint on the canvas.

Bored and fretful, Rosie wriggled on her bottom and plucked at the flowers.

Celeste screamed at her to sit still and Rosie sullenly obeyed, afraid of Hortense's sharp fingers and weary of Celeste's screeching. Each day, Hortense sat in the corner of the room, her tapestry on her knee and a disapproving look on her face.

Celeste's mood fluctuated from giddy happiness to screaming tantrums. One moment she was singing a silly little song as she wielded her brush, and the next, letting out a cry of despair, she was darting across the room to deliver a sharp slap or fiddle with Rosie's hair, her dress, or the cushions and flowers, and then back to paint some more.

The painting sessions invariably ended with Celeste tossing her brush across the room and wailing pitifully: 'My muse has left me.' Rosie didn't know what the muse was, but she was always glad when it left.

Yesterday, when the muse had gone, they'd played pick-up-sticks and hide-and-seek indoors, and the day before that they had gone out into the garden, Celeste challenging Rosie to see who could swing the highest. Whatever the game, Rosie soon learned that Celeste had to be the winner. This wasn't difficult considering the difference in their ages and, for the most part, Rosie played along willingly. Anything was preferable to the tedious, fractious hours spent in the studio.

In her innocence, Rosie had thought these two strange women might be her friends, but neither Celeste nor Hortense were kind and loving like Milo. Nor were they fun like he had been, and neither were they big sisters like Doria and Elvira Boswell. Celeste was utterly thoughtless to Rosie's needs and Hortense was joyless. She never offered a kind word or an ounce of comfort when Celeste's tantrums reduced Rosie to tears. Briskly efficient and supremely tidy she didn't play silly games. There was no squirting water when Rosie washed, or chasing after a stocking that had been whipped from her hand whilst she was putting it on. At times like this, Rosie missed Milo more than she could ever have imagined.

And so Rosie adapted to her strange, new world as only a child of tender years can. Milo and Pappa and Sheba and Flicker and the lurcher were gone and she didn't know where or why. She missed the horses and the lurcher. She even missed Eli, but it was Milo she missed most of all. Her only comfort was the old, blue cloak that Eli had put in the bag with her clothes. It smelled of the vardo, and Rosie had draped it over the pillows on her bed so that she could rub her cheek against its soft wool and go to sleep with its padded collar tucked beneath her chin. Then, she dreamed of Milo.

* * *

On the day Celeste declared the portrait finished there were ructions.

Rosie had no idea what the portrait looked like, Celeste having strictly forbidden her to go near the easel, and Rosie knowing better than to risk it. Celeste could be especially angry if she was disobeyed and Rosie, whose natural curiosity often overruled her wisdom, had been too afraid to take even a quick peek. Now, late one afternoon some six weeks after Rosie had arrived at Whitley Hey, she quivered with excitement as Celeste beckoned her enticingly to come over to the easel.

'Come, my sweet Titian cherub, see yourself in all your glory,' she cried, her cheeks flushed with success.

Rosie slid from her perch, her face alight with anticipation as she skipped across the room. Would she look like the beautiful angels and the pretty little girls in Celeste's big, shiny picture books? She drew a deep breath and held it as she stepped round the easel, planting herself squarely in front of it.

A lumpy, fat baby with arms too short and legs and feet that stuck out at awkward angles sprawled across the canvas. Rosie's breath whooshed from her lungs on a long, deep sigh as she peered closer. Did that foot have six toes? She knew hers didn't. She scrutinized the pasty-faced cherub with the overly big, misshapen head. It stared back through lopsided eyes, one much larger than the other and a different shade of blue. Its mouth looked like a mess of squashed strawberries and its nose like a plum. Only the tumble of bright red hair bore any resemblance to how Rosie saw herself.

'That's not me! That's ugly,' she exclaimed. She turned to

face Celeste. 'It's a horrid picture. It's silly and messy, and it's not like the pictures in the book because you can't paint properly; you don't know how.' As she angrily pointed out why she thought the painting was hideous, her foot caught against the leg of the easel. It toppled, the canvas crashing to the floor face down.

Rosie stamped on it.

Celeste's screech rattled the windowpanes. She grabbed at Rosie's hair with one hand and slapped her face with the other. 'You ungrateful, horrible brat,' she screamed. 'I should never have taken you in.' Still holding on to Rosie's hair, she tossed her like a rag doll, Rosie's head spinning as she sagged to her knees.

Hortense threw aside her tapestry, and leaping like a panther she crossed the studio. 'Stop it, you fool!' Hooking her own arms through Celeste's she forced her to break her grip on Rosie's hair. Rosie crawled into a corner, and pressing her hands to her face and peeping through her fingers she watched the women scuffle.

Hands flailing, Celeste clawed at Hortense's head, loosening long, dark strands of hair. Hortense grasped her round the middle, shaking her until her teeth rattled. Celeste kicked Hortense's shins and she lashed out, slapping Celeste's face so forcefully that Celeste reeled backwards and fell to the floor. Then, scrambling to her feet and wailing like a banshee, she fled from the room.

Hortense smiled smugly as she brushed the palms of her hands together.

She turned to face Rosie, her sleek chignon now tangled black curtains, and her usually impassive features twisted in a grim smile as she struggled to catch her breath. Then she walked towards Rosie. Rosie thought of the wicked witch in Florrie's book of fairy stories, and trembled.

Stooping and smiling, Hortense held out her hand. Rosie, heartened by this benevolent gesture allowed Hortense to pull her upright. Saddened to be the cause of Hortense's dishevelment she muttered a tremulous, 'Sorry', and feeling the need to justify her actions, she added, 'but it is a horrid picture.'

'It most certainly is.'

Hortense's emphatic response was accompanied by a malicious chuckle. *Out of the mouths of babes,* she thought wryly. Maybe now her foolish cousin would realise she had no talent for painting.

* * *

Summer days faded to blazing autumn. Out in the garden, Rosie sat under a huge, old chestnut tree, its leaves burnished russet and yellow and its fat, spiky fruits scattered in the grass below. Lonely and bored, Rosie prised open the prickly cases and tweaked out the shiny, brown conkers that nestled in furry, silver beds. Then she popped them back in again, liking the snug fit.

Milo likes conkers, she thought, biting down on her bottom lip to stem the miserable feeling in her chest as she recalled the conker fights they'd had the previous autumn. Dearly wanting to share again the fun they'd had, and wishing for him to come back, soon, she dropped a handful of the little, brown nuts into her apron pocket.

Dawdling across the grass, back to the house, Rosie tugged at the left armhole of her dress. It was too tight, its rough inner seams chafing the tender flesh of her armpit. However, the sleeve on the right was loose and baggy and whenever she wore this dress she felt quite lopsided.

Rosie entered the house by the front door, teetering on her heels in the hallway as she thought about what to do next. From below stairs, the rattle of pots and pans and Mrs Naggs's deep, jolly laugh reached her ears. Mrs Naggs and Florrie might like to see the conkers. Perhaps Florrie would have a conker fight with her. Ready to run down the backstairs and show off her treasures, Rosie's steps faltered as a piercing screech came from up above.

'Rosie! Rosie! Where are you? Come here this instant.' It was Celeste, yelling for her from the landing outside her studio.

Rosie considered pretending she hadn't heard and was tempted to slip down the backstairs to Mrs Naggs and Florrie. They were the only people in the house who were kind to her, and Florrie was fun to play with. But Celeste had ruled that below stairs was for servants only, and not wanting to get Mrs Naggs into trouble for allowing her to be there, Rosie reluctantly mounted the stairs to the studio.

By the time she arrived there, Celeste was back in the studio hacking at a length of maroon velvet on the table in front of her, scraps of it scattered at her feet. To Rosie it looked suspiciously like the curtains from her bedroom. She hovered in the doorway.

'Ah, there you are,' cried Celeste, brandishing a large pair of scissors. Coupled with the manic gleam in her eyes, she made quite a frightening spectacle.

'What are you making?' Rosie asked the question warily.

'I'm fashioning a sweet, little smock with a yoked bodice,' Celeste twittered, as she snipped haphazardly.

Rosie's heart sank into her boots.

Ever since Rosie had given her candid opinion of the 'Titian', Celeste hadn't so much as lifted a paintbrush. Instead, she had thrown herself into designing dresses. In the absence of any money to buy new material, she had refashioned some of her own outlandish garments, and had cut down one of her own dresses to make the one Rosie was now wearing. Rosie detested having to wear it, but she had outgrown the clothes she had brought with her to Whitley Hey.

'When the mothers of little girls see my creations I'll be the talk of the town, a celebrated fashion designer,' Celeste announced, brandishing the scissors again.

Rosie looked at her, nonplussed. What mothers and little girls? None ever came to Whitley Hey, and she never went anywhere to meet any. In the past few months she had been no further than the garden, and Celeste, Godfrey and Hortense rarely journeyed out.

Kicking aside the velvet scraps at her feet Celeste cried, 'Come to me, my Rosie Posie, let me hold this against you.' Rosie plodded over to the table.

Impatiently, she let Celeste pin pieces of maroon velvet over her shoulders and sides. Initially, she had been excited by the prospect of wearing pretty dresses instead of her rough, cotton smocks and woollen jumper, hand-me-downs from Sufina's daughters. Now, she knew what to expect. Sadly, Celeste's dressmaking, like her paintings, was botched and incongruous, leaving Rosie bitterly disappointed.

Twitching irritably and flinching painfully whenever Celeste inserted a pin too enthusiastically, Rosie prayed that Celeste would soon forget about making ugly dresses, just as she had forgotten about painting horrible pictures.

'Charming, perfectly charming,' Celeste gushed, stepping back to view the misshapen velvet pieces that swathed Rosie's figure. She clapped her hands gleefully. 'Now for the sewing,' she trumpeted, carelessly dragging the dress up and over Rosie's head. Pins scratched her bare flesh.

Excused, Rosie ran to her bedroom. Just as she had suspected, only one curtain now draped the window. Down on her knees, she took the conkers from her pocket. Setting the largest one aside to use as the shot, she arranged the others in a triangular pattern on the floorboards. Then, hooking her thumb behind her forefinger she flicked the shot, aiming it at the others just as Milo had taught her to do. The pattern diffracted. But it wasn't fun playing by one's self. Rosie left the conkers where they lay and climbed onto the bed, pulling the blue cloak up and over her head.

* * *

Hortense's shrill voice shattered Rosie's dream. The smell of horses and a campfire and the dark-haired boy with the ready smile were spirited away as she wakened. 'Did you hear me, Rosie? Time for dinner.' As Hortense turned to leave her foot landed on a stray conker.

Whoosh! Like a giant crow flapping its bedraggled wings, her desperately flailing arms grabbed for the doorframe. She caught it and righted herself. Without a backward glance, she stepped stiffly on to the landing. Rosie stuffed the corner of the cloak's collar into her mouth to suppress her giggles. The conkers had proved to be fun after all.

At the head of the stairs Hortense leaned on the banister to regain her composure. Anger burned in her chest. The child had made her look foolish. She'd make sure she paid for it.

* * *

Daylight hours shortened: no more exploring outside in the garden finding something, anything, to escape the house and its strange occupants. Snow fell, the land froze, and inside the house it was as bitterly cold as it was outside. Icy patterns formed on the insides of the windowpanes, Rosie tracing the whorls with her forefinger until they disappeared. Outside, under the eaves, icicles dangled and dripped. Wrapped in her blue cloak, Rosie sat on the windowsill in her bedroom and watched them melt, counting the drips like a condemned man counts the minutes to his execution.

Christmas came and went, uncelebrated, save that on Christmas Day they all ate together in the dark, dusty dining room; a miserable, false affair lightened only by Godfrey's feeble attempts to make Rosie smile. 'Cluck, cluck,' he said waving a chicken leg under her nose. Rosie, unsure whether or not she was allowed to have fun at the dinner table, risked a little giggle.

Godfrey looked across the table at Rosie thinking that whilst she was a pretty child she looked rather forlorn and uncomfortable in her hideous velvet dress, and he was saddened that neither Celeste nor Hortense showed any interest in her. He tried again to bring some cheer to the occasion and this time Celeste joined in, making silly remarks and becoming almost hysterical with excitement.

Hortense's blood boiled. Were they playing happy families? Were they now casting themselves in the role of proud parents entertaining their little daughter? An icy hand clutched Hortense's heart; she had never felt more excluded. 'Must you act like fools whilst we are eating?' she barked, slamming her cutlery onto her plate.

Celeste burst into tears and sulked. For Rosie's sake, Godfrey attempted to recapture the mood by pulling comical face and making silly remarks. Rosie tentatively played along with him, her smiles almost pitying. *Poor Mister Godfrey,* she thought, *he doesn't want to be here any more than I do.*

* * *

On one of those days in the depths of winter, Celeste announced that her fingers were pricked and sore; she would sew no more. Rosie inwardly cheered.

The maroon velvet dress made from her bedroom curtain, itchy with the dust of years, had prompted Celeste to turn a large, white tablecloth into a stiff, scratchy dress, and then one of Godfrey's old jackets into a tunic; each garment more uncomfortable than the last. Rosie yearned for the freedom of the simple smocks she had outgrown as much as she yearned for the company of other children, and one child in particular: Milo.

Like all solitary children, Rosie grew used to spending long, lonely hours lying on her bed imagining she was elsewhere, or pottering aimlessly about the house. Apart from the brief and happy interludes she shared with Mrs Naggs and Florrie at breakfast times and again in the early evening, Rosie's days were tedious. But being ignored brought with it a strange kind of calm, one that was preferable to Celeste's capricious demands. Therefore, she was wary when Celeste declared she would return to painting.

'Come, Rosie,' Celeste squealed one morning as she entered Rosie's bedroom. She was wearing her painting smock, her pale, lank hair tied up in tufts with purple ribbons. Lying on her bed, Rosie pushed aside the conkers that were her imaginary family and blinked her surprise. She hadn't seen Celeste for several days.

'Come along now, Rosie,' Celeste cried, 'I'm going to take up painting again, this time in the footsteps of Van Gogh.' She clasped Rosie's wrist, pulling her up from the bed and out of the room.

Rosie's nerves jangled.

Seated on the floor in the studio, she listlessly leafed through the book that Celeste had told her was filled with Mr Van Gogh's paintings. Turning page after page, Rosie's anxiety faded, and she decided that she liked Mr Van Gogh; he didn't paint pictures of little girls. He painted chairs and big yellow flowers, old men and women, and dark blue and purple nights.

I'm not any of these things, Rosie told herself gleefully. *Celeste can paint without me.* She looked across the studio at her guardian and rolled her eyes.

'A starry night, a starry night,' trilled Celeste, as she slapped purple and blue paint onto a used canvas, obliterating Mr Monet's cathedral and spattering the floor. Singing witlessly and smearing frantically she covered the canvas, leaving no time for the paint to dry before she splodged bright yellow blobs at random onto the dark blue. Rosie thought of little custard pies floating on water. She turned back to the book. According to it, Celeste's picture didn't resemble any of Mr Van Gogh's. Then, turning her attention back to Celeste's painting, she watched the custard pies dribble and dissolve into hairy yellow spiders.

SEVEN

WHITLEY HEY, 1904

Being a small child is scary enough, but being a neglected child makes it even worse. Whitley Hey was a rambling house, and above stairs it often seemed devoid of human habitation – except for Rosie.

Celeste shut herself in her bedroom or her studio, and Hortense in her own room or, on some occasions, in Godfrey's study or his bedroom. Rosie noted their comings and goings and wondered what it was they did behind the closed doors. Left to her own devices she played tea parties with the tiny cups and saucers in the glass-fronted cabinet in the dining room or made a pretend family with the cushions in the drawing room. Out in the garden, she flew back and forth on the swing until she felt sick. She chased birds or went in search of snails to race. For a child just turned seven, these were lonely pursuits.

Only Mrs Naggs was a constant. The purveyor of food and affection, she eased the loneliness that Rosie felt whenever she remembered Milo, and so Rosie frequently sought sanctuary in the kitchen whenever Mrs Naggs was there. She loved the warm, cosy atmosphere, so much calmer and friendlier than the tedious or frantic days above stairs. On most mornings Clara found Rosie waiting in the kitchen when she arrived from her cottage in the village. Clara came in for two hours each morning to make breakfasts and prepare a dinner and then again for an hour or so in the evening to serve it. On Mondays she stayed the whole day to do the washing and ironing. She always made Rosie feel welcome, and along with Florrie, the maid, Rosie learned to bake buns and biscuits.

One day, Rosie was in the kitchen when the farm manager delivered a basket of fresh vegetables to Mrs Naggs. Albert smiled at Rosie, and then lowering his voice he asked the cook, 'How's she getting on then?'

Clara raised her eyes to the ceiling and grimaced. Then, handing Rosie a dish of scraps, she said, 'Go an' give these to the cat.' Rosie trotted out into the yard, the cook and the farm manager watching her from the doorway. She was wearing her maroon velvet curtain dress. Albert didn't know much about little girls' clothing but he did know that when Florrie had been a similar age to Rosie, his daughter had looked winsome in pretty, gingham frocks. He was just about to remark on it, and Clara was just about to tell him about the sorry state of affairs when Rosie bent down to proffer the titbits to the cat.

'God bless us!' cried Clara, and Albert gave a great belly laugh as Rosie's plump, pink, bare bottom came into full view. 'Rosie!' Clara called out. 'Where are your knickers?'

'Ain't got none,' said Rosie, setting down the dish. 'Mine's too small and full of holes.' She went back to feeding the cat.

'It's a disgrace, that's what it is,' Clara said heatedly, 'and just like them upstairs not to notice that the child's grown out of 'em. They don't give a fig. Just look at her. Who in their right mind would dress a little girl like that?'

Albert growled his agreement.

A couple of days later, Albert brought Clara a sack of potatoes, and with it a bag filled with his younger daughters' cast-offs: knickers, petticoats and two dresses, one grey wool and the other green checked gingham.

'Let's be having you, lovey,' Clara said, stripping Rosie of her itchy maroon velvet and putting her into knickers, a petticoat and the green gingham dress.

Rosie, thrilled to be rid of the dress that smelled of dust, twirled giddily, holding out the dress's skirt and crying, 'Do I look like the princess in Florrie's book?' Sad to think that Rosie had no toys or books to amuse her, Florrie had brought the book of fairy tales from home.

Later, when Rosie went upstairs, neither Celeste nor Hortense seemed to notice her change of apparel, and if they did they didn't choose to remark on it.

However, when she later met Godfrey on his way to his study he said, 'My, you look pretty today.' Rosie gave him a smile, all teeth. Mister Godfrey was lovely. He smiled back and bumbled inside, pleased to think that his wife was looking after the child properly.

* * *

It broke Clara's heart to think of the unnatural way Rosie was being reared, and so she made it her business to rectify the matter. She could not afford to clothe her or buy expensive toys, but she found other ways to make the little girl's life less harmful.

'Off you go out into the yard and show Rosie how to skip,'

she said, handing Florrie a length of clothesline. Florrie went willingly, for she too pitied the little girl whose life was devoid of fun, unless she and Mrs Naggs provided it. Out of the pittance she earned, Mrs Naggs bought Rosie a ball. It warmed her heart to hear Rosie's whoop of triumph as she caught it when Florrie threw it.

Rosie loved Clara and Florrie, but they were too busy to entertain her all the time, and when they were not on duty she was bored and lonely. It made Rosie sad to think that the people upstairs had no time for her.

* * *

'I can skip fifty skips,' Rosie announced proudly, one bracing spring day as she burst from the yard into the kitchen, her cheeks ruddy and her eyes shining.

A bright sun shone through the kitchen window, glinting on the copper pans and the brass rail above the stove. A warm, sweet smell pervaded the air and Rosie sniffed appreciatively.

'Well done,' chorused Clara and Florrie. 'And now you've done your skipping you can help us,' said Clara. They were making a rhubarb tart. 'You can make some little ones just for us.'

Carefully, Rosie pressed an upended teacup hard down on the smooth sheet of pastry that Mrs Naggs had rolled out. She did this again and again until a pattern of perfectly shaped rings covered the pastry. Then, with a palette knife she prised the floppy, white circles out one by one and slotted them into a bun tray.

Now for the best bit, she thought, lifting a spoon ready to plop a blob of sweet rhubarb into each little nest, and anticipating licking the spoon when each nest was filled and the lids in place.

A shadow darkened the doorway. 'Come, Rosie, you're wanted in the drawing room,' Hortense ordered, a wicked gleam in her eye.

Rosie's heart sank; she knew what was coming. She scowled and carried on plopping rhubarb. Hortense tutted impatiently.

'Go on, lovey,' Clara said sympathetically, 'you can come back later.'

Trailing her feet, Rosie followed Hortense up to the drawing room.

'Oh, Rosie, my heart's delight, how sweet you are,' cooed Celeste, stroking Rosie hair and arms as though she were a favourite doll. Several weeks had passed since Celeste had last shown any interest in Rosie but now, in a tizzy of twittering and giggling, she scooped her into her arms and crushed her so tightly that Rosie gasped for air. Letting her go, Celeste squealed, 'Come, be my pretty playmate and let's have fun.'

She grasped Rosie's hand with both her own, and like a whirling dervish she forced her into a frenzied dance, cavorting round and round the room, her bony grip hurting Rosie's fingers, and her lunatic screams and yelps so frightening that Rosie was afraid of wetting her knickers. From a chair by the window Hortense looked on, a sneer twisting the thin line of her mouth.

Then, just as Rosie had learned to expect, her manic partner suddenly, and violently, pushed her away. 'Go! Go away! I don't want to dance anymore.' Celeste flopped into a chair like a burst balloon, whining, 'Take her away. I don't want her about me.'

No second bidding needed, Rosie scurried from the room, relieved to escape the close proximity of her guardian who now sat rocking backwards and forwards and making strange little mewing noises like a small, wounded animal. Hortense's lips curved into a malicious smile.

Out in the hallway, Godfrey started with surprise as Rosie burst from the drawing room. This didn't surprise Rosie. Whenever she chanced to meet him as he wandered, ghost-like, from his study to the dining room or out into the garden, he always looked at her with a puzzled expression as if he was trying to recall who she was, and why she was in his house.

Rosie gave him a perky smile. She rather liked poor, sad Godfrey; he made no demands on her. 'Hello, Godfrey,' she said breathlessly.

'Ah, yes. Rosie,' he said, smiling vaguely, 'and how is fair Helen today?' He'd asked her this before whenever their paths crossed, and it had taken Rosie some time to realise that he was enquiring after Celeste. At first, she had wondered at his inability to remember his wife's proper name. Now, it no longer puzzled her.

Godfrey was just as odd as his wife, but in a much nicer way.

She watched him mount the stairs to his study, his inky fingers trailing the banister rail as he ascended. Suddenly, she felt a great aching sorrow for him, and for herself. She clattered down the backstairs to the kitchen.

'Why do I live here in this house with Celeste and Godfrey and Hortense? I know I haven't always, 'cos sometimes I think about Milo and the horses and Pappa,' she cried, running and tugging at Clara's apron.

The knife Clara was using to chop carrots slipped from her fingers and her fleshy face crumpled. She shot Florrie a warning glance. Florrie, her mouth shaped ready for speaking, closed it tight. Rosie had lived with the Threppletons for more than two years now and in that time Florrie had voiced her opinion on the strange situation. 'She's never but once asked why she's here,' she'd said to Clara. 'If anyone took me away from my family I'd want to know why.'

Mrs Naggs pulled Rosie against her apron and stroked the top of her head. 'You live here because Madam wanted a lovely little girl like you,' she said gushingly. Florrie sniggered.

Rosie stepped back and blinked huge, disbelieving eyes up into Clara's face. 'But... but... she doesn't like me... and when we play the games it's like... she's angry and wants to hurt me. Then she sends me away like I'm something nasty.' Rosie hiccupped tearfully.

Clara sighed and pulled her closer. 'That's because she has things on her mind, lovey. It isn't that she doesn't love you,' she lied, patting Rosie's trembling little back to stem her hiccups. She didn't believe a word of what she had just said but she wasn't about to let the child know that. She thought it a disgrace for Celeste to have taken Rosie in and then abandon her just as she abandoned all her other whims and silly notions.

'I don't think she loves me,' Rosie said crossly, 'I don't think she loves anybody. She's nasty to Hortense and I don't think she likes Godfrey either.'

Gently, Clara cupped the little girl's cheeks in slightly damp hands and said, 'Never mind, lovey. You've got me and Florrie. Isn't that right, Florrie?' She waddled across the kitchen to check on the stringy lamb shanks she was roasting in the oven. 'I'll make you a jam sandwich when I've seen to this,' she said, desperate to raise Rosie's spirits, and inwardly seething at her cruel mistress. She vented her temper on the poor-quality meat she had taken from the oven, prodding it savagely with a fork. 'What sort of a woman is it spends money on paints before she'd leave enough to buy a decent cut of meat?' she said to Florrie.

'A mad one?' Florrie mouthed back cheekily.

But Rosie wasn't satisfied. 'Florrie has a mammy and a daddy to love her,' she said plaintively, 'and I know Celeste's not my mammy,' she cried, words tumbling out and tripping off her tongue, 'because she laughed and said "goodness me, no" when I asked her if she was, and Hortense says she isn't my mammy and wouldn't want to be. So where is my mammy?' By now she was screeching, tears streaming down her cheeks.

Clara tossed aside the oven cloth and plodded over to Rosie, her plump cheeks crumpling. 'Oh, my little love!' she wailed, scooping Rosie into her arms and cushioning her against her ample bosom. Rosie stopped screeching. With a heavy heart Clara set her down, and after wiping Rosie's cheeks with the corner of her apron she sat down in the rocker by the stove and pulled her up onto her knee. Then, rocking her like a baby and murmuring soothing words she held her until she felt Rosie's quivering body slacken and grow still. 'I can't find you a mammy, Rosie, but what I can do is love you like a granny, and that I will do so God help me,' she said, her voice cracking as she swallowed her own tears.

Rosie heard the sincerity in Clara's voice. She gave a wan smile, nodding her head solemnly as she gazed adoringly into the cook's face. 'I'd like a granny,' she whispered, her eyes like delphiniums washed with newly fallen rain.

* * *

Despite Mrs Naggs telling Rosie that she loved her, it wasn't enough to make her feel happy and wanted all the time. When the cook wasn't on duty the hours in between dragged, the days interminably long, and with no one else taking notice of her Rosie was frequently bored and angry. Today, she felt particularly cross. Even nibbling on the delicious scone that Mrs Naggs had just given her failed to make her feel happy.

'There, that's me done for now.' The cook untied her apron and went into the scullery, reappearing with her coat on and her basket over her arm. Clara was going home to care for her parents who were very old, and her husband who was very sick and couldn't be left alone for too long. Rosie knew this because she had heard Clara telling Florrie about them on numerous occasions. Florrie had already gone back to the farm to help her mother make jam and now, to Rosie, it seemed as though everybody but her had people to go to and things to do. She caught Clara's eye, giving her a long, soulful look. It tugged at Clara's kind heart.

'Play outside till I get back, Rosie. It's a lovely, sunny day even though there's a nip in the air. I'll be back in an hour or two to see to the dinner,' she said, smiling fondly at the lonely little girl. She stooped to give Rosie a peck on the cheek, wincing as acid bile burnt her chest. She suffered dreadfully with indigestion and no wonder, she thought, coming upright. Working for such ingrates as those demons upstairs was enough to curdle anybody's innards, and it wasn't right that they should make her feel guilty at leaving Rosie on her own. *After all,* she told herself, rubbing at her burning chest as she stepped outside, *much as I care for her she's not my responsibility. I've more than I can handle what with dashing between home and this place to earn a few shillings.*

Hurrying over the cobbles, Clara salved her conscience by

reminding herself that she had once offered to take the child with her when she went home at midday, but Hortense had pooh-poohed the idea as utter nonsense. 'You're employed to cook, Mrs Naggs, not entertain children. Rosie is not your responsibility,' she had snapped. Clara had tartly agreed, but it didn't prevent her from feeling neglectful where Rosie was concerned.

Rosie stood at the doorway, her mouth drooping at the corners as she sulkily watched the stout back in the brown tweed coat disappear. She didn't want to go upstairs. Celeste might involve her in one of her nasty games, and she didn't feel like playing in the yard with her ball, so what was she meant to do?

Feeling more than a little rebellious she ran out of the yard and into the lane. Mrs Naggs was nowhere in sight. Rosie kept on running until she came to a stand of beech and oak trees, and beyond them a dense thicket. She had never before been this far down the lane. Leaving the path, she trotted into the copse.

It was gloomy under the trees, and Rosie shivered and came to a stop. Then she heard a rushing, babbling sound. Curious, she ran to a gap in the thicket. A fast-flowing stream snaked its way between the copse and the fields, and Rosie hurried forward to stand on its bank. Clear, sparkling water swirled round smooth grey boulders and bubbled in the hollows, and in a pool close to her feet was a little shoal of minnows. They evoked a distant memory of Milo catching little fishes in a pond close to a campsite and then giving them to her in a jam jar.

Rosie glanced round, looking for something to put the fish in. Spying an old tin can in the reeds she lifted it and went back to the water's edge. She crouched, her shoes sinking in the soft mud and the hem of her dress trailing in the water as she leaned over. Startled, the minnows darted this way and that before swimming off downstream like tiny silver arrows. Without thinking, Rosie stepped into the stream to follow them. Her shoe soles slipped on the mossy stones.

Whoosh! Down she went, into a deep pool, the fast-flowing current carrying her with it. She let out a scream, thrashing the water and desperately trying to reach for a branch or a boulder to cling to.

* * *

At the same time as Rosie had walked down the lane, Hortense was walking back from Ha'penny Wood. She was in a foul mood. Godfrey had promised to meet her there, as he had done in the past, but today he had failed to turn up. *Damn the man, and my lunatic cousin and that blasted child,* she silently cursed, as she left the field and entered the lane. How much longer did she have to tolerate her miserable life before she and Godfrey made their escape? Her heart and her footsteps heavy, she trudged up the lane reflecting on how cruel the world was.

Being born out of wedlock was a curse in itself, and to be fathered by a soldier who had inconveniently died of typhus only weeks after her conception hadn't helped matters. Worse still was being be housed out of kinship and pity by her mother Claudette's younger sister, Marie. Beholden to Marie for food and shelter, their lives had been one long round of servitude and Hortense had detested it. Claudette had been a drudge, and the young Hortense had been expected to wait hand and foot on the needs of Marie's daughter, Celeste. Barely three years older than Celeste, Hortense abhorred the lowly position into which she had been thrust. But worst of all was still being at Celeste's beck and call in order to stay close to the man she loved.

Hortense glanced back over her shoulder to see if Godfrey had kept their tryst after all. There was no sign of him. For a moment she allowed her thoughts to linger on a young Godfrey Threppleton, the aspiring young writer new to the literary circles that she attended as companion to her cousin, Celeste. How thrilled she had been when Godfrey showed an interest in her, and how desolate she had felt when life had played her foul yet again.

Out of the blue, Godfrey had married Celeste.

The memory was so painful it caused her to stumble over a tussock of long grass. She kicked at it savagely, her heart crying out for him. By now she had reached the bridge over the stream and pausing to gaze into the fast-flowing water she wondered how long it would take for Godfrey to realise that she was the woman he should have married. Then they would go away together, leaving Celeste to her foolish whims. This thought brought Rosie to mind. Hortense scowled. Just lately, Godfrey was showing an interest the child, asking after her wellbeing or engaging her in conversation whenever their paths crossed. Did he now feel responsible for Rosie? Hortense's thoughts turned black. Was that gypsy brat about to thwart her plans? Cloaked in bitterness, she crossed the bridge and walked towards the copse.

A high-pitched wailing, carried on the breeze, reached her ears, and instinctively she hurried to where it came from. As she drew nearer the copse the screams grew louder and when she arrived beside the stream she saw Rosie in the water, clutching at reeds that broke loose in her grasp. Rosie saw her and cried out, her hopes of being rescued fading as she saw the look in Hortense's black, staring eyes and the cruel twist of her mouth. Hortense stood on the bank and watched her flail. Rosie screamed again.

How convenient, Hortense thought. *Let the child go, a terrible accident, no one to blame but the child herself and one less nuisance to deal with.* No sooner had these black thoughts crossed her mind than she heard a different shout. It was Albert, coming in from the field with his dogs. Leaping the fence, he was in the stream and then out of it with Rosie in his arms, soaking wet.

'She could have drowned,' he barked, a bemused look on his face as he walked over to where Hortense still stood, unmoved.

'She didn't though, did she?' Hortense turned on her heel, Albert following with Rosie sobbing against his shoulder.

Later, after Hortense had stripped her down and told her to get into bed and stay there until she was told to get up, Rosie thought of what might have happened had not Albert come along and rescued her. *I'd have ended up dead and been eaten by the little fishes,* she solemnly told herself. Shivering at the thought, she pictured Hortense's black eyes and twisted mouth as she had watched her struggle. Hortense had wanted her to drown. She began to tremble uncontrollably. She curled into a tight ball to still the tremors and tried not to think about it.

She dozed, and when she woke her tummy was rumbling with hunger, but she dared not go down to the kitchen for something to eat in case Mrs Naggs was cross with her. She had told her to play in the yard, and Rosie had disobeyed her. Eventually, exhausted by her near drowning and the horrible thoughts that plagued her mind, she fell into a deep sleep.

* * *

Early next morning, Albert called on Clara to enquire after Rosie.

'My good God, that's terrible,' Clara exclaimed, after he had related the incident of the day before. 'The child could have drowned.'

'And would have done had I not happened along. That Miss Hortense just stood there in her coffin shrouds, looking as true as I'm here like the grim reaper. You'd o' thought she wanted the bairn to drown.'

Later that morning, when Rosie went down to the kitchen for her breakfast, Clara took her to one side and made her solemnly promise not to wander off on her own ever again. Rosie promised. For now she had learned her lesson, no matter how bored or lonely she might feel.

* * *

Less than two miles from Whitley Hey, three vardos trundled along the roads. Eli and his clan had been picking cabbages in Lincolnshire, and were now working their way north to Appleby. Perched on the driver's seat next to his grandfather Milo recognised the familiar landmarks, a question that he dared not ask burning on his tongue. Rosie was but an hour's drive away. Should he risk suggesting they call and see how she was getting on?

He glanced at his grandfather, the set of his jutting jaw and the twist of his mouth letting Milo know that Eli was also aware of exactly where they were. *He's remembering what he did,* thought Milo, abandoning the words he wanted to say.

A mile and more down the road he threw caution to the

wind. 'Can we stop by and see Rosie?' he said, despising the quiver he heard in his voice: Pappa's anger was a force to be reckoned with.

Eli turned his head sharply, his eyes boring into Milo's. 'No point,' he growled, 'like as not she's forgotten ye.' They hadn't returned to Whitley Hey to pick potatoes or peas in the intervening years, Eli making excuses that there was more money to be had in Lincolnshire.

Tears sprang to Milo's eyes and he brushed them away with the back of his hand. Was Pappa right? Was it possible that Rosie had forgotten him? His heart felt empty. He'd never forget her.

Eli saw the tears and softened his tone. 'She be settled in the grand house by now,' he said. 'Ye'd not want to be upsetting her now, would ye? And folks like them'll not make ye welcome. Like as not they'll set the dogs on ye.' He flicked the reins, urging the horses to trot faster.

Milo craned his neck as the vardo bowled past the gates at Whitley Hey. Even a glimpse of Rosie would be better than nothing. He'd call out, let her know he hadn't forgotten her. But the grounds were empty, and maybe what Pappa said made sense. *She's no doubt a proper little lady by now; she doesn't need a gypsy boy for a friend,* he thought, *and even if she's unhappy Pappa won't let her come along with us.* He sank back in his seat and closed his eyes, visions of a mischievous little girl with hair like molten copper playing inside his head.

EIGHT

Autumn faded into winter. At the end of December a snow blizzard blanketed the yard and gardens at Whitley Hey. The snow lay crisp and white and tempting. Rosie had begged to venture out into it, but all she could do was gaze longingly at it through the window. Now, on New Year's Eve, as dusk was falling she crouched in the deep sill of the kitchen window and watched as the lights cast from the house windows turned the yard into a magical, shimmering white wonderland of shadows and shapes.

Behind her, at the stove, Clara lifted the lid of a large soup pot and stirred. Her cheeks were red with exertion and sticky wisps of greying hair clung to her brow from beneath her cap. 'I'll be glad when we've got this dinner over with,' she puffed, clanging the pot lid back in place. 'All this palaver just because Madam's decided to celebrate.'

'Aye, I were sickened when I heard 'cos we're having a bit of a do at home. Still, we'll finish early enough if Mr Godfrey keeps his word,' replied Florrie, wielding the masher in a pan of potatoes.

'I'll make damned sure he does,' said Clara, 'and then I'll be off to drink in the new year wi' my old man an' me mam and dad.

Clara checked the cheap cut of beef that was roasting in the oven and then reached for the pot of tea brewing alongside the soup. After plodding to the table she poured tea into three cups. 'Here, sit you down Florrie an' we'll have this before we make up the trays.'

Florrie opened the biscuit tin on the table and took one out. Then she lifted one of the cups and the biscuit and carried them over to Rosie. 'Here you are, love, have this. It'll keep you going till you get your dinner.' Her expression doleful, Rosie accepted the tea and biscuit. 'Thanks, Florrie.'

Clara flopped into a chair at the table and eased off her shoes. 'Phew! I'm ready for this,' she gasped, wiping sweat from her forehead with the corner of her apron. She lifted her cup and swigged appreciatively. As Florrie sat down opposite her, she nodded in Rosie's direction and pulled a pitying face. 'Poor little sod,' she whispered.

'It's shocking, that's what it is,' said Clara, deliberately kept her voice low. 'The child should have been out in it making snowballs an' a snowman, but she's got neither a topcoat nor boots. She's still wearing them old sandals your sister grew out of an' even they're too tight for her.'

Florrie pulled a face. 'They've never bought her a stitch since she arrived. If it wasn't for the stuff we give her she'd be running round bare-arsed. I don't know how they can fashion to treat her like they do.'

'Because they don't care,' Clara riposted. She took a deep swig of tea and swirled it round her mouth as if to rinse a bitter taste before adding, 'But then, they've not had nowt new themselves for years. Mr Hildred's allowance doesn't run to buying clothes when they spend it on paints and pens and paper, the barmy beggars. And for what, I ask you?'

'They should never have taken her in. She'd have been better off with the gypsies,' said Florrie, helping herself to a biscuit. She chewed contemplatively. 'I allus thought they might come back for her.'

Clara set down her cup and leaned closer. 'From what I heard the old man wa' glad to get rid of her. Like I told you afore, she were the result o' some trouble they had wi' a woman who weren't one o' them, an' like he said, Rosie were neither kith nor kin.'

Florrie sighed. 'An' now the poor little soul has to celebrate New Year's Eve wi' people who don't give damn about her.'

Clara drained her cup and got to her feet. 'Aye, an' the sooner we press on, the sooner we'll be away.'

Rosie climbed down from the windowsill. It was too dark now to see the snow. As she had gazed out at it, she had been dwelling on what lay ahead. Therefore, she hadn't heard a word of what Clara and Florrie had said, which was perhaps as well, otherwise it would have made her all the more miserable. She dawdled across the kitchen, her despondence hanging round her like wet rags.

'We're bringing up the trays shortly, so you'd better run along upstairs, lovey,' Clara said.

Rosie nodded and then slowly climbed the backstairs.

She didn't care that it was New Year's Eve and that they were going to eat a special dinner in the dining room. They rarely ate together, and when they did it was in embarrassed silence, the food in Rosie's mouth tasteless, and she wished she were eating it in the kitchen with Mrs Naggs. She pushed open the dining room door and slipped inside, her eyes popping when she saw Celeste.

Celeste had dressed especially for the occasion in a frothy white gown, its bodice cross-banded with a red and green striped runner that had recently graced the hall table. The militaristic sash and the untidy bow of purple voile that fastened back her hair were so at odds with the fussy white lace that Rosie had to hide her giggles behind her hand. Unaware as to how ridiculous she looked, Celeste posed artfully in front of the fireplace, one hand resting on the mantel and the other pressed to the back of her head.

'Why are you wearing your wedding dress?' said Godfrey, his eyes widening as he entered the room, 'and isn't that the thing from the hall table?' He looked and sounded utterly bemused.

Celeste stepped away from the fireplace, and flinging her arms wide she performed a giddy twirl. 'I'm celebrating in preparation for the new me. I am to be...' She faltered as Mrs Naggs and Florrie bustled into the room, each carrying a large tray.

Rosie glanced at Hortense and then at Godfrey, her eyes questioning. What was Celeste's new me going to be? She prayed it wouldn't involve her.

Mrs Naggs and Florrie set the trays down on the sideboard. Mrs Naggs filled four bowls with soup and Florrie brought them to the table. Celeste, Godfrey, Hortense and Rosie sat down to eat. 'There's beef on the platter and veg in the tureens. Pudding's in the bowl and custard's in the jug,' said Mrs Naggs, the words rolling off her tongue. 'You've all you need here so, begging your pardon, me an' Florrie'll get off home.' Flashing Godfrey a grateful smile and then shooing Florrie in front of her, she turned to leave.

Celeste squealed. 'Mrs Naggs, come back. You must stay and serve.'

Mrs Naggs closed the door smartly behind her. Celeste squealed again.

'I gave them permission to go home,' Godfrey said firmly. 'After all, it is New Year's Eve, and the roads are almost impassable. We can help ourselves.'

Celeste sulked, but Rosie considered how kind and thoughtful Godfrey was to let the cook and Florrie go home early. She gave him a wide smile, thinking how nice it was that Godfrey was taking more notice of her just lately. Godfrey smiled back then gave a sly wink. Rosie suppressed a giggle. Godfrey was fun, and whenever she met him wandering about the house he always had something to say that raised her spirits.

They ate in silence, three diners pondering on Celeste's interrupted announcement, and she irritably pushing food about her plate. It wasn't until Rosie handed her a helping of plum pudding that she shrugged aside her sulks and enlightened them.

'As I was about to tell you...' She paused dramatically, a manic gleam in her eyes. 'Tomorrow being the start of a new year, I am going to be a new person,' she announced pompously. 'I'm going to be a writer; a member of the Bloomsbury Group.'

Askance, Godfrey noisily swallowed a mouthful of pudding, and in between coughs and splutters he asked, 'Is that possible, my dear? Does one not have to be a writer of note before being invited into the Bloomsbury Group?'

'They do,' trilled Celeste, 'and tomorrow I will begin to write the first draft of my novel and I won't stop until I have succeeded in producing a literary marvel that publishers throughout the country will fight over. When my work is complete they'll accept me with open arms.'

That she had scant knowledge of what the Bloomsbury Group was, and had never written anything other than letters to her parents mattered to her not one jot. Godfrey often spoke of the Group with great admiration and that was enough for Celeste.

Hortense sniggered, her dark eyes sliding in Godfrey's direction as she said, 'It appears you have competition, my dear.' Godfrey kept his eyes on his plate and stirred his pudding listlessly, his appetite gone.

Rosie spooned up her pudding and custard. She had no idea who the Bloomers were, but she liked the idea of them taking Celeste into their open arms and whisking her away.

At Celeste's insistence, they spent the rest of the evening playing cards and charades and other futile games, each lost in their own thoughts; Godfrey half afraid that his erratic wife might yet prove to be the more successful writer, and Hortense cynically convinced it was another lost cause, but one that might encourage Godfrey to leave Celeste and go away with her.

For her part, Rosie had reached the conclusion that Celeste's new interest was to her advantage. She'd be of no use to Celeste as she didn't know how to read or write. Then, almost as though her thoughts had transferred themselves into Godfrey's mind, he gave her a piercing glare.

'Who educates you, child?'

* * *

Throughout the winter months Celeste shut herself away, scribbling frantically and discarding a mountain of screwed-up paper at the end of each day. Daffodils flourished and then withered, cherry blossom bloomed and fell and she was still writing. Cloistered in her bedroom, Celeste allowed nobody to enter save for Clara who went in to change the bed linen now and then. Florrie left her meals on a tray outside the door and collected them later, the food more often than not untouched. Hortense and Godfrey accepted her seclusion without any apparent alarm, and Rosie did much the same. Celeste no longer sought her out to play silly games. She had lost all interest in Rosie.

But Rosie didn't care. In Godfrey she had found a true friend and Godfrey had found his true vocation. Every day was now filled with new and wonderful surprises. She was no longer Esther in *Bleak House* because she had met Mr Dickens and his lively band of Pickwickians. She was exploring cities and jungles and deserts and climbing mountains in the turn of an encyclopaedia's pages or a spin of the globe's intricately drawn maps. Every page and every place had a story, and Godfrey knew them all. In the comfort of his study, Rosie's horizons broadened and her imagination ran riot.

Thus, her days were spent in the company of a disparate bunch of adults who each in their own way taught her a different way of life. She eventually forgot that once she had been Rosie the gypsy. Now, she was just Rosie Nobody.

NINE

YORKSHIRE, 1910

In the cluttered study at Whitley Hey, Godfrey spun the large, antique globe of the world and excitedly pointed to Mesopotamia. Rosie leaned forward, her eyes scanning the globe's multi-coloured surface as she picked out Jerusalem, Syria, Baghdad, Iran, Shiraz, and a long, blue line that marked the River Tigris. The 'r' rolled and the 'z' buzzed on her tongue as she read the fascinating names out loud. A slow, sweet smile lit her face as she met Godfrey's gaze.

Godfrey laughed and clapped his hands. 'You see, that's where it took place. A hot, desert land of silks and spices and the bloodiest warfare.'

They had just finished reading Byron's *The Destruction of the Sennacherib* and Rosie, her mind alive with 'wolves' and 'cohorts gleaming in purple and gold' laughed along with Godfrey. She loved the hours she spent with him amongst his weighty volumes and scattered papers.

It had been Godfrey's idea to educate Rosie. On the morning after the day of the New Year's Eve dinner six years before, the day Celeste announced she was to become a writer, Gregory had come across Rosie on the landing, his eyes popping with surprise when he saw her. Rosie had greeted him with a smile and a cheery 'good morning.' Godfrey had looked confused and then said, 'Yesterday, at dinner, how old did you say you were?'

'I think I must be seven,' Rosie had answered thoughtfully. 'I was near five when I came here so Mrs Naggs told me, and since then there have been two Christmases, so that would make me seven.'

Godfrey had widened his eyes at her logic.

Rosie had looked at him blankly, and Godfrey had hurried off to find Celeste. After that, lessons became an almost daily event, he delighting in his nimble-minded little pupil who, like an empty bucket, waited to be filled and she, grateful for the attention, absorbing all that he taught her. Godfrey almost abandoned Homer and *The Iliad*, diverting his efforts into concocting instructive and exciting tuition. The older and wiser Rosie grew, the more interesting these sessions were. Now, six years on, she was as educated as many a girl in a fine academy, and in Godfrey she had found someone to truly love. She knew in her heart that he felt the same.

It never occurred to Rosie that her life at Whitley Hey was dysfunctional; she barely remembered any other. Isolated from all but its inhabitants, and with no young people to play with – except for Florrie who sometimes took time out to catch a ball or skip in the yard – Rosie accepted each day as it came; she knew no other way. As time went by, Celeste's interest in her protégé having waned and her writing all-consuming, their paths rarely crossed, unless of course Celeste needed help with some whimsical notion or, feeling bored, wanted to play a madcap game. Rosie took all this in her stride, her life made meaningful by the hours she spent with Godfrey.

Now, she leaned forward, her blue-green eyes gleaming like tourmalines, and her expression one of thoughtful curiosity. When she spoke, her voice wavered with a wary expectation.

'Godfrey, there's something I've been meaning to ask you for ages.'

Godfrey looked puzzled. 'Fire away. Ask and I'll tell.'

'Will you promise to tell me the truth?'

Godfrey's frown deepened. 'Don't I always? What is it you want to know?'

Rosie took a deep breath and then asked him the same question she had asked Clara Naggs six years before. 'Where is my mammy?' Then, she had listened like a child. Now, at almost fourteen years of age, she listened like the intelligent young woman she had become.

Godfrey dropped his gaze and didn't reply immediately. Then, still avoiding Rosie's eyes he muttered, 'I should really have put a stop to it but I was being selfish.'

'Put a stop to what?'

'I should have stopped Celeste taking you from the old man. I should have known it was just one of her whims but...' He gave Rosie an agonised look. 'I wanted her to leave me alone to get on with my writing.'

'Tell me,' Rosie said impatiently, 'I don't care if the truth hurts. I have to know.'

'The old man didn't want to keep you. He made it quite plain that you were no relation to him. He said something about a woman leaving you with him and that he couldn't give you a proper rearing.'

Rosie digested his words, vague memories of Eli surfacing:

irritable, sometimes harsh but never downright cruel. Unlike Celeste and Hortense. She chuckled grimly. 'And you think I've had one here?'

Dismally, Godfrey shook his head. 'The boy didn't want to let you go,' he said encouragingly, 'if my memory serves me right he vociferously objected to leaving you here. He wept bucketsful, so Mrs Naggs told me.'

'That 'ud be Milo,' Rosie said. 'He was my friend. I loved Milo. He was like a big brother to me.' She paused. Her heart warmed to know that Milo had cried for her. 'I missed him more than anything when I was little. I cried for him nearly every night for ages and ages.'

Godfrey had the grace to look ashamed. 'Oh, my poor, little Rosie,' he said, 'what did we do to you?'

'You weren't to blame, Godfrey. Don't let it upset you.' She brightened. 'And now, because of you, I've lots to be thankful for.' Rosie gave Godfrey a perky smile to show that she didn't hold him responsible for anything that had happened in the past. But she wasn't yet satisfied, and the smile turning to a frown, she asked, 'But who was my mother?'

'I've no idea,' said Godfrey. 'Only the old man or the boy can tell you that.'

'Milo used to call me Rosie Nobody,' she said softly.

They sat quietly, each reflecting on what had been shared. Godfrey broke the silence. 'No matter how you came to be here, I want you to know that you have brought me the greatest joy in life, Rosie Nobody.' He reached out and patted her hand. Tears sprang to Rosie's eyes, and once again they sat silently, digesting the strange circumstances that had brought them together. Rosie thought, *I might not know who my mother is, or where Milo and Pappa are now, and living under the same roof as Celeste and Hortense is decidedly unpleasant, but Godfrey's more than good to me.*

Her eyes alight with enthusiasm, she asked, 'What will we do now?'

Smiling his relief, Godfrey suggested mathematics and Rosie reached for her books on calculus, her mind already eager to explore the summation of infinitesimal differences.

* * *

In the evening of that same day, some thirty miles from Whitley Hey, Milo stepped outside the vardo and walked across the camping ground to the edge of the copse. His heart felt too heavy inside his chest and he had a desperate need to be out in the cool night air, away from the claustrophobic atmosphere in the wagon where Sufina and Charity were fussing over Eli who, in his cot, fought for every dying breath.

Milo looked up into the vastness of the heavens, waiting for the clouds to move and reveal the stars. At his back, lamps on a dozen or so vardos marked a semicircle in the gloaming, the owners of these wagons having come to pay their respects and to travel with Eli on his final journey to the churchyard at Crakehill.

'Milo, Milo.' Charity's anxious voice rang out across the copse and Milo ran back to the vardo, panic rising in his breast. 'Eli's asking for ye,' she said, standing aside to allow him passage.

Milo climbed into the vardo and went and knelt by Eli's bed. Eli's eyes were closed, his hands folded across his chest above the edge of the blanket. His once swarthy face, now grey and etched with pain, resembled that of a granite statue whose strong features refused to be diminished by death's stealthy hand. Milo wiped tears with the backs of both hands and then gently laid one hand on the back of Eli's own. Eli's eyes fluttered open.

'I'm here, Pappa,' Milo said, gently applying pressure to Eli's hand.

Eli's rheumy eyes sought Milo's face. *So like Fennix,* he thought, gazing fondly at his grandson. *He has the same turn of lip, the same even curve of eyebrow that gives him the handsome expression of one who knows he is invincible.* But poor Fennix had not been invincible and Eli feared for the boy he was about leave alone in the cruel world. He drew a rasping breath.

'Mind ye take care now, 'tis a big world out there. Don't let it get the better of ye.' He gasped for air. 'I loved your father, and I love...' Eli's voice faded and his eyes closed. Milo closed his own, silent tears coursing his cheeks as he listened to Eli's final whispering breath and Sufina and Charity's sobbing.

* * *

They waked Eli for two days and two nights before burying him in the small, neglected graveyard in Crakehill village. As the diminutive, ageing priest led the brief ceremony Milo thought, *This is where my grandfather married the grandmother I never knew.* He gave a little smile. No jumping the broom for Eli; he had married Sabina in the eyes of God and was now lying along with her and their son, Fennix, in a plot marked with a slab of stone on which their names were etched. One day, Milo's own would be written there.

Milo glanced round at the congregation of men, women and children who had come to pay their respects, and after the priest had shaken his hand and wished him well, Milo led the mourners back to where they had left their vardo on a piece of waste ground at the edge of the village. There, he watched hungry flames lick through the bow-top canvas of Eli's vardo. Inside the wagon the fire spit and crackled furiously. Milo was saddened that this keeping with tradition was depriving him of a home and all that his grandfather had owned.

Flames soared and smoke swirled, and across the distance he saw Eli's horses flatten their ears and heard their shrill whinnying above the conflagration's roar. They too were mourning their master. He walked over to where the two piebald cobs were tethered and stroked their flanks. Apart from his own few miserable belongings they were all he possessed. *Not much to show for my seventeen years on earth,* he thought, as the bow top collapsed inwards with a fiery rush. He walked back to join the others.

'He was a powerful fellow,' Bosco said, clapping Milo on the back. 'We'll feel the loss of him.' Beside him, Charity snuffled into her shawl and wiped her tears. Milo was grateful for their sympathy but deep inside he felt a pain so great that he wanted to shout it to the heavens.

'You're welcome to ride along of us until such time as you get your own wagon,' Charity said, patting Milo's arm. 'You can move in with Shadrach and Ansil; they won't mind you bedding down with them, I'm sure.'

Milo essayed a smile and nodded. When he was younger, Shadrach and Ansil had been his sworn enemies. Now, they merely tolerated one another. He knew Charity was being kind, and there was no way he could move in with Clem Boswell and his family. A lad of his age couldn't share a vardo with Clem and Sufina's two teenage daughters, nor did he wish to share the tent their sons slept in. If he were to be honest, he didn't want to move in with either family but just at this moment, overwhelmed with sadness and confusion, he couldn't think of an alternative. He muttered his thanks to Charity.

The next day the travellers set out for Appleby, Milo astride one horse and leading the other. The wind carried swift, fluffy clouds across the sky, patches of blue appearing and disappearing and the steady jogtrot of the placid nags soothing Milo's troubled heart. He was out in the world without the shadow of Eli to shelter him.

The colourful procession of wagons creaked along the road, moving to their own music as the dangling array of pots and pans fastened to the outer walls jingled and jangled, attracting attention in the towns and villages they passed through. Boys and girls ran alongside, envious of the gypsy children perched on a driver's step or hanging boldly out of a half-leaf door, and at the same time derisory because as everyone knew, gypsies were to be despised.

'Mucky gypsies! Didicois! Sell us some pegs,' the local children chanted.

'Gorjers! Dirty Gorjers,' the younger gypsies catcalled back.

'Pikeys stink. Pikeys, pikeys, stinking pikeys,' came the reply.

'Come away,' called the housewives from their doorways, fearful that their children might be stolen from right under their noses. They didn't trust gypsies.

Milo heard the cries as though from a distance. He was deep in thought; if he sold one of the cobs could he buy his own vardo? Yet, he was reluctant to part with either Sheba or Flicker; they'd been with him for all of his life.

A flash of moving colour caught his eye and he pulled sharply on the reins. A small, red-haired girl in a blue smock had almost run under his nearside wheel. Time reeled back and, just for a moment, he thought it was Rosie. His heart lurched. Milo had never forgotten her, although his memory of her had faded with time.

The little girl leapt for the pavement. Tossing her bright, red hair back from her face, she turned and gave him a cheeky grin. *Rosie, Rosie, Rosie,* thought Milo as he flicked the horses on, common sense ruling that, like him, Rosie had grown up. She'd be all of fourteen, he ruminated, wondering how she'd turned out, and hoping she was happy.

For months after they were parted he had missed her and tried to keep the memory of her alive, Eli refusing to listen and stones of silence hanging round their necks should Milo say her name. When pea picking time came round, and later potato lifting, he had reckoned on seeing her again, maybe persuading Pappa to fetch her home, but Eli had refused to return to Whitley Hey; like Knaresborough, it was a place to avoid. As Milo matured he understood why. Knaresborough exacerbated Eli's grief and Whitley Hey his guilt.

TEN

At the same time as Milo was burying his grandfather, Rosie was sitting in the hallway at Whitley Hey. Today was the day Celeste and Godfrey made their annual trip to Wakefield and, much to her amazement, Rosie was to accompany them. They had never taken her anywhere before, and now as she listened to the rumpus up above she could barely contain her impatience.

It was always the same on 'Wakefield Day', as Rosie liked to call it, and she resigned herself to waiting and listening to Celeste's screams and shouts as she chose first one outfit and then another, always uncertain of how she should dress for their meeting with Godfrey's brother, Hildred.

Rosie was well used to Celeste's tantrums and tears, and thought the fuss over what she should wear ridiculous. Hildred Threppleton wouldn't care less. On his infrequent visits to Whitley Hey, she had witnessed the contempt he held for his brother and his outrageous wife.

Old enough now to be curious about the strange couple with whom she had lived for the past nine years, and tired of waiting for Celeste to announce she was ready, Rosie went down to the kitchen and Mrs Naggs. Perched on a stool at the large deal table, nibbling one of the cook's delicious scones, she asked, 'Why is it that Celeste and Godfrey are so in awe of Hildred? He only comes here twice a year, and then he spends most of his time with Albert Stubbs, so why, when they visit him, is there all this fuss and palaver?'

Clara Naggs, never one to miss the chance of a good old gossip, wiped her hands on her apron and flopped onto the stool next to Rosie. Putting her head close to Rosie's and lowering her voice, she said, 'A lot o' things hangs on these visits, lovey. They have to make a good impression or the boss won't pay up.'

'You mean Hildred? Pay up what?'

'The money he gives 'em to live here like they do. Hildred Threppleton pays for everything: mine and Florrie's wages, the food bills, a bit to Hortense and the rest to her ladyship and him that never did a day's work in his life.'

Rosie giggled at this reference to Celeste and Godfrey, and Clara nodded sagely. 'It's like this, lovey: when old Thomas Threppleton died, Mr Hildred took over the running of the brewery and all the other property old Tom owned. Mr Godfrey had taken himself off to London to do his writing and when he came back penniless and married, Mr Hildred let him come to live here. I think he hoped that Mr Godfrey would take an interest in running the farm but—' she sighed heavily '—he never has and he never will. It's a good job Albert knows what he's doin', otherwise the place would have gone to rack an' ruin years ago.'

'But why hasn't Godfrey got money of his own?'

''Cos he never earned any,' Clara said caustically, 'an' when he wouldn't go into the brewery 'is father disowned him an' left everything he had to Mr Hildred. Out of the kindness of his heart, he keeps 'em here. Not that Madam is one bit grateful; she's never done complaining.'

'Did Godfrey meet Celeste when he was in London?' By now, Rosie was intrigued and she wondered why she had never asked these questions before.

Clara sneered. 'Aye, she were supposed to come from some important family, half French they were on her mother's side, but they had no brass either. Mr Godfrey turned up here with her and that miserable cousin of hers and Mr Hildred 'as kept them ever since.'

'Rosie!' The shriek from the hallway had Rosie and Clara jumping to attention. Giving an impish grin Rosie said, 'They must be ready to leave.'

Clara smirked. 'Aye, off they'll go, begging bowl in hand asking for what neither of 'em deserves, the useless creatures that they are.'

Rosie hurried from the kitchen to find Celeste dithering in front of the long hall mirror. She had covered her hairline with a broad bandeau of brown velvet tied at one side in a floppy bow, the drab colour making her pale face look pasty and the bow like a rabbit with only one ear. Her dress was fashioned from a bed sheet that, at Celeste's insistence, Hortense had dyed with beetroot juice, her hands red for days afterwards. Rosie eyed the dress's patchy colour and its botched neckline. When Celeste draped a brown fur cape, faded and moth-eaten, about her shoulders Rosie raised her eyes to the ceiling.

'Do I look presentable?' Celeste squealed.

'You look delightful, my love,' said Godfrey, standing impatiently in the open doorway. 'Please hurry – we mustn't be late.'

'Hortense, what do you think?' Celeste turned imploring eyes on her cousin.

Hortense, stiff and starched in her plain black skirt and a jacket almost green with age, sniffed and didn't deign to answer.

'Come, come, hurry along,' Godfrey called, bouncing on his heels. He was wearing a faded blue velvet coat, a yellow cravat and wrinkled brown trousers.

Celeste vacated the mirror, and Rosie paused in front of it and assessed her own reflection. Her grey woollen dress – one of Celeste's cast-offs – was baggy and threadbare, and her knobbly tweed jacket two sizes too big. However, nothing could detract the beauty of her glorious mane of red hair. It hugged her temples closely and then swooped down over her ears in shining waves.

What an incongruous bunch we look, thought Rosie, following her guardians out to the waiting trap, and as she climbed into it she added, *and what an incongruous bunch we are: a dear, kindly man whose ambition to write has come to nothing; a madwoman whose mind is so disturbed she can settle to nothing; and a miserable drab who finds pleasure in hurting. And then there's me: a girl who belongs to none of them; a girl who can barely remember where she came from and will never understand why she's here with them now. I don't even have a surname,* she pondered. *I'm not a Threppleton, that's for sure; so who am I?*

* * *

Rosie sat in the rear of the trap with Celeste, and Godfrey and Hortense sat up front. Godfrey flicked the reins and the little pony trotted down the driveway to the road. Rosie's heart was beating fast. She, who could not remember journeying further than the farmhouse where Florrie lived, and that on foot, could barely contain her excitement and curiosity as the trap bowled along.

For the first mile or two they travelled along leafy lanes bordered with fields and woods, Rosie turning her head from left to right and back again as she drank in the sights. She commented on the trees and flowers and the sheep and cows in the fields. When they came to a cluster of cottages with pretty gardens close by a small church and a blacksmith's forge, Rosie cried out, 'Who lives there, and what's that place with a fire inside it?' She pointed to the forge.

Godfrey slowed the trap and pointed. 'Mrs Naggs lives in the cottage with the blue door,' he said, before going on to explain the forge's purpose.

'And that's a church, isn't it?' said Rosie, pointing again. 'I know that because it's like the ones in your *Ancient and Gothic* book, Godfrey.' He turned and smiled his approval.

'Oh, for goodness' sake,' snapped Hortense, 'are we to travel all the way to Wakefield listening to your idle prattle, Rosie? Shut up and sit quietly.'

Rosie sat back in her seat and scowled. Godfrey glanced over his shoulder at her and winked. A ray of sunlight flashed on his cheekbone turning his stubble to purest gold. Rosie thought how handsome and how kind he was. Next to her, Celeste sat silent and pensive, fiddling with the bow in her hair or the collar of her moth-eaten cape. A sickly odour wafted off her person. *She's sweating with fear,* Rosie thought. *Poor, mad thing. She spends so long cooped up in her room that fresh air and open spaces scare her.*

They arrived in Wakefield before midday, Rosie overwhelmed by the bustling town with its crowds of people and buildings of all shapes and sizes. She wanted to ask a hundred questions but Godfrey seemed so deeply preoccupied as he brought the trap to a halt in the yard at Threppleton's Brewery that she decided to wait until later.

So this is Hildred's empire, thought Rosie, gazing at the huge buildings and breathing in the pungent smell of fermenting hops. Godfrey climbed down from the driver's seat, and after he had handed down a dithering Celeste, he offered his hand to Hortense. She curtly refused it and sat on, staring haughtily into the distance. Unaided, Rosie jumped down and followed Celeste and Godfrey.

They walked by a high red-brick building that contained huge vats and snaking metal pipes. Rosie paused at the open doors to watch bursts of steam from the boilers and to listen to the gurgling liquid that eventually would turn into beer.

Godfrey marched purposefully over to the loading bay with Celeste mincing along at his side. Men in leather aprons were rolling beer barrels out of the bay and up the gantries onto the long drays that delivered the beer to the inns. In the shafts of each dray, huge shire horses swayed patiently on hooves as big as dinner plates.

'Oh! Oh! Oh!' squeaked Celeste, clinging to Godfrey's arm and clutching at her skirt as they walked past the horses, but Rosie stopped to stroke the nose of one. As she breathed in the scent of dusty hay, sweat and manure, an overpowering memory of an old man, two piebald cobs and a mischievous dark-eyed boy made her shiver: Milo and Pappa, and Sheba and Flicker and the vardo; she had almost forgotten them. Where were they now? she wondered.

Inside the loading bay, Godfrey, Celeste and Rosie dodged by the busy men in leather aprons rolling barrels. They slipped between stacks of crates filled with bottles until they came to a dingy office. Hildred watched their approach through a window thick with dust. Godfrey and Celeste went inside, but Rosie sat on a hard chair outside the door wondering why it was that they met with Hildred at the brewery and not at his home. Perhaps he didn't consider them grand enough to meet with his wife or take tea in his drawing room. The longer she sat inhaling the pungent smell of malt the heavier her head felt and she couldn't shake the memory of Milo and Pappa from her mind. It made her feel so desperately sad and lonely that her breath caught in her throat.

In a bid to clear her head, she stood and peered through the dusty window in the glass-panelled office wall. Hildred was standing, his considerable bulk dwarfing diminutive Godfrey who, seated, was gaping up at him. His jaw was slack and his eyes wide in disbelief. Although their voices were muffled, Rosie could tell that the words they spoke were heated. Celeste was shaking her head furiously, the ridiculous bow on her bandeau flapping like a bird's broken wing. Her cheeks were puce and her mouth pursed as though she was about to cry.

Hildred must be telling them something they don't want to hear, thought Rosie, listening to the low rumble of his voice and then glancing at Godfrey again. He was sitting rigidly upright, his face grey and his expression intense. Rosie thought he looked afraid. Then, quite clearly she heard Celeste squawk, 'Nooo, nooo, you can't possibly mean it. I won't tolerate such an indisposition.'

Celeste leapt from her chair, arms flailing, and the next minute she flew out of the office and scurried between the stacks of crates, her moulting cape and floppy bow bearing a striking resemblance to a furry creature fleeing from a hunter. Alarmed, Rosie ran after her.

Outside in the brewery yard, Hortense stood by the trap watching them come. Celeste threw herself on her cousin, screeching and crying hysterically. Hortense pressed her hands hard down on Celeste's shoulders, a tactic she often used to calm her, but she averted her eyes and gazed off into the distance as though the distraught woman in her arms was of no interest. At Rosie's approach Hortense raised her eyes heavenward as if to say: what do we do with the silly creature now? Without exchanging a word, they bundled Celeste into the trap and then sat either side of her to prevent her from thrashing about.

A short while later, Godfrey joined them. His shoulders sagged and he wore an expression of utter defeat. He climbed up into the driver's seat without a word, and with a flick of the reins he drove the trap out of the yard.

Rosie sat tightly against Celeste, hopeful that she would calm down before they reached the city centre. Godfrey had told Rosie that after the annual visit they celebrated with tea at the Strafford Arms and afterwards a walk to the cathedral. Rosie tried to imagine what it would be like and excitement swelled in her chest at the thought of doing and seeing something she had never done before. However, when he announced that they were driving directly home, her heart sank into her boots and she had to fight back tears. Celeste slumped against her, snivelling and moaning.

'What brought this on?' Hortense asked, when they were out on the road.

Godfrey glanced over his shoulder, a look of utter despair on his face. Then, in a voice that wobbled he replied, 'Hildred isn't prepared to fund my present lifestyle any longer, so he says. He is of the opinion that with three able-bodied young women in the house Mrs Naggs and Florrie are an unnecessary luxury. I am to dismiss them immediately.' He glanced behind him again, his expression one of disbelief.

This time it was Hortense's turn to shriek. 'What nonsense! Who will do the cooking and the cleaning?'

'The three of you apparently,' Godfrey said, although Rosie could tell by his tone that he thought it was a disaster waiting to happen. *He already knows that Celeste will be useless, and Hortense not much better,* she thought. Then she realised it would fall on her to keep them fed. Thank goodness Mrs Naggs had taught her to how to make soups and stews and bake bread and buns. But she knew in her heart that working alone in the kitchen would be miserable without Clara's witty chatter and Florrie's gossipy stories.

It was a sad little quartet that made their way back to Whitley Hey, Godfrey silent and tense and wondering how long it might be before Hildred turned them out of the house, as he had intimated. He'd been offered a good price for it by a gentleman seeking a country residence, and had still to reach a decision whether or not to sell it. Celeste knew nothing of this, having fled the office before Hildred had spoken of his intentions, and Godfrey refrained from mentioning it to Hortense in case she used it to try and persuade him to leave at once and take her with him. And he kept it from Rosie because he did not want to trouble her; she had suffered enough without having to consider the possibility of being made homeless at her tender age. But come what may, if the worst came to the worst, he silently vowed that he would support her in whatever way he could until she was of an age to make her own way in the world. She was too precious to be let go.

Hortense sat still and silent, her black eyes glittering as she made plans to persuade Godfrey to see the error of his ways. They must leave immediately and seek their fortune in some place where Godfrey's worth would be recognised; he would make an excellent schoolmaster. As for Celeste and Rosie, they could go to hell for all she cared.

Rosie was so bitterly disappointed at losing Mrs Naggs and Florrie's company that she ignored the sights that had intrigued her on the outward journey, and was simply thankful that Celeste had fallen asleep.

* * *

'Well, that's a turn-up for the books after all my years of service,' Clara exclaimed, when Godfrey told her of Hildred's decision. Godfrey apologised over and again and then shambled off, ashamed to be the bearer of such bad news.

'They'll not last a crack without us,' Clara told Florrie as Godfrey took his leave. 'They'll rot in their own filth or starve to death, for neither Madam nor Miss Hortense have ever so much as boiled an egg or washed a snot rag.'

'I think I know who'll bear the brunt of it all,' said Florrie meaningfully.

Two pairs of eyes turned to Rosie sitting dejectedly at the table and fiddling with a ball of pastry that Clara had abandoned.

Rosie met their gazes. 'You mean me, don't you?' she said. Clara and Florrie solemnly nodded.

* * *

In the few days that were left before Mrs Naggs's departure, Rosie kept close by the woman she now looked on as the grandmother she had never had, and Clara responded with the love and affection she had always shown her. In between tears and laughter, Rosie made the most of feeling loved and wanted. At one point she almost begged Clara to take her with her, but her loyalties were torn between the cook and Godfrey. Godfrey needed her.

On the day that Clara departed, angered at being deprived of the pittance she earned, and burning to vent her feelings of disgust, she gave Celeste and Hortense what she called 'the rounds of the kitchen' telling them exactly what she thought of their abysmal lifestyle and their appalling treatment of Rosie. Hortense met her reproach with haughty disdain, and Celeste had a fit of hysterics. Clara laughed them out of the kitchen, and after putting on her coat she clasped Rosie to her bosom, saying, 'You hang on, lovey. The time will come when you can leave Whitley Hey and make your own way in the world. You're a brave and lovely girl. You've weathered living here with this lot, and one day you'll realise that it's prepared you for tackling anything you choose. You'll make a success of your life no matter the poor start you've had because you're blessed with a sharp brain and a lovely nature.'

Clara spoke with such certainty that Rosie believed her.

ELEVEN

Rosie added a generous pinch of salt to the root vegetables bubbling on the stove in the kitchen at Whitley Hey. Albert had dumped a sack of carrots, turnips and parsnips on the doorstep earlier that morning, and now she was turning them into a tasty stew.

It was more than a year since Clara Naggs and Florrie had reluctantly quit their jobs amid tears and angry words, and Rosie had just as reluctantly stepped into their shoes. She didn't so much mind making meals; in fact she quite enjoyed concocting recipes from the ingredients that were delivered each week, courtesy of Hildred Threppleton. What she did object to was the lack of assistance with all the other household chores.

She turned from the stove to check if the gravy powder had completely dissolved, and finding that it had she was adding it to the vegetables, when she heard footsteps on the stairs. Her spirits drooped. Was it Hortense or Celeste? Most likely Hortense, she thought; Celeste rarely ventured below stairs unless it was to rant and rave over some imagined injustice.

'Not another of your stews,' Hortense moaned, wrinkling her nose as she stepped into the kitchen.

'You don't have to eat it. Nobody's forcing you.'

Hortense picked a freshly baked scone off the rack on the table and nibbled at its edges with her prominent front teeth. Rosie was reminded of the rat she had seen gnawing on a stray potato in the yard earlier that morning.

'Have you laundered Celeste's white shirtwaist and her chemise? She left them at the head of the stairs two days ago and now she wants to wear them.'

Rosie's eyes blazed. 'How many times do you need to be told? You both do your own laundry. I'll do mine and Godfrey's, but I draw the line at doing yours.'

Hortense scowled. 'You can't expect Celeste to wash and scrub. She doesn't know how.'

'Then you do hers when you do your own, and whilst you're at it you can wash the entrance hall floor. It's filthy. And the dust in the dining room is so thick I could write my name in it.' Rosie tossed her mane of red hair and threw up her hands in sheer frustration. 'I'm not your servant and never will be. I'll gladly cook because we have to eat, and I'll keep the kitchen and my own room in good order, but as for the rest of the house, it's up to you and Celeste.'

'How dare you,' Hortense squawked. 'I'll not stay to be spoken to in such a vulgar manner.'

'Then take yourself off,' cried Rosie. 'The little you contribute will not be missed.' She gave Hortense a defiant smirk before turning back to stir the stew.

Hortense flounced up the stairs, and Rosie smiled wickedly. During the past year, she had made several vain attempts to persuade Celeste and Hortense to take responsibility for the housework and their own needs, and far too often she had found herself acquiescing to their demands for the sake of peace and quiet; but not today. She had made her objections perfectly plain, and that was the way she intended to carry on. She'd care for Godfrey who was oblivious to the chaos, for they still spent enjoyable hours each day in his study, but as for Celeste and Hortense, they could go hang.

* * *

Not too many miles away, at a fair on the outskirts of Wakefield, Milo was plying his wares to the townsfolk there to enjoy the rides and make purchases from the stalls. It was a pleasant evening in late September, the fairground crowded and trade brisk. Now, he stood amidst a variety of finely crafted stools, carved animals and birds, wooden bowls and spoons, pleased to see that his stock was rapidly diminishing as he made sale after sale.

From an early age, his grandfather had taught him how to make pegs and spoons, and in the months since Eli's death he had sought comfort in sitting each night whittling at pieces of wood he collected on his journeys. Whilst pegs and spoons were a staple of his trade they offered little in the way of creativity.

One day, he'd chanced on a piece of wood that loosely resembled a rabbit, and then discovered that he could use his whittling skills to produce things that would earn him far more than pegs and spoons ever would.

'That's a lovely rabbit,' Charity Doe had remarked. 'It looks almost real.' Milo, pleased by her reaction, had carried on whittling.

After Eli's death he had travelled along with the Boswells

and the Does, too stunned with grief at the loss of his grandfather to make any decision as to what he should do or where he might go. Suffering from an inertia that prevented him from summoning the courage to buy his own vardo, Milo still shared with Shadrach and Ansil Doe, but of late tempers had been fraught.

To escape Shadrach and Ansil's company, when the wagons pulled off the road for the night Milo went in search of fallen branches and, finding a quiet place away from the camp he carved small woodland animals or crafted little stools, surprising himself by his aptitude for creating these lifelike creatures or useful pieces of furniture. There was always a good demand for them at the fairs. Milo's money belt was never empty, and the leather bag hidden inside his mattress was comfortingly fat.

'How much for the squirrels?' A rosy-faced woman with a large, open purse pointed to the cute little carvings, and when Milo told her the price she bought two of them. As stars began studding a purple sky and a chill wind started to blow, the crowds grew thinner and his wares became fewer. With only one stool and couple of rabbits left, Milo packed them into a sack and rolled his canvas groundsheet. He was making his way back to the vardo when Shadrach caught up with him. The strong stink of ale on his breath made Milo wary.

Shadrach glanced down at the almost empty sack. 'Had a good day then? Made plenty of *vonga*?' He eyed Milo's money belt.

Milo grunted. He paid the Doe brothers for his share of the vardo, and regularly lent them money, most of it never repaid, but tonight he wasn't going to fall for Shadrach's bullying ways. He quickened his pace, only to be brought to a staggering halt as Shadrach thumped him between the shoulders. The sack and the canvas went flying, a sharp crack letting Milo know that the little stool had most likely lost a leg or two. He spun round to face Shadrach.

'Come on, hand over some of that cash,' Shadrach growled, grabbing at Milo's waistcoat and pulling him close. Milo punched his fist into Shadrach's paunchy gut and Shadrach's knees buckled. Milo towered over him.

'Get up and fight like a man,' Milo yelled, all the pent-up frustration that had plagued him for the past few months bursting from every pore.

Shadrach staggered to his feet and flung a wild punch at Milo's head; Milo deflected it with a punch of his own that landed squarely on Shadrach's jaw. Like a felled tree, Shadrach sprawled in the dirt. Milo left him where he was, and picking up his sack he hurried back to the camp.

Inside Shadrach's vardo, he stowed his clothes and a blanket into an old saddlebag and into the sack he put his favourite carvings: an owl, a long-legged lurcher and a small statuette of Eli. Then taking the leather pouch from its hiding place he ran to where he had tethered the horses. Astride Sheba, and leading Flicker by the reins he clattered out on to the road. He'd make his peace with Clem and Sufina Boswell and Bosco and Charity Doe at a future date. He had no quarrel with them, but he wouldn't spend another night in Shadrach's vardo. Kicking the horse into a canter he left the encampment and all that he had ever known behind. From now on he was on his own.

* * *

'I'm worried about Celeste,' Rosie told Godfrey one evening as they sat over a cup of tea and a copy of Emily Brontë's *Wuthering Heights*.

Godfrey raised his gaze from the book, his sad grey eyes meeting Rosie's.

'I am too,' he said, his voice wobbling pathetically. 'I have pleaded with her to leave her bedroom and find a worthwhile project to occupy her time but she pays me no heed.' He covered his face with his hands to hide his misery.

'I know you have, and so have I,' said Rosie, 'but it's useless. She's even stopped washing herself or combing her hair, and she won't let me change the bed sheets. The room stinks, but she seems not to notice it, and if I didn't take her meals up to her she'd starve. Even so, she eats like a bird. She left her breakfast *and* dinner untouched.'

Rosie heaved a great sigh, her pity for the poor demented creature who skulked like a trapped bird in the confines of her bedroom, and her love for the broken man now sitting beside her, tugging at her generous heart. She had realised a long time ago that Godfrey had no deep love for Celeste, but being the kindly, decent soul he was, he still felt duty-bound to care for her.

'What does Hortense say of the situation?' Godfrey sounded as though he was clutching at straws.

Rosie sniffed. 'Hortense says nothing. She goes about her business as though none of us exists.' She gave Godfrey a meaningful look. 'You must have noticed that she no longer eats her meals with us – just takes the food I've made up to her room – and whilst she does her own laundry and occasionally takes the notion to do a spot of cleaning here and there, she ignores me for most of the time. As for Celeste, she seems to have given up on her. I don't know when she last did anything for her.'

Godfrey shook his head. 'I can't understand it. When first I met them and married Celeste they were so close that it was unthinkable to leave Hortense in London and not bring her here with us. In those days she would have done anything for Celeste.' *And for me,* he thought guiltily, although it was years since he had last shared her bed. *She's also given up on me,* he silently concluded.

'Perhaps the demands became too great to tolerate,' Rosie said wryly, as she recalled Celeste's high-handed dealings with Hortense. Then, bursting with curiosity, she said, 'How did you meet them?'

Godfrey gave a glimmer of a smile. 'I was trying my hand as a writer in London and was introduced to them at a party. The company was made up of academics and minor aristocracy, all vying to outdo one another in their search for fame.' Rosie chuckled, and Godfrey had the grace to look sheepish for he knew she suspected that that was exactly what he had been doing.

'It was Hortense who first attracted me, but over time I found her rather dull. On the other hand I was smitten by Celeste's vivacity,' he continued. 'She was interested in everything that was going on at that time and seemed to know everyone.' He shuffled in his seat, an embarrassed flush suffusing his neck and cheeks. 'To my shame I saw her as a gateway to the world of academia and all that I thought I might become.'

Rosie saw the pain in his eyes as he acknowledged his failure, and her heart went out to him. 'Go on,' she said softly. 'What happened next?'

Godfrey got up and wandered across the room, speaking

with his back to her. 'You've no doubt reached the conclusion that it was all false and fleeting. Celeste wasn't really accepted by those people, for all she pretended to come from an aristocratic French family with important connections in the arts. Her father was simply a clerk in the embassy and her mother of no consequence. By the time I came to my senses we were married and my writing had been dismissed as insubstantial drivel.' He swung round to face Rosie, a sorry smile on his face. 'So you see, just as my father predicted, I crawled back home with egg on my face and threw myself on Hildred's mercy.'

'Why didn't you join the family business and make a living that way?'

Godfrey's laughter was brittle. 'Hildred wouldn't allow it. He paid me to keep as far away as possible in fear that my addled brain would affect his profits – that and his contempt for Celeste. He hated her from the start.'

'But you loved her?' Rosie looked into his face, seeking confirmation.

Godfrey shrugged. 'I thought I did, but as she flitted from one hare-brained scheme to another, always demanding, demanding, demanding, I found it hard to be in her company. I think she felt the same way about me, and so...' He seemed to run out of steam, his shoulders sagging as he came and flopped down beside Rosie. She reached for his hand and squeezed it.

'You each went your own separate ways. Celeste to whatever took her fancy and you to your writing. Tell me, Godfrey, why did you choose to rewrite *The Iliad*?'

Godfrey grimaced. 'Foolishness. Or so it now seems. I wanted to prove I could write as excitingly as Homer. As he said: "Life is largely a matter of expectation." Now, I know that it was pure vanity on my part.' He paused, musing for a moment on his abandoned work, before adding, 'It's also a weighty tome to tackle, one that I thought would keep me occupied and out of Celeste's hair for a long time, and whilst ever she thought I was going to prove that I was a great academic and make our fortune she left me alone to get on with it.' He gave a sad, little laugh. 'How wrong she was.'

'But why, if you knew you were flogging a dead horse, did you continue to work on it? Why not try to write something of your own?' Rosie's impassioned tone of voice made Godfrey laugh again, bitterly.

'Because I have no imagination, no story to tell. It's as Homer said: "Even a fool learns something once it hits him."' His voice was heavy with the truth of his words.

Tears pricked Rosie's eyes. Godfrey was such a kind, unworldly, lost soul, she badly wanted to say something to cheer him, but she didn't know what.

Instead she said, 'I'll go down and make supper for everyone.'

TWELVE

Milo woke to shafts of sunlight glancing through holes in the barn roof. For a moment he wondered where he was and then, his knuckles still stinging from where they had connected with Shadrach's jaw, he realised why he was here. Giving a wicked smile, he pulled the blanket up to his chin and gazed up at the rafters, contemplating his next move.

He had ridden through the night with no particular destination in mind, angry thoughts and a deep sense of loss spurring him on. Just before dawn, the horses weary and his own backside aching, he had arrived at the barn on the edge of a village. He'd seen the church tower in the distance and realised that he had reached Eggleston, a place he'd passed through many times before with Eli. He reckoned that he had slept for no more than a couple of hours.

In the far corner of the barn the horses munched on a pile of hay. Milo's throat was parched and his hungry belly rumbling. He cursed himself for not having thought to bring any food or water. *What sort of a traveller am I?* he thought wryly. *Eli will be turning in his grave at my stupidity.* He rolled over and got to his feet, and folding the blanket he went over to the horses and prepared to move out. Cautiously, he pushed one of the barn's large doors back on its hinges. After making sure there was no one about he led the horses out into the sunlight.

He was closing the barn door when he heard a shout, and swinging round he saw an old woman coming towards him. She was waving a stout stick. For a fleeting moment Milo thought about leaping into the saddle and riding off, but just as quickly he decided to stand his ground and brazen it out. Maybe she'd give him a drink of water and a bite to eat. Slowly, he walked to meet her.

The woman halted and flourished the stick. *She must be ninety if she's a day,* thought Milo, admiring the brave expression on her wrinkled face. For all her great age, her pale blue eyes were crystal-sharp. He smiled endearingly and then came to a stop about two feet away from her. 'Beg pardon ma'am, I hope you don't mind me taking shelter in your barn. I lost my way in the dark and the horses were weary.'

Her eyes narrowed and she pursed her lips against her toothless gums before opening her mouth wide and bawling, 'Nero.'

Milo wasn't going to hang around long enough to meet Nero so he turned on his heel and was ready to mount and make his escape when an ancient, shaggy mongrel shambled into the yard. Milo wanted to laugh out loud.

'He'll tear you limb from limb if I give him the word,' the old woman said in a voice that made Milo think of cawing crows, 'so hand back what you stole from my barn.' She waved the stick threateningly.

'I stole nothing. Sure, there's nothing to steal but a pile of hay and a rusty ploughshare. Check my pack if you please.'

He gestured to the saddlebag and the sack that was tied to the saddle's pommel.

The old woman approached, the dog at her heels. She unhooked the sack. First she shook it, and hearing a rattle she pulled at the string tied round the neck and then upended it. Out tumbled a stool with a broken leg, three rabbits, an owl, a dog and a little wooden man. She stared at them, curious. The mongrel plodded over and sniffed at them. Then she stooped and picked up the carving of the lurcher, holding it out for the dog to see.

'This is you, Nero,' she told the mongrel, and indeed it was a fair likeness. Nero wagged his tail. Then her eyes pierced Milo's face. 'Where'd you get these things? Stole 'em did you?'

'I made them,' said Milo, 'that's what I do. I carve wood.' He picked up the owl and the statuette. 'This old owl sat above our wagon night after night when we were lifting potatoes near Driffield, and this—' he proffered the statuette of Eli '—this is my grandfather.' And thinking to soften her heart into giving him something to eat and drink he solemnly added, 'I'm just after burying him.'

The woman handled the little wooden man and the lurcher carefully. Then, giving the statuette back to Milo she stuffed the lurcher into the pocket of her capacious black apron. 'I'll keep this one. Them's fine work you've got there.'

Milo grinned. 'Maybe you'll see your way to giving me a bite to eat in exchange for the carving,' he said hopefully.

It was the old woman's turn to grin. 'Pick up your bits and pieces and come this way, lad.' She turned and hobbled towards a gateway. Milo refilled his sack, and leading the horses by the reins he followed her out of the barnyard and into another yard behind a small cottage that had been hidden from view by tall trees and a dense hawthorn hedge. He wondered if he was letting his dry throat and his rumbling gut rule his better judgement, for it had crossed his mind that she might have a lusty son or grandson lurking somewhere.

'Leave the horses here,' she said, and as Milo tethered them to a stout sycamore she added. 'No one will bother them. There's only me and Nero bides here.'

Milo breathed a sigh of relief. He looked into the smiling face whose features were desiccated by extreme old age, and saw only kindness coupled with a lively sense of humour. He followed her into the cottage.

* * *

At Whitley Hey, Rosie too had risen early. She was making breakfast when Godfrey entered the kitchen looking grey and bedraggled. He sat down heavily at the table, his elbows resting on it, and his clasped hands propped under his chin.

'Couldn't you sleep either?' Rosie said, setting a boiled egg and two slices of toast in front of him. They had suffered three disturbing incidents during the night, Celeste ranting and raving as she roamed between her bedroom and the studio. On each occasion, Rosie or Godfrey, and sometimes both of them had forcibly returned her to her bed then trudged wearily back to their own, ears cocked for the next outburst. Strange though it may seem, Rosie willingly cared for Celeste in a way Celeste had never cared for her.

Godfrey shook his head. 'In between the forays I tossed and turned all night, and when I did doze I wakened under a blanket of sour dreams, Celeste playing on my conscience. Less than an hour ago, I got up and found her pacing the floor like a caged animal. I put her back to bed and tried to reason with her but...'

Words failing him, he sliced the top off his egg and then shrugged disconsolately.

'I'll take this up to her before I sit down to my own,' Rosie said, placing an egg and some toast on a tray and then mounting the backstairs.

Godfrey had barely eaten a mouthful when he heard Rosie's distraught cries.

'Godfrey! Godfrey! Come quick.'

His lethargy forgotten, Godfrey bounded up the back-stairs and then up the main staircase to where Rosie waited on the landing. She was trembling visibly, her face masked with fear and revulsion. She pointed a finger to Celeste's open bedroom door. 'I-In there,' she stuttered.

Godfrey stepped inside, Rosie at his heels. He let out a wail. 'Oh no! Oh, my God. What have you done?'

Celeste was sitting in the middle of the bed, clumps and wisps of greying hair strewn over the pillows and bedspread. Pinpricks of bright red blood mottled the pale, bald patches on her scalp, and watery, red rivulets trickled like spidery veins on to her forehead and cheeks. Her smile was demonic as she yanked another handful of hair out by its roots.

'No! No!' yelled Rosie and Godfrey, simultaneously leaping towards the bed, Rosie to the right side and Godfrey to the left. They each grabbed an arm, Celeste laughing hysterically as, with the strength of ten she struggled to free her flailing limbs. Baring her teeth she lunged at her captors, snapping at them like a rabid dog. Rosie and Godfrey held on. As she fought them off, loosened hanks of hair like fledgling birds took flight. A blood-streaked clump stuck to the sweat on Rosie's upper lip. She swiped it away, and as she swallowed her revulsion Celeste's bloodied head butted her in the face. Praying that her stomach would not betray her, Rosie battled on until she felt Celeste's body go limp.

Battered and breathless, Rosie and Godfrey stood over the inert body and exchanged looks of horror. Gently, Godfrey eased his wife into a comfortable position in the bed and drew up the covers. She sank back on the pillows, her eyelids fluttering and a vacant smile twisting the corners of her mouth. She looked like a doll that some peevish child had disfigured in a fit of pique, and Rosie felt an overwhelming rush of pity for the poor, broken creature. Godfrey's eyes were riveted on Celeste, his own wild with fear and desperation.

A movement at the bedroom door diverting their attention, Rosie and Godfrey turned and saw Hortense lolled against the doorframe. How long had she been there? They looked at her with unveiled dislike. Obviously, she had heard Rosie's cry for help and Celeste's hysterical screams. Why had she not come to assist?

Impassively, Hortense surveyed the scene, only her eyes betraying her repulsion. Then she turned on her heel and walked away, leaving Rosie and Godfrey to look at one another and shake their heads.

'I'll drive to the village and get the doctor,' Godfrey said, his voice wobbling and his face grey. He shook his head in disbelief as he shuffled from the room.

After he had gone, Rosie bathed Celeste's wounded head. Soothed by the warm water and Rosie's gentle strokes, Celeste dozed. Judging it safe to leave her, Rosie went to Hortense's room. She rapped the door and turned the knob, intent on marching in and speaking her mind, but the door was locked. She could hear Hortense moving about inside, so she called out, 'Celeste needs you. Will you sit with her while

I make us something to eat?' Receiving no reply, she kicked the door for good measure and yelled, 'Come out, you heartless bitch, and lend a hand in caring for your cousin.'

Godfrey came back alone. The doctor was elsewhere, but his wife promised to let him know he was needed at Whitley Hey. 'All we can do is wait, and hope he comes soon. I've left the trap at the front door in case I have to go again,' he said. Then he went and knocked on Hortense's room door, begging for her to come and help attend Celeste. When she didn't respond he rattled the knob, repeating his request to no avail.

For the rest of the morning Rosie or Godfrey, and sometimes both of them, stayed with Celeste. In between bouts of raving she slept, or if she was awake she lay like some dead thing, as though her spirit had already departed.

About midday, Rosie took Godfrey a cup of tea and a sandwich to where he sat keeping guard over his demented wife. 'I see that Hortense is still in hiding,' she said vehemently, 'I've a good mind to go and break down her door and drag her out by the hair.'

Godfrey's hand trembled as he accepted the tea, the cup rattling against the saucer. Nervously, he glanced at Celeste. She was sleeping fitfully. 'I don't understand,' he said wearily. 'Hortense's lack of compassion has me shocked and disappointed.'

'I'm more than disappointed. I'm bloody raging,' cried Rosie, marching from the bedroom and along the landing to Hortense's room. She gave the door a violent kick and yelled, 'Open this bloody door!' She twisted the knob. To her amazement the door swung open and she barged into the room. Seconds later, she hared back to Celeste's room, a look of utter bemusement on her ashen face.

'She's gone,' she cried, 'taken her belongings and left.'

'Surely not,' Godfrey gasped, tea slopping into the saucer as he jumped up.

'She has,' Rosie affirmed. 'Her drawers and cupboards are hanging open and empty, and her dressing table bare.'

'But where would she go?'

Rosie shrugged. 'I've no idea, and I can't say I care.'

'But how would she travel?' Godfrey was struggling to make sense of it.

Rosie dashed from the bedroom, and running the length of the landing she peered out of the window. 'She's taken the pony and trap,' she shouted.

Godfrey hurried from Celeste's bedroom. 'But I might need it to fetch the doctor,' he said, looking like a sulky child who has lost his favourite toy. 'We must get a doctor. Celeste needs professional help – and soon,' he added, as his wife gave a bloodcurdling scream.

Rosie groaned. 'In God's name, we all need help, Godfrey.'

THIRTEEN

EGGLESTON AND WHITLEY HEY, 1913

Milo kept his head down against the blasts of icy wind as he rode back to Bridie Newell's cottage. He had been to the market in Wakefield to sell his carvings and although Christmas was only two weeks off, a time when shoppers should have been buying his little stools and plate racks or his birds and animals as gifts for friends and family, trade had been poor. He put it down to the harsh weather – people only too willing to stay indoors out of the icy rain that had fallen for much of the week – rather than the quality of his goods. Having reluctantly sold Flicker to buy chisels, a lathe, three spoon gouges and a set of knives, his carvings were fine and intricate; Milo was proud of them.

In the three years that he had been living with Bridie he had made enough money to keep himself and the old woman in comfort. This he did willingly because he had grown extremely fond of Bridie. She reminded him of Eli. She had the same inner strength of character that spits in the face of hardship and a wisdom gathered from all that life had thrown at her. She kept him amused with her wry sense of humour and caustic witticisms, but it was her rough way of giving him her love that touched his heart. This was something Milo had not experienced before, never having had a mother or a grandmother to show him affection as Bridie did, day in and day out.

Now, as he led Sheba into the barn, Milo was eager to get indoors and spend the evening with Bridie. He knew she'd have a tasty stew simmering on the fire and maybe some of her home-made shortbread for afters. Quickly, he unhitched the sacks containing the unsold carvings and then gave the horse a good rub-down before feeding and watering her. Sheba comfortable and the sacks safely stored, he ran across the yard to the cottage. An icy blast accompanied him into the warmth of the little house.

'Shut that door and be quick about it before it freezes my arse off,' bawled Bridie, lifting an iron pot from the fire and setting it on the hearth. She had been waiting and listening for Milo's approach for the past hour as she tended the tasty stew she had made for the lad she had grown to love.

Milo laughed. He had grown used to Bridie's blunt way of speaking. 'Sure, you haven't an arse big enough to freeze,' he retaliated taking off his jacket and muffler. This remark was true for Bridie was birdlike, her small body shrunken with age.

'Never you mind my arse. Sit yourself down an' get this into you.'

Milo lowered his long, sturdy frame down onto a stool of his own making at the left hand side of the fire, stretching out his frozen fingers to the blaze, his blood tingling pleasantly as his hands warmed. He rubbed them together vigorously before accepting the bowl she handed him. Milo smacked his lips and began spooning stew into his hungry mouth and

Bridie sat down in the ancient armchair at the opposite side of the fireplace, her sharp eyes alight.

'Well, how did ye do today?' Bridie always asked the same thing on his return from the market, not for any pecuniary reasons but because she was proud of Milo's skills and wanted him to be successful. Before he could answer she added, 'Did you hear any interesting gossip or see anyone worth mentioning?' This too she always asked. Bridie loved gossip.

'The butcher's wife's run off with the chap that delivers the carcases,' Milo said, before spooning up another mouthful of stew.

Bridie cackled raucously. 'She always was a flighty one was Maggie Simms. She left him once before for the chap what made the sausages, but she came back an' she will do again. That one knows what side her bread's buttered – or should I say her steak minced.' She crowed at her own wit.

Milo swallowed and then laughed out loud. He enjoyed relating the events of the day in detail, particularly those that appealed to Bridie's sense of humour and her inquisitive nature. Although she now rarely ventured further than the cottage yard, Milo understood that she liked to be conversant with all that went on in the district so he dwelt on the interesting and spicy bits of gossip he had gleaned in the town.

'The council are going to build houses in Westgate for the working classes,' he said, refilling his bowl from the pot on the hearth. 'Dr Gibson says that the slums are causing disease and that people need clean, decent housing, so they're going to demolish 'em. Somebody told me that Hildred Threppleton is objecting.'

'Pshaw! Hildred Threppleton; him what owns the brewery. He's objecting 'cos he'll be losing the rents on them ratholes he owns. Greedy so-and-so owns half the town.' Bridie went off on a rant about the haves and the have-nots and Milo finished his stew. It never failed to amaze him that Bridie seemed to know everyone in the town for all she hadn't visited it too often in the past few years.

'Any shortbread?' he asked, knowing fine well there was for he could smell the hot buttery biscuits that she had baked in the side oven.

'Is your belly never full?' Bridie asked tartly, but Milo could tell she was delighted, her gummy smile wide as she handed him a plateful of the golden morsels. Milo took one, sinking his teeth into it and giving a rapturous sigh as he munched. His mouth emptied, he asked, 'Did Sam call for the rent today?'

'He did, Milo, and he asked after you. Said he hoped business was good.'

Milo chuckled. 'He would, seeing as how he put your rent up once he knew I was staying with you.' Bridie had told the landlord that Milo was her great-nephew, and although he didn't believe a word of it Sam had just nodded and then raised the rent a week later.

In the time that Milo had lived with Bridie she had ferreted into his background, sighing when she learned that his mother had died giving birth to him, and voicing her disgust when he told her about his father's untimely death.

'Eeh, you've had it rough, lad,' she had said, Milo quick to correct her by telling her about Eli and the loving care he had given him.

'He was the best,' Milo had said fondly and pausing thoughtfully before he'd added, 'That's why I found it so hard to understand what he did to Rosie.' Then he'd told Bridie all about the little red-haired minx he'd grown to love.

'Bearing in mind what you've told me, I suppose he had

his reasons,' she had said ruminatively. 'We all does things we regret.' Speculatively, she'd gazed into Milo's face. 'It sounds as though ye were awful fond of little Rosie.'

'I was – I still am. I think of her often.' The expression on Milo's face had been achingly sweet. Bridie's heart had gone out to him.

'Why did ye never try to meet up with her again? Ye knew where she was,' she had said, almost accusingly.

'I was afraid she wouldn't want to know me,' Milo had growled, his cheeks reddening, 'that she might have forgotten me. It would be like losing her all over again.' He'd wiped his hands over his face, frustrated by his lack of courage.

'Aye, that it might,' Bridie had said, 'but everybody needs somebody by them that they knows care's about 'em. Maybe she's thinking of you.' She'd left it at that.

But now, as then, she didn't like to think that Milo would be alone in the world once she had gone, and at her age that day was fast approaching. Like all good mothers – for that's how she saw herself – she'd like to see the lad settled with someone who loved him.

'An' how's the lovely Lily doing?' Bridie said, a wicked twinkle in her eye.

Milo grinned. 'She's pestering me for something I'm not yet ready to give her.'

'She's not the one then?'

Milo shook his head. 'She's a grand girl, but I'm not ready to settle down. There's other things I want to do before I saddle myself with a wife and childer.'

He'd had quite a few dalliances with girls from the market but, as yet, none of them had appealed enough for him to make any promises.

'Aye, you play the field, lad; you'll know when the right

one comes along, an' in the meantime you stick wi' old Bridie an' have the best o' both worlds.'

She gazed fondly at the handsome, dark-eyed boy and secretly wished that he would stay with her until the end. It would be easier to die if she were not alone when the time came; she had been alone too long.

* * *

Rosie lifted the pan of warmed milk and filled two large beakers, each of which contained a generous spoonful of Fry's Cocoa. Then she added two even more generous spoonfuls of sugar to Godfrey's and as she stirred each drink to a frothy consistency she pondered on what the future might hold.

These days, the house moved to a different rhythm now that Celeste was incarcerated in the lunatic asylum in Kirkburton and Hortense had gone to nobody knew where. Since their departure, Rosie and Godfrey had formed the habit of organising their lives to suit themselves. Most mornings, Rosie attended to the household chores and Godfrey to his writing. Afternoons were spent in the study, Rosie continuing with her lessons or, if the weather was fine, roaming the gardens or the farm fields. One glorious afternoon in early autumn, Godfrey suggested they forego the lessons and take a walk to Cotterley.

'Cotterley? Where's that?' Rosie had never heard mention of it.

'Two or three miles down the road. We can explore the ruins of the old church.' Godfrey's enthusiasm shone in his pale, grey eyes. 'Or, if you prefer nature to history we can cross the fields behind the farmstead to Ha'penny Wood. It'll be magnificent at this time of year. The beeches will be at their best, and there'll be fungus galore...' He paused dreamily before saying, 'Such fascinating, magical life forms, don't you think?'

Rosie didn't know what to think. 'Ha'penny Wood,' she echoed curiously. For a man who had rarely left the confines of his study in all the years she had known him Godfrey seemed awfully knowledgeable about places further afield. She, on the other hand, knew virtually nothing about what lay beyond the gardens and the farm at Whitley Hey. There had been no further annual trips to Hildred's brewery since he now brought Godfrey's allowance to the house and apart from that one-time fateful trip to Wakefield she had been nowhere.

'How come you know about... er...' she searched for the unfamiliar names '...Cotterley and Ha'penny Wood? You never go further than the house and farm,' Rosie said accusingly.

Godfrey looked slightly embarrassed. 'In the past I'd slip out of the house at dawn to roam the countryside in an attempt to gather my thoughts. I didn't go off when Celeste was ill,' he hastened to add. 'I would never have left you to cope on your own.'

Rosie shook her head. So he hadn't been cooped up in his study for all those years. What a strange, surprising man he was, and yet she didn't blame him for wanting to escape the house and some of its inhabitants. She had wanted to do the same on a hundred occasions, and had contemplated it just as often but had been too afraid of losing her way. Now, she realised just how insular her life was and that she must do something about it.

'Let's go,' she cried, dashing off to fetch her coat and boots. Godfrey followed at a more leisurely pace, his smile wide. He loved pleasing Rosie; and why hadn't he taken her to these places before now? he asked himself.

Since Celeste's departure, Rosie had raided her wardrobe to replace her own outgrown garments and footwear. Grateful that Celeste's boots and shoes were the right size, and despising the flounces and bows that Celeste had favoured, Rosie stripped the dresses and altered them to fit. They were still dated and worn, but she had never before been so well dressed.

* * *

That first outing to Cotterley and another to Ha'penny Wood had been wonderful experiences, Rosie awed by Godfrey's knowledge of plant life and the history of the land. After that, weather permitting, they ventured out daily, Rosie's horizons broadening by the hour. However, with each passing month she grew hungrier and hungrier for the world beyond Whitley Hey and its immediate surroundings, disappointed that there were limits to how far they could travel on foot. And, winter approaching, even these short journeys had to be curtailed.

Now, in December, an icy blast rattling at the kitchen window and thick snow blanketing the yard and garden, Rosie acknowledged that winter's iron hand would yet again make her a prisoner. Heaving a sigh, she lifted the cocoa cups and went upstairs to the study where Godfrey sat toasting his feet at a blazing log fire and reading Conrad's *Heart of Darkness* for the umpteenth time. He glanced up as Rosie entered the room, a warm smile on his face. Secretly, he often thought of Rosie as his daughter, and knew deep down in his heart that he would be lost without her.

* * *

The foul weather persisted and once again the house closed in round them, Rosie often feeling as if she too was just as incarcerated as poor Celeste. She yearned for companions of her own age, and yet she worried that if she were to find some she wouldn't know how to behave. It frightened her to think how narrow her life was, and that whilst her head teemed with the knowledge Godfrey had helped to put there, she knew nothing about how other people lived, or how she would find her way about a busy town. She had never been shopping although she had listened enviously to Florrie excitedly describing the purchases she had made on her monthly trips to Wakefield. In fact, Rosie's social circle was so small that she imagined she would probably find large crowds intimidating, and yet she dearly wanted to experience these things. She dreamed of living elsewhere, but when she wakened she knew she would never leave Godfrey alone, with nobody to care for him.

* * *

Milo stamped the snow off his boots before entering the cottage, a pile of logs in his arms. 'It's blowing a blizzard out there and the snow's so deep I'll not be able to get into town for days if this keeps up.'

Bridie hobbled to the fire and then the table with none of her usual ribald comments or ready wit. She set the plate down, her crabbed hand shaking. Gravy slopped onto the cloth. 'Aagh!' she moaned, and then shuffled back to her chair by the fire.

Milo was busy stacking logs in the alcove at the fireside,

but now he turned troubled eyes on Bridie, fear clutching at his heart. Shoving the last log into place he swivelled on his knees and took her hands in his, the paper-thin skin and knobbly bones like two dead birds against his palms. He gazed up at the face he had grown to love and saw the grey tinge to her cheeks and the maroon sacks below her eyes, exaggerated by the fire's glow. They had not been there a week ago. Milo's heart ached.

'What ails ye, Bridie?' He spoke softly and urgently.

Bridie managed a weary half-smile. 'Nothing but old age, lad. I feel my time is drawing in – an' there's not a damned thing I can do about it.' Her spirit flared as she spoke the last few words and she gave a gravelly cackle before adding, 'And this bloody weather doesn't help. I can't seem to get warm these past three days.'

Still on his knees, Milo turned and poked at the fire on which he had put fresh logs. Flames soared up the chimney. He stirred the logs to let the heat escape into the chilly room, and then coming upright he went and fetched a blanket from his bed, wrapping it about Bridie's frail, little body until she resembled a cocoon.

Bridie gave a throaty chuckle that turned into a hacking cough, and when she had caught her breath and wiped her rheumy eyes she ruffled Milo's hair. 'Ye're very good to me, lad,' she said warmly. 'I bless the day I caught ye thieving from my barn.'

Milo gulped his relief. Bridie was back to her old self. 'I did no such thing,' he riposted. 'You had damn all to steal. T'was you did the thieving when you pocketed my lurcher.'

Bridie's eyes strayed to where the carving of the lurcher sat beside a battered old clock on the shelf above the fire. 'Aye, t'was me that saw the talent ye had an' set you on the road to making yer fortune.'

Milo ate his supper and then they sat on for an hour or so, the lively banter and the gossip of the day seeming to revive Bridie, but when at last they retired for the night, Milo insisting that she keep the blanket from his bed, he stayed awake listening to her rasping breath.

* * *

The next day, Milo strapped a shovel to the horse and battled through the snowdrifts along the road to Eggleston, bringing back with him a rather irate doctor whom he had coerced into making the journey. A fat young man with a pompous attitude, he had baulked at driving his pony and trap out of the town and on to country lanes heaped with snow, but Milo's threatening stance had changed his mind.

'You'd let an old lady die because you're afraid of getting your boots wet?' Milo had sneered. 'I thought your sort saved lives.'

Shamed, the doctor had followed Milo to the cottage, Milo making his passage easier on several occasions by shovelling a path through the drifts. He cursed at their slow progress, afraid to leave Bridie alone for too long. He had insisted she kept to her bed and did no chores, but knowing how stubborn she was he doubted she would obey him. However, she had made no attempt to rise before he left and that troubled him all the more.

Bridie was still in bed when Milo led the doctor into the cottage. Hearing the door creak on its hinges she opened her eyes, widening them when she saw that Milo was not alone. She gave him a quizzical glare.

'I've brought the doctor,' he said.

Bridie curled her lip. 'Then ye've wasted good time an' money,' she growled.

'I'm Dr Arbuthnot,' the plump young man said, moving closer to the bed. 'Your son insisted I come to see you.' Bridie didn't bother to correct him.

'Arbuthnot, ye say. Is old Compton dead then?'

Surprised by the abrupt question, Dr Arbuthnot mumbled that he was his assistant. 'Perhaps I should take a closer look at you,' he said, the tremor in his voice making the corners of Bridie's mouth quirk.

'Ye'll do no such thing. I'm not ill. The only thing wrong wi' me lad is too many birthdays. I'll be ninety-nine come summer, an' I don't expect to make it to a century. So you be on your way an' do summat for them as can be helped.' Bridie closed her eyes and pressed her lips together signalling that the consultation was over. Dr Arbuthnot, looking somewhat relieved, shrugged his shoulders, and bidding her good day he walked to the door, beckoning for Milo to follow him.

Seething inwardly at what he had allowed to take place, Milo stepped out into the chill air feeling as though he wanted to punch someone or something. He should have forced Bridie to let the doctor examine her, and yet, in his heart he knew he could never humiliate her in such a manner. He looked balefully at the doctor. Dr Arbuthnot met his gaze warily.

'She's dying of old age, nothing more.'

'How can you be sure?'

'Her skin is paper-thin and mottled. No doubt her heart is failing. You told me yourself that she falls asleep during the day, and that she cannot get warm. All these are signs that the body is giving in, and after almost ninety-nine years it's not surprising.' Dr Arbuthnot sounded very sure of the facts. Milo bowed to his superior knowledge.

'What should I do?' he asked fervently.

The doctor smiled sympathetically. 'See that she drinks plenty and eats little and often, and keep her warm. From what I've seen, she's a tough old bird. She's not ready to go just yet.' He accepted his fee and climbed into the trap.

Milo left him to find his own way back to Eggleston and hurried inside to Bridie.

'Doctor indeed, he was barely wet behind the ears.' She cackled.

FOURTEEN

Golden daffodils trumpeted along the edges of the lawn and the trees in Whitley Hey's garden, and the neighbouring woods burgeoned forth with buds and blossom; spring had come at last. Rosie welcomed it gladly, seeing as how the first three months of 1913 had had far too many days of lashing rain and blustery winds, thus preventing walks in the country-side. It seemed to Rosie that she and Godfrey, like a pair of old hens, had been cooped up indoors for an eternity. She pulled on an old caped coat that had belonged to Celeste and headed for Godfrey's study.

Once again they trekked the lanes and woods, this time venturing further from the house. Out on the road, Rosie turned her head when she heard the rumble of wheels. A cart was coming towards them, and when it was in hailing distance Rosie stuck out her arm and flagged him down.

'Can we take a ride with you?'

'Where be you going?' the carter asked curiously. 'I'm for Eggleston meself.'

'Then that's where we'll go,' Rosie cried, her excitement palpable.

Godfrey looked askance. 'That's miles from Whitley; how will we get back?'

'The same way. There are bound to be carts going back through Whitley.'

'That's right, miss. I'll be coming back this way meself at about four, so if you looks out for me at the Bull and Ram you're welcome to ride along o' me.' At Rosie's insistence Godfrey agreed, and laughing at their daring like two truanting schoolchildren they climbed aboard.

Godfrey having overcome his doubts and Rosie's enthusiasm infectious, sat back and enjoyed the journey, although his mind was plagued with regrets. He would dearly have liked to be the one taking her on this venture but, sadly, they had no means of transport since Hortense had misappropriated the pony and trap, and Hildred refused to replace it. That Godfrey regretted the wasted years spent in self-inflicted confinement at Whitley Hey went without saying. Now that he thought of it, he should have been introducing Rosie to all manner of things other than book learning, and as the cart trundled along he pondered on how insular the girl's life had been in her formative years, and how it still was, and she sixteen years of age. Silently, he promised to amend his negligence.

The carter dropped them at the Bull and Ram, reminding them to be back by four. Rosie could barely contain her excitement as, fascinated by everything and everyone she saw, they progressed slowly through the narrow, winding streets to the centre of the little town. However, she did feel dowdy when she saw the fashionable clothing worn by the young women who passed by, her dated cape coat a sorry comparison to the neat, high-collared coats they were wearing.

They window-shopped in Church Street and then visited the church that gave the street its name. As they walked round the outside of All Saints, Rosie gazed in wonder at its Gothic architecture and asked a hundred questions. When they stepped inside she was spellbound, the cloistered silence and the fragrant scent of incense making her blood tingle.

'What's this?' she whispered, firstly at the font and then at numerous objects that caught her interest, and Godfrey answering in his usual didactic manner.

At the altar, Rosie gazed in awe at the magnificent stained glass window that filled the gable wall. 'Marvellous! Beautiful!' she said, her words gushing out on her breath. She would have liked to linger, but outside there were so many other places to see and unfamiliar things to do that she tore herself away, following Godfrey out of the peaceful gloom and into the sunlit, busy street. They turned the corner into Market Street.

'Oh, look,' Rosie cried, clapping her hands gleefully when she saw the stalls that lined either side of the street, their canvas awnings flapping in the gentle breeze and their gaily bedecked counters piled high with all manner of goods. She set off at a trot, lured this way and that as she inspected brightly coloured scarves, pottery, sweet meats and a host of foodstuffs. Godfrey dearly wanted to purchase something for her, but having only enough money in his pocket to pay for something to eat, and by now they were hungry, he led her to a pie stall where they feasted on crusty pastry filled with mince and hot gravy.

* * *

Across the street, Milo lifted a beautifully carved crane and handed it to the woman who was admiring it. It was one of his more expensive pieces and he was keen to make a sale. The woman held the bird in her left hand, carefully stroking the finely carved feathers with the tip of her right forefinger. 'It's so lifelike,' she commented, turning to hold the bird in the direct rays of the sun. Milo's eyes followed her movements, his attention suddenly deflected as he caught sight of a glorious tumble of copper hair. It hung down the back of a young girl standing at the pie stall. She turned sideways, and something about the way she tilted her head and lifted her hand to her mouth made him shiver.

Rosie. It could be Rosie, he thought, torn between dashing across the street to see the girl's face or staying put and making a sale. The woman spoke, and whilst he hadn't quite made out her words he tore his gaze from the girl and paid full attention to his customer, cleverly negotiating the sale of the crane and a frog on a lily pad. When he next looked over at the pie stall, the girl had gone. Crushed with disappointment, he served another customer.

* * *

Godfrey and Rosie walked away from the stalls to the far end of the street, Godfrey keen to show Rosie the window display in an ancient apothecary. 'It fascinates me,' he said, as they gazed at large red and blue flacons with bulbous bottoms and narrow necks that were flanked by an assortment of amber flasks, demijohns and neatly labelled bottles of all sizes. 'A cure for all ills,' he said dreamily, and then pointing to the narrow boxes of sharp, shiny surgical instruments he added, 'I once toyed with the idea of becoming a doctor.' He sounded sad.

'You'd have made a good one,' Rosie said encouragingly. She didn't want Godfrey to dwell on 'what might have been' and spoil the fun of the day. 'You'd have been kind and gentle and very learned,' she continued, 'finding new cures and saving lives.' She paused reflectively. 'Funnily enough, when I was tending Celeste's cuts and bruises I found it satisfying to watch them heal. Maybe *I* should become a doctor.' She chuckled at the idea.

'There's no reason why you shouldn't,' Godfrey said, his eyes flashing as he caught her hands in his and waltzed her round. 'You know what we'll do? When we get back home we'll hunt out all the books on the human body and medicine and start you off on your career.' Rosie burst out laughing at his enthusiasm.

'You really believe I could be one, don't you?'

'You can be anything you want, Rosie. Never forget that.'

They retraced their steps, Rosie spying the display of wooden animals and birds as they strolled past the stalls. She tugged at Godfrey's sleeve.

'Oh, look! Aren't they lovely?' A tall, dark-haired, young man, head down, was busily rearranging some of his wares on his counter. As he stepped back to view the display he raised his hand, flicking his forelock away from his eyes.

Something in this simple action stirred Rosie's memory and she felt a sudden compulsion to go over to the stall and take a closer look at the young man and his wares but Godfrey, his eye on the clock in the church tower, urged her on. 'If we're to meet the carter at the Bull and Ram we had better keep moving,' he said, quickening his pace. Reluctantly, Rosie complied.

Milo raised his head just in time to see the back of a shapely young girl with bouncing copper tresses disappearing into the crowd, and once again a feeling deep inside told him to run and enquire who she was.

'Hey, Lily, mind my stall for a minute,' he called to the girl selling embroidered mats on the next stall. Lily agreed willingly. She had been walking out with Milo for almost two months now and her heart was set on marrying him.

Milo pushed his way through the throng of late afternoon shoppers, keeping a sharp eye out for a head of copper curls, but he didn't spot the girl again.

In the yard at the back of the Bull and Ram, Rosie and Godfrey waited for the carter to finish his pint of stout.

* * *

Milo packed up his stall, stowing his unsold carvings into the basketwork panniers he had bought specially to transport his wares. Much to Lily's disappointment, he refused to accompany her home for tea, and with a pannier slung over each shoulder he walked to the farrier's yard to collect his horse. As he walked he thought about the red-haired girl.

In the intervening years he had often thought about Rosie, anger spurting in his chest whenever he recalled the day Eli had given her away. He had never forgotten the way she had looked that day, a pink and white cherub with a scattering of freckles across her pretty little nose, and those greenish-blue eyes that had looked on innocently as the madwoman and his grandfather decided her future. Now, having seen the red-haired girl in the market, he couldn't get her out of his mind.

The evening was pleasantly warm and the hedgerows on either side of the road back to the cottage sweet smelling and effulgent with red campions and bluebells. Here and there carpets of germander speedwell winked their tiny blue eyes under white parasols of wild parsley, Milo breathing in the scented air with deep satisfaction and remembering a giddy little girl who had picked bluebells and placed them in jam jars inside the vardo.

During the years he had lived with Bridie, it had occurred to him more than once that Whitley Hey was not all that many miles away. Sometimes, on nights when sleep evaded him, he contemplated paying a visit to the house and enquiring as to Rosie's wellbeing, but the memory of the madwoman's dislike for him – he hadn't forgotten the way she had snapped at him to keep quiet and not to interfere as she and Eli negotiated Rosie's future – had him reasoning that it would be a wasted journey. Fear of rejection still haunted him.

Now, as his horse trotted along the same road that Rosie and Godfrey had travelled an hour or so before, Milo thought it more than likely that Rosie would by now be a grand young lady. After all, the Threppletons were rich. Didn't they live in a mansion and own a thriving farm? He pictured her wearing beautiful gowns and attending parties and balls with the daughters and sons of wealthy landowners, doctors, merchants and the like. *She's hardly likely to want a gypsy for a friend,* he told himself sourly.

* * *

'What a day,' Rosie exclaimed, flinging her hat in the direction of the hallstand. 'I can barely believe I've seen and done so much in so few hours.' She turned to Godfrey, who was picking up her hat and then hanging it with his own coat. 'Thank you for taking me to Eggleston, Godfrey.'

'I believe it was you who took me, or should I say the carter,' Godfrey replied, the twinkle in his eyes letting her know he too had enjoyed the day.

'Wasn't the church magnificent?' Rosie cried. 'It's the most splendid building I've ever seen. And all those people – I've never seen such crowds.'

Yet again, Godfrey felt a tug of guilt.

Rosie skipped to the head of the basement stairs, calling out as she clattered downwards, 'The gravy pie in the market was delicious but I'm hungry again. Will we have boiled eggs or cheese sandwiches?'

Smiling indulgently, Godfrey followed her into the kitchen.

'Next Friday is payday,' Godfrey said, as they ate cheese sandwiches thick as doorsteps. 'I'm going to beg Hildred to replace the pony and trap. If he agrees, we can travel whenever and to wherever we choose.'

'Oh, yes please,' Rosie spluttered through a mouthful of bread and cheese. Mindful of how they had come to be without transport she asked, 'What was it that made Hortense so bitter and vile?'

Godfrey's eyes darkened. 'Lack of expectation,' he said morosely. He then went on to tell Rosie about Hortense's unfortunate childhood, and neglecting to divulge his own involvement he concluded, 'That and a disappointment in love made her the way she was.'

Rosie snorted. 'It doesn't excuse the way she treated me,' she cried, 'but why are we even bothering to discuss her? We don't want the day to end on a sour note.'

They sat on, Rosie recalling all they had seen and done and not wanting to let go of what she thought was the best day in her life. Then they went up to Godfrey's study and dug out the medical books, flipping pages and swapping scraps of information, taking great pleasure from yet another shared experience.

That night, Rosie in bed and the excitement of the day making her restless, she again relived the hours spent in Eggleston. When she pictured the market stalls and the wonderful variety of goods on offer, it was the stall selling carved animals and birds that she saw most clearly. As she dwelt on the mental image, the strangest feeling came over her. In her mind's eye Rosie saw the young man whose dark hair flopped over his forehead and curled round his ears. She pictured the way in which he had flicked back his forelock, the action so familiar that she felt she knew him. The notion made her smile.

FIFTEEN

Bridie Newell died in Milo's arms on a glorious late spring evening just one week after Milo had seen the red-haired girl at the market. He'd thought of her often, but since that first sighting he hadn't been back to Eggleston to tend his stall. He had stayed at home instead to tend Bridie. With each passing day he had watched her spirit flickering and fading, knowing that soon she would leave him.

In those last few days she only left her bed to answer nature's call. Then, Milo had helped her, lifting her twig-like body in his arms and carrying her out to the closet in the yard. She'd give him a gummy smile and croaked, 'I'm a useless old bugger, as helpless as a newborn babe,' her attempt to make light of the situation bringing tears to Milo's eyes. Whenever Bridie saw his tears she'd say, 'Away out o' that! I'm not weeping so why should you?'

On the evening of her death, Bridie asked Milo to open the door and both windows to let in the warm breeze and the fiery rays of the setting sun. When he had done that, he went and sat by the bed and held her hand. They both knew it wasn't long now.

'I'm not afraid,' said Bridie. 'I can meet my maker with a clear conscience for I've allus done a good turn rather than a bad'un. I've had a grand life even if no man ever wanted to marry me and give me childer, but you've made up for it these past three years, an' for that I'm grateful.' Her voice grew fainter by the second and Milo held both his breath and Bridie's hand like a man clinging to a crumbling cliff edge.

Bridie closed her eyes, a gentle smile lighting her face, and Milo got down on his knees so that he could put his arms round her. Sighing happily, she snuggled into him and didn't speak again. It was as though she had decided the time was right to let go.

* * *

Godfrey stood beside Rosie, a woebegone expression on his face. Rosie blew her nose noisily and then reached for the glass of linctus on the bedside table.

She sipped the noxious syrup in the hope that it might ease her swollen throat.

'It can't be helped, Godfrey. It's not your fault I've got this awful cold.'

'But you were so looking forward to it.' He shook his head despairingly. 'I'd rather not go at all.'

'Hildred's expecting you,' Rosie spluttered, an attack of coughing preventing her from saying more. She too had been looking forward to going to Wakefield. It would have been her first visit since the disastrous trip that precipitated Celeste's descent into madness. She blew her nose and then, trying to sound cheerful, she added, 'I was looking forward to the ride in the car he's sending to fetch you more than anything, to be honest. I can't say I'm sorry not to see your brother, even if he does put a roof over my head and pay for every mouthful of food I eat.' Facts that played on Rosie's conscience.

Godfrey gave a wan smile and a little shrug. 'Then I'll go and be at my most grovelling and see if I can't persuade him to provide us with a pony and trap. Business must be thriving if he can afford to purchase a motor car.' He stooped to drop a kiss on Rosie's brow. 'The car should arrive shortly,' he said, coming upright and then glancing at his pocket watch. 'Now, you keep warm and I'll be back in the late afternoon.'

Rosie gave an enormous sneeze. 'Bless you,' said Godfrey.

She wiped her nose and then waved the handkerchief dismissively at him. 'Go on with you,' she said, 'and enjoy the ride. I'll most likely sleep for the rest of the day and dream of the smart pony and trap your persuasive charm will force Hildred into giving us. Quote to him from Homer: tell him "the journey is the thing".'

Godfrey laughed, and giving Rosie a farewell wave he ran downstairs and was standing by the front door when the sleek black and cream Standard drove up to the house. He felt childishly excited to be taking his first ride in a motorised vehicle, yet at the same time he was anxious about why Hildred needed to see him and disappointed that Rosie was too poorly to share the pleasure.

'The car's here,' he called loudly before stepping outside, hopeful that Rosie would hear him. 'Wish me luck.'

* * *

After Godfrey had gone, Rosie continued reading Bennett's *Anna of the Five Towns* and as she read she drew parallels with Anna's narrow existence and her own. Not that Godfrey was like Anna's harsh father – he was anything but – yet like Anna she felt deprived of choices and the more she read the more Rosie determined to discuss her future with Godfrey when he returned. She couldn't stay cloistered in Whitley Hey until she grew old and grey, or go mad like poor Celeste. It wasn't natural for a healthy young woman to let a man she barely knew support her for the rest of her days. She needed to leave and find a job that would support both herself and Godfrey. It never occurred to her that Godfrey should find work, but she knew she couldn't bear to leave without him.

Tossing the book aside, she got out of bed and on trembling legs went down to the kitchen to make a hot drink to soothe her aching throat. As she waited for the kettle to boil, her thoughts tumbled like stones inside her head, each one heavier than its predecessor. What sort of work could a girl like her do? Who would employ someone with so little experience of the world outside Whitley Hey?

How would she pass herself in society? And what would she say if they asked about her family background? She'd never had a family. She didn't even have a surname that she could truly call her own. A quote from *The Iliad* about Odysseus and the Cyclops came to mind: '*I am Nobody.*'

'That's me,' she said aloud to the steaming cup of honey and lemon juice. 'I'm Rosie Nobody.'

Disillusioned by these thoughts she climbed the stairs. Lying back against her pillows, her head thumping, she sipped her drink and tried to think more positively. She knew she was clever, that Godfrey had taught her well. Perhaps it was time to put her knowledge to use. If she could meet someone who would take time to listen, maybe she could convince them that nothing was beyond her capabilities, but how was she to meet such a person if she stayed here? With this thought in mind she put her cup on the bedside table and snuggled down under the covers to think some more. Minutes later, she fell sound asleep.

When she wakened, the room was in complete darkness, the open curtains letting her know that night had fallen whilst she slept. Curious as to why Godfrey had not wakened her to report on his visit to Hildred, she climbed out of bed and went in search of him.

The lamps on the landing and in the hallway remained unlit and she wrinkled her forehead, puzzled. What time was it? And why hadn't Godfrey lit the lamps? She tottered along the corridor to his study. It too was in darkness. He must be down in the kitchen making something to eat, she told herself, descending the stairs to the hallway, and gasping when the face of the long-case clock told her it was five minutes past midnight. When she opened the door at the head of the basement stairs, her nose didn't detect any appetising smells or her ears the rattle of pots and pans. Neither was there a crack of light shining from under the kitchen door.

Her legs decidedly unsteady and her thoughts grim, she tottered downwards.

As she stepped into the dark, empty kitchen, fear clutched at her empty stomach. She was alone in the house. Godfrey hadn't come back.

SIXTEEN

Hildred Threppleton stood in the hallway at Whitley Hey, twisting his bowler hat round and round in his large, beefy hands, his features ravaged with grief as he gave Rosie the news. She hadn't slept since discovering Godfrey's absence and now, cold, hungry and dishevelled she stared vacantly at Hildred, too stunned to speak or move.

'He didn't suffer,' Hildred said gruffly. 'His death was instantaneous, so I've been told.'

'He was so looking forward to riding in the car,' Rosie said, her voice barely a whisper. Feeling foolish at making the remark, she hung her head and covered her face with her hands.

'Had I known the driver was incompetent I would never have let him near the vehicle,' Hildred growled, and then, as though giving vent to his anger would somehow assuage his grief and his own culpability, he said, 'Apparently the fool was bowling along the road when he collided with a farm cart coming round the bend. Poor Godfrey was thrown from the car and hit the road with great force, so the carter informed us. By the time the carter had untangled himself from the wreckage of his cart and his dead horse, Godfrey was beyond help.' Hildred's shoulders heaved and he looked as though he might collapse.

Rosie pressed her eyes shut and screwed up her face, clamping her lips together to stem the tide of tears that surged from her throat to her eyes. She was afraid to feel. Numbness was far safer. It didn't hurt. She opened her eyes, and looking directly at Hildred she asked, 'What will I do now?'

Hildred walked by her into the drawing room and sat down heavily on a sofa.

Rosie followed, feeling ridiculously vulnerable in the nightdress she was still wearing. Her sore throat throbbed as she blew her blocked nose into an overworked handkerchief. Hildred nodded for her to take a seat. She sat facing him, her trembling hands wedged between her knees as she waited for him to determine her future.

'You can't stay here,' he said. Rosie was shocked by his bluntness although he hadn't spoken unkindly. 'I'll take you back to Wakefield with me, find you accommodation and a suitable occupation.' He shook his head. 'I cannot begin to imagine how or why you came to be here in the first place, other than that it was some foolish whim of that dreadful woman. However, poor Godfrey told me you have been very good to him and...' he gulped back a sob '...it's only right that I take some responsibility for you now that he's no longer with us.'

He fell silent, shrouded in guilt. The reason he had sent for Godfrey was to inform him that he was re-letting the house to a wealthy merchant and that Godfrey would have to find alternative accommodation. That decision had killed his brother, and Hildred felt bound to make reparation. He stared hard at Rosie. 'How many years is it that you have lived here? I seem to have forgotten.'

'It must be more than ten. Mrs Naggs told me I was about four when I arrived.'

'*Tempus fugit*,' Hildred muttered.

'Time flies,' Rosie translated automatically, as she would have done during her lessons with Godfrey. A lump came into her throat at the memory.

Hildred's eyes widened. 'You know Latin, do you?'

'Yes, Godfrey taught me that, and French and a bit of Spanish. We studied every day. Mathematics, the Classics, science and geography, we covered them all.' Talking about Godfrey and all that they had done together somehow helped to ease the terrible ache in her heart. But it didn't last.

'My, my,' said Hildred, his eyes popping and then clouding with concern as Rosie burst into tears. He let her cry, and when at last she could cry no more he gently advised her to pack her belongings. Out in the hallway, she unhooked the awful cape coat from the stand and then slowly climbed the stairs.

In Godfrey's bedroom Rosie found a large, leather valise in which to pack her things. Back in her own room, she emptied drawers and the wardrobe but when she took stock of the hand-me-down garments that had once belonged to Celeste, she was overcome with anxiety. Like the cape coat, they were shabby and old-fashioned; hadn't her visit to Eggleston let her know as much?

Panicked, she rushed to Celeste's room, but the wardrobes there were stuffed with more of Celeste's outlandish creations, none of them fit for wearing in the city. She helped herself to two silk scarves and a pretty embroidered waistcoat. Next, she dashed to Hortense's old room. Perhaps she had left something behind. In a drawer she found a black shirtwaist, and thrown over the back of a chair was a long, black skirt. Neither of them were in good condition, the shirtwaist missing buttons and the skirt tattered at the hem, but both garments were preferable to Celeste's and whatever Rosie had.

Back in her own room, she quickly washed her face, ashamed that Hildred must have seen the dribble of snot smeared on the side of her reddened nose. What must he think of her? Then, dressed in Hortense's cast-offs, she packed underwear and nightclothes and two of her least offensive dresses and the waistcoat and scarves in the valise. On top of these she scattered her few personal possessions: a hairbrush, some ribbons bought by Mrs Naggs, a rag doll Florrie had given her, and a handful of shiny conkers. Finally, she folded the blue cloak from her bed and draped it over her arm. Picking up the bag she left the room and didn't look back.

Outside Godfrey's study her heart fluttered uncomfortably. How she longed for him to be in there sitting at his desk, pen in hand. She closed her eyes to stem the tears and thought longingly of the happy hours spent in that room with the man she had grown to love. An idea blossomed and she hurried downstairs to share it with Hildred. He stood as she entered the drawing room.

'Ah, I see you've dressed for the journey,' he said, looking approvingly at her sombre black outfit. 'Have you everything you need?'

Rosie took a deep breath. 'I wondered if I might take some of Godfrey's books,' she said, her voice wobbling with uncertainty.

Hildred's bluff features softened. 'Why not,' he said gently. 'Off you go and help yourself.' He followed her up to the study, and Rosie not wishing to appear greedy chose a dozen of her favourite books. Hildred roamed about the room, pausing every now and then to lift an item or look at a book. When Rosie indicated she had what she wanted, he said, 'I'll be clearing the house. Is there anything else you would like to have?'

Rosie would have liked to take everything but reasoning that it wasn't possible she replied, 'If I might, I'd like Godfrey's pens and the globe.'

Hildred nodded. 'Take the pens with you, and I'll have the globe delivered to you when we bring the contents of the house to Wakefield.'

Rosie's heart swelling at his generosity, she scooped up the pens and put them in her skirt pocket, and emboldened by Hildred's kindness she added to the books she had already chosen, stowing them in the valise, on top of her clothes. Hildred lifted the bulging bag and went downstairs. Rosie lifted the blue cloak from where she had hung it over the back of Godfrey's chair, and with it draped over her arm she gazed fondly and tearfully round Godfrey's study for the very last time. She was leaving Whitley Hey.

* * *

Hildred took Rosie to Wakefield: not to his own home but to a house close by the brewery. There, Rosie was introduced to Miss Agatha Wimpenny, owner of a boarding house for young ladies. Miss Wimpenny, a small, plump, homely woman of middle years welcomed Rosie with a warm, friendly smile, Rosie feeling immediately easier than she had felt on the journey from Whitley Hey.

Before Hildred left, he gave Rosie instructions to meet him at the brewery the next morning at eight o'clock sharp.

Miss Wimpenny showed Rosie up to a small, pleasant room at the back of the house. 'This is all yours, Miss Threppleton. You don't have to share, what with it being the smallest. The bathroom is at the end of the landing. When you've unpacked come down to the kitchen for a cup of tea.' As she trotted out of the room Rosie followed her with her eyes, thinking that if everyone was as nice as her landlady then getting used to living in Wakefield might be easier than she had imagined.

Then her mouth turned up at the corners at the name Miss Wimpenny had called her. Miss Threppleton indeed, she thought, amused. What had Hildred told Miss Wimpenny? Had he passed her off as his late brother's daughter? Rosie didn't care; she didn't have a surname, and she could hardly go about calling herself Rosie Nobody.

* * *

The next morning, Rosie dressed carefully in the black shirtwaist and skirt.

She had replaced the shirtwaist's missing buttons with some she had snipped off the pretty waistcoat and she had tidied the ragged hem on the skirt. It was a bright, breezy morning, Rosie pleased to find it warm enough not to have to wear the awful cape coat. Instead, she draped one of the scarves about her shoulders, its dark red colours contrasting nicely with the black. She had rolled her hair into a neat chignon, and when she looked in the mirror in Miss Wimpenny's lobby a tall, slender girl with tidy red hair and lively greenish-blue eyes stared back at her. She looked efficient and ready for anything. At a quarter to eight she left the boarding house and walked through unfamiliar streets to the brewery, her steps brisk and her heart in her mouth.

Hildred greeted her pleasantly, and once again she saw the look of approval in his eyes. Silently, she thanked Hortense for her cast-offs. Hildred led her to an office in a building across the yard from the loading bay, and there he put her to the test.

'What do you make of this?' he said, handing her an invoice written in French.

Slowly at first and then with increasing alacrity, Rosie translated the invoice.

Beaming, Hildred clapped his hands. 'Godfrey did teach you well,' he cried. 'Now, what about this?' He pushed another invoice with a long column of figures on it into her hand. 'Does it tally correctly?'

Rosie totted the figures and then declared, 'It's four pence too little.'

* * *

A few streets away from the brewery, Milo was busy displaying his wares on a stall in the market. He had been lodging in Wakefield since Bridie's death, the city providing him with better custom than that in Eggleston Market, and easing the loss of the woman he had looked on as a grandmother. He missed Bridie's wry wit and wise words and the rough love she had freely given. Now, it was time to start afresh.

Another reason for leaving Eggleston was Lily Dawson. Milo was too kind-hearted to let her believe they had a future together so, by putting distance between them, he had gently ended the friendship. He missed Lily's lively chatter and warm kisses, just as he missed the friendly banter of the other stallholders on Eggleston Market. He had yet to make friends in Wakefield and once the market closed for the day, the evenings were lonely.

At the end of the day he returned to his lodgings in Back Lane, a street of small terraced houses close by Wakefield Gaol. There was nothing fancy about Gertie Briggs's house, but Milo's rent was cheap and the meals she provided edible. The window in his sparsely furnished, dank and dismal room looked out on the gaol's ominous grey walls and Milo had shuddered when he first saw them. He would hate to be locked up.

After eating the watery stew Gertie served up, Milo went to his room and spent an hour or so carving a couple of owls; they were popular with his customers. Then, finding the silence in the room oppressive, he changed his shirt and neckerchief and went out. He wasn't a drinking man but, just lately, he had taken to making regular visits to the Wagon and Horses pub more for the company than the ale. Walking down Ings Lane and then into Westgate, Milo pondered on whether or not to stay in Wakefield.

* * *

Rosie closed the ledger and then stretched her aching shoulders. She had stayed behind in the office long after the other clerks had left for home to work on an account that had been overlooked. She enjoyed performing the tasks Hildred set. They were varied and interesting because Hildred had several other businesses as well as the brewery. He regularly praised her for her diligence, and more importantly he paid her a decent wage at the end of each week. She often worked late. It made the long, lonely evenings pass more quickly, and she had nothing to hurry back to her lodgings for; as yet, she hadn't made friends with Miss Wimpenny's other lodgers.

In fact, Rosie had yet to find any companions of her own age, the other clerks in the office being two elderly men, and whilst Miss Wimpenny was pleasant enough she was far too nosy for Rosie's liking. An hour in her company was like the Grand Inquisition. As for the three young women who lodged along with her, two had young men to occupy their free time and the third, a hoity-toity civil servant, had shown no interest in making friends.

Now, it being a warm, balmy evening, as Rosie left the office she decided to take the longer route back to her lodgings, calling in at the Public Library in Drury Lane. She was a regular visitor, the love of books that Godfrey had inspired filling many a lonely hour. She fished in her bag for a pair of cream crocheted gloves that matched the pretty beret she was wearing. Its broad band sat low on her forehead, and her glorious mane of copper curls fanned out from under it and over the shoulders of the smart navy blue coat she had bought after receiving regular wages for one month.

Having also purchased a new navy blue skirt and two new blouses and a pretty pale blue cardigan in the preceding weeks, she had gleefully consigned Hortense's black shirtwaist and skirt into a charity box for the destitute that her landlady would then take to the church she attended. As she walked towards Westgate, Rosie had no misgivings about her appearance. Her clothes suited the city and the city suited her. Compared with the solitariness of Whitley Hey, Wakefield offered an abundance of new things to see and do. And hopefully, she told herself as she strolled into Westgate, she'd soon make friends with whom she could share the pleasure.

* * *

Milo saw her from across the street and his heart somersaulted. He was sure it was the same red-haired girl he had seen in Eggleston Market although now she looked considerably better dressed. She had the same graceful swing of her hips and the tumble of coppery hair was the same colour. He quickened his pace and as he closed the distance he took a deep breath and then called out, 'Rosie.' If he was wrong he'd apologise, he told himself. He called again, louder this time.

'Rosie!'

The girl hesitated and glanced over her shoulder. She stopped, turned, and stared, a look of incredulity widening her eyes and making her lips part as she gaped at him. 'Milo?'

It was barely a whisper, but he heard her say his name. He hurried towards her, his arms reaching out for her, but when he was at her side he let his arms fall and just stood drinking in the loveliness of her. She looked awfully grand and he hesitated, unsure what to do next.

Rosie continued to stare and then, in a distinctly wobbly voice, she said, 'Milo, is it really you?' Tears sprang to her eyes as she waited for him to confirm what she desperately hoped was true.

'It is, Rosie. It's me, Milo. You remembered me after all this time.'

Then she was in his arms as they hugged and jigged in a happy little dance.

Both of them now close to tears, they stepped apart to

gaze into each other's faces as if to confirm that they weren't dreaming. When Milo scissored the first two fingers on his right hand and flicked his hair back from his forehead in that old familiar way, Rosie gasped.

'I saw you at Eggleston Market,' she cried. 'You were selling lovely little carved animals. I thought I should know you but couldn't think why. It was that thing you do with your hair made me think that.'

Milo laughed out loud. 'And I saw you. It was your fiery curls made me think it was you; that's why I ran after you.'

'You ran after me?' Rosie looked immensely pleased.

'Yes, but I lost you in the crowd. Since then I've never stopped thinking about you.' His expression serious, he said, 'I've never forgotten you, Rosie.'

Rosie blinked back tears and then said, 'When you left me behind I missed you so much I cried in bed every night, for ages.'

Milo's cheeks blazed. 'It was Eli gave you away, not me,' he cried. 'I begged him not to do it but he reckoned it was for the best and...' he ran his eyes from her head to her toes and back again '...maybe he was right. Look at you now – you're a grand lady.' He clasped her hand and started to walk. 'We've a lot of talking to do, Rosie, and we can't stand here all night. Let's go to Clarence Park. We can sit and talk there.'

They found a bench in the park close by the fountain, and as the shadows lengthened they each told their stories. At Rosie's insistence Milo went first, telling her that Eli had died and that he had left the clan and had lived with Bridie Newell until recently. Rosie was delighted to learn he made a good living from his carvings. 'You were always good with your hands,' she said.

Milo was infuriated to learn that, contrary to what he had

imagined Rosie's lifestyle would be in a big house with people with money, she had been a lonely, neglected little girl who never knew what to expect from Celeste and Hortense. He did, however, take some comfort from hearing that Clara Naggs and Godfrey had been kind to her.

'I knew we should never have left you there,' he cried. 'I told Pappa she was a horrible, madwoman but he wouldn't listen.'

'It wasn't all bad,' said Rosie. 'Godfrey was lovely and kind, and he taught me everything I know – and thanks to him, Hildred gave me a job that pays good wages. Perhaps Pappa did me a favour after all.' She paused, her eyes clouding and her mouth turning down at the corners. 'I loved Pappa, even though I made him cross. Tell me he didn't suffer before he died.'

Milo told her how they had buried Eli with his wife and then burned the vardo, before he'd ended up living with Bridie Newell. Rosie giggled when he told her about Bridie accusing him of stealing, and about her other witticisms. 'I'm glad you met up with her. She sounds to have been a lovely woman.'

'She was,' Milo replied fondly. Pleased to talk about her, he regaled Rosie with yet more of his time with the woman who had shown him nothing but kindness. Rosie listened, but hearing about Bridie, who had been like a grandmother to Milo, only aroused her curiosity about the man she had thought was her grandfather: Eli.

'Milo, tell me this, because I've often wondered about it. Who do I belong to? I know it wasn't Celeste or Godfrey, but what I don't understand is why, if I belonged to Pappa, did he give me to them?'

Milo didn't answer immediately. Instead, he rubbed his

hand over his jaw as he considered what to say. He didn't want Rosie to feel she was in any way to blame for the circumstances that had led to her living with Eli. When he did speak he chose his words carefully.

'When you came to us, I was too young to remember how it came about. I only know what Sufina Boswell told me when I was older. One night Dadda brought a lady back to the vardo.' Nervously, Milo flicked back his hair. 'I do remember her. She wore that dark blue cloak with the fancy collar, the one Pappa sent with you when he gave you away.' He gazed at Rosie. 'She had hair like you. Anyway...' he took a deep breath eager to have done with what he had to say '...Sufina told me that the woman gave birth to you, and after that some men came looking for her and took her away. They killed my father, Fennix.' Milo screwed up his face and clasped his hand to his mouth.

Rosie gasped. 'Killed your father,' she reiterated in a whisper. 'But why?'

Milo shrugged. 'Gorjers have never liked us gypsies and it seems as though they thought he wasn't going to let them take her. Sufina wasn't there, so she never saw what happened, and Pappa refused to talk about it.'

Rosie placed her hand on his arm comfortingly. 'I'm so sorry, Milo, so terribly sorry, but please go on. I have to know.'

Milo struggled to regain composure. 'When the men took the woman away she left you behind and Pappa raised you.' He told her how Eli had fashioned a feeding bottle for her and paced the floor of the vardo with her in his arms, and that as she grew he, Milo, had helped nurse her. 'I loved caring for you, Rosie,' he said affectionately.

By now, hot tears were streaming down Rosie's cheeks, so

hot that she felt they might leave tracks in her skin. 'Who was she?' Rosie cried.

Milo shrugged. 'Nobody knows. Sufina said that my dadda met her at a fair in Knaresborough – but she wasn't his woman,' he hastened to add. 'You're not his child. You're no kin to us and that's why Eli gave you away.'

For what seemed an age, Rosie and Milo sat in silence, Milo regretting the loss of his father and hopeful that his divulgence had not overly distressed Rosie. She sat utterly overwhelmed and striving to make sense of it.

'So that blue cloak I have was my mother's?' Rosie said, her tone suggesting she was struggling with contentious thoughts.

Milo nodded. 'Pappa used to wrap you in it to keep you quiet,' he said, and grinned. 'You were a noisy baby.'

'But why didn't she take me with her – or come back for me?' Rosie sounded extremely forlorn.

'I don't know,' Milo said flatly.

'She mustn't have wanted me,' said Rosie, hollowly.

Milo, drained of emotion, merely nodded.

After another long silence, Rosie took Milo's hand in hers and gently squeezed it. 'It's all right, Milo. Please don't be upset. None of it was our doing and in the end here we are, and in a funny sort of way we've both been blessed. You had Bridie's love and I had Godfrey's, and now—' Rosie gazed adoringly at Milo and squeezed his hand all the harder '—we have each other. I'm so glad you found me.'

They had talked and talked without realising that any light there was came from the moon and not the setting sun. The warm, balmy air had cooled and Rosie gave an involuntary shudder. Milo drew her closer.

'What time is it?' Rosie sounded anxious.

Milo took his pocket watch from his waistcoat pocket. He'd purchased it from a cheapjack at the market and was quite proud of it. 'Almost a quarter to ten,' he said, his spirits sinking. He didn't want the evening to end.

Rosie jumped to her feet. 'I must be going. Miss Wimpenny locks the door at ten and I don't have a key.'

'I'll walk you home,' said Milo, linking her arm through his. They set off at a brisk pace, Milo telling Rosie about his carvings and she talking about the work she did for Hildred.

They arrived at Rosie's lodgings just in time to find Miss Wimpenny peering up and down the street, door key in hand. 'Ah, there you are, Miss Threppleton. You're late out tonight.' She perused Milo from head to foot, noting the long, dark hair, his bright red neckerchief and leather waistcoat.

Milo was surprised to hear her call Rosie 'Miss Threppleton' and then he reasoned that it was as good a name as any; but he still thought of her as Rosie Nobody. 'Meet me tomorrow at six by the fountain,' he said hurriedly.

Rosie stood on tiptoe to peck his cheek. 'I'll be there,' she said warmly.

Milo reluctantly walked away, Rosie and Miss Wimpenny gazing after him, the latter thinking perhaps she should have a word with Hildred Threppleton. She pulled Rosie inside, locked the door and then gazed at her sternly.

'Miss Threppleton, it's not my place to choose your acquaintances but you do know that that young man's a gypsy.' She sounded shocked.

Rosie smiled. 'Yes he is. He's a gypsy all right.' She skipped up to her room, not caring one jot for her landlady's disapproval. She had found Milo. What was more, she knew something about where she came from. She was still Rosie Nobody, but at least she had her mother's cloak. She sat down on the bed and pulled the cloak up to her face, rubbing the soft, velvet collar against her cheek and thinking how wonderful her life would be now that Milo was here to share it.

* * *

Milo jogged back to his lodgings, his joy at being reunited with Rosie causing him to whoop and laugh out loud, uncaring that passers-by might think he was drunk or crazy. In fact, with all that had happened in the past hours he did feel slightly crazy but it was a wonderful feeling.

He had found Rosie, and this time he would make sure that nobody took her from him ever again.

SEVENTEEN

Miss Wimpenny stood in Hildred's office, shifting nervously from foot to foot as she gave the reason for her visit. Hildred listened impatiently.

'It's not my business to interfere, but I thought I should let you know,' Miss Wimpenny twittered. 'Maybe the girl is making unwise friendships because she's lonely. She hasn't made any other friends as far as I can tell.'

Hildred nodded thoughtfully and then said, 'Thank you for your concern, Miss Wimpenny. Leave it with me and I'll do something about it.'

'She's met up with him these past few evenings. I know that for a fact because he leaves her at my door.' She pursed her lips distastefully. 'One has to be careful with people like that. We all know what gypsies are like.'

'Yes, yes, Miss Wimpenny, as I've said, leave me to deal with it.' Eager to get on with his business, Hildred ushered her outside. After he had got rid of her he sat down and pondered on what she had said. He had noticed that Rosie no longer worked late, and that she seemed to be in extremely high spirits these past three days. Still, he couldn't have her wandering about the city with any Tom, Dick or Harry. *I should have kept a closer eye on her,* he thought. *After all, the girl had so little opportunity to make acquaintances when she lived at Whitley Hey that she more than likely has no idea who is, and who is not, acceptable company.*

Hildred didn't mention Miss Wimpenny's visit to Rosie, neither did he ask her about Milo. Instead, he arranged for Rosie to be introduced to the son and daughter of his chief clerk, Norman Shortcross. 'It's like this,' he said, 'Rosie knows nobody in the city and working here hasn't given her the opportunity to mix with young people, so what do you say to arranging a meeting with your Peter and Grace? They're of a similar age, and that way she'll be mixing with the right sort of company.'

Flattered, and keen to please his employer, Norman arranged for Rosie to visit his home and meet his children on the next Sunday. When Hildred told Rosie about the invitation she wasn't one bit pleased, but she didn't show it. Hildred had been so kind to her that she didn't like to refuse.

'Thank you very much,' she said politely, although her heart wasn't in it. She glanced across the office to where Mr Shortcross was sitting at his high desk diligently totting columns of figures. The sunlight shining through the window bounced off his round, bald head. It hadn't taken Rosie long to think of him as 'short' and 'cross', for he was a small, plump man with an unpleasant temper, fond of picking holes in her work. Now, she wondered how the invitation had come about. No doubt it was Hildred's doing, she thought, just another kindly act, but she would have preferred it if he had sought her opinion before making the arrangement. It made her feel rather like a stray dog needing a home: one to take pity on, and she didn't like being pitied.

* * *

'I'm sorry,' she said to Milo when they met by the fountain that evening. 'I don't want to go, but on the other hand I don't want Mr Threppleton to think I'm being ungrateful. I'd much rather go to Nostell with you.'

Downcast, Milo shrugged his disappointment. 'I suppose we can always go another day,' he said, the clutch of fear in his chest making him think that yet again he might lose Rosie; this time to grander company than he could ever offer.

* * *

On Sunday afternoon, Rosie presented herself at the Shortcrosses' front door feeling apprehensive about what to expect and sorry to have let Milo down.

When the door opened, two almost identical round faces beamed at her and she was welcomed inside with a volley of chatter.

'Hello, I'm Peter and this is Grace, and you must be Rosie. We're so glad you could come.' The moon-faced boy stuck out his hand. Rosie clasped and found it rather damp and limp. She thought of Milo's firm, calloused grip whenever he took her hand, and then found herself comparing Peter's lank, mousy hair with Milo's glossy dark curls. A flutter of guilt at not having gone with him to Nostell moved through her chest, but she pushed it aside and returned the boy's smile.

'Yes, we've been looking forward to meeting you, particularly me,' said Grace, tucking her arm through Rosie's and pulling her close in what Rosie thought was a show of female solidarity. 'I've been dying to meet you ever since father told us Mr Threppleton had asked him to invite you.'

Ah, so it was Hildred who'd arranged this and not crabby old Shortcross, thought Rosie and tongue in cheek, she told them how pleased she was to be invited. She looked from Peter to Grace and then asked, 'Are you twins?' Neither Hildred nor their father had mentioned this and once the words were out of her mouth Rosie felt gauche and rather impudent.

Peter and Grace smirked. 'Two peas out of the same pod,' Peter chortled.

'But I'm the nicest pea,' chirped Grace. 'Peter can be annoying at times.'

Peter aimed a friendly swipe at his sister's shoulder crying, 'Me? Annoying? Just you wait, Rosie. You'll soon realise what a splendid chap I really am.'

Although Rosie was nervous and unsure of how to behave, Peter and Grace seemed like fun, and she felt the tension in her neck and shoulders relax. She smiled from one to the other, fascinated by their similarity. Apart from their clothing and the way they wore their hair, they were the same height and shape and their gestures and facial expressions mirrored each other.

Peter led the way into a comfortable sitting room and introduced Rosie to Mrs Shortcross. A plump, sweet-faced woman, she was just as welcoming as her offspring, Rosie concluding that the Shortcross twins took after their mother and not their sour-faced father. He greeted her with a curt nod. 'Off you go and entertain Rosie. I'll call you when tea is ready,' said Mrs Shortcross, smiling fondly at the three young people.

They trooped across the hall into a small room with a table where, after teaching Rosie the rules, they played a hilarious game of Ludo and then Chinese Checkers, Peter and Grace cheating their way to victory and Rosie laughing at their antics as they did their utmost to outdo one another. She couldn't recall a time when she had had so much fun. All her misgivings flew out of the window as she joined in merrily, whooping with delight when she won a game.

After a delicious tea of ham sandwiches and home-made sponge cake, Rosie was more than glad she had accepted the invitation. Behaving properly in the company of other young people had just come naturally. She hadn't made a fool of herself or been completely tongue-tied, and furthermore, they had liked her. With promises of doing it again soon, Rosie made her way back to her lodgings as happy as a dog with two tails.

* * *

'I'm glad you enjoyed your day with Peter and Grace,' Milo said when he met Rosie the next day, Rosie having regaled him with the fun she'd had. He had been slightly fearful for her, and disappointed that she had chosen to spend her time with them rather than him. But knowing how lonely her childhood had been he was genuinely pleased for her and suppressed his niggling jealousy.

On the following Saturday, when Rosie brought Peter and Grace to meet Milo at his stall in the market, he soon realised why she enjoyed their company. It being late in the afternoon and trade slack, at Rosie's insistence Milo closed his stall and went with them to the ice cream parlour. Hiding the discomfort he felt, for he too was unsure how to behave in the company of young people whose background was so different from his own, he paid for four ice-cream sundaes and then sat in between Rosie and Grace at a little table on the pavement.

'Peter, you messy pig! You've got ice cream on your chin,' Grace exclaimed.

Peter grunted pig-like and then, his eyes boggling and his tongue sticking out, he attempted to lick off the offending blob, his contorted features so grotesque that the girls howled with laughter. Milo joined in, and before he knew it he was enjoying the banter.

'Dad says you're a gypsy,' Grace remarked, her eyes and her tone suggesting that she thought it very romantic. Milo glanced at Rosie, as if to say, 'Did you tell them that?' but Rosie denied it with a shake of her head, and wondered who it was had told Mr Shortcross.

Milo sat back in his chair and stuck out his chest. Then he tucked his thumbs into the armholes of his waistcoat and gave Grace a dazzling smile. 'I am,' he said proudly, 'once a gypsy always a gypsy. You can't deny your breeding. I don't much travel the roads these days but whenever I have the mind to I can be up and off and nothing to stop me.'

Rosie's spoon halfway to her mouth, she let the ice cream plop back into the glass. Panicked, she gaped at him. Was he thinking of moving on and leaving her behind? She reached out with her free hand and clutched at his sleeve. 'You're not thinking of moving on are you, Milo?' she asked, her voice high with anxiety.

Milo's heart swelled in his chest. 'For the time being I'm settled here. Business is good so I'll stay a while.'

Rosie's breath whooshed from her lungs so noisily that Peter thought she was choking on her sundae and slapped her heartily on the back. That set them laughing again.

'I envy you,' said Peter. 'You must have seen so many places and done so many things that I've never even thought about. I'm stuck here, apprenticed in a miserable office to an equally miserable solicitor.'

Pressed into relating tales of his time on the road, Milo was in high spirits. Not until he was walking Rosie back to her lodgings did he come down to earth with a jolt. Just before they reached her door, Rosie halted and looked at Milo in such a way that he knew he wasn't going to like what she had to say.

'Milo, I've been thinking. If you didn't wear that leather waistcoat and a neckerchief you wouldn't look like a gypsy. Why don't you buy yourself a jacket like Peter wears?'

Milo couldn't remember when he had last felt so offended. He tossed his head and turned on his heel, and leaving Rosie where she was he called back, 'Once a gypsy always a gypsy.'

* * *

Yet again Miss Wimpenny was standing in Hildred's office making the same complaint. 'She's still associating with that gypsy boy,' she declared, her cheeks blooming with self-righteousness.

Hildred was busy tackling an awkward contract for a property he was looking to purchase and he waved her away impatiently. 'I'll have a word,' he said, showing Miss Wimpenny the door and then stomping from his office to Rosie's.

'What's this about you associating with a gypsy lad, Rosie?'

Rosie looked up, surprised. She glanced over at Norman

Shortcross but he kept his eyes on the adding machine. Peter and Grace must have mentioned Milo to him. Rosie wouldn't put it past the crabby old beggar to interfere. If so, she had nothing to be ashamed of and she'd let Hildred know just that.

'Milo is like a brother to me,' she said calmly. 'I lived with him and his grandfather before I went to live at Whitley Hey. I owe my life to them. Had they not nursed me as a baby I might not have survived. I met Milo again two weeks ago and I'm glad I did because I'd missed him dreadfully. Now, he has his own business in the market and is a perfectly respectable young man—' she threw Mr Shortcross a challenging glance '—so it would be unfair of you to object to my seeing him.' She met Hildred's gaze directly, a hint of defiance in her voice.

Hildred's lips quirked; she was a most determined young woman, and a valuable asset to his business, he couldn't deny that, and furthermore he liked having her about the place. 'Then I think it only right that you introduce me to him,' he said.

* * *

Milo met Rosie's smile with a stern face. 'Have you come to tell me to buy a jacket and a top hat?' he asked sarcastically, as Rosie arrived at his stall.

Rosie flushed. 'I didn't mean to insult you, Milo, and I'm sorry for what I said.'

'It's me who's sorry, Rosie. Sorry that the way I dress offends you.'

'Please, Milo, don't be angry with me. It was cruel and thoughtless of me, and I can't bear for us not be friends.'

Rosie's abject expression tugged at Milo's heart. He could

tell that she was genuinely sorry and so he stepped out from behind the stall and gave her a brief hug. 'Let's forget about it,' he said.

Forgiven, Rosie's spirits perked and she smiled winsomely up into his face.

'I've a favour to ask,' she said sweetly.

Milo immediately looked wary. What now?

'I want you to meet Mr Threppleton,' Rosie continued. 'He asked after you and I said I would bring you to meet him. We're to go to the Strafford Arms at six o'clock this evening.'

Milo frowned. 'Why?' To Rosie's disappointment he was cross again.

'Because Mr Threppleton has been very good to me, and I told him that you were the dearest person in the world to me,' she gabbled, desperate for Milo to understand how important it was for him to meet Hildred. 'I told him you were like a brother, and I want him to know what a wonderful person you are.' Rosie's shoulders sagged as she ran out of steam. She began to beseech him again, but Milo was one step ahead.

'Like a brother, a wonderful person, and not some common gypsy who'll lead you astray? Is that it? Is he about to check me out to make sure I'm good enough to associate with you?'

Rosie blanched. 'No,' she cried, neither convincing herself nor Milo.

Milo turned away from her to serve a customer. 'I'll think about it,' he growled. 'Now let me get on with my work.'

Rosie walked away, thoroughly disheartened.

* * *

Rosie and Hildred sat in the foyer at the Strafford Arms waiting for Milo to arrive. Rosie was nervous, still unsure that Milo would keep the appointment, and that if he did what would Hildred think of him. Anxiously, she twisted her hands in her lap whilst unpleasant thoughts tumbled through her mind. What if Milo behaved in a surly, uncouth manner towards Hildred? If Hildred advised her to stop associating with Milo, she would have to ignore Hildred and risk losing favour with him. Come what may, she knew in her heart that she'd never let Milo go. When he walked through the door, Rosie gasped and said, 'Oh, Milo.'

Milo grinned. He was wearing a smart black jacket over a crisp white shirt, and although he still wore his grey moleskin work trousers he looked extremely presentable. He walked confidently towards where she and Hildred were sitting and held out his hand. Hildred looked from Milo to Rosie, confused by her surprised exclamation. He shook Milo's outstretched hand. Milo, interpreting his confused expression, grinned again.

'This was Rosie's idea,' he said, flicking the lapel of his jacket. 'At first, I was angry when she told me to stop dressing like a gypsy but afterwards I saw the sense in it. If one businessman is to meet with another businessman then it's only right to show him respect by dressing like one.' He turned and smiled wickedly at Rosie. 'I'm still a gypsy, Rosie, for all the fancy clothes.'

Rosie flushed and didn't know what to say. Hildred, somewhat flabbergasted at Milo's little speech, hid a smile and then said, 'I couldn't agree more, young man. Shall we go and sit in the lounge?'

When the two men were settled, Rosie said, 'I'll leave you to it,' and before either of them could respond she skipped out of the hotel, her heart fluttering like a bird who has just learned how to fly.

Milo and Hildred shook their heads, bemused, and both started to talk at the same time. 'That young lady has a mind of her own,' Hildred said, as Milo said, 'That's Rosie for you, always getting you to agree to something you're not sure you should be doing.' They started to laugh, the ice broken, and as they talked over a pint of good stout Milo's respect for Hildred grew, and in turn Hildred admired Milo's business sense.

'I generally do a good trade for the better part of the year, but the winter months can be lean,' said Milo. 'What I lack is space to set up a workshop and make a wider variety of goods. I don't have room in my lodgings to craft anything bigger than fireside stools, which is a shame because I've lots of ideas for pieces of furniture and ornaments. I'll never make a fortune from the little carvings even when there's a demand for them.'

Hildred listened without interruption. *This lad's no fly-by-night waster,* he thought. *He's a lad who one day will make his mark in the world.* Filled with the need to help Milo on his way and perhaps benefit financially from a business point of view, Hildred said, 'I think I can solve one problem for you. I've just recently purchased a small warehouse. I intend to use the larger part of it for housing woodworking machinery to make crates for the bottled beer I produce, but there's a smaller part I have no use for. It's yours if you want it. For a sensible rent, of course.' He sat back, big and bluff, his folded hands resting on his considerable paunch and a genial smile on his face.

Milo's dark brown eyes gleamed as his mind registered what Hildred was offering. 'Yes, sir,' he blurted, 'I'm more than happy to accept it.' He stuck out his hand, and when

Hildred grasped it, Milo sealed the agreement so heartily that Hildred was afraid his wrist might be dislocated.

'You can also have use of the machinery if you wish,' said Hildred, 'and maybe in return you'll oversee the crate making now and then? Make sure the crates are sturdy and the machinery used properly.'

Milo could barely believe his luck. With machinery, the chairs and tables that were just drawings in his notebook could now become solid objects. He couldn't wait to get started and neither could he wait to tell Rosie the wonderful news.

* * *

To celebrate his good fortune, Milo took Rosie to Nostell Priory the following Sunday. They wandered through the beautiful gardens that were open to the public, gazing in awe at the magnificent mansion house from across the lake.

'I'll have a house like that one day,' Milo said.

Rosie laughed and then retorted, 'And I'll come and live with you.'

Milo knew then that there was nothing he'd like more than to spend his life living with Rosie, and it need not be in a grand mansion; a little house or even a vardo would do, as long as she was by his side. He no longer thought of her as the red-haired, mischievous little girl whose funny antics had made him laugh. She was a beautiful young woman and when he was with her she stirred his feelings in a romantic way. *I'm glad we're* not *blood kin,* he thought, feeling the heat rise inside him as it did just lately whenever she was near him. He wanted to take her in his arms and kiss her. Afraid that she would see the naked truth of everything he felt for her writ large on his face and that she might find his kisses disgusting, he turned away from her gabbling mindlessly about the house's fine architecture.

Inside her head, Rosie also weaved a little dream of living with Milo, but not in any way romantic. It was simply that there was nobody she'd rather be with than Milo. He was part of her, she belonged to him, and not having to share him or herself with anyone else right now was just wonderful. She slipped her hand into his and walked along as contented as a cat with cream. The sun was going down, a rosy glow warming the shimmering waters of the lake. Rosie breathed in the sweet smell of flowers and the musky scent that was particularly Milo's, and thought it a pity that the magical day was drawing to a close.

EIGHTEEN

What a year it had been. Had anyone told Rosie and Milo, in the spring of 1913 when they were first reunited, that they would find themselves in such happy circumstances one year later, neither of them would have dared to believe it. Now, as Rosie and Milo sat in Clarence Park with Peter and Grace on a sunny Sunday afternoon in the summer of 1914, they revelled in their good fortune. At that moment Rosie believed that every part of her life was just wonderful.

Hildred, quick to recognise her abilities, had promoted her to managing his expanding property portfolio. She was still needed in the office to translate documents from France and Germany, but much of her time was spent inspecting houses that were for sale in the city and then finding suitable tenants and making sure the rents were paid. Rosie loved the freedom this work entailed as she dealt with Hildred's growing empire.

It was on one of these expeditions that she came across a charming little house in Milton Street. She was tired of living in lodgings, and irritated by Miss Wimpenny. She was a busybody. Keen to have her own place, she had asked Hildred if she could rent the property. Now, the two-bedroom house was home to Rosie and Eileen, a quiet Irish nurse who worked at the Clayton Hospital, and to whom Rosie had rented out a room to offset her expenses.

Milo now lived and worked in the warehouse he rented from Hildred. Throughout the latter months of 1913 he crafted quality furniture, the lathe that he had added to the machinery Hildred had installed enabling him to turn fine spindles for the chairs and tables he made. He still continued to carve small pieces for the market stall and had recently employed an elderly ex-carpenter to man the stall when he was busy in the workshop. Ned Jackson had lost several fingers in an accident and could no longer follow his trade, but he knew about wood. Milo was more than happy to give him a job. With an ever-increasing list of clients, Milo's furniture business was flourishing.

'This is the life,' said Peter, throwing himself down on the grass and stretching out to soak up the sun. 'Thank God for Sundays, sadly followed by bloody Mondays.' Milo and Rosie laughed.

'Peter!' Grace expostulated. 'Mind your language. Ladies present.'

'Where?' Peter retorted cheekily. 'I can only see you and Rosie.' He glanced up at the bench on which the girls and Milo were sitting, Grace plump and pleasing in a pink skirt and tunic. Rosie looked delightful in a long green skirt and a finely knitted green and bronze top, the colour and the soft, fluid lines of the fabric enhancing her tall, slender figure and flaming hair.

'You impudent so-and-so,' cried Rosie, reaching down to playfully slap at him.

Peter grabbed her outstretched hand, tugging hard. Rosie plopped down across his middle, her skirts flouncing about her knees and exposing cream, silk-clad legs. Peter stole a quick kiss as she sprawled on top of him. Milo jumped up, jealousy flaring in his gut as Rosie and Peter romped on the grass. He pulled her to her feet, harder than intended.

'Ouch!' Rosie shook her injured wrist and glared at Milo. 'There's no need to be so rough.' But for him there was a need. He wanted to be the one whom she had kissed, the one who felt her tumble of wild hair on his cheek as his hands snaked round her tiny waist to strengthen on the small of her back and pull her in, close. He loved Rosie – and not in a brotherly way – but he was at a loss as to what he should do about it. Grumpily, he apologised. For him the afternoon was ruined.

Peter leapt to his feet and swung Rosie in his arms, and before setting her down he kissed her cheek. Rosie giggled and kissed him back then stood lolling against him, laughing up into his flushed, sweaty face. Peter might not be handsome, she thought, catching sight of Milo's glowering face, but he was sweet and fun to be with, and furthermore he adored her. It was exciting to think that he found her attractive enough to want to kiss, and so, despite Milo's apparent disapproval, she pecked Peter on the forehead.

Milo turned on his heel and strode away; it was perfectly obvious where Rosie's affections lay.

On that same afternoon as Milo resigned himself to losing Rosie to Peter, the Archduke Ferdinand and his wife were assassinated in Sarajevo. When, in the following days, Milo read about it the newspapers, and the doom mongers on the market rumoured that a war was pending, he paid little heed to the gossip.

However, by the end of July there was no ignoring the situation; Britain was going to war.

* * *

'It's so peaceful and lovely here, but everywhere you go these days everyone's talking about the war,' Grace said dolefully, as she, Rosie, Peter, Milo and Eileen strolled through Clarence Park one Sunday in early autumn. By the lake, the dogwoods were flashing bright red berries and in the distance bronzed beech and golden chestnut gleamed through a nebulous haze. Rosie thought of Keats' seasons of mist and mellow fruitfulness, at the same time wondering why mankind never seemed satisfied with a world as beautiful as this, and choosing instead to despoil it by going to war. She voiced her thoughts out loud.

'How is it that in a world filled with beauty, men can want to kill each other?'

'Greed,' Milo said. 'Wanting what's not rightly yours. And whilst the fighting might still seem far away from us, we'll be in the thick of it before you know it.'

'But why?' Rosie wanted to know as, hand in hand with Peter, she walked towards the bandstand, Grace alongside and Milo and Eileen, the pretty Irish nurse, walking a few steps behind them, though not hand in hand. Milo liked sweet, gentle Eileen but he knew that like was all it would ever be.

Peter didn't immediately answer Rosie's question. His attention and his eyes were on two pretty girls sitting in the bandstand. They both wore their hair piled high on their heads and topped with frothy little hats in the latest fashion. Their skirts in the new shorter length showed off their ankles. As he drew nearer Peter ogled them, and giving a cheery wave he called out, 'Good afternoon, ladies. Isn't the weather glorious?' The girls giggled and fluttered their fingers.

Milo felt the skin on his cheeks tighten. Why did the buffoon humiliate Rosie in such a fashion, and why was she content to let him? Peter flirted with any female under thirty, so Milo had noticed, and he thought it disrespectful to Rosie. If she was his he'd have eyes for no other girl.

Rosie appeared not to notice Peter's roving eye. She simply found him highly amusing and was flattered by his obvious affection for her. Sharing kisses and tender moments with someone of the opposite sex was something Rosie had never before experienced, and whilst she would not have said she was in love with Peter she loved the heady sensation of having a romance. It was what girls of her age did, she told herself. Now, clinging to Peter's hand, she basked in the pleasure of feeling wanted at the same time feeling slightly disconcerted by Milo's surliness. He looked on with barely disguised jealousy.

Peter led the way onto the bandstand, carefully choosing seats that gave him a good view of the pretty girls. He pulled Rosie down beside him then sprawled back, his legs casually crossed and his eyes on the girls opposite. Once they were all settled, Rosie impatiently asked, 'Is no one going to answer my question? Why are we going to fight the Germans?'

'To stop them invading our shores,' said Milo. 'The Austrians are fighting the Serbs, the Russians are fighting the Germans who are also fighting the French, and it's our job to stop them beating the Belgians and sailing across the channel to England. You don't want to wake up one morning and find Germans marching through the streets of Wakefield, do you?'

Rosie was impressed by Milo's grasp of the dreadful situation.

'My, aren't you the knowledgeable one,' Peter said sarcastically, wishing he had been the one to provide such a succinct answer. He tried to top it by giving his own garbled opinion, his voice raised in an attempt to impress not only Rosie but also the girls he had his eye on.

'Clear as mud,' chortled Rosie, giving Peter a bemused glance and then turning to Milo, her serious expression letting him know that it was his opinion she most valued. Peter glowered, and turning his attention back to the girls he winked saucily. Milo glanced at Rosie, to ascertain if she was aware of Peter's roving eye and his disregard for the gravity of her question. She didn't seem to have noticed.

'As yet I've avoided reading about it,' Rosie continued, 'but I do know that Mr Threppleton's extremely concerned. He says it'll ruin overseas business and the businesses at home if all the men have to go and fight.'

At the word 'fight', Peter tore his eyes away from the girls at whom he had been winking suggestively and crowed, 'What fighting? Who?'

Rosie gave Peter a withering glance. 'All the men who will have to go off and defend us,' she cried, her voice high with concern.

'Oh, that fighting,' Peter said nonchalantly. He gave Milo a challenging look. 'Will you go? Do your sort join the army?'

Milo met Peter's gaze with steely eyes. 'I'll go if I have to. *My sort* won't just sit back and let the Germans take over.' His harsh tones grated threateningly, and the three girls looked anxiously at one another, eager to pour oil on Peter's offensive remark and avoid an argument.

'That was extremely rude of you, Peter,' Grace hissed.

Rosie, desperate to soften the insult, valiantly exclaimed, 'It'll be up to all of us, men and women, to pull together and do what we can.'

'That's right, we'll all be needed,' Eileen said, in her lovely Irish lilt. 'The doctors in the hospital are already talking about sending aid to the Belgians and the French. They say that some of us nurses will be expected to go and man what they call field hospitals to deal with the casualties.' She seemed quite excited, as though she would like to go.

'It'll not come to that,' Peter said, his tone pooh-poohing the information.

Eileen dropped her gaze and flushed, embarrassed.

Milo jumped to her defence. 'I'm sure Eileen knows a damned sight more about it than you do, Peter.'

Rosie flinched. *Here we go again,* she thought, *Peter making thoughtless remarks and Milo taking umbrage at whatever he says.* Just lately, she struggled to overlook their antagonism towards each other. To lighten the mood, she suggested they walk down into the town for ice cream.

On the way, Milo contrived to walk with Rosie, leaving Peter to flirt with Eileen. 'If it came to the worst we could always run away together,' he said lightly, 'buy a vardo, hitch the horse, and off we'd trot into the sunset, free as birds.' He still kept Sheba in the farrier's yard, occasionally riding her out to the larger fairs in the district to sell his wares. 'There's still a bit of the gypsy in me, and I'm sometimes tempted to travel the roads and discover new places.'

'What! And leave all you have here?'

'What I have here is maybe not enough, Rosie.'

Rosie gave him a quizzical, troubled look, but by now they had reached the ice cream parlour and she was left wondering.

* * *

Each day, on his way from the warehouse to the market, Milo saw the posters calling him to war. The man with the pointing finger and the flashing blue eyes particularly intrigued him. Did his country really need him – Milo?

One day, on his way to buy glue and sandpaper, he passed by the Drill Hall and had to push his way through the crowd of young men queued on the pavement. Happy and excited, their shiny faces lit up, they cheered as one after another their comrades exited the Drill Hall waving the required papers and clutching a Bible. Milo thought: *Is that what I should do?* Rosie's words echoed back to him.

What! And leave all you have here?

Three weeks later, two entirely separate incidents made up his mind for him.

* * *

Milo lifted the brass knocker in the shape of a horseshoe on the Shortcrosses' front door and rapped it smartly. He was wearing a brand-new dark grey jacket and trousers, his crisp, white shirt looking even whiter against his tanned skin. He looked extremely handsome. This was his third visit to the house, and each time Helen Shortcross had welcomed him as a friend of Peter and Grace. Milo liked the dumpy little woman with her gentle smiles and cheerful disposition. Unlike her husband who tended to look down his nose at him. Still, regardless of Helen, he hadn't felt wholly comfortable on his previous visits and now he hoped that Rosie had arrived before him to ease the way.

Mrs Shortcross answered his knock, Milo immediately

noticing the absence of her usual cheery demeanour. Her eyes were red-rimmed and her lips trembled as she spoke. 'Come in, Milo, dear.' She gazed at him long and hard, as though sizing him up and then shook her head despairingly. 'All you lovely boys,' she muttered, before standing aside to allow him into the hallway. Embarrassed, Milo didn't know how to respond. 'In there,' Mrs Shortcross said, her voice wavering as she pointed at the sitting room door. Milo pushed it open and stepped inside. Mrs Shortcross scurried into the kitchen.

Rosie and Grace were sitting close together on the couch by the window, Grace's pale hazel eyelashes sticky with recently shed tears. Drooped against the arm of the couch, Rosie sat with her gloomy face cupped in both hands and her eyes fixed on Peter. He was standing in the centre of the hearthrug, his back to the fireplace, a proud, haughty, self-satisfied expression on his beaming face.

When he saw Milo, he clicked his boot heels together and saluted cockily.

'Peter's enlisted in the Duke of Wellington's,' Grace said tearfully.

'Yes sir!' Peter brayed. 'You are now in the presence of Second Lieutenant Peter Norman Shortcross, 1st Battalion, Duke of Boots.' He saluted again.

Milo gazed at the pompous young man a full head shorter than himself and smiled slowly. 'I suppose I should congratulate you,' he said flatly.

Deaf to Milo's lack of enthusiasm, Peter barked, 'Accepted, sir. My country needs me. I've answered the call.'

Rosie leapt from the couch. 'You're treating it as some silly game when it's nothing of the sort,' she cried, glaring into Peter's face. 'You have no idea what you're letting yourself in for.' Her voice rose hysterically. 'You could be killed.'

Peter sobered, pulling a face like a small boy being sent to bed too early, his moment of glory shattered. Grace began to gulp and snuffle tears into a tiny, overworked handkerchief. Norman Shortcross entered the room, marching straight over to Peter and clamping an arm about his son's shoulders.

'Well, Milo, has he told you? He's made me proud, I can tell you that. The Duke of Wellington's Regiment will be privileged to have him.' He slapped Peter's back. 'That officer cadet training at school wasn't wasted after all. You'll go in as an officer and rise through the ranks in no time, if I know you.'

Mrs Shortcross wobbled into the room, teacups rattling on a loaded tray in her unsteady hands. She set it down on a low table, and then wiping her eyes with the back of her hand she said, 'Tea, anyone?' and in a firmer voice: 'No war talk. We've had quite enough of it for one day.'

They drank their tea and made subdued conversation about the glorious hot weather. As Milo sipped, a gamut of emotions coursed through him, half of him feeling as though Peter had stolen the limelight, and the other half telling him Peter was a crass fool. He gazed at Rosie. She was gazing at Peter, her woebegone expression making Milo's blood curdle. He couldn't wait to escape the cloying atmosphere in the room, and as soon as it seemed no longer impolite he made his excuses.

'I have to go to the farrier's, check on Sheba and pay my dues before he leaves for home,' he said.

To his surprise, Rosie set down her cup and also made her excuses. She pecked Grace's cheek and then gave Mrs Shortcross a brief, comforting hug before going to stand in front of Peter. He stood, and taking her in his arms he kissed her firmly on the lips. Rosie broke free, her cheeks flaming, but Mr Shortcross let out a cackling laugh. 'That's a soldier for you. Kisses the girls goodbye, and off to war he goes.' Rosie ran from the room.

Out on the pavement, she linked her arm through Milo's and they walked along in silence. Just before they reached the farrier's yard Rosie said, 'Do you think Peter's done the right thing? He's awfully brave about it, but I can't help feeling afraid for him.'

'It's not up to me to say whether he's right or wrong,' said Milo. 'Are you saying that because you think I should join him?'

Rosie shook her head.' I don't really know what I think. I'd prefer it if none of you young men had to fight but I don't have a say in the matter.' She sighed heavily. 'All I know is I'll miss him when he goes.' She gazed up into Milo's face, her own willing him to answer positively. 'Do you think the war will be over in a few months' time? Peter says it will.'

At any other time, Milo would have answered in a way that pleased Rosie, but feeling the way he did he told her what he honestly believed. 'There's so much at stake and so many countries mixed up in it, none of them are going to give in easily. It could last for years.'

'Years!' Rosie echoed, her eyes widening and mouth drooping at the corners. 'Peter's asked me to wait for him,' she said, her voice barely above a whisper. 'He says we're unofficially engaged, and when he comes back we'll make it official.'

Milo stopped in his tracks. His chest felt bruised, as though he had been kicked, and he sensed such a deep feeling of loss it made his breath catch in his throat. 'I didn't know you and he were so...' He struggled for words but none came.

Rosie gave a sad, little giggle. 'Neither did I, but I suppose it's only to be expected. We've grown very close.'

Milo recalled the confident way in which Peter had taken

Rosie in his arms to deliver the kiss. How many times had they done that before? he wondered.

'If it's what you want,' he mumbled, suppressing the urge to declare his own feelings for her; he'd left it too late.

'I think it must be,' said Rosie, sounding decidedly unsure, 'but I know you don't approve. I can tell by the look on your face and it confuses me. I'd have thought a brother would want his little sister to be happy.'

'I'm not your brother!' Milo cried, his words scorching the air. 'I'm no kin of yours, Rosie. Never was, never will be.'

Rosie, shocked by his anger, stopped in her tracks. 'I know that, Milo,' she replied, her voice wobbling. 'Eli always made that perfectly clear, but you're the only person who's like family that's all.'

Milo saw that she was close to tears. 'If it makes you happy to wait for Peter then that's what you must do,' he said, despising himself for hurting her and making his tone as conciliatory as he could manage.

Rosie shrugged. 'These days I don't quite know what makes me happy,' she said in a little sad voice, 'but I do know that I want us to always be friends.'

They parted at the farrier's gate, Rosie promising to meet Milo the next evening. Milo's heart breaking, he pushed open the heavy gates and went into the yard. He stopped and stared in amazement. The five horses in the farrier's care were out of their looseboxes, two smartly uniformed soldiers moving from one to the other, running their hands over the horses withers and legs. A third, wearing an officer's uniform, stood watching with a practised eye. The inspection completed, the soldiers gave their verdict.

'We'll take them all,' barked the officer, addressing Sam Jagger, the farrier. Sam looked as though he was about to cry.

‘’Tis only these two are mine,’ he cried, pointing to a bay mare and a handsome roan. ‘I can’t let you take ’em without the owners’ permission.’

‘Then notify the owners and we’ll be back tomorrow. The cavalry needs ’em. There’s a war on, you know,’ the soldier sarcastically replied, slapping the hindquarters of the mare.

Sam saw Milo and hurried towards him. ‘They’re here for the horses, lad. I’ve told ’em they aren’t all mine but it’s not making a damned bit o’ difference. He says they’ll have to take ’em whether or not ’cos the army needs ’em.’

Milo let out a strangled cry. ‘But Sheba’s too old to go to war! What use could she be?’ He hurried over to where she stood, head down as though she already knew of her impending fate. He addressed the officer. ‘I’m not letting you take her, she’ll be of no use to you.’

‘Makes no odds how old they are, so he says,’ cried Sam, jerking his thumb at the officer. ‘They’ll work the poor buggers to death an’ shoot ’em if they don’t drop dead first. Cannon fodder, that’s what they’ll be. Bloody cannon fodder! There’ll not be a horse left i’ this country by t’time they’ve done.’ He wrung his gnarled hands despairingly.

The officer gave Sam a disparaging glare and then turned to Milo. ‘I’m under orders to acquire as many horses as I can. At present we’re paying for them, but if the engagement’s a long one we’ll be taking them for nothing so you might as well let her go now. I’ll make it worth your while.’

Milo placed his arm round Sheba’s neck and laid his cheek against hers. She whickered contentedly. His thoughts jangling, Milo addressed the officer. ‘Will you be back tomorrow?’ The officer’s answer affirmative, Milo said, ‘Let me think about it.’ Patting Sheba’s flank he strode out of the yard.

He didn’t sleep that night. Tossing and turning then

pacing the warehouse floor he carefully, and heartbreakingly, weighed up his situation. Rosie had given her heart to Peter and the government were about to take his last tie with Eli – what did he have left? Let her go now, the officer had said as they stood in the farrier's yard. Let her go. He'd have to let Rosie go, he thought bitterly. She belonged to Peter, so why not let the officer take Sheba? Let Peter bloody Shortcross and the British Army deprive him of everything he loved; he just didn't care anymore.

The next day Milo walked to the farrier's yard, his heart and his feet leaden. 'Take her. I'll not be needing her in future,' he told the officers when they arrived. Feeling like a traitor, he tenderly rubbed Sheba's nose.

The officer plunged his hand into his pouch and withdrew a handful of coins. Extracting what he considered to be Sheba's worth, he handed the money to Milo. Reluctantly, Milo took it. It felt dirty in his hand. He couldn't bear to look into Sheba's soulful brown eyes, so without a backward glance he walked briskly out of the yard, the heat of the afternoon making him sweat, and yet inside he felt as cold as ice.

On his way back to the warehouse, he thought of Sheba straining under the weight as she hauled cannons across the mud of Flanders. He'd seen the newspaper photographs of men and horses struggling through quagmires in torrential rain, and now he thought seriously about what being at war meant: the rattle of gunfire and the roar of cannons, men and horses boldly marching onward, the mud, the blood, and the dying. There were men who, at this very moment, were giving their lives so that he, Milo Simmonite, could be a free man in a country ruled by an English king and not the Kaiser. He had never before felt a hint of patriotism but now he thought he understood General Kitchener's words: *Your country needs you.*

And who else needed him? he thought. He had lost Rosie to Peter and Sheba to the War Office. There was nothing to keep him here for a moment longer.

NINETEEN

Milo didn't tell anyone what he was about to do. He simply went along to the Drill Hall and presented himself to the recruiting officer. The officer's eyes lit up when he saw the strapping young fellow standing in front of his desk; he was just what Kitchener's Army needed.

'And what makes you want to be a soldier?' he asked jovially.

'An enlisted man took my girl and the War Office took my horse, so you might as well take me,' Milo said wryly.

The officer grinned; a sense of humour as well as plenty of muscle, he thought.

He began to take Milo's details. 'Milo Simmonite! That's a name I haven't come across before,' he said, and Milo grinned as he spelled it out for him, at the same time thinking that, contrary to his argument with Peter, perhaps *his sort* didn't enlist in the British Army after all: lots of families in the travelling community were named Simmonite.

'Date and place of birth?' continued the officer. Milo was

tempted to tell him he'd been born in a lay-by on the Great North Road. Instead, he said, 'Boroughbridge.'

Before Milo had time for regrets he was in a back room, stripped naked and coughing as a man in a white coat cupped his balls in his hand. 'King and country's got you by the bollocks, lad,' the man jested but Milo couldn't raise a smile. More filling in of forms, and then he was out on the street with a Bible in his hand. He was now a private in The King's Own Yorkshire Light Infantry Regiment. Two more days and he'd report to a training camp in Doncaster.

Walking to the brewery he began to have second thoughts. Would he ever get to finish the finely turned spindles for the chairs he was making, and what about the three pheasants he was carving? He'd take his small tools with him; carve in the empty evenings like he had after Eli's death. Carving was comforting. He played the name of the regiment over in his head; he liked the sound of it, and the shorter version the recruiting officer had used: KOYLI. Another thought occurred to him. He wouldn't have to put up with that pompous flirt, Peter Shortcross; he was in the Dukes.

* * *

Hildred was bitterly disappointed when he learned of Milo's decision, but stirred with an almost compulsory feeling of patriotism he didn't show it. 'I'll keep an eye on your woodworking business, and with luck you'll return when this blasted war is over.' They shook hands, and then Milo went in search of Rosie. He wouldn't leave without telling her. Neither would he leave without putting up a fight. He'd tell her that he loved her, had always loved her, and that he wanted her to wait for his return, not Peter's.

Milo tapped on the office window, and when Rosie raised her head he beckoned for her to come outside. She knew something was afoot the moment she saw the tightness in his jaw and the gleam in his dark, brooding eyes.

'What is it, Milo?' she said anxiously as they walked across the brewery yard.

She had slipped her arm through his and now she squeezed it hard, afraid. 'Has something awful happened?'

'Can we go somewhere and talk?' Milo wasn't sure his legs would support him if he were to tell her all that he needed to say. They walked across the street to a little square and sat on a bench under a stunted sycamore tree. Milo took Rosie's hands in his, and with his thumbs he fondled the soft skin as he began to speak.

'I've enlisted,' he said hollowly. 'I leave in two days' time.'

Rosie gasped. 'Oh, Milo, not you as well.' Her face crumpled. She freed her hands to throw her arms round him, burying her head between his neck and shoulder. Her hair smelled of meadow flowers, or maybe hops from the brewery. Milo grew dizzy as he breathed in the scent. He closed his eyes and clasped her to him, holding her for what he thought might be the very last time.

'Oh, Milo, I can't bear to think of not seeing you every day. Who will I turn to when I want to laugh, or complain? You coming back into my life has made me happier than I ever could have imagined. You're part of who I am.' She said all this through muffled sobs against his neck, her warm, moist breath like a balm.

Buoyed by her words, Milo drew a very deep breath.

'Rosie, before I go there's something I have to tell you. I don't know where they'll send me or where I'll end up but I can't leave without...'

Rosie lifted her head and pulled away from him. 'They're sending Peter to India, would you believe it. India! It's thousands of miles away. If I'm already missing him and he's not twenty miles from here, how am I going to feel when they send him to India?'

There it was then. Milo's trembling heart turned to stone. Rosie thought only of Peter, and the words of love he had been about to say turned to ashes on his tongue. Rosie continued to bemoan 'poor Peter's' lot, Milo cynically wondering if her unofficial fiancé would find the women in India as attractive as he obviously found any others who chanced his way.

Milo kept his thoughts to himself, and lost himself in the greenish-blue depths of Rosie's eyes. Her lashes sparkled with unshed tears, and her cheeks were flushed. She had never looked more beautiful. Gently he stroked the tumble of fiery curls, the silken softness catching on his roughened fingers. He closed his hand round the tresses at the nape of her neck. Suddenly, his lips were on hers, his tongue seeking access to the sweetness of her mouth.

Rosie's lips parted, and with equal passion she returned the kiss. He felt her heart beating against his own, even through the thickness of her coat and his own jacket. He held her all the tighter, his lips now kissing the soft flesh of her neck and then up to her ear. She made sweet, little moaning noises as his mouth moved against her skin and then back to her lips, the quivering of her body reminding Milo of a tiny bird that he had once held captive in his hands.

When, at last, they drew apart, Rosie gasped. 'Oh, goodness me, Milo.' She gazed at him as though bewitched, her entire body tingling from head to toe. 'What was that all about?'

But Milo wasn't listening. Unable to bear her reproof, he was on his feet and running like the wind down the street. Rosie stared after him, her head spinning and her blood pulsing through her veins. What a marvellous sensation, she thought, running her tongue over her lips to taste again the sweetness of his kiss. Utterly bemused by the wonder of it all, and saddened by Milo's hasty departure, she sat on for some time and tried to sort out her feelings.

* * *

The next day, Milo packed the things he would take with him and then, using the warehouse's small handcart, he delivered a table and two chairs to one of his customers. He talked with Ned Jackson and the crate makers, asking them to keep an eye on his rooms in the warehouse and the unfinished furniture, joking that if they felt like it they could complete the work for him whilst he was away.

When Rosie arrived at Milo's workshop at midday asking for him, Ned, following Milo's orders, told her that he wasn't there. From his hiding place, Milo heard the disappointment in her voice as she asked Ned to tell him she had called and would come back later.

That evening after the crate makers had gone Milo lay on his bed in the room at the back of the warehouse, every fibre of his being tensed as he listened for Rosie's knock on the door. When it came he steeled himself not to answer. When she called out his name he almost relented, and in the silence that followed he struggled to convince himself he had done the right thing; she didn't love him, she loved Peter.

* * *

Early the next morning, standing on the platform at Kirkgate Railway Station he was still trying to convince himself, even though it seemed that every other recruit waiting to board the train had someone seeing him off. He watched enviously as a pretty girl in a bright red coat flung her arms about a spotty youth and gave him a passionate farewell kiss. Milo thought about the kiss he had shared with Rosie, wishing he were doing it again, right now.

He boarded the train, a lost and lonely figure in amongst all the other fellows piling aboard still clinging to the hands of tearful girls, their cries of 'come back safe' and 'I'll miss you' ringing in his ears. Would anyone miss him? he wondered, thinking of Rosie. He gazed out of the window at the waving, cheering, tearful crowds on the platform and he wanted with all his heart to jump off the train, go and find Rosie, tell her he loved her and then take his leave of her in a proper fashion; if he had done that in the first place he might now be leaving sure in the knowledge that she would miss him just as much as he now missed her.

The guard blew his whistle and the train lurched into motion, steam swirling up to the station's canopy as metal ground against metal. Clunking and clanking, the train snaked out of the station.

Milo slumped against the window. Rosie had promised herself to Peter and it was too late to do anything about it even if she had returned his kiss with the same fervour it had been delivered. He decided he'd done the right thing after all; better that they part this way with no recriminations. Maybe, one day, they would meet again and go back to being what they had always been; a brother and sister in all but name: Milo Simmonite and Rosie Nobody.

TWENTY

WAKEFIELD, 1915

'I can't believe he just left without giving me a forwarding address so that we can keep in touch,' Rosie moaned as she sat with Grace in the Shortcrosses' sitting room two days later.

Grace patted Rosie's hand comfortingly, the threatening tears and the two red spots on Rosie's cheeks letting her know just how upset she was and prompting her to ask, 'Didn't he come to see you and say that he was going?'

Rosie thought of the meeting in the park and the kisses. Her cheeks reddened further. 'Sort of,' she muttered, 'but... but something happened... and he left without telling me exactly when he was leaving, and when I went to the warehouse he'd gone. I wanted to see him off, to let him know...' Words failed her. She could hardly tell the sister of her intended about the kiss, and how it had made her feel.

Grace patted Rosie hand again. 'He'll most likely write to you as soon as he's settled. Then you'll know where he is,' she said cheerfully. 'Now, I'll go and make us a cup of tea. There's nothing like a good cup of tea to make things look better.'

The tea and the sympathy did little to soothe Rosie's

confused feelings. One minute she was seething with anger at Milo's secretive departure, and the next she was reliving the heady sensation of his lips on hers, and the feel of his warm, rough cheek as he nuzzled her ear. She desperately wanted to talk to him about it so that it would help her to understand what had happened between them.

* * *

Two weeks dragged by with no word from Milo, and Rosie was restless. It was the end of another tedious day in the office, the job she had once found so fascinating now seeming humdrum and rather pointless. The longer the Germans continued to storm through Belgium and France the more useless she felt. To add to this she worried for Peter and Milo's safety. If anyone had asked her whom she missed most she couldn't have honestly answered, but she knew which one she thought of most often.

And then there was Hildred. He was increasingly irascible with each passing day. Too old to go to war, he was fighting his own battles, constantly worrying over the lack of raw materials to keep his brewery functioning efficiently. 'Although I don't know why I bother,' he told Rosie. 'My brewery and my property will be stolen from under my nose once the Germans invade England.'

She was tired of hearing him moan and now – as he stamped into the office, his expression sour – she steeled herself to listen to more complaints.

'The hops haven't arrived yet and it's more than two weeks since I ordered them,' he grumbled, running a distracted hand over his balding pate.

Rosie, having no pressing work to occupy her, was reading

the latest copy of *The Gentlewoman*. In it was an article on the role women could, and should, play to give Britain the victory. She thought of Milo and Peter training to go to war, and all the poor boys already fighting for their lives in France. She felt like telling Hildred that if hops were the only thing he had to worry about, he was lucky man.

'The roads are jammed with military manoeuvres and the trains are loaded with troops. "Mobilisation" they're calling it, everything on the move but not my hops,' Hildred continued, giving Rosie a frustrated glare before asking, 'Heard anything from Peter lately? How is he?'

Rosie grinned. 'A bit like you, Mr Threppleton. Thoroughly dissatisfied with the state of affairs,' she teased. 'The weather's too hot, the food is awful and the locals don't speak English.'

Hildred harrumphed. 'I suppose I shouldn't grumble then, but I do need those hops. We can't brew beer without them.' He stomped out of the office and across to the brewery, leaving Rosie to contemplate what she had just said.

Peter's letters were a litany of complaints, every sentence about himself and his discomforts. He never responded to her news, and there were no vivid reports of the colourful, mystical country that Rosie imagined India to be. Neither were there any loving words apart from 'wait for me' and 'all my love, Peter.' Never having been the recipient of a love letter she had waited impatiently for Peter to write, but now when the postman called, her heart didn't flutter and by the time she had received the fourth letter she merely skimmed through it before committing it to the bottom drawer of her tallboy.

She had yet to receive a letter from Milo.

Rosie tidied her desk and put on her coat. As she walked

across the brewery yard the lorry that delivered the hops pulled in through the gate. *Thank God for that,* she thought, and gave the driver a cheery wave.

Eileen was already in the little house in Milton Street by the time Rosie arrived. She was a delightful lodger and Rosie sniffed appreciatively as she walked into the kitchen. Eileen, neat and efficient in her smart grey nurse's dress, was stirring a pot of soup on the stove, her fluted white cap on the table and her bright red cape slung over the back of a chair. Rosie eyed them and their owner enviously. Eileen did something worthwhile every working day.

'Do yez want a cheese sandwich with the broth?' Eileen's Irish lilt and quaint way of speaking still charmed Rosie even though they had been sharing the house for almost a year.

'I don't mind if I do, and whilst we're eating tell me something funny that happened in the hospital today to cheer me up. I've had to listen to Hildred moaning all day long.' Rosie slipped off her coat, and then after carefully moving Eileen's cap to the far end of the table out of harm's way she fetched bowls from the cupboard and cups and saucers from the draining board. Drying dishes was a job they both avoided, Eileen believing it was more hygienic to leave them to dry in the air and Rosie simply disliking the task. She'd washed and dried enough dishes in Whitley Hey to last a lifetime.

Sandwiches cut and bowls filled they sat down facing one another. In between mouthfuls Eileen asked, 'Is ould Hildred still tearing the nerves out of yez?'

Rosie nodded. 'He went on about the blooming hops for so long I felt like going to Kent and fetching them myself.' She groaned noisily. 'I've got to get out of there before I go crazy.'

'Yez could always volunteer at the hospital. They're cryin' out for more help now that the lads are coming back in hundreds wi' their arms an' legs hanging off an' their lovely faces smashed to bits,' Eileen said pragmatically.

'Do you think they'd take me?'

'Sure, they're that short-staffed they'd take the organ grinder's monkey.'

Rosie laughed. 'I'd be just about as much use, but at least I'd feel as though I was doing something worthwhile.' She helped herself to another sandwich.

'Ye'll not be nursing now. It'll be cleanin' floors an' makin' beds an' maybe a turn in the canteen. The VADs get all the dirty jobs,' Eileen said, using the initials for the Voluntary Aid Detachment. 'Tis only the trained nurses like meself that tends the wounded, an' that can be dirty enough. There's some pretty gruesome sights, let me tell you.' Eileen gave Rosie a challenging look.

'They can't be worse than Hildred's miserable face. Tell me, who do I see about volunteering?'

* * *

'Threppleton, is it? Any connection to the brewery?' Rosie nodded, and noting the matron's satisfied smile, she thought: *That name obviously carries some weight in these parts.* She could hardly tell someone like matron that she didn't have a surname, that her mother hadn't stayed around long enough to give her one, or that she had no idea what her father was called.

The matron scribbled something on the form that Rosie had completed earlier and then eyed Rosie thoughtfully.

'No previous experience, I gather, but you seem bright enough. If, as you say, you've been handling accounts and managing property you must have some capabilities.' She didn't sound convinced. 'As a nurse in the Voluntary Aid Detachment you will be expected to obey rules, Miss Threpleton,' Matron continued sternly and rather doubtfully as she appraised Rosie. 'To begin with, you'll have to do something about that.' She pointed to Rosie's coppery curls. 'We don't want it dangling in food or contaminating sterile equipment. Make sure it's rolled tight and kept covered.'

Rosie didn't know whether to feel insulted or pleased. She hadn't given a thought to her appearance and she mentally kicked herself as she asked, 'When do I start?'

* * *

Rosie plunged the mop into the bucket and gave it a firm twist. Soapy spirals squirted upward, and she gave it a final twist before swishing the mop under and around the empty beds at the end of the ward. As she mopped, the scuffs and stains on the pale grey linoleum disappeared leaving the floor gleaming wetly. Rosie felt a deep sense of satisfaction that, at last, the work she was doing was vital.

At Rosie's induction more than a month before, Sister Foster had instilled into all the newly recruited VADs the importance of the work they would be doing. 'Cleanliness, as well as being next to godliness, is the only way to combat infection,' she had said in her strong Scots accent. 'To a wounded soldier infection is as great an enemy as are the Germans.' She referred to the VADs as 'girrrls'. Rosie struggled to suppress her smiles whenever she heard the rolling r's trip off Sister Foster's tongue as she delivered her instructions.

Before Rosie had applied to be a VAD she had spent long hours in the library reading medical books and copies of *The Nursing Mirror*. She had passed the First Aid and Home

Nursing exam with flying colours – much of her success down to the hours she had spent studying medical matters with Godfrey – and now here she was in the Clayton Hospital, her hands red-raw and the smell of Lysol as familiar as her daily breath.

'Ah, Threppleton, when you've finished in here report to the canteen.'

Sister Foster's brisk voice brought Rosie to attention, and leaning on her mop she smartly replied, 'Yes, Sister.' She waited, hoping for a few words of praise. None came. Sister Foster marched to the other end of the ward where the beds were occupied. Rosie shrugged as she watched her go. She didn't need thanking; she knew she was doing a good job.

Sister Foster attended to the dressing on a young man with a head wound and then left the ward. Rosie lifted her bucket, about to follow her. As she walked past the occupied beds to the ward door a voice called out, 'If you're waiting for a kind word from Frosty Foster you'll have a long wait.'

Rosie giggled and walked over to Bert Senior's bedside. 'Well, Bert, how's the leg today?' The young corporal had sustained severe injuries to his right leg. The doctors were desperate to try and save it from amputation.

'Killing me,' Bert groaned, 'but the sight of your lovely backside as you swing that mop round does me a power of good.'

Rosie's cheeks pinked, but she was used to the men's banter and retorted, 'Never mind watching my bum, just watch your tongue or else I'll report you to Frosty,' the grin on her face letting the young lad know she'd do no such thing.

She plumped Bert's pillows and then combed his lank, fair hair back from his forehead with her fingers. 'See you later, handsome.'

She lifted her bucket, and deliberately swinging her hips in a provocative manner she walked from the ward. A chorus of laughter from the men in the beds alongside Bert's followed her out, just as she intended it should. She looked on it as part of her job. Cheering up these broken men was just as important as washing them and easing their pain, but Rosie's ultimate aim was to gain enough qualifications to tend their wounds; that was proper nursing.

On her way to the canteen Rosie met Sophie Forsythe. Sophie was on her way back to the ward, having left it earlier to dispose of soiled dressings. 'It's dinnertime,' Rosie said.

Sophie grimaced. 'Sorry I took so long,' she moaned. 'I hate having to handle all those gory bandages, and when I went to wash my hands I had to queue to get to the sink.' She shuddered and waved her hands as if to rid them of something unspeakable.

Like Rosie, Sophie was a new VAD, but unlike Rosie she was striving to come to terms with tasks she had never before been expected to perform. Whereas Rosie had experienced having to cook meals and clean the house when she lived at Whitley Hey, Sophie had lived with her parents in a grand house in South Elmsall and had been waited on by servants.

Rosie gave a sympathetic grin and tucked her arm through Sophie's. 'Never mind, you won't have to do it again – until tomorrow,' she chuckled.

'Are you on tonight?' Sophie sounded weary.

'No, it's my night off, thank God,' replied Rosie, wrinkling her nose at the ripe stink of mashed turnip as they entered the canteen. 'After we've served this up I'm off home.'

Sophie sighed. 'You're lucky to live near enough to go home. I hate living in the nurses' quarters and having to share everything with all those other girls. Even the bath water's rationed.'

Rosie and Sophie each grabbed a trolley and joined the queue of VADs who were waiting at the long counter for the girls behind it to dish up the patients' evening meal; a dollop of mash, a roast potato and a wafer-thin slice of corned beef drowned in lumpy, brown gravy.

'If this doesn't finish 'em off, nothing will,' Rosie commented, loading plates of the unappetising mush onto her trolley. Sophie was doing the same, and the tiers of their trolleys filled they clattered back to the ward Rosie had recently left.

'You girls going dancing tonight?' a lad with injuries to both his arms enquired as Rosie spooned mashed potato and turnip up to his mouth.

'Dancing! Not a chance,' said Rosie. 'I'm off to the knitting bee to rest my aching feet and knit socks for your mates at the front.' She giggled. 'Not that they'll be glad to get 'em. They'll be marching backwards the way I turn a heel.' Laughing, the young lad spluttered turnip onto his bed sheet. Rosie wiped it up.

'My dancing days are done,' the man in the next bed said wistfully. He'd lost a leg at the Battle of Ypres. 'I never thought I'd be saying this, but I'd give owt to be back marching, even through all that bloody mud in Flanders.'

Rosie gave him a sympathetic smile.

'What about you, lass?' a veteran who was recovering from a bad bout of dysentery asked Sophie. Sophie flushed. She was nervous around the men, some of them rough and outspoken, and not at all like the men she was used to.

'I'll go back to the quarters and sleep,' she said, her misery plain to hear.

'You could come knitting with me,' Rosie said, sensing that the last thing Sophie wanted to do was spend an evening in the nurses' home.

Sophie flushed again. 'Could I really? Would nobody mind?'

'Mind? They'd be glad to see you, especially if you can knit. It's a chance to have a good natter and a bit of a laugh. They're a nice bunch of women.'

'Aye, an' while you're at it you can knit me a sock,' said the man with one leg. 'Think on, now, I only need one.' He laughed at his own wit.

The men fed and other duties performed, Rosie and Sophie left the ward, and whipping off their white caps, cuffs and aprons they hurried along the corridor, hopeful that they wouldn't meet either Sister Foster or Matron in their haste to escape the hospital. To be seen half-undressed would incur a severe reprimand.

Still wearing their long, grey dresses under their navy blue coats the two pretty girls walked to the Shortcrosses' house, the armbands emblazoned with a red cross on their coat sleeves attracting admiring glances and encouraging comments.

'Three cheers for the VADs,' one of a group of soldiers home on leave shouted as they passed by the Red Lion pub. 'Do you lovely girls want to join us?'

Rosie and Sophie smiled and waved but kept on walking.

'Good on you, lasses, keep up the good work,' said the old chap selling newspapers on the corner of the street.

'It's nice to be appreciated now and then,' said Rosie, stepping up to the Shortcrosses' front door and rapping the knocker.

Grace answered, her round face lighting up when she saw

Rosie. For an instant Rosie thought of Peter, so alike were the sister and brother, but she didn't feel any sad yearning for him. It made her feel at fault.

'Oh, I'm so glad you've found time to come,' Grace said, giving Rosie a brief hug. She turned to Sophie. 'And who's this with you?'

'Grace Shortcross, meet Sophie Forsythe.' Rosie made the introduction then taking a nervous Sophie by the hand she said, 'Come on and meet the others.'

Grace led the way into the sitting room and introduced Sophie to the group of women sitting chatting and knitting. Helen Shortcross sprang to her feet crying, 'Rosie, how lovely to see you.' She enveloped her in a warm embrace, and then letting her go she proudly announced, 'For those of you who haven't already met Rosie, she's Peter's intended.' Her eyes twinkled as she bestowed a fond smile on Rosie. The women, ranging in age from eighteen to eighty, made complimentary noises, one old lady remarking what a lucky fellow Peter was to have such a lovely, dedicated girl to come home to.

Rosie's cheeks reddened, not with embarrassment but guilt. Helen's unexpected announcement had brought home to her the seriousness of the commitment she had made. She still exchanged letters with Peter but the pressures of learning her new role and studying to advance her position meant that she wrote less often and, if she were completely honest, he was not uppermost in her thoughts.

Grace, Rosie and Sophie sat down in a corner of the room. Grace, kind and jolly and quick to sense Sophie's shyness, gave her a half-finished sock to work on, soon putting her at her ease with her merry chatter.

Rosie, desperate to think of something to take her mind off what Helen had said, asked, 'How's the clerical work going?'

Grace pulled a face. She was working for the government, documenting the movement of troops from one training camp to another and then, inevitably, to the front line. 'It's tedious beyond belief. Lists and lists of names, addresses and next of kin but—' she shrugged '—somebody has to keep tabs on the poor blighters. What about your lot?'

'They come and go and we do what we can for them whilst they're with us, bless 'em.' Rosie poked her needle in, round, and out, the thick grey wool itchy against her tender fingers. She didn't feel like talking about those poor, hurt lads tonight. She didn't feel like talking about anything. For the rest of the evening, as she knitted and listened to the gossip, she felt like a fraud.

TWENTY-ONE

BOULOGNE, APRIL 1915

'Where do you think we're going to from here?' Milo asked Harry Oldroyd as they lined up on the dock at Boulogne. The sea trip had been horrendous and Milo, still feeling nauseous, was glad to be on dry land.

'Haven't a sodding clue,' replied Harry, 'but you can bet your last shilling it'll be somewhere bloody awful.'

Milo liked Harry. He liked his pragmatic outlook on life and wry humour. It reminded him of Eli, and Bridie. Although Harry was thirteen years older than Milo they had teamed up at training camp, first in Doncaster and finally in York before being shipped to Boulogne. When Milo had asked Harry why he'd enlisted he'd replied, 'It seemed the right thing to do,' but he hadn't said it in a tough-guy sort of way. Now they were on their way to only God knew where and would soon be involved in proper fighting, not the pretend stuff they'd done in camp. Milo knew he could rely on Harry to cover his back and that he would do the same for Harry. It was good to have a mate at times like this.

They filed off the dock, long lines of men clanking and

groaning under the weight of their packs as they marched to a railway station. Then they stood on a windswept platform and waited, smoked, and grumbled when it started to rain. Smoking was new to Milo but Harry had been doing it for years, and when Milo tried it he found it comforting. Lighting another Woodbine, Milo gazed down the track and into the distance. Through the drizzle he could see a cluster of houses with grey slate roofs, lights winking from windows, families going about their business.

He wondered what Rosie was doing right now. He often thought of her, and more than once she had crept into his dreams, kissing him as she had on that day he ran away from her. However, whenever he wakened he wondered if he was exaggerating his feelings for Rosie and that kiss simply because he was missing everything he had been used to. Was he imagining being in love to ease the misery of what he was now doing so that, like lots of other lads in his unit, he could get through every day knowing he had a girl waiting for him? Whatever it was, he couldn't stop thinking about Rosie.

He'd even told Harry about her. 'I think I'm in love with her but she's in love with somebody else,' he had said. 'Even so, I'm sorry I left her the way I did.'

'Then write to her, just a few lines to let her know where you are,' Harry had advised. But the fear of not receiving a reply, or worse still receiving one that told him she had been shocked and disgusted by his behaviour, deterred Milo. Better to leave things as they were. He had enough to contend with without having to deal with a broken heart as well.

The afternoon wore on, and with no train in sight the soldiers slumped on their backsides on the platform. Some played cards, but Milo took his knife and a little statuette from his pack; whittling was comforting.

'Whose dog's that?' Harry always showed an interest in Milo's carvings.

'Captain Horner's. It's a wolfhound,' said Milo, deftly flicking his knife against the wood to create the dog's rough coat.'

'Can you carve one o' me wi' me gun to send to me mother?' asked a cheeky young lad sitting close by. He was no more than sixteen if he was a day.

'You'll have to get in t'queue,' Harry said. 'I'm his manager an' he has umpteen orders to do.' Milo grinned and whittled away. At training camp he'd carved any number of requests for his comrades to carry on their person or send home to their loved ones: favourite dogs or horses for the animal lovers, rabbits for children, and heart-shaped tokens bearing entwined initials for sweethearts.

'Aye, wait your turn,' said another soldier, watching Milo at work. 'He's doing one o' Kitchener next so's I can send it to him an' get promoted to a general.'

'Not bloody likely,' Milo said. 'It were him that got me into this mess, him and his pointing finger. I'd more like cut his head off, given chance.'

'Me an' all,' said the young lad. 'It were them eyes in that poster that seemed to be looking at you made me join up. I must have been bloody barmy.'

The banter lightened the mood, but as another hour passed the hungry and thirsty men fell silent. Lost in his own thoughts, Milo carried on carving.

Harry got to his feet and stretched his arms, yawning noisily. 'If this bloody train doesn't come soon I'm buggering off back home,' he said. The soldiers within hearing distance laughed.

'That's what I liked about being on the road,' said Milo,

'you didn't need to wait for anything. You just hitched up and you were off to wherever you wanted.' He had told Harry about his earlier life as a traveller. Harry had been interested and envious of Milo's gypsy life. He had been a factory worker and had never travelled more than ten miles from his own doorstep.

Harry smiled ruefully. 'With a wife and three children I never got the chance to be adventuresome, an' if somebody had told me that when I did go off to do summat different that I'd end up sitting on a station for bloody hours waiting to shoot Germans, I'd never have bloody believed 'em.'

'I don't want to find any of the buggers when we get to wherever we're going,' said a spotty young lad, his voice wobbling pathetically. 'I don't like the idea of having to kill anybody, not even a bloody German.'

There was a rumble of agreement from several of the men. Then a grinding roar further down the track captured their attention. Milo stowed his tools and the wolfhound into his pack and watched the train snake into the station. Some of the men cheered half-heartedly.

In the next few minutes the scene on the platform resembled a gigantic, disturbed anthill as soldiers scrambled to their feet. Hoisting their packs and pushing and shoving, the troops boarded the train. Crammed into filthy carriages they stood, or sat if they were lucky, and rattled further into the country that was to become their home for the next three years. Not that any of them knew that as they chattered or dozed or gazed out over the landscape.

Milo was wedged against a grimy window, and with no opportunity to do anything else he watched the countryside slide by: scattered farmhouses surrounded by muddy enclosures and mangled fields, little towns with narrow streets and tall church spires, and woodland covered with ancient trees. Then they were there. Wieltje.

Milo gazed partly in awe and partly in horror at the sprawl of tents, the huge stacks of boxes and piles of coal, planks and sacks. The camp teemed with men, carts, and horses. He thought of Sheba. Was she there in this muddy hellhole? He'd go and check, the first chance he got.

Captain Horner barked out instructions and then led the way to the tents, past the field kitchens and the stinking latrines to the canvas city that would be home for the next few weeks. Milo and Harry bunked in beside each other along with Spotty Williams, a puny young lad with a bad complexion, and Charlie Sykes, a bookish young man who had been a schoolteacher. These four had been drawn to one another during training, their shared interests in wildlife, birds and books good enough reason for them to stick together. It also kept them out of the clutches of the rougher, smart-mouthed bullyboys and gamblers who would take the few bob they earned in the toss of a coin.

'It's not t' Palace Hotel, is it?' Harry said, dumping his pack on a narrow bed with a straw-filled mattress. 'If you turn over quick in this—' he kicked the bed '—you'll be on t'floor afore you know it.'

'I'm used to sleeping in a small space,' said Milo, thinking of his cot in the vardo. It seemed like a lifetime ago. He fished his mess tin and cutlery out of his pack and growled, 'I wonder when we'll get something to eat. I'm starving.'

'If it tastes as bad as it smells I'm not sure I could stomach it. There were a right stink coming from that field kitchen when we passed it,' said Charlie. He'd been plagued with constipation since leaving England and blamed it on the stodgy food served up at every meal.

'Come on, you lazy lot, we haven't got all fucking day,' Sergeant Baker roared from the door of the tent. 'Get a bloody move on.' A short man with a barrel chest, Sergeant Baker had been christened 'Big Buns' by Spotty Williams. Although they grumbled, the men knew that Big Buns' bark was worse than his bite, and that his soldiering skills might one day save their lives. As one, they quickly vacated the tent.

After they had unloaded ammunition boxes, sandbags, rolls of barbed wire and reassembled Lewis guns they made their way to the canteen where they ate bully beef and jam sandwiches, followed by hot coffee. Milo lit a cigarette, and leaving the canteen he strolled across the muddy terrain to where the horses were corralled for the night. Huge shires with hooves as big as dinner plates swung their massive heads alongside sleek stallions and plucky little cobs. Sheba wasn't amongst them. *She probably never made it as far as Dover,* thought Milo, feeling guilty at selling her because he'd had his world kicked from under him on the day he lost Rosie to Peter. He leaned on the enclosure's rail breathing in the warm smell of horseflesh, his eyes misting as he recalled the years he and Sheba had travelled together.

* * *

For the next few weeks, Milo fell asleep each night to the distant rumble of guns and woke to them each morning, and in the hours in between he lifted, shifted, stacked and packed equipment ready to be taken to the front line. On a dry, sunny day in May he marched out of camp with his companions, the loaded pack on his back making it heavy going and the thoughts tumbling through his head making him barely aware of boarding the lorry that was taking him to Bazentin Ridge. He was going into battle.

* * *

Rosie walked the length of the ward, her expression fraught with anxiety. A new lot of casualties had arrived on the ward during the night and she was scanning their faces and the names on the boards above each bed. It wasn't something new that she was doing; she'd been doing it all along with a strange feeling of dread that was coupled with a terrible yearning.

Unconsciously at first, and then very much aware, she realised that she had been looking for the dark, handsome face and the name of someone who rarely left her thoughts; and it wasn't Peter Shortcross, the man she had agreed to wait for. It was Milo Simmonite.

Ever since the night of the knitting bee in the Shortcrosses' house, when Helen had introduced her as Peter's future wife, Rosie had known that something was terribly wrong. She rarely gave Peter a thought. She didn't worry over his safety, not even when he wrote that he had been involved in 'a hairy skirmish' whilst quelling civil disobedience in some Indian town. She just perfunctorily answered his letters, letters that had become briefer and fewer as time went by.

And now, with Peter's latest letter from India stuffed in her skirt pocket, she wondered if he too regretted asking her to wait for him. He certainly sounded more cheerful. For the second time he had mentioned Penelope Chisholm, the daughter of his commanding officer. He wrote that he'd just returned from 'a jaunt up country' with Penelope and her parents and 'what an absolutely smashing girl she was'; the same girl he had escorted to a regimental ball only a few weeks ago so a previous letter had informed Rosie, the one who 'danced the tango and the fox-trot amazingly'.

Milo wasn't among the new casualties, much to Rosie's relief, for although she longed to see him again she dreaded finding him bloodied and disfigured. She went over to the workstation at the end of the ward, and as she covered a tray with a crisp, white cloth and then laid out scissors, clamps, swabs and Acriflavine ready for the doctor's rounds, her thoughts were jumbled. She didn't know quite what she hoped for.

The night staff had stripped and washed these underfed, stinking, lice-ridden men, tended their wounds and now, save for the odd groan and the snoring and snuffling of exhaustion, an eerie quiet hung over the ward. Rosie prepared a second tray, her movements automatic but her mind juggling with her troubled thoughts. Once again she recalled Milo's kisses and the thousand questions they raised. She desperately needed answers.

'You're quiet this morning. Didn't you sleep well?' Sophie asked, as she piled rolls of bandages onto the trolley next to the trays Rosie had laid out.

'I don't think I will ever again. My mind's playing tricks on me, and my feelings are all over the place.' She shook her head. 'And coming into this every day isn't helping one bit.' She waved a hand towards the sleeping men.

'I must admit it is depressing, but don't let it get to you.' Sophie's voice was full of concern. She was unused to seeing Rosie anything but cheerful. It was Rosie's lively chat and her ability to stay calm and efficient in the most dreadful circumstances that gave Sophie the confidence to continue doing a job she found far more daunting than she had imagined.

'Oh, don't listen to me,' said Rosie, heading for the large

sink behind the workstation, Sophie at her heels. 'I'm just being a crackpot.'

'It's you being a crackpot that has me still doing this job,' Sophie said. 'I still go weak-kneed at the things we have to see and do. I thought I'd have grown a thicker skin by now but it only seems to get thinner, and the casualties' injuries are so appalling that I...' Words petering out and tears threatening, Sophie turned on the taps, afraid to say more.

'Aye, I know what you mean, and some of this lot are in worse shape than the last lot,' Rosie whispered to Sophie, as they filled large metal bowls with hot water and made sure the carbolic soap and clean towels were to hand for the doctor's rounds.

'I don't think Corporal Jackson's going to last much longer.' Sophie's voice wobbled. 'His breathing's very shallow.'

'So I'd noticed.' Rosie tried hard not to let her emotions interfere with her work but each death on the ward left her feeling angry and diminished; such a terrible waste of lives – and for what? She was no longer sure.

A strangled cry had Rosie hurrying to attend to a soldier whose head and eyes were covered in bandages. 'Can't see, can't see,' he cried, clutching feverishly at his dressings. Rosie clasped both his hands in hers and held them tight as if to imbue some of her own strength into him. 'Doctor's coming now,' she said soothingly. 'Let me give you a cool drink then I'll settle you more comfortably.' She held a glass of water to his lips and he gulped it down, dribbling like a baby.

'I'm fucking helpless without my eyes,' he moaned. Rosie had no answer to that. Sadly, she envisaged his future; lost and struggling in a world he could no longer see. A dull ache pulsated at the back of her head as she plumped his pillows and then sat to hold his hand again; in return, he squeezed hers. Some small comfort, thought Rosie.

Sister Foster bustled into the ward, closely followed by Dr McDaniel, and at their heels a team of nurses and doctors who were there to begin the serious task of repairing, if possible, the injured soldiers. For the rest of the morning Rosie handed up swabs, bandaged wounds and, on one occasion, assisted in irrigating a pus-filled wound. As the antiseptic fluid penetrated deep into the gaping hole in the leg of a young, semi-conscious officer, Rosie deftly picked out grit and bits of shrapnel.

'Well done, Threppleton,' Dr McDaniel praised after the particularly tricky procedure. He had noted Rosie's efficiency and her understanding of the more complex medical terms he used, surprised that a recently appointed VAD's capabilities appeared equal to that of a qualified nurse. Therefore, he didn't hesitate to add to her knowledge and develop her skills. Rosie absorbed everything he said and was keen to learn more.

At the end of her shift she trudged wearily homeward, stopping to buy a newspaper and then calling in on Hildred. Whilst she waited for him to finish haranguing Norman Shortcross about an overdue account, Rosie turned the pages of the *Wakefield Express* until she came to the 'Fallen in Combat' lists. She scoured them regularly. Columns lined the page but, fortunately for Rosie, the names were printed in alphabetical order. She went straight to the 'S' section.

Hildred finished his tirade and came to sit with her at his desk. 'You look weary,' he said, noting the purple shadows under her eyes. Rosie shrugged and gave a half-smile. She was, but it was a satisfying weariness that she felt she had earned from doing the right thing.

'I'm off tomorrow so I'll be able to sleep in,' she said. 'Sophie's off too. I've promised to show her Nostell Priory. We'll walk in the gardens, do something normal for a change.'

'I've forgotten what normal is,' Hildred said bitterly. 'There's no decent meat in the butcher's, butter's become a luxury and what with the servants all gone to work in munitions, life just isn't the same.'

Rosie looked at Hildred, portly and well fed, and thought of the wasted, wounded men on the ward. Their lives were no longer the same either, and not for the lack of meat or butter but for the horrific sights they had seen and the terrible things they had been ordered to do that had ripped their bodies and minds to shreds.

'Never mind,' Rosie said, 'it might soon be over.' She liked Hildred, but her feeble attempt to cheer him up brought with it a flutter of annoyance. What were his losses compared to those of the men she nursed daily? Their lives would never be the same again.

* * *

Rosie and Sophie went to Nostell Priory, but it didn't have the same magic for Rosie that it had had on the day she had spent there with Milo. The beech and chestnut trees had long since lost their bronze and golden canopies, their bare limbs black against a cold, grey sky. The grass that earlier in the day had been rimed with a light frost was still wet, and in no time at all Rosie and Sophie's shoes were soaked.

'My feet are sopping,' Sophie said, as they walked past the grand mansion. 'Let's go and find somewhere to get a warm drink. It's lovely here but it's not the best of days to make a visit.'

Rosie readily agreed, her heart as heavy and damp as her shoes. 'It's at its most beautiful in autumn,' she said dreamily, recalling the perfect day she and Milo had spent there. She glanced back at the mansion, Milo's words sharp in her head: *One day I'll have a house like that.* And what had she replied? *And I'll come and live with you.* The memory didn't cheer her; in fact it did quite the opposite. She missed him more with each passing day and bitterly regretted that she had no means of contacting him. Just a note to let her know he was alive and well would ease her aching heart and mind.

TWENTY-TWO

SPRING 1916

Peter was coming home on leave. Rosie read his letter with mixed feelings. Should she tell him that she regretted her hasty promise to wait for him, or would the fondness she had felt for him before his departure spring to life again on his return?

'I did find him fun to be with,' she confided to Sophie. 'He's a jolly decent fellow with a smashing sense of humour. I suppose I could do far worse but...' she paused and thought of Milo's kiss '...not long after Peter went to India something happened that made me think I didn't really love him at all. He never took my breath away, and my heart didn't beat like the clappers when he kissed me, and, honestly, I've hardly missed him at all.'

Sophie's blue eyes grew round. 'Have you fallen for someone else?' Her eyes ranged the row of beds as if she thought it might be one of the occupants, or a previous soldier Rosie had nursed. Rosie saw the look and read her mind.

She grinned and shook her head. 'No, not one of our

chaps. And anyway, I don't think I even know what love is.' She pulled a face. 'But I know what it isn't.'

Over the past few months Rosie had asked herself time and again if the love she felt for Milo was a figment of her imagination. Did she think she loved him because he was the closest thing she had to a family member? Was the way she felt like the feelings a mother has for a lost son, or a sister for a brother? She had never had a family to love or grieve, so she just didn't know. Or was it because she presumed he was fighting for his life in France? And whilst her romance with Peter had seemed like love, Milo's kisses had wakened something deep inside her; something she couldn't ignore.

Now, as she made her way across the town Rosie mulled over all these aggravating feelings, her anxiety rising with every step. By the time she arrived at Kirkgate Railway Station she still hadn't reached any conclusion, and walking beneath the arched entrance she had no idea of what she would do next.

'Isn't this just wonderful?' cried Helen Shortcross as Rosie appeared at her side. Helen's smile was ecstatic although her eyes glittered with unshed tears. Rosie returned the smile, hopeful that it looked suitably wide enough. Standing on the station platform awaiting the arrival of Peter's train, Rosie wished she were any place else other than here.

'I wonder if he's still as daft as he always was,' his sister Grace remarked rather ungraciously. Her father harrumphed and gave her a reprimanding glare. Rosie hid a grin behind her gloved hand. She had dressed for the occasion in a long, green skirt and matching tunic with a scooped neck and long, narrow sleeves, the soft knitted fabric enhancing her slender figure and its colour the coppery tumble of her hair. Out of uniform, she felt strangely glamorous, at the same time wishing she had worn the drab grey dress after all; let Peter see what her life was all about these days, let him know she wasn't the same naïve girl he had left behind.

The train clunked into the station. Doors flew open disgorging uniformed men and civilian passengers. Looking weary and dishevelled, the soldiers' elation at being home on leave shone through as they fell into the waiting arms of loved ones. The crowds jostled, screams of delight mingling with tears of joy, and Rosie wondered how she should react when Peter alighted the train.

Further down the platform, Rosie saw a tall, distinguished man in a colonel's uniform gallantly handing a fashionably dressed lady of a similar age to himself down from the train. He then did the same for an equally fashionable and strikingly pretty girl with white-blonde hair.

Peter followed close behind. He looked handsome in his dark blue uniform, his naturally pale complexion tanned by a foreign sun. As the colonel's party gathered on the platform, Rosie noted that Peter was paying courtly attention to the pretty girl. Grace noticed too. 'Oh, look at him,' she scoffed, 'he's probably just met her on the train and now he's all over her. He never could resist the chance to flirt.'

But Rosie suspected they hadn't just met. She was almost certain the girl was the 'amazing, fox-trotting, smashing Penelope'. For the first time that afternoon, Rosie was glad she had taken the trouble to dress for the occasion.

Helen let out a squeal and ran towards Peter. He saw her and the others, and making hurried excuses to Penelope and her parents, he came to meet his family and Rosie. Helen enveloped him in a motherly embrace and his father slapped him on the back roaring, 'Welcome home, son.' Released from his mother's arms, Peter stepped forward and hugged Rosie. 'Hello, old thing,' he said, and pecked her cheek.

Rosie held on to him, and barely aware of what she was doing or why, she kissed him full on the lips, a hot kiss that took Peter by surprise. It also surprised Rosie, and when she let him go she gave a triumphant little smile. *There now, Miss Penelope,* she thought, *you see who he belongs to.* But as quickly as the kiss and the thought registered in her brain, she realised she had acted purely out of jealousy; a jealousy that was instinctively feminine and one that, deep in her heart, she did not truly feel.

'Hey, steady on, old girl,' gasped Peter. 'Let's save it for later shall we?' He glanced nervously in Penelope's direction.

Rosie flushed, but she linked her arm through his and held on to him whilst he introduced the Chisholms to his family. *Why am I behaving this way?* Rosie asked herself. *What am I trying to prove?* Feeling utterly discombobulated, she watched Peter and the colonel supervise the loading of their trunks onto trolleys, Peter barking orders at the porters. *No doubt, he's trying to prove how indispensable he is to the Chisholms,* Rosie thought cynically.

The two families walked out of the station together, Norman Shortcross doing his best to ingratiate himself with the colonel, and Peter, linked to Rosie, casting furtive glances at Penelope. The Chisholms' chauffeur was there to meet them and they climbed aboard a large, sleek Wolseley. The Shortcrosses and Rosie walked back to the Shortcrosses' home, Rosie confused and shrouded in guilt. For the rest of the day she plastered a smile on her face and shared in the joy of Peter's homecoming, relieved when the time came for her to leave.

'You don't have to walk me home, Peter, stay here with

your family,' Rosie insisted. But Peter was just as insistent. Arm in arm, they walked along the street in silence, Peter taking Rosie by surprise when, at the entrance to alley between the houses he yanked on her arm, dragging her into the dark, narrow space. Pressing her against the wall he covered her lips with his own, his teeth grinding against hers and his hands roaming her body. Breathless, Rosie pushed him away. 'What do you think you're doing?' she gasped.

'What's up?' Peter wasn't pleased. 'You were all over me at the station and now, at the first chance for us to be alone, you're pushing me away.'

Rosie sagged against the wall. 'Sorry, I'm tired and I have to work tomorrow.' She prayed he would accept her excuse.

'You're a volunteer; you don't *have* to go,' he said, pushing her back against the wall to kiss her again.

Rosie averted her head to deflect his lips. 'It doesn't work like that,' she said wearily. 'I have to go, otherwise they'll be short-handed.'

Peter stepped back, prepared to argue, and seeing her chance to escape Rosie hurried back onto the street. In high dudgeon Peter followed her. 'To say you promised to wait for me, that we have an understanding, you don't make a chap feel at all welcome,' he grumbled. They walked on, Rosie quickening her pace. At her door Rosie unlocked it but she didn't invite him in. 'Come on, Rosie, you know I love you,' he wheedled. 'Let me come in and I'll prove it.'

Rosie shuddered. What on earth had the army been teaching him, and what sort of a girl did he think she was? Without waiting to find out she slipped inside, closing the door in his face as she said, 'Goodnight, Peter. Welcome home.'

* * *

'I felt awful,' Rosie confided to Sophie the following morning, as they carried out their duties on the ward. 'I didn't know how to behave towards him, and I made a foolish mistake the moment we met.' She told Sophie about the streak of jealousy and the passionate kiss. 'It obviously gave him the wrong idea.'

'What will you do now?'

'I'm not sure. I don't know how I feel. He's changed so much, and I did love him in a funny sort of way before he joined up. I'll see him again and make my peace, and maybe I'll find out where my heart truly lies.' Rosie groaned. 'Lack of experience is what it is, Sophie. I never knew any other boys before I met Peter...' She paused. 'Well, except for Milo, and I thought of him as a brother – and now I'm not sure what I think.' She chuckled wryly. 'You make sure you get bags of experience before you go promising yourself to any man, my girl – that way you won't end up like me.'

'I think I might have met one that I can practise on,' Sophie whispered, a mischievous grin on her face.

'Who?'

'The bed by the window,' Sophie said mysteriously.

Rosie glanced over to the window. 'What? Lieutenant Dalrymple?'

Sophie blushed. 'You know he's leaving tomorrow to go back to the front. Well, he's asked me to write to him and I said I would. He's such a lovely, gentle soul and I do get the flutters whenever he looks at me with those gorgeous grey eyes.'

Rosie giggled. 'Now you mention it, I had noticed you giving him more attention than the others, but how are you going to gain any experience with men if he's off tomorrow? Writing's not the same as doing.'

* * *

Rosie did make her peace with Peter, and over the first ten days of his leave she let him take her to the Theatre Royal and the newly opened cinema, as well as an evening walking in Clarence Park. Although they recaptured some of the fun they had once shared, laughing at Charlie Chaplin's antics in the darkness of the back row of the Picture House where Peter stole a kiss or two, or lingering late by the Chantry Bridge under a romantic moon, Rosie could not forget the kiss she had shared with Milo.

One day, Rosie was on the ward attending to a soldier who had just been transferred to her ward. Harry Oldroyd was older than most of the other patients and had suffered a serious stomach wound that would prevent him from returning to war. However, he seemed to be making steady progress, and as Rosie settled him in she asked, 'Where were you when it happened?'

'Bazentin Ridge, lass,' he replied, a wry smile on his face. 'A place an' a name I'm not likely to forget. We were part of what the high command call "The Big Push" trying to drive the Germans back an' take the Somme.'

Rosie always felt privileged to be in the presence of men who had fought at the strangely named places she read about in the newspapers; she often looked them up in her atlas wondering if Milo had been in these places too.

'You wouldn't do us a favour, lass?' Harry said, once he was comfortably in bed.

'If I can,' Rosie said, and smiled.

'I'm not much at writing an' in my condition I don't feel up to it, but I'd like to send a letter to me wife. They sent that card telling her I wa' injured but it doesn't say much so I'd like her to know it's looking as if I might make it home. Will you write an' let her know? I'll tell you what to say.' Rosie's heart went out to him, and as she left to attend to another patient she prayed that Harry would be proved right, and that he would make it back to his wife and family.

Later that day, in a quiet moment Rosie sat by Harry's bed, pen and paper in her hands. With Harry dictating, Rosie had filled one page and was on to a second when Harry said, 'There's a bit o' summat in me locker I'd like to send her along with the letter. Will you get it out?' Rosie knelt and lifted out the bag containing Harry's personal bits and pieces. She laid it on the bed.

'Look inside, lass. There's a little wooden ornament of a wren in there. Me wife's called Jenny—' his face softened '—an' just in case I don't make it home I'd like her to have it 'cos I allus call her my little wren.'

Rosie delved into the bag. In and among his shaving tackle, some photographs and his service book was a small wooden bird. Rosie withdrew it, her breath catching in her throat. She held the bird in the palm of her hand, her heart racing. Fingertips tingling, she traced the finely crafted feathers on the perfect likeness of a wren. Then, in a voice that was barely a whisper she asked, 'Who made this?'

Harry smiled. 'A very good mate of mine; he has a grand eye an' hand for crafting stuff does Milo.'

Rosie's heart missed a beat. 'What did you say he was called?'

The urgency in her voice startled Harry, and his smile slipped as he said, 'Milo.'

Blood sang in Rosie's ears. 'Milo! Milo who? What was his last name?' Rosie was almost in tears.

Harry looked perplexed. 'Simmonite. Why?'

'Oh, Harry, I could kiss you.'

'Nay, don't be doing that. I don't think Frosty Foster 'ud approve – an' I am a married man,' he jested, a twinkle in his eye.

'I wouldn't care what she thought. You've just answered my prayers.'

Harry looked even more bemused, but as Rosie explained he smiled warmly.

'I reckon you must be the lass he told me about. He thinks a lot o' you, he does.'

Rosie's heart swelled and she said, 'So he hasn't forgotten me?'

'Forgotten you!' Harry chuckled. 'No he hasn't, an' I don't think he's likely to.'

Rosie couldn't have wished to hear anything more heart-warming, and thrilled to be in the company of a man who had fought alongside Milo she said, 'Tell me about him. It'll bring him closer.'

Harry settled his head back into his pillows, pleased to talk about his friend. 'Well, as you know, he's a grand lad is Milo. Me an' him took up together from the start. We stuck by one another an' saved each other umpteen times but...' He shrugged and then groaned as the movement tugged at his wounds. 'He couldn't do owt about that bloody shell that ripped me guts apart. I've heard nowt since I were shipped back to England so I only hope he's come to no harm.'

So did Rosie.

'How can I get a letter to him?'

Harry gave her the name of the regiment and Milo's

number and the British Army Postal Service address from which all letters started their journey to France. 'It might take a while for him to get it,' he said, 'but he'll be right glad to hear from you. I gather from what he told me that you an' him had some unfinished business.' He winked knowingly and Rosie giggled.

'I think you could be right, Harry. Now, let's get your letter finished before I clock off,' she said breezily ''cos I've another to write before this day's done.'

For the next hour, Rosie worked with a song in her heart. Later, on her way home, she called at the post office, and happy to know that Harry's letter and the little wren were winging their way to his Jenny, she skipped her tea and started writing as soon as she got indoors. Not long after, her heart feeling lighter than it had felt for some time, she left the house and ran to the corner of the street. She placed a kiss on the envelope before dropping it into the post box. Her letter to Milo was on its way to France.

* * *

'I've discovered Milo's whereabouts,' she told Peter the following evening when they met to go to the Picture House. 'I've already posted a letter to him. I do hope he gets it.'

Peter didn't seem all that interested in Milo. In fact, he was distracted for much of the evening. As they walked back to Rosie's house, he said, 'I won't be able to see you for the next couple of days. I've wangled an invitation to spend the weekend at the Chisholms'. It could be good for my career. Move me up the ranks.' Rosie listened to his excuses with a calculating look on her face. Peter saw the look. 'They have a country house in Wharfedale, and the colonel has a shoot there so it should be good sport,' he concluded rather pathetically.

Rosie wondered if Penelope was a good sport. Did she allow him to kiss and maul her like he tried to do with Rosie? Is that what they did in India? She decided she didn't care. She had better things to think about than to worry over Peter's peccadillo with Penelope Chisholm. She was welcome to him.

TWENTY-THREE

JULY 1916

Milo marched along the Albert-Bapaume Road, the thud of boots and the clank of equipment mingling with the voices of the men who liked to sing as they marched.

'What are we fighting for? What are we fighting for?
To win the bloody war,
Whizz bang! Fire your gun, shoot and kill the bloody Hun,
And win the bloody war.'

What they had to sing about Milo couldn't imagine; no doubt it kept up their spirits, but not his. It was warm July day, sunlight dappling the rutted road through the branches of elm and chestnut trees. Rooks cawed, and every now and then he heard the sweet, piercing song of a blackbird. He thought of Eli and sleeping in the vardo and waking in the early morning to that same call. What was it Eli used to say whenever he heard it? 'Oh blackbird what a boy ye are.' Yes, that was it. Then, that sweet singing had cheered Milo, but with the memory of what had happened at Bazentin Ridge still burning in his heart and mind he doubted he'd ever feel cheerful again.

'How much further to Pozières?' Spotty Williams panted, sweat glistening on his pimpled forehead. He always suffered on route marches.

'No idea,' grunted Milo, 'and if we never get there it'll be soon enough.'

'Only a couple of miles,' Charlie Sykes answered. Charlie, the ex-schoolteacher, always seemed to know these things.

The three of them plodded onward, but for Milo it wasn't the same without Harry. He sorely missed Harry Oldroyd's witty comments and ribald humour. Up until now it had made him feel safe, as though there was nothing they couldn't overcome as long as they stuck together. But all that had come to an end at Bazentin Ridge. He wondered if Harry was still lingering in the field hospital desperately waiting for the harried doctors to treat his wounds with the scant equipment at their disposal. Or had he made it back to England, to a hospital that had facilities and doctors that could heal a gaping hole in your stomach... or was he dead? The last thought made him shudder. He pushed it from his mind, and forcing himself to think of something pleasant he recalled the day he had spent with Rosie at Nostell Priory.

Once again, he pictured her greenish-blue eyes wide with amazement as she'd admired the mansion house and the shimmering lake: *I'll come and live with you,* she had said. He thought he could almost smell the scent of her coppery hair and feel the softness of her hand in his as he stumbled along, blind to the road under his aching feet.

As the shadows lengthened and the rosy glow of the setting sun warmed the distant hills, the weary soldiers' thoughts turned to home, a strong, sweet tenor voice airing the sentiments of many a man.

'I left a rose in my garden back home, the fairest you'll ever see,

I kissed her goodbye with a tear in my eye, but I know she's waiting for me.'

I left my rose, but she's not waiting for me, thought Milo sadly, as he joined in the chorus.

They reached Pozières as darkness fell and they climbed the hill on which the village sat. Most of the houses had been reduced to rubble. Huddled in a trench, Milo listened to the thud of mortars and the rattle of gunfire from the German machine gun nests to the north. Orders to eat and rest came down the line. Milo removed his boots and massaged his aching feet. Then he took off his tunic, and with his fingernails he raked lice out of its seams and did the same with his shirt and singlet.

Rubbing his torso clear of the tiny, venomous bugs he mentally calculated that he hadn't changed his clothes for almost a month, and that he'd been wearing the same socks for more than two weeks. Gingerly replacing his singlet, shirt and tunic he settled down in the bottom of the trench, and when food came he loaded his mess tin and filled his belly, hopeful that his delousing and a full stomach would help him get a good night's sleep.

Milo hadn't slept properly since the night Harry was wounded. When he tried to sleep the whole ghastly nightmare reeled behind his closed eyes, as clear as it had been on the night that it had happened. They had been fighting from early morning, driving the Germans back, and as dusk fell they crawled through the detritus of mud, bodies and spent shells towards the German lines. Milo kept his eyes on the darkening horizon, blinking as shells burst open like sunflowers in full bloom and bullets whistled like fireflies; shooting stars in a crazy cosmos.

Harry was to the left of him, jesting that the knees of his trousers were wearing thin, when a stray shell exploded a yard or so in front of them. Milo recoiled, rolling into a nearby shell hole. When he peered over the edge of it he saw Harry, flat on his back, a lump of shrapnel sticking out of his middle. Milo leapt to his feet, heedless of his own safety, and lifting Harry up into his arms he set off at a drunken trot, staggering beneath the weight as he carried his mate back to the trench.

The officer in charge had immediately ordered Milo to return to duty. Blood-soaked and seething, Milo had gone back the way he had come cursing the officer, the Germans, and the generals and politicians who had ordered the war. Damn them all that they had sent a decent man like Harry Oldroyd into the jaws of hell and more than likely killed him.

Now, Milo's thoughts bitter, he shuffled into a more comfortable position and waited for the night to pass. Delving into his pack, he took out his whittling knife and the skylark he was carving. Sergeant Poole had asked him to make it to remind him of the birds that flew over his father's field back home in Shropshire. Further down the trench someone started to sing. Milo recognised the voice as that of the new padre: a country boy with a calling from God and a liking for a good tune was how he had described himself to the men.

Softly, but loud enough for the strains of the song to reach Milo's ears, he sang the words: *'There's a long, long night of waiting until my dreams all come true, till the day that I'll be walking down that long, long trail with you.'* Was there any chance he'd walk the 'long, long trail' with Rosie? he wondered.

Before an uneasy sleep claimed him, Milo prayed for

Harry's survival and that, one day, he'd meet Rosie and Harry again.

* * *

Rosie applied an impregnated dressing to the wound on Private Johnson's back, placing it carefully so that it would receive the full benefit of the antiseptic. Very aware that Dr McDaniel was closely observing her, she hoped he hadn't detected the tremor in her hands. He had been keeping a keen eye on her for some time now, not because he fancied her in a romantic way, she was sure of that, and not because he thought her work was shoddy – he frequently praised her – but his scrutiny still made her nervous.

'Well done, Threppleton. You cleaned the wound and applied the correct antiseptic dressing most capably.' He smiled as he turned away. 'We'll make a nurse out of you yet.'

Rosie glowed under his words, the pleasant feeling staying with her until she met Peter later that evening. He was tipsy again.

He had returned from Wharfedale in an extremely disgruntled mood and had spent the last few days of his leave drinking heavily. Now, two nights before he was due to return to India, his mood swung from maudlin to angry.

'Is it because you're afraid to go back?' Rosie asked, although he had told her that his service in India was nothing like the horror of being in France.

'Of course I'm not afraid,' he blustered, 'what have I to be afraid of? I'm an officer, a leader of men.' He didn't add that in Colonel Chisholm's eyes, Peter's lowly rank and the lack of a wealthy background were a stumbling block in his pursuit of Penelope. He'd learned that at the house in

Wharfedale. Amongst the colonel's titled and affluent friends, Peter was nothing; he was simply a lad the Chisholms had befriended because the daughter they doted on had requested it.

When Peter, in his cups, had boldly suggested to the colonel that he wanted to marry Penelope, the colonel had swiftly and stringently disillusioned him. His ambitions in tatters, on the journey home he he'd consoled himself that he still had Rosie; she'd do for the time being.

Now, as they arrived at Rosie's door, he gazed at her like a soulful puppy. 'It's the thought of leaving you. I can't bear it,' he whined. Rosie smirked inwardly. It hadn't bothered him to leave her and go off to Wharfedale. 'We're meant to be together, Rosie, and we've so little time left to show what we mean to one another,' he continued pleadingly as she unlocked her front door. Rosie was sorry that Eileen was on night duty.

Peter stumbled through the door, Rosie already regretting his presence. 'I'll make some tea. Sober you up,' she said, heading for the kitchen. 'Go into the sitting room.' She gave him a little push towards the door, keen to put distance between them.

'Sod the tea!' Peter grabbed Rosie's arm, dragging her into the sitting room. 'I want to show you how much I love you,' he cried, pushing her backwards onto the small couch under the window. Rosie landed with a thump on the cushions. Peter lunged forwards intending to cover her body with his own, but she was too quick for him.

Rolling sideways, she was up on her feet in seconds. 'No, Peter!'

He grabbed her again, crying: 'Let me, Rosie. Let me make you mine. Now!'

Spittle flew from his lips on to Rosie's cheeks. She yanked herself free, leaving him staggering on the hearthrug.

'I never was yours, Peter, and I never will be,' she said, her harsh, grating tones foreign to her ears. 'When I promised to wait for you I was young and foolish. I don't love you. I don't really know what love is, but I do know that what I feel for you is no more than friendship, a friendship you want to ruin with your filthy ways.' Two bright spots burned on her cheeks and tears flecked her lashes.

Peter slumped onto the couch, his head in his hands and his ears bright red with shame. 'I'm sorry, Rosie,' he mumbled, 'it's just that I love you so.'

'No, you don't, Peter. Like me, you don't know what love is. You just like the thrill of conquest. Now, please go before we hurt one another any more.'

Peter rose unsteadily and bumbled out of the sitting room. In the hallway, as Rosie opened the front door he said, 'You will wait for me, won't you, Rosie?'

Exasperated, she shook her head and then gently pushed him out onto the pavement. She watched him slouch down the street, a sad figure of a man.

* * *

'I could have done with you here last night,' Rosie said the next morning, as she told Eileen about her altercation with Peter. 'It's a good job he was tipsy, otherwise I might not have managed to fight him off.'

'Ach, men, they're all the same. Dirty ould beasts just out for one thing. Don't let him in again.' Eileen gave Rosie a concerned look and then added, 'An' that goes for any other fellas that might walk ye home an' me not here to protect you.

I was meanin' to tell yez, I'm off to France at the end of the week. Six of us are goin' to a hospital in Calais, so ye'll be on your own for a while. I'll be sorry to leave you, Rosie, but I really do want to be where the fightin' is.'

Rosie's look of dismay said it all. She knew she'd miss Eileen, and furthermore she envied her. To be there in the thick of it made working at the Clayton seem rather tame. Rosie yearned for something more challenging than scrubbing floors or emptying bedpans.

* * *

On the day of Peter's departure back to India, Rosie didn't go to the station to see him off, and a few days later when she met Grace in the street she found she had no need for excuses. Peter had confessed to her that he had wanted to marry Penelope but that the Chisholms didn't think he was good enough.

'That's Peter all over,' Grace said. 'He always wanted to better himself, be somebody, and he probably thought he could do that by marrying up. He's as fickle as the weather, but he does care about you.' She gave Rosie a pleading little smile. 'Don't think too badly of him.'

'I won't,' Rosie said. 'I do care for him as a friend, and I don't want this to spoil our friendship, Grace, because I appreciate yours and your family's kindness towards me when I knew nobody in Wakefield.'

Grace patted Rosie's arm. 'Of course we'll remain friends, although you won't be seeing much of me in the future. I've been posted to HQ in Leeds. I'm off next week.'

Rosie and Grace parted with promises to keep in touch.

* * *

High on the hill in Pozières, Milo crouched in a dugout that looked down on what remained of the houses and barns: the villagers were long gone. In what was left of the roof of one building, its grey slates and rafters smashed and mangled, two great gaping holes stared back at him like the eyes of a blind giant, and in what had once been orchards stunted, blackened trees spread their burned limbs; a hideous crucifixion. He reloaded the Lewis gun, an automatic response to Charlie Sykes' urgent cry, and its clattering roar reverberated yet again in his eardrums.

Word had it that the Germans were falling back. 'Keep this up, lads,' Big Buns had said late the night before, 'and we'll have the bastards on the run within the next twenty-four hours.'

Shells, mortars and bullets fired from the German lines bit into the hillside above and below him, but Milo wasn't afraid. Not even when an explosion at the far end of the dugout took out two of the twenty-nine men crammed in there. He had Spotty Williams on one side and Charlie Sykes on the other, and a letter in the breast pocket of his tunic. If, at that very moment, the Kaiser himself and the entire German army were to appear and face Milo they wouldn't have quenched the joy in his heart or wiped the smile that appeared every now and then from his face. He reloaded the Lewis again.

Orders came to stand down, and leaving a fresh threesome to man the gun, Milo, Spotty and Charlie shuffled off for a welcome rest. Leant against the clay banking, Milo carefully withdrew the letter from his pocket. The envelope was stained with his muddy fingerprints and he wiped his hands on his trouser legs before taking out the pages. He'd received it the day before and almost knew its contents by heart, but the sheer thrill of reading Rosie's words and holding the papers that she had touched filled him with unmitigated joy. Once again, he read:

My dearest, dearest Milo,

I can't tell you how happy I am to think that this letter will find you safe and well. I have missed you more than you will ever know, for you mean the world to me. You always have and you always will.

Rosie told him how she had met Harry Oldroyd, yet another reason for Milo to rejoice when he learned that Harry had survived, and she went on to say how sad she was whenever she recalled the day she and Milo had parted.

Although I do recall a very strange moment that, at the time, was wonderful and exciting; a moment that sent my head spinning and my heart beating like it never had before. Since then, I've thought of it often, but I wonder if I'm reading more into it than it really meant. Perhaps it was just the heat of the moment.

When Milo first read this he knew she was referring to the kiss and his own head spun to think that it had meant something to her, but then she had gone on to dismiss it and each time he read the letter he didn't know what to think.

Rosie did not mention Peter.

Milo carefully replaced the letter into its envelope and tucked it deep into his pocket against his heart, determined to write back as soon as he got the chance.

TWENTY-FOUR

WAKEFIELD, AUGUST 1916

The papers were full of it. Day after day heart-rending news reports and hideous photographs covered the pages, the killed-in-combat lists growing longer and longer. Rosie folded the broadsheet and pushed it across the canteen table to Sophie. 'It's heartbreaking but I feel compelled to read it,' she said.

'We don't even know if what we're reading is the truth,' Sophie complained. 'Look at the way they reported that the first day of the Battle for the Somme was a victory, and within a week we learned that it had been absolute carnage.'

'And we're now reaping the results of it,' Rosie said, referring to the latest batch of new patients on the ward. 'It galls me when I see young lads like Private Simpson lying there with his legs blown off. Nineteen, and he'll never walk again.'

'He'll most likely live though, whereas poor Corporal Hughes is unlikely to see tomorrow,' Sophie said sadly. 'His mother's in a dreadful state. He's the eldest of nine and the breadwinner. His dad was killed three years ago in that awful pit disaster in Glamorgan. Do you remember that, Rosie?

Over four hundred men killed, and that was an accident. Now, they're sending them to their deaths on purpose.' She banged her cup down on the table.

On this miserable note the girls finished their tea, and replacing their cuffs and smoothing their aprons they walked back to the ward. 'I still haven't had a letter from Milo,' Rosie said disconsolately. 'I'm beginning to think he never got mine.' She didn't want to think that he had chosen not to reply because she had promised to wait for Peter. She regretted not having told him in her letter that she had changed her mind.

'Give it time. It takes ages for Toby's letters to reach me.' Sophie had kept up a flow of correspondence with Toby Dalrymple since he'd returned to the front. 'He's been promoted to captain and he's asked me to marry him,' she said proudly.

Rosie offered her congratulations at the same time thinking, *Oh dear, Sophie. Here you are, thinking you're in love with a man you hardly know.* Out loud she said, 'Don't go making the mistake I made by committing yourself to something you might regret. Don't promise anything until you know what he's really like.'

Undeterred, Sophie dreamily said, 'Oh, but I already do. He's lovely.'

Back on the ward Rosie moved from bed to bed, kidney dish in hand, gauze swabs at the ready as she assisted Dr McDaniel on his rounds. He was irrigating a flesh wound in a soldier's side, bits of Flanders mud and German shrapnel floating up from a wound that had already been treated at a field hospital in France.

'The blasted stuff's buried so deep it's still finding its way to the surface,' he remarked, stepping back to let Rosie swab the filth away and apply a dressing.

He watched closely, and when she had finished he said, 'Come to my office at the end of your shift. I've a proposition to put to you.' He strode out of the ward.

'What do you think it is?' Rosie asked Sophie a short while later.

'Maybe he's going to ask you for a date, take you dancing.'

'Don't be ridiculous!'

'He's had his eye on you for ages. You said so yourself.'

* * *

Milo handed his letter to the postal sergeant in the Field Post Office. That morning his unit had been stood down for two days' leave and within an hour Milo had replied to Rosie's letter. He had chosen his words carefully, using similar phrases to the ones she had written. He had wanted to write that she was his heart's desire and that he loved and needed her more than anything in life, but whilst Rosie's sentiments had made his heart sing she had made no mention of loving him in the way he loved her. For all he knew, she was still promised to Peter.

He let her know how pleased he was that Harry had survived, and told her about Spotty and Charlie and the lice and the awful food. He deliberately kept it light-hearted. He wouldn't burden her with the horrors he faced every day, although she must be familiar with the results of them now that she was a VAD. He finished by saying:

Should you choose to write to me again, your letters will keep me strong and give me hope. Your letter has made me happier than I have been since I left you that day. You are the dearest person in the world to me. I will always keep you in my heart.

My deepest love, Milo

He hadn't wanted to stop writing, the very act of putting pencil to paper making him feel close to her, but time was pressing and the lorries were waiting to take the unit to a town nearby for relaxation.

In the town there was a small bar selling wine and bottles of French beer at an exorbitant price. Milo drained his third bottle and pulled a face. 'This stuff tastes like witches' piss,' he said, but it didn't stop him from sinking several more, and later, in the footsteps of Spotty and some other lads in the unit he tottered out to the rear of the bar. There were three small huts and three queues. Milo joined one, but when it came to his turn in the hut he just stood there staring stupidly at the scantily clad young woman on the bed.

She looked bored and weary, and her heavily rouged cheeks and kohl-black eyes smudgy and wrinkled. When he didn't move she stood and embraced him, a cloud of cheap perfume and the acrid stink of semen making his head swim. He pulled away. 'I love Rosie,' he mumbled, staggering back outside.

'That were bloody quick,' a voice yelled, followed by ribald laughter. 'You must have needed that badly.'

It's the last thing I need, thought Milo, as he spewed against the yard wall.

* * *

Rosie looked round the bedroom that had been hers for almost two years in the house in Milton Street. The dressing table stood bare and rather forlorn now that she had denuded it of her hairbrushes and pots of cream. They were packed in the brown leather bag along with the clothes and books she was taking to France.

'Do you think you've got everything?' Sophie eyed the bulging bag and then the fine woollen, dark blue cloak with the padded collar that was draped over the bed. 'What about this?' She lifted a corner of the cloak. 'It's beautiful, isn't it, but quite out of fashion. Where did you get it?'

Rosie smiled sadly. 'It was my mother's. The only thing I have that belonged to her. I never knew her, you see.' Sophie looked surprised, for whilst Rosie had told her she was an orphan and that the Threppletons had been her guardians she hadn't elaborated on the subject.

'That's so sad,' tender-hearted Sophie replied. 'I don't know what I'd do without my mother. She's as much a friend as a parent.' Then thinking the remark unkind, she said, 'Sorry, Rosie, I didn't mean to rub it in.'

'I know you didn't, and I'm not hurt. I've grown used to never having had a mother. I can't say I miss her because I don't have any idea what sort of person she was or what she even looked like. Milo's the only person I know who has seen her and he was too young to remember much. He told me she had hair like mine so I have her to thank for this unruly mess.' Grinning, she tossed her glorious mane of copper hair back from her face.

'I'd give anything for hair like yours,' Sophie said, twirling a hank of her own mouse-brown hair round her fingers. She lifted the cloak. 'So, what are we to do with this?'

'I don't want to take it with me in case I lose it. It's precious. Would you keep it safe for me, Sophie? Perhaps you could take it home with you the next time you go to Elmsall if you think your mam wouldn't mind you keeping it there. Then I can collect it when this awful war is over.'

'You've been such a good friend to me I feel privileged to keep it for you.' Sophie folded the cloak and held it to her chest. 'I hate to think of you leaving, and things won't be the same without you, but I know you're keen to go so I'll just have to bear it. We will keep in touch, won't we?'

Rosie reached out and hugged Sophie, her own cheek brushing against the soft folds of the cloak just as it had so many times before in the past. 'I'll write as often as I can, and you carry on the good work on our ward. Look after those poor lads for me.' By now, both girls were in tears.

'What time's your train?' Sophie asked as they let go of each other.

'I'm to meet Dr McDaniel and the rest of the team at twelve outside the station. We'll travel down to Dover and then cross the channel to Dieppe early tomorrow morning.' Rosie gave a bemused grin. 'I still can't believe I'm going.'

She had been thrilled and honoured when Dr McDaniel had asked her to be part of a team he was taking to a field hospital in France. Not only because she thought that was where the really valuable work was done but because it made her feel as though she'd be closer to Milo. She had yet to receive a reply to her letter.

* * *

Stars twinkled in the midnight sky above Pozières, a peaceful canopy of purples and darker shades of blue. Milo was crouched on his hunkers, his rifle across his knee. Charlie was slumped against him. He was used to the feel of Charlie's and Spotty's bodies, he knew the shape and smell of them and took comfort from it. The artillery on both sides had stopped, the deafening roar that had pounded their eardrums throughout the day diminishing to an occasional burst of machine gun fire or the crack of a sniper's rifle. Milo kicked out at a rat that in the lull was bravely foraging close to his feet. The toe of his boot sent the rat flying to his right, a voice calling out, 'Oy, don't be sending your bloody vermin down here; we've enough of us own.'

Spotty Williams dropped down beside Milo in the trench that only a few hours earlier had been cleared of the bodies of Australian troops. They had arrived the week before to carry out the first major offensive on Pozières. 'I hope them bloody Aussies are making mincemeat over there,' Spotty said, jerking his thumb in the direction of the German trenches.

'My thoughts exactly,' said Charlie. 'I hope there's not a sodding Hun left alive by the time we move up.'

'It won't be long now,' Milo said, and felt the palms of his hands turn clammy. Officers were moving up and down the trench issuing orders for the night raid.

When the signal came, Milo's unit were to go forward into No-Man's-Land and rush the German trenches. Every now and then, Very lights illuminated the sky, the glare lighting up the stretch of scrubland they were about to cross. With each flare, Milo scanned the rutted ground looking for shell holes or ridges that would provide cover. As the minutes ticked by, he could feel the tension in the air increasing. It seemed to run through his body like an electric current.

Beside him, Spotty began to shake. 'I'm scared,' he whimpered, pushing closer to Milo. 'I think me number could be up.' He started to cry great heaving sobs.

Milo placed his arm about Spotty's shoulders, pulling him closer still. 'You made it through Bazentin and Fromelles and you'll make it through this,' he said, and trying to lighten the moment he added, 'Only the good die young, Spotty, and you've been a bad bugger ever since I met you.'

Spotty gulped on his tears and gave a grim chuckle. 'You'll stick by me, won't you, you an' all, Charlie?'

'Like shit to a blanket,' Charlie replied. 'You'll be sick of the bloody sight of me an' Milo before we're done.'

Orders came to 'Stand to'; they were moving out. Milo felt a trickle of cold sweat run down his spine. He shouldered his rifle and shuffled into line. Leaving the trench was like leaving home. At a blast from a whistle he scrabbled up the ladder, his weight like a rag on the rungs. Then he was over the top, crawling on his belly to the wire, found a break in it and crawled into No-Man's-Land. The starlit heavens hung above his head, and the earth shook as a huge mortar exploded somewhere up ahead. The sound was thrown back from the sky. Milo felt it inside his ears and down his spine.

All around him were the stooped backs of men, keeping low, moving forward under the incessant clatter of artillery and the crash of shellfire. Milo kept moving. Nearer now and nearer, the first of the German trenches in sight. Milo came upright and ran full tilt, diving for cover into a shell hole as bullets whistled past his head. Spotty slid in beside him.

'It dun't look like them Aussies have had much luck getting rid of Jerry. There must still be a load of 'em down there,' panted Spotty, his breath coming in short gasps and his eyes wide with fear.

'Then it's up to us to clear the buggers out,' Milo replied stoutly, trying imbue courage he didn't feel into the quivering lad.

Spotty glanced over his shoulder. 'Where's Charlie?' he croaked.

Milo didn't know so he said, 'He must be in front of us.'

He got to his knees, ready to run. 'Come on, Spotty, let's find him.'

Clay and blood clogged Milo's fingers as he crawled. It squelched under his boots when he ran, leaping over corpses or trammelling in their slime. They had almost reached the German trench when Milo's boot came into contact with the spilled guts of an Australian. He skidded, threw out an arm to keep his balance and caught Spotty's sleeve, bringing them both crashing to the ground as a hail of bullets from a German machine gun nest whizzed over their heads.

'That were too bloody close for comfort,' Milo gasped, as he sank into the churned earth. He rested his chin on a ridge of mud and wiped the back of his hand across his eyes. To his amazement he saw a clump of small, blue flowers inches away from his nose. They reminded him of the bluebells Rosie had been fond of picking. He got to his knees and then his feet, adrenaline and a sense of invincibility surging through his veins. If tiny blue flowers could survive this carnage, so could he. 'Come on, Spotty,' he yelled at the top of his lungs, 'let's go an' finish the buggers off.'

TWENTY-FIVE

Milo's letter lay on the doormat inside Rosie's empty house in Milton Street.

Rosie was in Dieppe. The sea crossing had been horrendous. Although she had managed not be sick, she felt decidedly nauseous and could still feel the pitch and toss of the ship as she stood on the dock with her bag at her feet. It was raining, a fine drizzle that seeped into every crevice. She glanced round for Sally Owens, a VAD who Dr McDaniel had recruited in London. Sally was a cheerful cockney with a ripe turn of phrase and she and Rosie had immediately struck up a friendship. Now, Rosie was anxious to find her.

Earlier in the crossing, thinking she was about to vomit, Rosie had dashed to the side of the ship and stayed there taking in great gulps of salty air and gazing out over the dark waters. It had such a calming effect on her stomach that before she knew it the ship was about to dock, and in the melee of embarkation she and Sally had been separated.

'There you are,' Sally cried, rushing up to Rosie and dumping her own bag beside Rosie's. 'For a minute I thought you'd bleedin' well thrown yourself overboard. You were ten shades o' green when you dashed off.'

Rosie gave her a sickly grin. 'I did think about it, but I can't swim.'

'Even if you could the water 'ud be bleedin' freezing. You'd never have made it back to Blighty,' chirped Sally, as she shivered in the chill breeze blowing off the sea. She pulled her scarf up over her head. 'An' it's bleedin' raining. I thought the weather on the continong was supposed to be better than ours.'

Rosie chuckled at Sally's mispronunciation of the word 'continent'. She was glad they would be working together. It would make getting to grips with this strange, new place all the easier. By now, Rosie felt cold and damp inside and out, and her heavy coat was giving off that cloying smell of wet wool. She didn't know what she had expected, but it hadn't been this foul weather and the chaos all round her. Sailors and soldiers were thronging up and then down the gang-planks unloading equipment, the dock piled with boxes and swarming with people.

Dr McDaniel, looking harassed and slightly seasick, called out to Rosie and Sally. 'Over here, girls, follow me.' He strode ahead, leading them and the rest of his team to the lorries waiting to take them to Beaulencourt Hospital.

The lorry Rosie and Sally were travelling in jounced over the rutted roads, and when some of the other passengers lit cigarettes, Rosie's nausea returned. Fortunately, she had been one of the last to board and the rain had eased off so she leaned against the tailgate, her head sticking out under the rolled-up canvas. Gulping mouthfuls of fresh air she watched the scenery flash by.

Bumped and shaken, they passed through little towns and

villages torn apart by shot and shell and through countryside that still maintained its natural beauty; trees in full leaf, and lush meadows with cattle knee-deep in wild flowers, grazing contentedly in the early morning drizzle. To Rosie, these pockets of calm in a land that had already seen too much violence and bloodshed seemed almost surreal. She tried hard not to dwell on the families that had fled the tall narrow houses in the towns or the pretty cottages in the hamlets, albeit they were lucky that they had not been victims of the bombardments that had flattened their homes.

Dusk and another heavy downpour heralded their arrival in Beaulencourt. Again, Rosie hadn't known quite what to expect. A large stone building was what she probably had in mind so she was unprepared for the straggle of tents and ugly, green Nissen huts scattered over a muddy acre of land in the centre of which stood a more substantial building that resembled a church hall. Dozens of men moved to and fro, some bearing stretchers from which limbs dangled helplessly. Dirty, mud-caked soldiers queued outside the larger canvas structures, a girl in a uniform similar to Rosie's own allowing them admittance two at a time.

'Cor blimey,' Sally Owens gasped, 'I think they've brought us to the end of the bleedin' world.'

Rosie had to agree. The contrast between the Clayton in Wakefield and what she now saw couldn't have been more different. It looked as though life was going to be a lot harder from now on. Keeping to the duckboards that prevented them from ending up ankle-deep in mud and puddles, the girls trudged across the rain-soaked camp to their accommodation.

Rosie and Sally were billeted in a Nissen hut along with seven other girls, the narrow beds a cupboard width apart; one little cupboard in which to keep their possessions. At one end there was a rudimentary tea station complete with kettle and cups, cocoa and biscuits and a small, pot-bellied stove. The two girls were quick to bag two beds next to it. Stashing some of their belongings into their cupboards and stowing their bags under their beds, they were ready for duty.

* * *

'If I have to haul another gallon of water from over there my arms'll drop off.'

Groaning dramatically, Rosie clanked the bucket of hot water on the floor. It was the umpteenth she had fetched that day from the central building that housed the cookhouse and the boilers. It was their second day at Beaulencourt and Rosie and Sally were scrubbing out a Nissen hut, ready for the arrival of new casualties. Yesterday, they had helped to transfer thirty recovering soldiers from this hut to elsewhere, and were now preparing to receive the next batch of new casualties that were being brought up from the front line.

'You know what they say?' replied Sally, down on her knees scrubbing at the stained floorboards. 'Cleanliness is next to godliness.'

'Aye, Sister Foster always says that and she's right. We can't risk transferring infection. It does its worst without us helping it.' Rosie began to wash down the panelled walls, removing all trace of the hut's previous occupants.

By midday the freshly sanitised hut resembled something like the ward that Rosie had worked on at the Clayton: neat, clean beds on either side of the long hut and a doctors' and nurses' station complete with surgical equipment and dressings in the middle of the room. When Dr McDaniel and Sister Foster arrived to inspect it, Rosie and Sally glowed under Dr Dan's praise. However, Sister Foster pointed out that some of the beds were not an equal distance apart. Rosie gave Sally sly wink, letting her know that Frosty's fault-finding was the norm.

An ambulance rumbled into the compound and the grizzly off-loading began.

'All action stations,' Sister Foster barked as a couple of weary stretcher-bearers clumped into the ward carrying what, to Rosie, looked like a blood-soaked heap of blankets until an arm slid out from underneath. Rosie took a deep breath and then hurried to assist in lowering the injured man onto a bed.

More ambulances arrived, stretcher after stretcher unloaded, and the ward echoing with screams and groans as the beds were filled. Rosie steeled herself against the nauseating sights and sounds as Dr McDaniel, Sister Foster and two trained nurses swiftly assessed each man's injuries and prioritised their needs. Orders came thick and fast.

Rosie cut away mud-caked tunics to expose ghastly wounds, helped staunch bleeding, and held buckets for men to pee or vomit in.. She held out kidney dishes or wrapped clamps in gauze and passed over antiseptic swabs to the nurse she was assisting as they moved from bed to bed. At other times she carried armfuls of soiled dressings to the incinerator and bedding to the huge laundry bins.

On her way to the bin with yet another pile of stinking sheets she passed Sally on her way back from the incinerator. She gave her a weary grin. Sally waved her hands distastefully. 'Why is it we always get the bleedin' shitty jobs?' she asked.

''Cos we got the shitty end of the stick,' piped Rosie.

Back and forth they worked without ceasing as, wounds assessed and emergency treatment delivered, it was time to make each man as comfortable as possible. Some of these men had not slept in a proper bed for a year or more. Cleaning mud and blood from their bodies, easing their pain and giving them hope was what Rosie liked best. It was what she was here for.

Swiftly but gently, Rosie stripped a young boy of his bloodstained uniform. He was filthy from head to foot, hadn't been bathed in months, but the angry rash that covered his body was still visible through the dirt. Rosie gagged at the sight of a mass of livid, suppurating pustules where he had scratched himself raw. An ugly gash on his thigh was a shrapnel injury. He lay there, puny and shivering, and watching her with pale blue eyes that were close to tears.

'How old are you?' Rosie said, as she washed away clay and grit and deftly removed slivers of shrapnel from his thigh.

Cautiously, the lad slid his eyes to left and then right and whispered, 'Sixteen, but don't be saying owt. I told 'em I were eighteen.' Rosie glanced at the hastily ascribed card attached to his bed: Gibbs, Robert 1 KLR, No.273654. Pte.

'Well, Robbie, your secret's safe with me,' said Rosie, as she gently washed French clay from between his toes. 'Tell me though, how long have you had this rash? It looks as though its driving you daft, what with all the scratching.'

'It is. I've had it nearly two weeks, ever since I ate them mushroom things. We were starving, you see, an' Tucker said they were safe to eat. I'd never had 'em afore 'cos Mammy allus cooks plain stuff like meat an' tatie pie.'

At his use of the word 'mammy' Rosie's heart went out to him; sixteen years of age and here he was, filthy and wounded, and more than likely a witness to things nobody should ever have to experience.

'Dr Dan'll know how to treat it,' she said confidently.

'Now, let's see if we can make this leg better.' Just then, Dr McDaniel arrived by her side. As she helped him irrigate the flesh wound on the boy's thigh she told him about the mushrooms.

'Lucky they weren't a deadly poison variety,' said Dr Dan. 'It's just an allergic reaction. Lather him in zinc oxide once we've dressed the leg. In the meantime keep on with the Carrel-Dakin's and I'll be back with you shortly.'

Rosie was inordinately pleased that Dr Dan trusted her to use this method for cleansing the wound and continued to transfer the Dakin's solution from the large glass bottle via rubber tubes into the deepest part of Robbie's wound.

'This antiseptic will prevent infection,' she said, proud to have mastered the technique.

'Thanks for being good to me,' Robbie said, as Rosie applied an impregnated dressing on the cleansed wound.

'No bother at all, Robbie lad,' Rose replied. She gave him an encouraging grin and moved on to the soldier in the next bed.

* * *

Milo was exhausted. In a haze of phosgene and mustard gas they had stormed the German trenches at Pozières and were now resting in the Salient. The battle for the Somme was still raging but for the moment Pozières was quiet, the territory won: but at what cost?

'I hope to God they can do something for Spotty,' Charlie said bitterly.

'I think I'd rather be shot than gassed,' Milo replied, picturing the half-crazed, breathless men who had been taken away in ambulances along with those with gaping wounds from shells and bullets. He shivered. 'I told him to put his hood on but he said it made his head itch and he couldn't see properly.'

Charlie groaned. 'Daft young sod.'

The postal sergeant came huffing and puffing down the trench. Milo perked up and got to his feet to join the shattered, grey-faced men clustered round him; some with certainty and others anxious. Milo slumped off, empty-handed. Rosie wasn't going write back, not after all this time.

* * *

Rosie's days and nights seemed to run into an endless revolving spiral of fetching and carrying, washing and scrubbing, changing dressings, spoon-feeding the helpless and holding the hands of the dying. On night duty, she sat listening to moans, groans and mutterings, easing pains and calming nightmares, and to strengthen her spirit she pretended that each man she tended was Milo. Where was he now? If only he'd answered her letter before she left for France. She still scoured the list of names of the wounded men admitted to the field hospital and looked into the faces of each new patient just as she had when in Wakefield, always on the lookout for him. He rarely left her thoughts.

Rosie liked night duty best of all. Sitting in the darkened hut, with the lamps turned low and the stringent smell of Lysol tingling her nose, she could hear the distant boom and roar from the battlefield if the wind was in the right direction. Sometimes she thought she felt the earth shake and she prayed for the men out there; Milo could be one of them.

When she was off duty, she kept to her own company or Sally's. She had little in common with most of the other

VADs: the posh girls who declared it was their duty to king and country but were afraid to get their hands dirty; the rough drinkers and smokers looking for excitement; and the saintly, sentimental, sweet girls who believed a cup of tea and a biscuit were the cure for all ills. Sally was her only friend. Unfortunately, they were rarely off duty at the same time so Rosie filled her free hours with reading. When Godfrey Threppleton had taken her under his wing and given her a love for literature he had given her a most precious gift, and Rosie often thought of him fondly. She still wrote and received an occasional letter from Peter, in India, and Grace, Sophie and Eileen all kept in touch with her. Letters were a lifeline at times like this. However, the one letter that she had most wanted to receive whilst she had still been in Wakefield had never arrived.

One afternoon when she was feeling particularly low Rosie sat with her writing pad on her knee deliberating whether or not to write another letter to Milo, a silly sort of pride deterring her from just getting on with it. Had her first letter gone astray or had he chosen to ignore it?

'Who are you writing to?' Sally asked as she entered the hut and flopped on the bed beside Rosie's.

'I'm thinking of writing to Milo again,' she said glumly, 'but I could be wasting my time. I don't know where he is, and now that I am here he doesn't know where I am. We'll probably never meet again.' She tossed her pen aside and wailed, 'We're star crossed, that's what we are.'

'Hark at Sarah Bernhardt.' Sally mockingly placed the back of her hand across her forehead and struck a theatrical pose then getting up off the bed she said, 'He might not know where you are, but you know how to contact him. Just get on with it, and stop moping.' She walked over to the tea-point. 'I'm making cocoa. Do you want some?'

Rosie grunted her reply and uncapped her pen.

* * *

Later that night, sitting at the bedside of a grievously wounded soldier with his hand in hers, Rosie wondered if another VAD in some other field hospital was sitting holding Milo's hand. She prayed it wasn't so; that he was unscathed.

The soldier moved restlessly in the bed, and opening his eyes wide in a lucid moment he looked directly into Rosie's. 'Susan,' he gasped, 'is it you, love?' His cracked, dry lips curved into a slow, heartbreakingly tender smile. 'I knew you'd come. I did think you'd forgotten me.'

'Aye, it's me, love, your Susan. I'm here. You should have known I'd come when you needed me.' Rosie didn't mind telling the lie if it brought him comfort in the short time he had left.

'Give us a kiss, lass,' croaked the soldier, 'I've sorely missed your kisses.'

Leaning over, Rosie placed her lips on his and they shared a tender kiss. Rosie thought of Milo's passionate kiss. The soldier gave a deep, satisfied sigh, a smile lighting his gaunt face. Moments later, still smiling, he took his last breath.

* * *

'Hard night?' Sally asked, as Rosie entered the Nissen hut early the next morning, her night duty ended.

'Something like that,' said Rosie, beginning to strip off her uniform.

Sally, just up and out of bed, was making a cup of cocoa before she went on duty. 'Want one?' she asked.

'Please,' Rosie replied, climbing into bed.

Sally brought the two mugs over and perched on the end of Rosie's bed. As they sipped their cocoa, Rosie told Sally about the kiss. 'It was only a white lie, wasn't it?' she said, her conscience troubled at having duped the dying soldier.

'If it brought him comfort and he died happy it were a blessin', so don't you go worrying that it was wrong,' Sally replied firmly. She drained her mug, and after taking off her nightgown she put on her uniform. 'I'll have to go, see you later.' Sally walked out of the hut and Rosie pulled the blankets over her head and fell fast asleep. She wakened shortly after midday. Dressed and hungry she stepped outside in need of fresh air, the chilly weather that had set in during the past week blowing away the last vestiges of sleep. She was walking across to the canteen when she heard someone calling her name.

'Letter for you, Threppleton.' The VAD in charge of distributing the post hurried towards Rosie and shoved an envelope in her hand. Rosie recognised the sloping script immediately. It was a letter from Hildred. Trying hard to quell her disappointment, and telling herself that she couldn't possibly expect it to be from Milo – he didn't know where to write to her – and that she should be grateful Hildred took time to write, she tucked the letter in her pocket and went to the canteen.

After eating an unappetising, dried-up meat and potato pie served with watery cabbage, she went back to the hut and sat on her bed to read Hildred's letter.

She opened the envelope, surprised to find another envelope inside it along with his letter. Curious, she withdrew it, her heart leaping and her fingers trembling as she gazed at the childlike, carefully formed letters spelling out her name and the address in Milton Street. She felt a tightening in her chest. She couldn't be sure if the letter was from Milo – it could be from one of the VADs back in Wakefield – so before she allowed herself to be plunged into despair she scanned Hildred's letter.

Hildred had gone to check on the house in Milton Street and found the letter on the mat; it had lain there for some time judging by the postmarked date, he explained. Anxiously, Rosie peered at the faint grey stamp in the top corner of the envelope. 'Milo,' she cried, tossing Hildred's letter aside and ripping open the envelope with the British Forces postmark. How had she not spotted it before? She withdrew two flimsy sheets of paper, and her blood tingling and her hopes soaring, she began to read.

My dear Rosie,

I can't begin to tell you how happy I am to have got your letter. I am sorry I left you without saying a proper goodbye. I still think of the day I left you in that little park and ran off like a fool after I had kissed you. I shouldn't have done that because you are the dearest, most precious person in my life. You always were and you always will be. I have missed you a great deal and it is only the thought that one day I'll see you again that keeps me going.

Rosie paused then read the lines again. Milo had remembered the kiss, but what did he mean by 'I shouldn't have done that'? Was he apologising for running away or for having kissed her? Did he think it was wrong to kiss her because she was Peter's girl? Tears sprang to her eyes. Poor Milo. Had that kiss confused his feelings just as it had her own? Rosie read on.

What luck that Harry made it back to England and ended up in your hospital. I hope that he has made a good recovery. Harry kept us going with his kindness and his good sense of humour. He's very wise too. I miss him but I still have my mates, Spotty and Charlie. We stick together. We even scratch each other's backs when the lice are driving us crackers. I haven't had a good wash in weeks so you'd find me pretty smelly if you were here.

We've just been stood down for a couple of days and it's good to be away from the fighting. It's scary when the shells and bullets are flying all round you but you just have to get on with it and hope for the best. I'm writing this letter sitting in a trench with my belly full of hot stew, so life's not too bad. When we go back into battle I hope you will be thinking of me and say a prayer for my safety. I think about you whenever I'm afraid. Sometimes, when I'm on night watch, I pretend I'm at Nostell Priory with you. Do you remember that day?

Should you choose to write to me again your letters will keep me strong and give me hope. Your letter has made me the happiest I have been since I left you on that day. You are the dearest person in the world to me. I will always keep you in my heart.

My deepest love, Milo

Rosie held the pages to her lips. Dear, darling Milo. He hadn't said he loved her in the way that she now knew loved him, but his letter was much more like a love letter than any she had received from Peter. Opening the drawer in her bedside cupboard, she took out her writing pad and pen; she'd finish the letter she had started the day before and post it straight away whilst she was off duty.

Her heart filled with love, she scribbled page after page, signing it: *Your own darling ever-loving Rosie.* There, she thought, that should give him a clue as to how she really felt; that it wasn't sisterly love but a truly, deeply romantic love. She tucked Milo's letter into the pocket of her grey dress. She'd keep it close and read it again and again when she went on duty tonight. On feet as light as a feather, she ran along the duckboards to the post sergeant's depot.

* * *

Milo was in Flers-Courcelette, or 'Flo's Corsets' as Charlie called it when he received Rosie's letter. Crouched in a trench, his fingertips tingled with the intimacy of holding the paper that Rosie had touched. He read her words, marvelling at her description of a working day and smiling at the witty comments she made about her superiors, but the words that made his heart sing were the ones that told him that she had made a silly mistake.

It was only after he had left for India and then again when he came home on leave that I realised I don't love Peter at all, and I don't think he loves me. I still think of him fondly as a friend but I know now that he is not the man I want to marry. When he asked me to wait for him I was silly enough to think I loved him, but now I know I was in love with the idea of being in love, if you know what I mean.

'Oh, yes Rosie, I know what you mean,' Milo whispered to himself. To Charlie he said, 'I never knew how much I loved her until it came to losing her. But now—' he waved the letter under Charlie's nose '—I think I've found her again.' He folded the letter and tucked it into his breast pocket next to the other one.

Charlie gave him a friendly nudge and winked. 'They say love conquers all, an' if we blast the bloody hell out of Jerry an' Flo's Corsets you'll be able to go back an' show your Rosie just how much you love her.'

Milo was still in a romantic haze when the order came to 'stand to'. He shuffled along the trench to the fire step, ready to go over the top, his blood tingling and his hands clammy, but his heart was beating with a new tune. His 'ever-loving Rosie' had renewed his hopes and dreams, and he wanted nothing more than to survive this day to return that love. Would God be kind to him? he wondered. He dearly hoped so.

TWENTY-SIX

BEAULENCOURT, SPRING 1918

God was kind. Milo had survived the battle of 'Flo's Corsets' and at the first opportunity he had replied to Rosie's letter. From then on, despite Milo moving from one scene of carnage to another under constant threat of shelling and deadly phosgene, and despite the hordes of wounded and dying men that dominated Rosie's daily life, their letters always reached their destination.

As words flowed back and forth and one year rolled into the next they brought with them an understanding so deep and true that tentative sentiments of love blossomed into full-blown declarations. Come spring 1918 and the war still raging, Rosie and Milo were writing passionate love letters.

* * *

It was just another day in Beaulencourt, and Rosie performing her duties with the same fortitude that had carried her through the last two grim years. Out at the incinerator, she viciously prodded its contents with a long stave, encouraging the flames to devour the bloodstained dressings and sheets and have done with the job. The early morning was chill, but with a bright, brittle sun shining on her back and the heat from the large metal vat on her face, Rosie sweltered. As she poked at the detritus of smouldering cotton, oxygen filled the gaps and flames leapt high. Rosie jumped back to avoid the fiery tongues. This was one job she detested.

Today was her first day back at work, having spent the last week on leave in Armentières. Along with a nurse called Margaret and two VADs, Vera and Ann, she had viewed the sites, visited churches and drank coffee at pavement cafés. In the two years she had been at Beaulencourt, this was only the second leave she had taken, the first spent in St Omer – Rosie had no desire to return to England for her leave. And although she had welcomed a change of scene Rosie hadn't particularly enjoyed either trip. On each occasion she was overwhelmed by the sheer devastation of the towns and the countryside.

She had tried not to look at the empty homes, many without roofs, their inner walls sad with peeling wallpaper and broken furniture, but her eyes were drawn back to them at every turn in the road. This evidence of destroyed human lives had cut her to the quick, as did the abandoned farms where fields that had once flourished with crops were now potted with craters of glimmering water. Rosie imagined undetected bodies buried in the mud. Therefore, rather than boost her spirits, the leave had left her feeling depressed, as though she was suffering from an overload of mud, blood and misery.

She threw an armful of dressings into the blaze, and was playing the game of pictures in the fire when the rumble of an engine alerted her. A lorry swung into the compound and came to a stop by the cookhouse. The VAD driver climbed out and stretched wearily. Rosie hallooed and waved to her. The girl plodded over to Rosie, her eyes puffed from lack of sleep.

'Back-up to replace those going on leave,' she said, jerking her thumb at the doctors, nurses and VADs who, having alighted, were now lifting their bags and gazing speculatively at their new surroundings.

'You look shattered, Mary.' Rosie liked this hefty girl who had been brought up on a farm close to Eggleston, and now she was filled with concern. Mary had lost weight and her once bonny face was grey.

'Dead on me feet,' said Mary, 'but we're short of drivers, an' I've not had a proper sleep for forty-eight hours. I wa' down at the casualty station last night bringing in the lads from Hébuterne. You'll most likely be getting some of 'em later today.' She sighed heavily. 'I'd best be getting back. See you again soon.'

'You make sure you get some sleep, and soon,' Rosie advised. She watched Mary trudge back to her lorry. *How much longer can this awful bloody war go on?* she asked herself. *And how much longer can girls like me and Mary continue to perform the arduous tasks expected of us without us ending up as two more casualties?* She wiped her hand over face, sooty streaks smearing her hot cheeks.

Curious as to the new arrivals, she scanned the small group of men and women clustered around the accommodations sergeant. Three men and four women, Rosie's eyes were drawn to a tall, angular woman standing slightly apart from the others, her back to Rosie. Her blue-grey cape edged with bands of scarlet signified that she was a qualified Territorial nurse.

Rosie's breath caught in her throat. She'd recognise that long, straight back and the arrogant way the woman held her head anywhere. Without a second thought, like a pin drawn to a magnet, Rosie set off walking towards the woman. As she drew nearer, the woman swivelled on her heels until she was facing Rosie.

Across the distance their eyes met, the woman's jaw dropping as she stared in disbelief. Rosie halted, but her eyes remained fixed on the woman's face as she tried to come to terms with the tumult of emotions now flooding through every vein. Rosie stood her ground.

The woman excused herself from her companions, and adjusting her nurse's cape she picked her way precariously along the duckboards towards Rosie. Insolently, Rosie watched Hortense Leger approach.

Hortense eyed her coldly. 'What are you doing here?' Her voice was just as Rosie remembered it: harsh and imperious.

'Same as you, I suppose,' Rosie replied nonchalantly, although she felt anything but. 'I've been here two years.' She made the remark in an attempt to show priority, but at the same time silently cursing her weakness at allowing Hortense to make her feel inferior. Memories of her younger days surged back.

'You're a VAD then,' said Hortense, her tone of voice disparaging as she looked Rosie up and down. Rosie was annoyed that her uniform was smudged with soot. Hortense fingered the silver badge pinned to her cape, her eyes glittering maliciously, and Rosie aware that she was signifying her superiority.

Rosie's temper flared. 'I never knew you had nursing qualifications, Hortense.'

The way she said it suggested she didn't believe it. It was

a known fact that several women purporting to be nurses had lied about their qualifications.

Hortense flushed. 'There's an awful lot you don't know about me' she snapped.

'I know you didn't stay to nurse your cousin, Celeste, when she needed you most,' Rosie retorted. 'You disappeared like a thief in the night leaving me and Godfrey to do the nursing.' She paused deliberately. 'You do know that both Celeste and Godfrey are dead.'

The colour drained from Hortense's face.

'Ah, I see you didn't,' Rosie said, taking satisfaction from having shocked her. 'Celeste died in the lunatic asylum, and poor Godfrey was killed in a car accident. But I'm sure that's of little importance to you. As I remember, you couldn't wait to get away from them.'

Hortense froze. For a moment she looked stunned and then, swinging on her heel she marched off to join her companions who were now making their way to the accommodation huts. Rosie was glad to see the back of her. With the camp being as big as it was, if luck was on her side their paths would rarely cross.

On the ward later that night, as Rosie flitted from bed to bed offering cooling drinks, plumping pillows and easing pains, she wondered what hand of fate had brought Hortense to Beaulencourt.

* * *

Milo was in Bapaume.

'How long now, Charlie?' Milo, his muscles taut and the palms of his hands clammy leaned against the breastwork of the trench, the clay's cold dampness penetrating his tunic and intensifying his fears.

'Another minute or so, I reckon.'

Milo patted the breast pocket of his tunic, thick with the bundle of Rosie's letters; his good luck charms. The feel of them above his heart reviving his courage, he flexed his knees and then put one foot on the bottom rung of the ladder. The whistle blew.

'Watch out for yourself, Charlie,' whispered Milo.

'You an' all, Milo, take care.'

'I will, Charlie,' Milo replied fervently. He had to survive now that he knew Rosie loved him. What was more, according to his map, she was nearer to him now than she had been at any point in the past four years. That had to mean something.

Then they were off, up over the top and through the wire. The sun was shining brightly in their eyes as they ran through shell shot and gunfire. They slowed, tripping on roots of dead trees and the bodies of men from the first wave. Milo had no breath left and he slumped into a shell hole, Charlie along with him and a lad he didn't know. The lad wept, and Milo and Charlie had no words of comfort.

Then they were up and off again, the taste of metal and blood in every breath.

Nights of wakefulness followed days of mayhem until, on the eighth night they were on a wooded hill, muddied and bloodied from crawling for cover through the leafy mould and the lifeless bodies of their comrades. Word had it that the Germans were on the run, driven back by the force of the attack.

Exhausted beyond bearing, Milo sank to the ground as orders came to stand down. Pushing a headless body wearing a German uniform away with his boot, he rested his head on his bent knees. He thought of Rosie. Lovely Rosie who had told him she loved him and wanted to spend the rest of her life with him. *As the crow flies, she's less than seven miles away from me,* he calculated, *but right now it might as well be a million.* He wept.

In the morning, a party from Milo's unit were ordered to recover the bodies of their fallen comrades, the fighting having moved forward and the officer in charge deeming it safe to do so.

'Great success, chaps, the place is clear of Huns and at this jolly rate we'll have them beaten in no time.'

'Do you think they stamp that last bit on their tongues when they train 'em to be officers?' Charlie said, his sarcasm making Milo smile as they prepared to join the recovery party. His tears of the night before and a few hours of restless sleep had brought relief and now, having survived the worst nine days of his life, he was ready to carry on. A mild drizzle began to fall as they set out to perform their gruesome task.

So many soldiers – husbands, sons and sweethearts – now nothing but broken, bleeding carcases, and those who still had faces staring through lifeless eyes into a grey, wet morning under a foreign sky. Milo stooped to lift the legless body of a Lewis gunner, staggering under his weight as he heaved him onto a stretcher.

He heard the crack before he felt the searing pain that set the space between his shoulders alight. The pain radiated up into his neck, his head and then his brain. He fell forward onto the body of the gunner, and just before a terrifying blackness descended he heard someone shout, 'Sniper! Sniper in the trees.'

* * *

Rosie hurried from her billet, and sliding along the duckboards to the ward she felt the now familiar pulsing in her veins that always preceded the arrival of the ambulances bringing in badly wounded men from the battlefield. Already, the camp was a roaring, seething mass of vehicles, stretcher-bearers and medics, but in Rosie's ward there was the same calm, efficient urgency that always followed an intake of new casualties. Rosie stripped away uniforms, set up drips, washed bloodied wounds and applied dressings.

'Over here, Threppleton.' The doctor who had called for her assistance was standing by a bed reading from a card that had been pinned to the wounded man's trousers. When Rosie joined him he said, 'Apparently they removed the bullet from his back at the dressing station but the wound's infected. Strip him down, remove the dressing, clean him up and then set up the Carrel-Dakin's.' Orders delivered, the doctor moved on to the soldier in the next bed.

Rosie lifted a pair of scissors and began carefully slicing into the back of the soldier's filthy tunic. Peeling the two halves apart, and gagging at the fetid smell she revealed the pus-stained dressing. Tenderly, she peeled it away to expose his ravaged flesh. Ragged flaps of skin – black and green – surrounded the hole from where they had gouged the bullet, dark red lines of poison snaking across his back. Rosie caught her breath and began to wipe away clotted blood and filth. He was a muscular lad, his healthy skin smooth and tanned. Rosie, more used to washing the flaccid, white skin of men who never exposed their bodies to the sun thought, *This chap's spent time under God's good sunlight.* Fleetingly, she wondered if he was a farm boy. Gently dabbing and swabbing, the sharp smell of Lysol biting her nose, she continued cleansing the wound.

The soldier, who all this time had been lying face down on the bed, groaned loudly and then slowly and painfully he eased onto his shoulder and turned his head. For the first time since starting her task Rosie saw his face.

Her hands became flaccid and useless, and a hammering inside her chest was so loud that she thought the soldier must hear it. Blood sang in her ears and she had to force herself to stay upright. Leaned against the bed, she gazed into the soldier's face, a mixture of wonder and fear on her own. His eyes were closed but Rosie knew exactly what colour they were.

'Milo,' she whispered. 'Milo, it's me, Rosie.'

Milo's eyes stayed closed, but a smile curved the corners of his mouth before a racking pain had him groaning and rolling his face back into his pillow.

'For God's sake get a move on,' the doctor snapped, as he turned back to Milo's bed. 'Get the Carrel-Dakin's.'

Rosie jumped. She must keep her mind on saving Milo, she told herself, and leaving the doctor to inspect the wound, she fetched the trolley that held the bottles and tubes and the antiseptic. Swiftly, she began to apply the fluid to the inflamed, pus-filled area between his shoulder blades, removing filth from deep inside the wound. She felt Milo's muscles relax and heard him give a deep sigh.

'Oh, you know how to use it,' said the doctor, his surprise showing.

'Yes, sir, Dr McDaniel who was here before you showed me how it was done,' she replied, and carefully sluicing the wound she silently added, 'and I'll wash away every bit of infection from this wound because this is the man I love.'

All the while Rosie tended his wound Milo remained in a semi-conscious state, only a twitch and a groan letting her know that he was aware of her ministrations. Several hours later, the time came for the doctor to check Milo. Rosie held her breath as she removed the dressing for the doctor's inspection.

'It's much improved,' he said, prodding gently and remarking that the inflammation had lessened, and then pronouncing, 'I think we might yet save this chap.' As he plunged his hands into a bowl of hot water and worked up a lather with carbolic soap, Rosie's breath came out in a whoosh so loud that the doctor lost his hold on the soap and gave her a curious look.

From then on, in between caring for other soldiers Rosie spent as much time as she could at Milo's bed, and when Sally came on duty she called her over.

'This is Milo,' she told her, tears hovering on her lashes. Milo was lying perfectly still, and in her heightened state of anxiety Rosie was unsure whether he was unconscious or simply sleeping. Agitated, she turned to Sister Foster. 'He's a bad colour, isn't he? And his breathing's too shallow.'

Sister Foster leaned over Milo and placed a practised ear to his chest. Then she laid the palm of her hand on his forehead and then the back of it against his cheek. 'Seems to me like he's sleeping peacefully, and yes his breathing is a bit shallow but his temperature is fine.' She gave Rosie a sympathetic smile. 'And if it had been anybody else but Milo you'd have known that for yourself.' She patted Rosie's arm. 'Don't go imagining the worst. He looks like tough stuff to me.'

'The doctor said the bullet was close to his heart and that he might have blood in his lungs,' Rosie persisted.

'And he might not. He'd not be breathing so regularly if

he had.' Sister Foster walked off to attend to a soldier who was crying out for help.

Heartened by the nurse's no-nonsense attitude Rosie visibly brightened, but throughout the next few days as Milo drifted in and out of consciousness she watched him like a hawk, delighted when a faint blush of colour reached his pallid cheeks and his breathing steadied. To allay her fears she asked Sally to swap duties with her so that she could be with Milo in the long, dark night-time hours should his condition deteriorate. It seemed to Rosie that the majority of soldiers who lost the battle with life, died during the night; that the angel of death was more active in the last few hours before dawn.

'Course I will,' said Sally, 'but you'll have to check it out with Frosty.'

Sister Foster smiled at the request. 'By all means,' she said gently. She had grown to admire this clever, willing VAD but she was careful not let it show and now, in her usual brisk manner, she said, 'Don't neglect the others at the expense of your sweetheart, Threppleton.' Rosie assured her she would do no such thing, and now as she sat in the darkened ward, her ears alert to the needs of all the men, she thanked God for sending her to Beaulencourt.

Milo moved restlessly in the bed, his head turning from side to side as though he was searching for something although his eyes were closed. Rosie placed her hand on his brow, flicking back the long dark locks just as she had seen Milo do so many times before. He opened his eyes and blinked rapidly, and as his vision cleared he settled his eyes on Rosie's face. A sweet, slow smile stretched his lips and he lowered his eyelids, his long, dark lashes stark against his pallid cheeks. He started to speak, his voice that had been silent for days now no more than a croak. Rosie's heart leapt, and she leaned forward placing her ear close to his lips, anxious to hear every word.

'I was dreaming of my girl, nurse. When I felt your hand on my brow I thought she was here with me.'

'She is, Milo,' urged Rosie, her heart and stomach turning somersaults. 'It's me, your Rosie, right by your side.' She placed her hand on his cheek, stroking gently.

Milo's eyelids fluttered and then he opened his eyes wide. 'Rosie, is it you?'

He struggled to sit up, Rosie gently pushing him back against the pillows.

'It is, Milo. I'm here, love, so just keep calm and don't disturb your wound.'

Milo felt the thudding in his chest and wondered if his heart was about to burst and finish him off. Rosie was here, holding his hand, stroking his brow. He hadn't been dreaming. The tension seeped from his muscles and the frown lines on his forehead grew smooth. He closed his eyes, the corners crinkling as he smiled and gave a huge, satisfied sigh. Rosie let silent tears fall unheeded. She knew then that her Milo was going to be all right.

TWENTY-SEVEN

'Sister Foster's going on leave as of today,' Sally announced as she entered the billet carrying a bucket of water. She plonked it down noisily next to her bed.

Rosie sat up in bed and stretched sleepily; she was still doing night duty.

'Good for her – it's long overdue. She might be a frosty bitch at times but she's a dedicated nurse and I respect her for that – and there are times when I think she really has a kind heart hidden beneath the ice.'

'Sister Voyard's taking her place,' Sally continued as she stripped off her uniform. Standing in her vest and knickers, she dipped a flannel into the bucket sloshing warm water up over her face and neck and under her armpits. 'I'm going for a drink with that ambulance driver, the good-looking one with blond hair,' she said, towelling herself dry and then pulling on a pink cotton frock and cardigan. 'Does this look OK?'

'You look lovely,' Rosie replied, and then asked. 'What happened to Lenny the stretcher-bearer? You change your boyfriends as often as I change my knickers.'

'Love 'em an' leave 'em, that's me.' Sally laughed.

'By the way, which one's Sister Voyard?' Rosie looked puzzled.

'The tall, stiff snotty cow who's been working with Dr Farrell. The one you said you knew when she first came here.'

'That wasn't what she was called when I knew her,' Rosie said, puzzled as to why Hortense was using a different surname. 'She was called Hortense Leger when I was a kid.'

'Perhaps she got married,' Sally said, giving a final brush to her hair.

'Well, if that's the case, God help the poor soul who was daft enough to marry her,' Rosie replied with feeling. Up until now hers and Hortense's paths had rarely crossed. Rosie was thankful for that. Now, she was going to be her ward sister. She groaned out loud. 'God, I don't fancy having to work under her. She never liked me when I was young, and I can't say I much care for her. She's spiteful at the best of times.'

Although Rosie had admitted to knowing Hortense, she had chosen not to divulge the whole sorry story and had passed Hortense off as a friend of the family. Sally didn't need to know about her dysfunctional upbringing with the Threpletons. Rosie preferred to forget about Celeste and Hortense, but she always remembered Godfrey with affection.

* * *

Later that evening when Rosie went on duty Hortense met her with a cool glance. As the night shift progressed, Hortense watched Rosie like a hawk. Rosie tended to her work in her usual efficient, friendly and gentle manner, Hortense quick to see how popular she was as she made the soldiers laugh at her comical remarks or eased their pain and soothed their fears.

Like a radiant angel she moved through the ward, her glorious red hair a beacon of hope around her pretty, smiling face. The soldiers followed her with their eyes, smiling whenever it was their turn to receive her ministrations.

Hortense began her duties, her thoughts tumbling. Had Rosie gossiped to the other nurses about their relationship? Had she entertained them with horror stories of her childhood? Hortense felt a stab of fear. Rosie had already voiced her suspicions regarding her qualifications as a nurse, qualifications that had belonged to the deceased daughter of the man whose housekeeper she had been. After his death she had assumed his daughter's identity to obtain a senior nursing post in a London Hospital. *Rosie can't possibly know I stole them,* she told herself as, her hands shaking, she poured Lysol into a kidney dish.

However, she had never imagined that one day she would be working alongside Rosie and now, her mind working overtime as she moved from bed to bed, she knew she had to act, and quickly. Smiling grimly she reached a conclusion. *I'll get rid of her before she ruins my reputation.* With renewed alacrity she ripped off a dressing, the soldier howling pitifully.

'Let Rosie do it,' one man grumbled as Hortense went to change his bandages. Ignoring him, she roughly applied a clean dressing seething when he shouted, 'Bugger off, you heartless bitch.' Hortense stormed back to the nurses' station.

Rosie struggled to hide her disgust.

'Give us a wiggle, nurse,' one cheeky lad from Barnsley called after her as she walked away from his bed. Rosie exaggerated the swing of her hips as she crossed the ward to where Hortense was now sitting. The soldiers cheered.

'Enough of that nonsense, nurse,' Hortense snapped.

* * *

When the soldiers were settled for the night, Rosie sat by Milo's bed holding his hand, talking softly until he fell asleep. She dropped a kiss on his brow before going to calm a lad having a nightmare.

Hortense was still sitting at the nurses' station the dim light from the lamp casting her shadow grotesquely against the white wall. Rosie thought of a wicked witch as she walked towards her.

'You spent an inconsiderable amount of time with Corporal Simmonite. Might I ask why?' Hortense's black eyes glittered malevolently.

'I've known Milo all my life. He's the man I intend to marry once this war is over,' Rosie replied, her tone curt. She lifted a water jug and walked off to replenish the glasses by each bed.

Hortense's resentment bubbled through her bony frame. Young, beautiful Rosie was yet again threatening her position. The indignity of the men favouring Rosie's gentle hands over her own cut through her like a knife. And now it seemed that Rosie had found something she, Hortense, had never had: love.

Sister Foster had told Hortense that Rosie had especially requested night duty – and why. Hortense smiled grimly as she exacted her revenge. 'After tonight you will return to day duty,' she announced at the end of the shift, smirking as she added, 'I will also be on the day shift.'

'But... but... I need to be with Milo,' Rosie blurted, thinking of the long night hours when death came stalking. Then, no longer in control of her animosity she cried, 'Godfrey told me all about your disastrous childhood, Hortense, and I know from experience you tried to ruin mine, but I won't let you spoil the rest of my life. I'll...'

'Enough!' Hortense barked, hustling Rosie out of the ward. 'Get out of my sight whilst you still can.'

Rosie pulled away from Hortense and marched off, her hands itching to swipe Hortense's smirking face.

Hortense watched her go. She really must get rid of Rosie.

* * *

'It's just like the spiteful cow to disallow it. That's how she gets her pleasure,' Rosie wailed as she crawled into bed, exhausted and demoralised.

'She really is a rotten bitch,' Sally replied, yawning loudly as she heaved out of bed to start the day shift. 'I'm not looking forward to working with her.'

* * *

For the next few days, Hortense gave Rosie all the worst jobs, and contrived to keep her away from Milo. 'There are other patients in the ward who need you, Nurse,' Hortense sneered, as Rosie plumped Milo's pillows and exchanged a few loving words.

Rosie noted that Hortense never referred to her by her surname as she did the other VADs. She clearly didn't think her worthy of the name Threppleton. Rosie resented Hortense's devious animosity and wondered where it might lead. Sister Foster had turned a blind eye whenever Rosie sat and talked with Milo. As long as she performed all her other duties the kindly sister had seen no harm in letting them catch up on old times and discuss their future; unmarried, and likely to stay that way, Moira Foster was a romantic at heart.

Milo was making good progress, his strength increasing day by day. Due mainly to Rosie's meticulous care he had suffered no further infection, the killer of so many men on the ward, although Rosie was just as thorough in her treatment of them. One day, Hortense off duty and Milo feeling particularly strong, he asked the sister on duty if he might go outside for a breath of fresh air.

'Why not,' said Sister Carey. 'It's a lovely day. Take a VAD with you. You'll probably be unsteady after being so long in bed.' Milo chose Rosie.

Rosie's heart leapt. Time together away from the ward was a dream come true. She helped Milo out of bed and draped a blanket over his shoulders, and with him leaning on her arm she led him to the door and then outside. Slowly, Rosie measured her pace to Milo's although she wanted to skip for joy, and Milo, his tread heavy and his breathing a little laboured kept pausing to gaze about him in sheer wonder as they made their way behind the Nissen huts to a place where a few trees formed a small copse. It was the beginning of October and burnished leaves crunched under their feet and a watery sun lanced through the branches overhead.

Milo took a deep breath. 'God, but it's good to be out in the air. There were times when I thought I'd never smell it again,' he said, his voice shaking with pure pleasure.

Rosie took the blanket from his shoulders, and spreading it on the ground beneath a gnarled elm she lowered him gently down onto it. When he was settled she sat down beside him. Milo held out his arms to her. Carefully, Rosie moved into them, and resting her face in the hollow of his neck as he embraced her, she brushed her lips against his roughened skin.

They stayed this way for a while, each of them content to feel the closeness of cheek against cheek, and entwined limbs. Then Milo placed his fingers under Rosie's chin, and raising her head he placed his lips on hers. Tenderly at first, and then with increasing passion, he kissed her in much the same way as he had on that day in 1916.

Rosie returned his kisses, her heart leaping somersaults. Until now, under the watchful eyes of the nurses and men on the ward, they had only exchanged fleeting expressions of their love; whispered words, a careful embrace or a swift brushing of lips late at night when nobody was looking.

Now, Milo was kissing her eyes, her cheeks and her neck. Rosie could feel the thud of his heart against her own and she felt a loosening inside as though Milo had pulled a string and banished all her worries and her fears. Breathless, they broke apart even though Rosie wanted to hold him tightly and never let him go.

'You've no idea how I've longed for this moment,' Milo whispered against her hair. 'I don't think you know it, Rosie Nobody, but I've loved you so long and so truly it came near to breaking my heart.'

'And I thought I'd lost you forever,' Rosie gasped, 'that I'd never be able to show you how much I love you.' She gazed deeply into Milo's eyes. 'I've always loved you like a sister should, but when you kissed me on the day you came to tell me you were leaving, you wakened something in me and I never forgot it. It took me quite some time to realise what it was.' She leaned forward to brush her lips against his. 'Now I know it's you I've loved all along – and nobody else,' she added, both of them understanding she was referring to Peter.

'I knew it almost from the minute I met you again in Wakefield,' Milo said. 'And I don't mean in a brotherly way,' he hastened to add.

Rosie smiled impishly. 'I should hope not after kisses like that.'

She snuggled back into Milo's arms, feeling warm and safe. For the first time since meeting him again, she felt free to talk about Peter. 'I never really loved him, nor he me. We were just two young, foolish people who thought we were in love.' She paused thoughtfully before saying, 'And I wanted to be loved.' Her smile wistful she fleetingly recalled her early, loveless years, Milo instinctively knowing what she meant.

'And you are loved, more than you'll ever know,' he said softly.

Rosie returned his words with a passionate kiss.

They talked and kissed until the sun was lost in threatening rain clouds. 'Best get you back inside,' Rosie said. 'We don't want you catching a chill when you've come so far.' She helped him to his feet, and draping the blanket over his shoulders they exchanged a last, hungry kiss before walking back to the ward. As Rosie and Milo arrived at the ward door Rosie's spirits sank, the joy of what she and Milo had just shared rapidly evaporating when she saw Hortense.

'And where may I ask have you been?' She sounded positively outraged.

'I gave him permission to get a breath of fresh air,' Sister Carey called out. 'It's as good a medicine as any.'

Milo looked defiantly at Hortense and said, 'It is indeed, and after that little outing I feel absolutely bloody marvellous.' His lips quirking he added, 'VAD Threppleton's little airing has done me a power of good.'

Hortense sniffed and let it go. Then, glaring meaningfully, she went off about her business.

Rosie breathed a sigh of relief, but a spike of fear pricked her insides. There was no way of knowing what Hortense might do to gain retribution. If Rosie's memory served her right there never had been.

She and Milo had talked about the time Rosie had spent as a child in Hortense's care and he hadn't liked the sound of it.

'You need to watch her. She seems to have it in for you good and proper,' he said as Rosie helped him back into bed.

* * *

Early in the morning a few days later, Rosie left her billet and walked to the ward dreading having to work another day with Hortense. She was weary from carrying out the unremitting, arduous tasks that Hortense somehow managed to put her way.

'She's an absolute bitch where you're concerned,' Sister Carey said, the other nurses and VADs having noticed Hortense's unfair treatment of Rosie. Even the qualified nurses resented Hortense. Her arrogance and constant criticism, and the way she fawned over the male doctors rubbed them up the wrong way. She was brisk and unsympathetic with the patients, handling them callously and ignoring their pleas. Nobody liked Hortense.

This morning, however, Hortense greeted Rosie with a smile; a smile that Rosie knew all too well. She hadn't forgotten the malicious gleam in those cold, dark eyes whenever Hortense was up to something.

'Ah, there you are. You won't be working on the ward

today. You're to accompany Captain Hetherington to Dieppe. Dr Vaughan and Nurse Bristow require your assistance to transport him back to London.'

Rosie's jaw dropped. Why her? Milo needed her here.

Hortense smirked at Rosie's obvious dismay. 'You are to travel as far as Dieppe to help put the captain onto a hospital ship that will take him across the channel. You're to return here immediately once that's done. You'll be away for two or three days so go and get whatever you need for the journey.'

Rosie's eyes were pools of sadness as she gazed in Milo's direction. He gazed back at her, his eyes darkening with sorrow and anger. She saw his pain and took two steps towards him, only to be brought to a sharp halt as Hortense caught her by the arm. 'Do as you're ordered,' she barked.

Rosie wrenched her arm free, and disregarding all consequences she dashed over to Milo. 'I'll be back in a couple of days. I love you,' she gabbled as Hortense loomed up behind her.

Milo looked stricken, and addressing Hortense he shouted, 'Why Rosie?'

'Calm down, Corporal Simmonite. Orders are orders,' Hortense said smugly. She chivvied Rosie from the ward, Rosie looking back at Milo with tears in her eyes. Sadly, Milo watched her go.

Back in her billet Rosie considered seeking someone in authority who might rescind Hortense's orders. But Dr McDaniel and Sister Foster were no longer at Beaulencourt, and she hadn't formed any close contact with any other senior personnel. After stuffing her possessions into her leather bag she trudged back outside.

An ambulance waited close by, its driver's door hanging open. Billy Cooper leaned out, calling, 'Are you the VAD accompanying Dr Vaughan? 'Cos if you are, get a bloody move on. We've a ferry to catch.' Rosie hurried over to it, prepared to do her duty.

* * *

The journey to and from Dieppe was horrendous. On the outward trip, as they struggled to keep the grievously injured captain alive they were twice driven off the road by shot and shellfire. Arriving in Dieppe, they learned that the hospital ship had been delayed, Rosie cursing the bad weather and the powers that be for everything and anything that was keeping her away from Milo.

Three days later, Captain Hetherington safely aboard the ship, Rosie made the return journey with only the ambulance driver for company. Billy Cooper was the blond-haired fellow Sally was dangling on a string.

'She's a heartbreaker is that mate of yours,' he told Rosie as they bounced along the rutted roads. 'I really do have feelings for her but she laughs when I tell her and seems to think it's funny when I say it hurts me to see her with another chap,' he complained, swinging the ambulance round a crater in the road so fast that Rosie jolted into him. 'You're all the same, you VADs. One chap's not enough for you.' He accelerated along a straight clear stretch of road.

Above the roar of the engine, Rosie said, 'No we're not. I've loved one man since the day he went off to war and I still love him, so slow down, Billy, before you get us both killed, because I have to get back to him.'

Several hours later, Billy brought his ambulance to a grinding halt in the camp at Beaulencourt. 'Don't give up on

Sally; she really likes you,' Rosie told him as she leapt from the passenger seat. 'She's just playing hard to get.'

Leaving Billy to ponder on her advice, Rosie dashed across the duckboards oblivious to the slime and the fact that it was almost pitch black. On reaching Milo's ward she slowed her pace, and catching her breath she cautiously pushed open the door. It wouldn't do to disturb the men at this time of night.

In the dim light, she gazed lovingly at the hump beneath the blankets on Milo's bed and then crept across the ward to where Sister Carey was sitting at the night station, her head rested on her arms on the desk. Rosie tapped Sister Carey's shoulder.

Startled, the sister reared up and swiftly adjusted her cap. She blinked and then said, 'Oh, it's you, Threppleton. You're back. I wasn't asleep.' She flushed guiltily and got to her feet.

'I wouldn't blame you if you had been,' Rosie said. 'Is it all right with you if I let Milo know I'm back? I won't stay long.'

Sister Carey looked puzzled. 'He's not here.'

Rosie's blood ran cold. 'Not here?' she gasped.

Sister Carey, now fully awake, began to explain. 'He's been transferred – back to his unit, I think – we needed the beds so they sent him and two more to...' She faltered, frowning. 'I'm not sure where. Sister Voyard did the organising with Dr Luscombe. Milo left this morning.'

Rosie was consumed with a burning anger. 'The wicked, wicked cow!' Her forceful cry was so heartfelt that it made Sister Carey draw a sharp breath. But Rosie didn't care. Keeping her voice low so as not to waken the men, she said, 'She sent him away on purpose to spite me.'

Sister Carey sighed. 'You could be right. It was a toss-up between him and Sergeant Harper, a malingerer if ever I met one. I'm sorry you didn't get chance to say goodbye, Rosie. Ask Sister Voyard in the morning. She knows where he's gone.'

Rosie trudged to the billet, her heart broken into a million pieces. Just when she and Milo had found each other again, she'd lost him, and all because of that malicious, hateful woman.

* * *

Under-slept and furious, Rosie approached Hortense first thing the next morning. 'Where is Milo?' she blurted, not caring that the men on the ward heard her.

Hortense smiled smugly. 'Might I remind you where you are.' She glided over to attend to a man who apparently didn't need her. Rosie asked her again, louder this time, the men in the beds perking up, amused by the exchange; anything to lighten the boredom.

'Don't you dare raise your voice to me. I won't tolerate such unprofessional behaviour. Now, take those to the incinerator—' Hortense pointed to the baskets of soiled dressings '—and if there are any further outbursts I'll have you disciplined.'

Frantic to find out where Milo had gone, Rosie ran, flinging the dressings into the incinerator, basket and all, before going in search of Dr Luscombe.

'I need to speak to Dr Luscombe. It's urgent,' she said to a nurse she met outside the operating theatre.

'He went on leave yesterday morning,' the nurse replied.

Rosie felt like screaming.

Seeing her distraught expression, the nurse asked her what it was about.

Rosie told her about Milo, and finished off by saying, 'And Sister Voyard refuses to tell me where they sent him.'

'Oh, oh, Sister Voyard.' The nurse pulled a sour face. 'Look, it's none of my business but if she won't tell you, maybe the sergeant in charge of manoeuvres will.' She patted Rosie's arm. 'Best of luck.'

But Rosie's luck was out. Gruffly, the sergeant told her, 'I can't divulge military information to the likes of you.'

Rosie left his office cloaked in despair. Once again, she had no idea where Milo was but, she brightened at the thought of it, Milo knew where she was. All she had to do was wait for a letter. Her anger dissipating, she went to her billet, smartened herself up and then went back to the ward. An icy tension persisted for the rest of the day, Hortense finding fault in everything Rosie did.

'Don't let her get you down, love,' said an older soldier who had told Rosie that she reminded him of his daughter. Like most of the men who had been on the ward for some time he knew about Rosie and Milo's love affair. 'She's just jealous. Her sort don't know what love is. She's probably never had a chap, an' with a face an' an attitude like she's got, it's understandable.'

Rosie smiled wanly, but she knew she hadn't heard the last of it. Hortense would find some other way of hurting her; she was sure of that.

The next day, at the end of her shift, Rosie learned what it was.

'Threppleton, you're wanted in Matron's office straight away.' The young VAD who delivered the message made a throat-slitting action with her finger. As Rosie trudged across the camp to see the matron, she presumed Hortense had reported her for behaving unprofessionally the day before and that she was now about to be reprimanded.

Standing to attention in Matron's office, Rosie awaited her punishment. She no longer cared what it might be. She'd accept it and get on with it. Across the desk, Matron observed her over the metal rims of her spectacles, her features pinched. No mercy here, thought Rosie.

'Miss Threppleton, you surprise me.' Matron sounded more disappointed than angry. 'Up until now, I have had nothing but favourable reports on your conduct. However, Sister Voyard tells me that you are in the habit of forming unhealthy relationship with the patients and some of the male workers. In her opinion you have been too long at Beaulencourt.'

Rosie opened her mouth to protest, but Matron waved her into silence. 'Once these dalliances start to interfere with your efficiency you put the patients and yourself at risk,' she continued, severely.

Rosie drew herself up to full height and set back her shoulders. She was determined to keep calm, as much to save her reputation as to stay in Beaulencourt. 'It's all lies,' she said firmly. 'Ask anyone other than Sister Voyard and they'll tell you it's not true.'

Matron sighed wearily. 'Miss Threppleton, I have neither the time nor the inclination to conduct an inquiry. I trust Hort...' The matron flushed as she hastily corrected herself. 'I trust Sister Voyard's judgement. Therefore, I'm transferring you to Étaples – see what they make of you there.'

Knowing it was pointless to argue, Rosie left Matron's office seething with rage and heartbroken. Milo's letters might never reach her in Étaples.

On her way back from Matron's office Rosie nipped into

the billet, pleased to see that Sally was awake. She was on night duties. Rosie flopped down on the end of her bed. 'They're posting me to Étaples,' she said forlornly. Then she told her what Hortense had told Matron. She was almost crying with aggravation.

'The rotten cow,' cried Sally. 'She really must hate you.'

'She does. She always has and I don't know why.' Rosie looked mystified. 'I was only a little girl when I first met her, and she never once showed me any kindness.' Rosie's anger intensifying, she warmed to her theme. 'One day, I fell in a river and she just stood there on the bank watching, waiting for me to drown.'

Sally gasped. 'The heartless bitch! She must be a psychopath.'

Rosie nodded her agreement, and said, 'She's as evil as Satan.' The fire went out of her then, her shoulders slumping and her voice coming out in a pathetic wobble. 'And what's more, Milo will write to me and I won't be here to get his letters. We'll probably never find one another again.' Tears streamed down her cheeks.

Sally pulled Rosie close, comforting her like a child, and as she hugged her she had an idea. Her face lit up. 'Course you will. I'll still be here with the bitch, God help me, and I'll collect Milo's letters and post them on.'

Rosie freed herself from Sally's arms and sat back, blinking away her tears. 'You are absolutely bloody brilliant, Sally Owens,' whooped Rosie. 'Why didn't I think of that?'

'Because Beelzebub's bleedin' daughter has got you in such a state that you can't think straight.'

Rosie visibly brightened, her eyes twinkling as she said, 'So the bitch won't win after all. I'll go and tell the postal sergeant that I've given you permission to collect my mail, and

I'll write to you the minute I get there and let you know exactly where I'm based.'

'When do you leave?'

'Tonight, so I'll say goodbye now before you go on duty.'

They hugged again. 'Take care of yourself in Étaples,' Sally whispered.

'And you,' replied Rosie. 'Maybe we'll meet again one day.'

TWENTY-EIGHT

Her bags packed and the transport waiting, Rosie popped into the ward to say goodbye to the soldiers, many of them sorry to see her go.

'Take good care of yerself, lass. You've taken good care o' me,' said one.

'Aye, them buggers in Étaples 'ull soon know how lucky they are to get you,' cried another one. Before long, a chorus of heartfelt farewells echoed round the ward, Rosie choking back tears at their kindness and Hortense watching balefully as Rosie moved from bed to bed.

The last farewell delivered, Rosie went and stood by the door. She gave Hortense a meaningful look and said, 'May I have a word, Sister Voyard?'

She stepped outside, leaving Hortense with no option but to follow her. When she did, Rosie glared defiantly into her face. 'You might think you've spoiled my life again, Hortense, and in some ways you have but in the end I'll be the winner.' The words shot out like bullets. Hortense opened her mouth to retaliate but Rosie silenced her with a sharp prod to her chest.

'I don't know what it is makes you such a miserable, scheming bitch or why you take pleasure from hurting people. Had you ever taken the time or trouble to be kind you might not have ended being what you are: a lonely, friendless, old spinster.' She looked Hortense up and down disparagingly.

Hortense's cheeks flamed. She began spluttering viciously imperious threats, only for Rosie to wag a threatening finger under her nose, silencing her yet again.

'When I was a child you never once showed me any kindness, and instead of using your intelligence to influence Celeste you did nothing but mock her. Oh, I know she was unstable, but for Godfrey's sake you could have done so much more. Instead, when we needed you most, you thought only of yourself. Poor Godfrey was devastated when you left him.'

Hortense blanched. A gamut of emotions spread across her face, as though she was recalling times of pleasure and of pain. She shook her head as if to dispel her thoughts and then hissed, 'Celeste used me.' She licked her lips as if to take away the taste of the name. 'She treated me like a servant rather than the cousin I was, and in the end Godfrey betrayed me.'

Rosie frowned, puzzled as to how Godfrey had betrayed Hortense. Curious now, she nodded for her to continue, and was shocked to see that Hortense's cold, obsidian eyes were moist. 'Go on,' Rosie muttered.

Hortense appeared to shrivel, as though her spine had suddenly folded in on itself. Her face adopted a strange, shut-off expression as though a curtain had been drawn over it and she was in another time and another place. And then, as if speaking to the air and not to Rosie, she said, 'Godfrey should have been mine but Celeste stole him from me. I thought that he'd come to realise it was me he needed after all. I only stayed because of him.'

Hortense fell silent and gazed into the distance. Rosie also gazed across the camp, silently struggling to make sense of what she had said; in what way had Godfrey needed Hortense? He barely seemed to notice her. The seconds ticked by. Then, her composure regained, Hortense turned her attention back to Rosie. Her dark eyes – now dry – glittered and her smile was supercilious.

'You didn't know that Godfrey and I were lovers, did you?' she gloated.

This time it was Rosie's turn to blanch. 'Lovers? Then why did you leave him?'

'Because of you,' Hortense snarled. 'He wouldn't abandon you.'

Rosie's jaw dropped. 'Whatever do you mean?' she gasped.

'You became one of *his* fascinations. Once he started to tutor you he could think of little else. I wanted him to come away with me, but he wouldn't leave you alone with Celeste. He adored your cleverness, and the madder Celeste became the more he felt it his duty to stay for both your sakes. You and my insane cousin stole him from me and I'll never forgive you for that.'

'I was just a child,' cried Rosie. 'You can't punish me for that.'

'I already have,' Hortense scoffed. She turned on her heel and went back into the ward. Rosie let her go. There was nothing more to say.

Rosie stayed where she was for a while marvelling at her own ignorance. *Granted, I was only a child when I lived at Whitley Hey, but not for one minute did I suspect that Hort-*

ense and Godfrey were lovers. Is that what drove Celeste into madness? And what of Godfrey's duplicity? How could that sweet, kind man have had an affair with someone as horrible as Hortense? Rosie shook her head in disbelief. *I lived with those three strange people for ten years,* she thought, *and yet I didn't really know them. But then,* she told herself, *is it any wonder? Living at Whitley Hey was like living in a bubble. Until Hildred whisked me off to Wakefield I didn't really know what living was.*

Rosie walked across to the lorry that was waiting to take her to Étaples. On the journey, she didn't engage in conversation with any of the other passengers: two VADs and a young doctor. She was still mulling over what Hortense had said, and reflecting on her own time at Whitley Hey, and in between these thoughts she was thinking about Milo.

Goodness me, thought Rosie, as the lorry rumbled on through the night and she was beginning to doze, *I'm an absolute know-nothing. I didn't know Godfrey and Hortense were lovers; I have no idea where the man I love has gone; I don't know who my parents are, and I don't even know my proper name. I surely am Rosie Know-Nothing. Rosie Nobody.*

* * *

Shortly after Rosie left Beaulencourt, Hortense paid a visit to the postal sergeant's office. She gave him a saccharine-sweet smile and adopted a mildly flirtatious manner. 'What an important job you do, Sergeant,' she gushed. 'Keeping people in touch with their loved ones is vital for morale.' She stressed the words 'loved ones' and fluttered her eyelashes.

The postal sergeant – a big, ugly fellow with a boozer's nose – was unused to women's flattery. He glowed under her words and her admiring gaze. Puffing up his chest he asked, 'What can I do for you, Sister?'

'My dear, dear friend, VAD Rosie Threppleton, has been sent to Étaples for a week or two. Before she left, she asked me to collect her mail and keep it until she returns.'

The sergeant scratched his balding head. He vaguely remembered a young VAD asking him to give her mail to a friend. He gave Hortense an understanding nod. Another dazzling look of admiration had him reaching into the pigeon-hole marked with a T.

'Thank you so much – you're wonderful! I'll no doubt call again, so until next time...' She gave him a smile full of promise, and clutching the letter she swished out of the office leaving the sergeant gazing longingly after her.

The next day, Sally dropped by the post office. A spruce, young soldier was manning the desk. Sally eyed him admiringly as she asked, 'Any letters for VAD Threppleton?' The soldier flicked through the pigeonhole marked T.

'None,' he said, 'but if you're off duty tonight I'll meet you in the canteen, if you like.'

Sally grinned. She'd finished night duty the day before. 'I do like,' she chirped. 'I'll see you about seven.'

When she called at the post office again, and again, there were no letters for Rosie; Milo wasn't going to write to her after all.

In the weeks that followed, Hortense collected seven letters, five of them from Milo, one from Peter and another from Grace. Vicariously, she read each one, smirking triumphantly when she threw them into the incinerator. Watching the pages curl and turn to grey ash pleased her immensely.

TWENTY-NINE

NOVEMBER 1918

Étaples was by the sea; a scruffy, smelly little fishing village as Rosie found out on a walk she took on her second day there. She was disappointed. Never before having spent any time on the coast, she had imagined rocky cliffs and a great expanse of clear blue water stretching for miles and miles. Instead, all she saw was a dirty little harbour and run-down houses. She had enjoyed watching the trawlers come in and land their catch, but other than that she hated Étaples.

Neither did she like the hospital. In some ways it was similar to Beaulencourt, only bigger. A great sprawl of prefabs had been erected around a larger corrugated iron building on a vast patch of scrubland, and the billet she shared with nine other girls was next to the railway line, trains rumbling past every ten minutes or so, day and night. Rosie slept badly, the clanking of wheels and the trembling of the billet's walls so disturbing that each morning she went on duty feeling tired and tetchy. Even so, she carried out her duties as efficiently as she could, but for much of the time her mind was elsewhere.

Day after day she waited for a letter from Milo. She firmly believed that he would write to her at Beaulencourt, and she prayed that Sally would send it on to Étaples.

She worried that he had been sent back to his regiment, that he was in the thick of it again, fighting for his life. Not even the news that the Germans were on the run and that the war would soon be over lifted her drooping spirits. A fellow VAD, Sylvia Gordon, was just as unhappy as Rosie. Her fiancé, Roland, had been killed at Vimy Ridge.

'I'm thinking of quitting,' she said, as she and Rosie carried baskets of soiled bedding over to the laundry. 'There seems little point in being here now that Roland's dead. I might as well go home and try to start a new life without him.' She tried to make light of her situation. 'Not that I'll find anybody else, I don't suppose. After all, I'm no beauty.' She shrugged. 'Roly didn't care how I looked; he said he just loved me for myself.'

Rosie felt a lump forming in her throat. 'I'm so sorry, Sylvia. I don't know how you've managed to keep going. Losing Roland must be terrible for you. I don't know what I'd do if I knew Milo had been killed.'

They dumped the baskets inside the laundry doorway and now, her arms free, Rosie embraced the small, dumpy girl with a face like a full moon and eyes that were too close together. She held on for a while before letting her go, as much for her own comfort as for Sylvia's.

'Looks aren't everything, Sylvia,' said Rosie, keen to raise her morale. 'You've got a lovely smile and a kindly nature – so who knows? You might meet someone else who loves you just as Roland did. I'm sure he wouldn't want you to be lonely and unhappy for the rest of your life.'

Sylvia gave a grim chuckle. 'It's easy for you to talk, you

still look gorgeous even when you're splattered in blood and caked in some chap's shit.'

It was true. Lots of the men admired Rosie's trim figure and her pretty face, and even though she had to wear her lustrous copper hair scraped back from her face and covered with a white cap the men still fancied her. And, whilst Rosie joshed with them to raise their spirits, she knew that there would never be anyone but Milo for her.

'Thank God we've got a rest period,' Rosie said, eager to change the subject as they trudged between the prefabs back to their billet, sand spurting up and dusting their stout, black shoes. When they reached the market garden they slowed their pace to call out greetings to the men who were considered fit enough for gardening duty.

'Skiving again?' The soldier who had called out leaned on his spade and laughed.

'If you worked as hard as we do you'd know what hard work is,' Rosie called back perkily. 'Be sure and plant plenty cabbage; I like cabbage.'

'An' I like you, love. If you're not doin' owt tonight I'd be pleased to show you just how much.'

'See what I mean?' Sylvia said dismally as they walked on.

Rosie shrugged. She had reached the stage where the only thing she liked about her work was caring for the men; holding their hands when they were afraid or lonely, writing letters to a loved one for those who couldn't do it for themselves or listening to a dying man's last words and giving him comfort before he made his journey into the unknown. Those little acts made the work worthwhile, but she had grown weary of the sheer drudgery of scrubbing and cleaning. She wouldn't be sorry to give that up.

The girls reached their billet just as a train thundered

past. 'Bloody trains,' Rosie said, 'I'll not miss them when I leave here.'

'We can leave whenever we like, Rosie. We're only volunteers, remember. And anyway, everyone's saying the war will soon be over, so I'm going to tell Matron I'm leaving at the end of the week. I'm sick of this place, and if she objects I'll tell her there'll be no men left here for us to nurse if we've won the war.' Sylvia sounded very determined for one usually rather timid.

Rosie frowned at Sylvia's skewed logic. 'No, but there'll still be hundreds who need nursing before they can go back to England. I'd feel a bit of a cheat if I just walked off now.'

'Well, I for one wouldn't,' Sylvia said, her voice ringing with asperity. 'I've done my bit for this war and all it's done for me is kill the man I love.'

She flopped down on her bed.

There was no answer to that, so Rosie didn't attempt one. The war had damaged so many people in a hundred different ways that nothing would ever be the same again. She sat down on her own bed and then put up her aching feet and lay back. Sylvia was right. She had done her bit, and for what? *I've done mine too,* thought Rosie, *and in the end it hasn't done me any favours either. I've lost Milo and he's lost me.*

'If you come back to England with me you might find out that Milo's already there waiting for you,' Sylvia said, propping herself up on one elbow to give Rosie an encouraging look.

'Do you think that's where he could be?'

'There as well as anywhere,' piped Sylvia.

For the rest of the day Rosie thought about what Sylvia had said and what she was about to do. Sylvia could be right. Milo might be in Wakefield waiting for her.

The next day, when Sylvia went to speak to Matron, Rosie went too.

* * *

The lorry bounced along the road to Calais, Rosie and Sylvia sitting in the back of it with three soldiers, and the driver and another soldier up front. The soldiers were in great spirits, joking and laughing at their good fortune. They were going home. Rosie marvelled at their courage, for all three had sustained injuries so severe that they were considered unfit for duty. The lad sitting next to her had lost his left ear and part of his cheek, yet his eyes twinkled and he appeared to be smiling.

One of Godfrey's quotes from *The Iliad* sprang to mind: 'A man who has been through bitter experiences enjoys even his suffering after a time.' She supposed it must be so for these men.

'My kids'll think I'm a bloody pirate when they see this,' said the gaunt-faced soldier with a patch over one eye. He tapped the patch with his forefinger. 'When I tell 'em I've got me eye on 'em they'll know which one it is.' He chuckled merrily at his own wit. 'An' if our lads an' the Allies keep going the way they've been doing, we'll win this bloody war hands down.' He rubbed the palms of his hands together with glee.

'Yes, one of those chaps they brought in from Amiens was telling me that the Germans are in such disarray and unwilling to fight that they're retreating fast. With help from the Canadians and the Aussies we've broken the Hindenburg Line and cut off Jerry's rail network, and we've had successes at Cambrai and Selle; the French are getting their towns and villages back.'

The young man who delivered this piece of information wore an officer's uniform, the cuff of its right sleeve pinned up to his elbow. Rosie wondered if he had been left- or right-handed, and hoped for his sake that his left hand was the one he had used to write with or perform the daily acts of shaving and such like. The officer and Eye-Patch carried on talking about German failures and British successes, the young lad with the disfigured face contributing an unintelligible remark now and then. Rosie marvelled at his companions' patience as they let him speak. As she listened to all that was said she felt a swelling inside her chest, which she thought must be hope rising. Their enthusiasm for a war they seemed to think was almost won took away the niggling guilt she had felt at resigning her post. When the war talk petered out, Eye-Patch turned his attention on Rosie and Sylvia.

'Are you lasses going on leave?'

Rosie fleetingly considered saying 'yes' because she didn't want him to think she was running out on the wounded men, but before she had chance to voice it Sylvia told him in no uncertain terms that they were giving it up for good and going home.

'And so you should,' said the officer, bestowing a smile on each of them. 'War's no place for a woman, although...' he grinned appreciatively '...we chaps are extremely grateful for your services. We couldn't do without you.'

Rosie smiled at the compliment: the second that week. Matron had been displeased when they resigned and had tried to dissuade them, but when she realised that they were determined to leave she praised them glowingly for their duty to king and country. The soldiers each added their own thanks, and Rosie stopped reproaching herself and joined in the banter and laughter. For the first time in weeks she felt happy; she was going home to find Milo.

Near to the port of Calais, the lorry driver had to slow down to let a cart loaded with timber get by. Thick trunks and sturdy branches were sticking out of the sides of the cart and narrowing his passage, so the lorry driver pulled over onto a patch of waste land. As the lorry's tyres churned up earth softened by recent rain, there was an almighty explosion. Clouds of smoke followed by leaping flames engulfed the lorry's bonnet and as the windscreen shattered the driver and his companion leapt from the vehicle. Shards of glass flew into the back of the lorry, the passengers diving for cover.

'Out! Out!' shouted the officer lunging for the rear doors and using his good hand to throw them wide open. He leapt to the ground, Rosie cannoning into him as she tumbled out. Eye-Patch jumped clear dragging Sylvia with him, and the disfigured soldier pushing her from behind. They rolled on the muddy verge in a tangle of arms and legs.

'Run for it,' yelled the officer. 'Get as far away as you can.'

Scrambling to their feet, Rosie and Sylvia ran back down the road, the soldiers and the driver behind them. Bang! With a mighty roar the lorry's petrol tank ignited, chunks of metal flying into the air and flames licking at the wreckage.

'Oh, my God!' Sylvia, having regained her breath, began to screech at the top of her lungs.

Rosie grabbed her by the arms and shook her. 'Stop it. Stop it now, Sylvia,' she said harshly, knowing from experience that the best way to deal with hysteria was to be firm. Sylvia slumped against Rosie, and her screams subsided into huge, gulping sobs. Gently, Rosie eased out of Sylvia's clinging arms. Swiftly, she counted the men huddled on the verge; all five were there.

'Is anyone injured?' she called out.

Rosie hurried over to the where the driver stood with his hand over his cheek. Blood seeped through his fingers from a deep, facial cut. The officer inspected the others. 'The chap with him up front has minor cuts to his forehead and cheeks,' he told Rosie. 'Apart from that everyone else is fine.'

'Fine be buggered,' said Eye-Patch. 'I'm shakin' like a bloody leaf an' I think I might have sprained me ankle.'

'You'll live,' the officer retorted.

'Does anybody have water in their bottles? And do any of you have your field first aid kit?' Rosie asked.

The replies positive, Rosie bathed and dressed the driver's cheek and Sylvia, having regained her composure, tended to his companion's face.

'What happened?' Rosie asked, as she finished her task.

'Stray mine, probably faulty,' replied the officer, 'otherwise we'd have been blown to kingdom come.'

It was then Rosie realised that all her possessions had gone up in flames in the burning lorry. Although the fire had subsided it was obvious that nothing could be saved. She slid her hand into her coat pocket feeling for her purse and her travel pass. Thank goodness she hadn't put them in her bag.

'What do we do now?' Sylvia sounded lost and afraid.

'We'll have to bloody walk,' groaned Eye-Patch. 'That's if we want to get that ship afore it sails.'

They hadn't gone far when the same cart, now minus its load of timber, came trundling back down the road. Maybe to hide his chagrin at having been the cause of their accident, the young French carter couldn't get them aboard fast enough.

'It's not exactly how I'd imagined arriving in Calais, but it's better than nothing,' said Rosie, squashing into the cart with her companions and breathing a huge sigh of relief. She was back on track, going home to find Milo.

* * *

It was late at night when the ship landed in Dover. There were no trains to take them any further so the officer arranged accommodation for them in a small guesthouse. Not for the first time, Rosie thanked God that the officer had been travelling with them; organisation was obviously his forte.

'Oh, Lord, proper beds,' cried Rosie as she and Sylvia were shown into a warm, pleasantly furnished bedroom. The two girls flitted about the room, admiring the bedside lamps, the little handbasin and the carpet under their feet. Having been deprived of such luxuries for so long they were giddy with excitement.

'The woman said there's a bathroom at the end of the corridor,' said Rosie, 'so bagsy I go first.'

'Go ahead!' Sylvia flopped on to the bed and kicked off her shoes. 'I'm going to lie here and feel what it's like to sleep on a bed that's not as hard as concrete.'

Rosie stepped into the bath and slid beneath the water, her hair lifting and floating like tangled rays of setting sun. She closed her eyes. *I could stay here forever,* she thought, soaking leisurely in lashings of hot water. She sponged her arms and legs and then her torso, delving deep into every crevice, washing away the dirt, the smell and the misery. She was safe, uninjured, and she was on her way home.

When the water grew tepid she stepped out and towelled herself dry. She felt clean and fresh for the first time in a long time. She picked up her vest and knickers. It seemed sacrilege to put these grubby garments on her clean body but she had no choice.

After Sylvia had taken her bath the girls climbed into bed, and lying between fresh, clean sheets smelling faintly of lavender, they talked. Even though Rosie had shared a billet with Sylvia for several weeks they'd had scant opportunity to really get to know each other. Their hospital shifts had only recently coincided, and at night, sharing a room with seven other girls left little opportunity for deep conversations.

'Where did you say home was, Sylvia?'

'Shropshire; but I'm definitely not going back there.'

'Then where will you go once we reach Dover?'

'I'll go up to London first. I've an aunt there who might give me a job.'

'Doing what?' Rosie yawned sleepily.

'She runs a charity for homeless families. It's likely she'll need an extra pair of hands because this rotten war will have widowed hundreds of women and left them to fend for themselves and their children. If you've no breadwinner in the house and can't pay the rent, you end up on the streets.' Sylvia gave a sigh that was almost a groan and then asked, 'What about you, Rosie?'

'I'll go back to Wakefield. I have a little house and a job in a brewery there, and Milo has a business. He carves the most wonderful things out of wood and makes furniture.' Rosie paused, thinking longingly of Milo's workshop and the sweet, spicy smell of newly lathed wood. 'Wakefield's the first place he'll look for me and I for him.'

'I'll most likely stay in London,' said Sylvia. 'I don't think I could bear going back to Shropshire now Roland's not there.' Despair coloured her words.

Rosie's heart went out to her. Poor Sylvia. *But what about me,* she thought, *what will I do if Milo doesn't come back to Wakefield?*

THIRTY

KNARESBOROUGH, YORKSHIRE

Milo stared into the distance at the beech and chestnut trees, their last few remaining leaves glinting like burnished copper as a brittle sun broke through the fine mist that blurred everything in front of him. It had been a day like this when he had last walked with Rosie in Clarence Park. Now, on the first day of November 1918, he was mooching round the gardens of the grand house that had been turned into a convalescent home, his thoughts as indistinct as the view.

Just as Rosie had feared, he had been returned to his regiment. A few days of vicious fighting in Amiens left him with a broken ankle and a bad bout of fever and dysentery. Considered unfit for duty, he had been shipped back to England. Today he was feeling much stronger, his guts and his ankle back in working order, and he hoped they would soon discharge him so that he could get on with his life. He yearned to be back in his workshop breathing in the familiar, friendly smells of wood, glue and paint, but most of all he yearned for his beautiful, darling Rosie.

It seemed like a lifetime since he had left Beaulencourt,

and since then she hadn't replied to any of his letters. Had he only imagined that she loved him, he wondered, and when she had nursed him so lovingly was it only pity she had felt because he was wounded? Yet, whenever he read the letters she had written in the past two years, he just couldn't bring himself to believe her affection for him had suddenly changed.

Finding nothing to please him in the garden, Milo returned to the house and went into the library. The owner had generously agreed to let the convalescents borrow certain books, and Milo made his way over to the section that held them.

He scanned the shelves, eventually settling on a worn copy of *The Wind in the Willows*; Rosie had talked about this book. He flipped the pages, reading a paragraph here and there. He wasn't a great reader and some of the text seemed rather silly – talking animals indeed – yet the thought of reading a story that she had praised seemed somehow comforting.

Over at a table by the door the owner of the house was acting as librarian, a job she had undertaken to safeguard the leather-bound volumes that were not on loan.

'*Riders of the Purple Sage*,' Celia Asquith read out loud, as she noted the details on the card handed to her by a young lad with a dreadfully disfigured face. 'You enjoy Westerns, do you?'

The soldier gave a travesty of a smile and nodded. 'Is it any good?' he slurred.

'I haven't read it,' she said, her tone suggesting that she never would, 'but it's very popular with your lot,' she added, nodding in the direction of the shelves that were lined with second-hand paperbacks; a donation from the local WVS who had organised the soldiers' library.

Milo stood and waited his turn, his eyes on the woman. There was something about Celia Asquith that intrigued him. Whenever he saw her about the house he sensed a curious stirring, as though he had met her elsewhere a long time ago, but this being his first visit to the library he had never yet spoken to her. Now, as he handed her his book, he wondered if perhaps she had been a customer at his stall. Or was it her red hair, so like Rosie's, that made her seem familiar?

She raised her gaze to meet his. 'Kenneth Grahame,' she said, her tone indicating surprise. 'He doesn't go out of here too often.' She studied Milo, noting his handsome features and dark, intense eyes. 'Is he a favourite of yours?'

Milo flushed. 'I don't know. I only chose it because a friend of mine used to talk about it,' and then for no reason he blurted. 'She has red hair like yours.'

Celia gave a half smile.

Thoughtfully, Milo studied her face and drew a sharp breath. Even her eyes were the same shape and colour as Rosie's, but they held none of the warmth or lust for living that he was so used to seeing in hers.

'Your friend has good taste,' Celia said, handing him the book. And dropping her gaze as if to dismiss him, she murmured, 'Enjoy it.'

Milo doubted he would, and walked away with the feeling that, just for a moment, he had almost slipped into another time and another place, a place achingly familiar and a time he had buried in the back of his mind.

* * *

Rosie travelled with Sylvia to London.

At Paddington Station, as the girls alighted from the train, a newsvendor bawled, 'Germans on the run. Hundred Days Offensive wins the war.'

'Listen to that!' cried Rosie. She grasped Sylvia's hands and there in the middle of the crowds thronging the platform the girls performed a little impromptu jig. This brought smiles to the faces of those waiting for trains, followed by a few cheers, for the girls still wore their VAD uniforms.

Someone called out, 'Where've you been, girls?'

'Just back from France,' Rosie shouted back. This resulted in an even louder cheer from the crowd. Rosie and Sylvia flushed with pleasure, and Rosie felt that her time in Beaulencourt and Étaples had been worthwhile after all.

'God bless you, lasses,' cried a uniformed chap on crutches, raising one of them aloft to emphasise his words, and almost overbalancing in the process.

'Thanks,' the girls called back and made their way along the platform.

'That was a nice welcome home,' Sylvia panted, the jigging having got the better of her. 'It's nice to feel wanted.'

'It's great to be back in England,' Rosie replied breathlessly, 'but I won't be truly happy until I find Milo. As soon as I find the ticket office I'm going straight on to Wakefield. Like you said, he might already be there waiting for me.'

Close by the exit, and across from the ticket offices, Rosie and Sylvia hugged each other and promised to keep in touch. Sylvia went to catch a bus to take her to Shoreditch and Rosie dashed to join the queue at the nearest booth to ask when the next train to Wakefield was and which platform did it leave from. 'You need to go to King's Cross, dearie,' the man told her. Rosie's face fell. Seeing her disappointment, he kindly gave her instructions on how to get there.

Out on the busy street, Rosie felt lost and slightly afraid. It was now late afternoon and the city was teeming with people who all seemed to know exactly where they were going as they hastily made their way through the streets. She told herself not to be so stupid. *You've been to France, you survived a war, and now you're panicking because you don't know the way to King's Cross Station.* Clutching her purse in her pocket, afraid to lose it, she hurried through the streets trying to follow the directions she'd been given. Fifteen minutes later, hopelessly lost, she stopped at a crossroads. Traffic roared by, more traffic than she had seen in the past two years. *Which way now?* she asked herself tearfully.

'Rosie! Rosie Threppleton!' The cry rose above the rumble of cars and buses. Rosie turned her head this way and that, looking for where it had come from. Then, her eyes popping with surprise, she saw Sally Owens hurrying across the road to meet her. 'Bleedin' hell, of all the people,' Sally cried.

'Sally,' Rosie gasped. 'Oh, Sally, am I glad to see you.' The girls fell into each other's arms, Rosie laughing with relief as they hugged. Sally was a Londoner; she'd know the way to King's Cross.

'What are you doing here?' Sally sounded delighted to see her.

'I was going to ask you the same thing,' said Rosie. 'I thought you were still in Beaulencourt.'

'I packed it in. When they transferred you to Étaples, they moved me back on to your ward with that bitch, Voyard. She made my life a bloody misery so I told 'em I was leaving and going back to work in London. I've been at The Royal Free nearly two weeks now. It's lovely to be back home.'

'I know just how you feel. I can't wait to get back to Wakefield.'

'You've time for a cuppa and a bite to eat before you go though, haven't you?'

Rosie hesitated and then said, 'I haven't eaten since yesterday. I'm starving.' And whilst she felt the urge to continue her journey, hunger gnawed at her insides. 'Go on then, if I don't eat something soon I'll most likely faint.'

Sally led the way to a Lyons Corner House and seated at a table in the warm, cosy café, they ordered tea and sardines on toast.

The 'Gladys', as the waitresses were called, smiled when she saw their VAD armbands on the sleeves of their coats. 'For you girls, cups of tea are on the house. Just pay for the sardines.' She winked and whisked off to fulfil the order, and Rosie and Sally began to catch up with all that had happened since Rosie had left Beaulencourt.

'I thought I'd swing for that cow, Voyard, 'cos once she knew I was your mate she came down twice as hard on me,' Sally said. She continued to moan about Hortense, Rosie interrupting her to ask about her mail.

'Did you ever go to the post office to collect my letters?'

'Course I did, but you never got any,' Sally said, flushing and hurriedly adding, 'I did mean to write an' tell you, but you know me, I'm not much of a writer. I called several times, and I must say I thought it a bit odd 'cos you always used to get letters. Then, one day when I mentioned it to that big, fat sergeant with the baldy head, he told me that he'd given them to your friend, Sister Voyard.'

Rosie's cheeks flamed. 'Hortense! She knew Milo would

write, and the spiteful cow intercepted them,' she cried. Tears sprang to her eyes. For the next few minutes both girls railed against Hortense's duplicity.

'I did ask her about them but she played dumb then nearly chewed the face off me,' Sally said. 'I'm really sorry, Rosie, and I'm sorry to hear you lost track of Milo again, 'cos I know how much you love him.' She patted Rosie's hand. 'But you never know, when you get back up north you might find him there waiting for you.' At the words 'up north', Rosie was more anxious than ever to continue her journey. She stood abruptly. 'It's been lovely seeing you again, Sally, and I promise to keep in touch. Now, if you'll point me in the direction of King's Cross I'll get off back to Wakefield.'

Sally looked disappointed. 'You don't have to go right now. If you like, you can always stay with me for a couple of days and see the sights.'

'It's lovely of you to ask, but I'm dying to get back to my little house and start living a normal life again,' said Rosie. She almost regretted bumping into Sally. 'Just tell me how to get to King's Cross,' she added, sounding rather desperate.

Seeing that Rosie would not be persuaded, Sally said, 'I'll walk with you. It's only up the road and round the corner.'

They threaded their way along the busy pavement, not always able to walk side by side. When next they could, Sally said, 'I reckon the next few days will be hectic. There'll be lots of fun now that it looks as though we've won the war.' She pointed to a banner hanging rather prematurely from a second floor window of a tobacconist's shop that declared 'Victory is Ours'.

The station in sight, Rosie quickened her pace. 'Look, I really must go,' she said, and pausing to thank Sally and promising to keep in touch, she hurried towards the station's entrance.

Inside the station, Rosie cursed inwardly at having delayed her journey and hurried to find the ticket office. The entire population seemed to be on the move. On the platforms, soldiers were boarding or alighting as trains arrived or departed and at the ticket office families with small children and piles of luggage queued impatiently. Rosie joined the queue, the noise and bustle making her irritable. She flinched when a guard gave a piercing blast on his whistle and covered her ears when a train screeched to a halt at the nearest platform. The taste of smoke, hot oil and human sweat caught in her throat and she felt the urge to escape, to be in a field of flowers and fresh air with Milo by her side.

At last, she faced the man behind the little glass window and enquired about a train to Wakefield. He glanced up at a timetable attached to the wall of his office.

'You've just missed the last one, and there isn't another one today,' he said. 'The next one leaves tomorrow morning at six-thirty from platform eight.'

Rosie wanted to scream. Why had she wasted all that time with Sally? She could have been halfway home by now. Miserably, she paid for her ticket and then trudged off to find the waiting room on platform eight. Fortunately, there was a tea stand on the platform, and after buying a cup of tea and a ham sandwich she went and sat in the crowded waiting room.

Trains chuffed in and out of the platforms. The tea stand closed for the night, and gradually the waiting room emptied until she was the only occupant. Still seething at having delayed her journey she took a copy of *Wuthering Heights* from her bag and began to read, although she almost knew the story by heart. It reminded her of the days she had spent in

Godfrey's study, and she closed the book and thought about Hortense's spiteful confession. Had they really been lovers, or was Hortense simply being malicious to upset her?

Then she thought about the stolen letters, hatred burning deep inside.

Her legs stiff and her backside numb, she stood and walked round the waiting room and then out on to the platform to rid her mind of unpleasant thoughts. Back inside, she read and dozed, willing the hours to six-thirty to pass by in a flash; wasted hours when she could have been back in Wakefield.

Shortly after midnight, a dishevelled man carrying a bulging, hessian sack shuffled into the waiting room. Rosie tensed, but apart from a cursory glance in her direction he paid her no heed. Tossing the sack onto a bench, he stretched out full length with his head resting on the sack and fell asleep. Even so, Rosie kept her eye on him and tried desperately to stay awake.

* * *

On the same day as Rosie had arrived in London, Milo was in the library at the convalescent home. Celia was at the table and he handed over the copy of *The Wind in the Willows* for her to note its return. At first, he'd thought the book silly and childish but the more he read the more he understood why Rosie had suggested he would like it.

'Well?' Celia said. 'Did you enjoy it?'

Milo flushed, somewhat embarrassed by the amusement he heard in her voice, but he had enjoyed it so he answered her honestly. 'Yes, I did. You see, the animals are really meant to be people. They live surrounded by nature and it made me think of the time I lived on the road, travelling from place to place.'

Celia raised her eyebrows. 'Lived on the road? How do you mean?'

'I belong to the gypsy community,' Milo said, and was taken by surprise at Celia's interest. At her insistence, Milo began telling her about his younger days as a gypsy. When other soldiers came into the library to change their books she dealt with them speedily, intimating for Milo to stay and talk. She patted the chair next to hers and Milo sat. He told her about Eli and Rosie, the little girl who lived with them and then was given away, and how when they had met again, he had fallen in love with her. He skirted round the subject of how they had come by Rosie, making no mention of the strange woman or his father's murder. They were far too personal and raw to tell. Even so, it felt good to talk about his past and about the war and his love for Rosie, as though he was unburdening himself.

'I can tell you love Rosie very much. She sounds like a wonderful girl.'

'Aye, she is,' Milo replied, his warm smile indicating his love for her. The smile broadened as he added, 'Funnily enough, you remind me of her. She looks very much like you.'

Celia drew a sharp breath then bit into her bottom lip as she tussled with her thoughts. Struggling to stay composed she said, 'Your story has me quite intrigued.' She twisted her clammy hands together afraid of what she was about to next ask. 'Tell me this. When you say Rosie came to you as a baby what exactly do you mean? Whose baby was she?'

Milo was shocked by the intensity in her voice and hesitated before answering, but the relief he had felt from talking about Rosie urged him on to further unburden himself.

'That's just it,' he replied, 'we don't know. That's why I call her Rosie Nobody.' Then, his voice low and shaking, he continued to tell her how his father had brought a lady back to the vardo one night and that she had given birth to Rosie the next day. 'We never got chance to find out who her mother was or where she came from. Some men came and took her away.' His expression sombre he said, 'They killed my father.'

Celia gasped and cried out, 'Oh, no! No!' Her body sagged and she buried her face in her hands, Milo quite taken aback that the death of a man she had never known should cause her such grief. Bewildered, and feeling decidedly uncomfortable he stood, ready to take flight, but then found himself gazing down at Celia's heaving shoulders, unsure what to do.

Eventually, she raised her tear-stained face, and swallowing noisily as though stones were sticking in her throat she mustered a wan smile. 'How silly of me,' she said, blinking away tears. 'I'm sorry if I embarrassed you, but for such a dreadful thing to happen...' She stood, and turning her back on him she gathered the books on the table and walked briskly over to the shelves of paperbacks. Milo took this as a sign for him to leave and he wandered back to his dormitory feeling somewhat disturbed.

* * *

The train chugged into Wakefield Station. Rosie leapt from the carriage and – cold, thirsty, hungry and feeling extremely dishevelled – she headed straight for Milo's workshop. He wasn't there, and the men making beer crates knew nothing of his whereabouts. She hurried across the town to Hildred's brewery.

'Rosie!' Hildred cried gathering her in a warm embrace. 'Thank goodness you're safe. I've missed you.'

'I've missed you too,' Rosie replied feeling secure as he held her against his portly belly. Hildred asked a hundred questions, Rosie answering them rather impatiently then asking the question burning on her tongue.

'The last I heard from him he was somewhere in France. He sent me a postcard,' Hildred said, concern creasing his face. 'I do hope he hasn't come to any harm,' he added sincerely.

Next, although it went against the grain to go to Peter's home, she visited the Shortcrosses, refusing Helen's offer of tea or to engage in lengthy conversation; her only desire to learn if they had heard anything about Milo. Wearing a look of disappointment, Helen told her that she had no idea where Milo was but that Peter was still in India and was expected home soon.

'You haven't written in ages,' Helen said accusingly. 'I hope you've kept in touch with Peter more often.' Rosie couldn't honestly say that she had, so making her excuses she dashed to the Clayton Hospital to see if they could tell her anything.

'He certainly isn't a patient here,' said the matron, 'nor has he ever been. He could be abroad or he might be...' She pulled herself up sharp.

'I know that,' Rosie cried, her angry tone making the matron blink. 'And no matter, I need to know where I can find him.' The matron saw the love and longing in her eyes and felt a rush of pity, but she was unable to help her.

Distraught, Rosie trudged through the town to her little house in Milton Street.

There was nobody else she could ask and nowhere else to

look. Now, as she stood in the cold, empty kitchen gazing forlornly at the once familiar kettle and the crockery that she had used to share a meal with Milo, tears sprang to her eyes. There was nothing for it but to wait and pray that he would find his way back to her.

THIRTY-ONE

Rosie spent a miserable six days wandering about the town and revisiting Milo's workshop and the brewery, always in the hope that someone had news of him. At the end of another fruitless day, she was making her way back to Milton Street when, outside the post office, she bumped into Helen Shortcross. Rosie, still feeling guilty about her previous visit and the way in which she'd dashed off, wished that the ground would open up and swallow her. She had no desire to talk to Helen. Helen didn't know where Milo was, and Rosie dreaded having to tell her that she had no intentions of marrying Peter.

'Rosie, how lovely to see you,' cried Helen, standing squarely in front of her with a warm smile on her face. 'Only this morning Norman and I were wondering why you hadn't called again on us.' Rosie's passage blocked, she had no choice but to stay and talk.

'Hello, Mrs Shortcross, have you been shopping?' Even to Rosie, the remark sounded inane, but she just couldn't think of anything else to say.

'I've just posted a letter to Grace. She's working at Forces

Headquarters in Leeds, still sorting out troop movements but —' she chuckled '—hopefully she won't be doing that for much longer.' She looked closely into Rosie's face, a frown on her own. 'I'm surprised we haven't seen more of you since you came home. You know you're always welcome in our house.' She giggled coyly. 'After all, you're soon going to be one of the family.'

Rosie felt her throat tighten and her mouth suddenly went dry. She ought to tell Helen that she wasn't going to marry Peter, but before Rosie could drum up the courage to do so, Helen chirped, 'I suppose you and Peter have been making all sorts of plans for the big day. His letters tell me nothing, but I imagine you and he have thought of little else now that he'll soon be home – but of course, I'm sure you already know that.' Fondly, she patted Rosie's arm, Rosie flinching as though she had been stung.

I must say something, she thought desperately, *but this isn't the place to break this woman's heart.* She took a deep breath. 'Actually, I haven't heard from Peter in quite a long time.' She wouldn't admit that she hadn't written to him for ages so she began to gabble. 'You see, they kept moving me from place to place and somehow his letters must have got lost.' By now, her cheeks were burning.

Helen looked shocked. Then her face crumpled in pity. 'Oh, you poor darlings. Peter must be distraught, but...' Now she looked puzzled. 'He never mentioned that he'd lost touch with you.' She laughed airily. 'As I said, his letters never say much at all.'

Rosie couldn't have agreed more. The last one she had received was no more than a few scribbled lines about playing polo and the weather being too hot.

'So you don't know that we're expecting him home any day,' Helen said. 'We got word only two days ago.'

Dumbly, Rosie shook her head, her heart sinking and her nerves jangling.

'Apparently he's being discharged early,' Helen continued. 'He'll be one of the first from his regiment to arrive home.'

Rosie plastered a smile on her face. 'That's wonderful,' she murmured.

'Isn't it just,' Helen gushed, 'but look, I can't stand talking any longer. Norman will be expecting his tea. Now, you make sure and call on us every day so that we're all there to meet him when Peter gets home.'

'I'll try,' Rosie said, her sickly smile and unenthusiastic tone causing Helen to look closely at her again.

'My poor dear, I do believe you're quite overcome. I know just how you must feel. Being reunited with the one you love after all this time is enough to take your breath away.' She gave Rosie's arm another fond squeeze, and as she dashed off she called out, 'I'll see you tomorrow, dear.'

Take my breath away, thought Rosie, *I feel absolutely winded.* She walked on, her mind in turmoil. She had to sort out her life, and quick. She couldn't go on letting that poor woman believe she was soon to be her daughter-in-law. Then there was Peter. Did he still expect them to marry? She just didn't know.

He hadn't written letters declaring his undying love for her as Milo had done, his letters were all about himself and the girls he'd danced with – she thought about the girl on the station, the one whose home he had visited on his last leave – and when he wasn't writing about that he was complaining about the food, the weather, and keeping 'the locals' in order.

Granted, he always signed off with the words 'wait for me', but wait for what? she asked herself angrily as she unlocked the door of the house in Milton Street.

In the kitchen, she banged the kettle onto the gas ring, and as the water boiled so did her thoughts. She'd go to the Shortcrosses' tomorrow and tell them the truth, and when Peter came home she'd tell him she'd made a mistake. She'd do it gently, she thought, but she was pretty sure he wouldn't really care. He'd probably be glad to have his freedom.

The tea made, Rosie sat down and was mulling over exactly what she would say when something Helen had said came into her mind. The tea she was pouring from the pot filled the cup and spilled over into the saucer as she recalled Helen's words. She stopped pouring, amazed not to have made the connection sooner. Grace! Grace was still sorting out where soldiers were based. She'd know where Milo was, and if she didn't she might know someone who did.

* * *

Rosie slept badly that night, tossing and turning and willing the hours to fly by. At first light she climbed out of bed, her heart full of anticipation. Today could be the day that she would find Milo. She ate a breakfast of tea and toast, the bread sticking in her throat, pent with excitement. Then she dashed upstairs, and wanting to look her best she delved into her wardrobe for clothes that she had not worn since she had travelled to France.

Flinging aside one garment after another she eventually settled for the green, fine woollen skirt and top – Milo had liked her in that – and then, the weather being cold, she topped it with a warm, camel-coloured coat she had bought with the money Hildred had given her to mark her eighteenth birthday. Three years ago, she thought, and I've hardly had a chance to wear it.

She appraised herself in the mirror and liked what she saw; such a change from the drab, grey dresses and the navy blue coat she'd been wearing ever since she became a VAD. And nice too to be able to leave her hair tumbling about her shoulders rather than have to roll it up and tuck it under a white cap. She saw that her eyes were sparkling; they hadn't done that for ages.

It was still too early to call on the Shortcrosses so she paced from the kitchen to the front room and then back upstairs to check her appearance in the mirror. Just before nine o'clock the impulse to start out on her mission became unbearable, and after gathering her purse and her gloves Rosie set off to see Helen.

* * *

'My, I wasn't expecting you so early,' Helen said, as she answered Rosie's knock. She was still wearing her dressing gown and her hair was in curlers.

'I'm not stopping,' Rosie said hurriedly. 'I only called to ask where I can find Grace.'

Helen looked disappointed and puzzled. 'Then you'd better come inside. I can't stand at the door dressed like this,' she said sharply. Rosie stepped inside.

'I'm sorry to call so early, but I have some business to do in Leeds for Hildred and I thought I'd pop in and see Grace whilst I'm there – maybe take her out to lunch.' Rosie gave Helen a winning smile, amazed at how easily the lie slid off her tongue.

Helen returned the smile. 'Oh, she'd like that, I'm sure. She's missed you these past two years and...' she sighed heavily '...I'm sure she's not the only one. We still don't know exactly when Peter will arrive, but I imagine he's also longing to see you.'

At the mention of Peter, Rosie's heart lurched.

But she didn't want to talk about him; she wanted to be on her way to Grace in Leeds. She smiled again and giggled nervously before saying, 'I was on my way to the station when I remembered I don't know where Grace's office is, so to save me searching for it I thought I'd call in and ask you for directions.'

'She's in Fenton Street, dear. Ask when you get to Leeds Station. Someone will direct you from there.' She pulled her dressing gown belt a little tighter as she said, 'You will call back later, just in case Peter arrives today?'

Rosie swallowed and said, 'Yes, of course. Thank you very much, Mrs Shortcross.' She waited impatiently for Helen to open the door and let her out. 'I'll have to dash if I'm to catch the next train.' And with that she hastily took her leave.

* * *

Frantic to find Milo, Rosie caught the first train to Leeds and then walked briskly across the city to Fenton Street. The city buzzed with anticipation, the entire population wanting to believe that the German army had been defeated. Newsboys on street corners yelled out the news: 'Kaiser Wilhelm to abdicate' and 'Armistice requested', their cries raising hopes, everybody excited at the prospect of peace. Strangers smiled at strangers, a warm, friendly feeling lightening Rosie's steps as she hurried towards her goal.

'I need to speak with Grace Shortcross,' she blurted to the man on duty at the door of the offices in Fenton Street. 'It's urgent.'

'Everything's urgent these days,' the man replied wearily. 'Have you any identification?'

Rosie whipped her VAD documents out of her purse and the man glanced at them and then opened the door. 'First on your left past the foot of the stairs,' he said, waving a hand in that direction.

Grace jumped up from her chair behind her desk the minute she saw Rosie, and hurried forward to embrace her. 'What a lovely surprise,' she cried. 'Thank God you're safe. We were so worried about you.' She let Rosie go, and drawing her further into the office she said, 'A strong cup of tea's in order.'

Over the welcome hot drink, Rosie answered Grace's eager questions about what it had been like in France. Rosie gave a broad outline of her time there. She purposely didn't mention Milo just yet. She needed to re-establish her friendship with Grace in order to seek her help, so she let Grace chatter on.

'You never replied to my last letter telling you that I've met a gorgeous man called Edward,' Grace complained.

'I never got it,' Rosie said dismally, 'or any from Milo – or Peter,' she added hastily, in case Grace thought it suspicious that she should miss hearing from Milo, but not Peter. 'Not that Peter writes often,' she added lamely. She had no intentions of furthering her friendship with him but she didn't want Grace to know that just yet so she said, 'Have you heard from him lately?' She asked this in order to take the heat out of the question she most wanted to ask.

'Not a sausage,' Grace said blithely. 'The last I heard, he

was having high jinks in the officers' mess and learning to play polo.' She pulled a comical face.

Rosie stopped feeling guilty at letting Peter down and casually asked, 'Have you heard any news of Milo lately?'

'Can't say I have,' Grace replied, equally casual.

'Is there any possibility you could trace him for me?' Rosie heard the near desperation in her own voice and saw that Grace heard it too.

'I could try, but it's a devil of a job keeping track of all those poor fellows. If their officers are thorough with the paperwork we usually manage to keep tabs on them, but in the chaos that's France it's easy for a man to go missing.' She waved a despairing hand over the piles of letters, forms and files on her desk. 'We're inundated with requests from people trying to find out where their loved ones are buried.'

Cold fear clutched at Rosie's heart. Was she about to learn where Milo had been buried? Any reserve she had had so far smashed through the barriers and she heard herself cry, 'Please, Grace! Please! I've got to find Milo. I love him so much I can't bear not knowing what's happened to him.'

Her request was delivered with such fervency it made Grace blink. She gave Rosie a quizzical look. 'Love? Do you mean as in love – like I am with Edward?'

Rosie nodded and whispered, 'Very much in love.'

Grace heard the desperate sincerity in her voice, and being very much in love herself understood how Rosie must feel. 'OK, give me his regiment, rank and number and I'll do my best,' she said briskly.

'Kings Own Yorkshire Light Infantry, corporal, number 19475,' Rosie said hollowly.

Grace went and lifted a huge file from a shelf. 'All the

details for the KOYLI are in here,' she said, thumping the file on to the desk. 'Let's see if Milo gets a mention.'

Rosie sat on the edge of her chair and watched Grace shuffle through the pages of record books and mounds of paperwork in her attempt to find out where Milo might now be. Rosie hardly dared to breathe. She twisted one hand round the other impatiently, so much that her fingers ached, along with her head. Grace pored over pages filled with lists of names and locations, her tongue sticking out of the corner of her mouth. She obviously knew what she was doing and Rosie admired her efficiency.

At last, Grace let out a whoop and said, 'Got him!' She waved a form in the air.

Then she began to read out loud. 'He was injured at Bapaume and transferred to Beaulencourt Field...' She stopped and gave Rosie a puzzled look. 'That's where you were, isn't it? You must have...'

'I did,' Rosie said, her voice barely a whisper. The words hung in the air, the expression on Rosie's face letting Grace know that when Rosie and Milo had met in Beaulencourt something monumental had taken shape.

'What happened?' Grace asked softly.

Rosie took a deep breath. 'We'd kept in touch by letter for ages, and long before he came to Beaulencourt we realised just how much we loved one another – and not in a brother and sister way,' she said, blushing. 'And then they sent me to Calais and when I got back he was gone.' Tears trickled down her cheeks.

'It's OK, Rosie. Please don't cry; I think I understand,' said Grace. 'I always thought you and Milo were well suited.' She didn't bother to add that she had also thought that Rosie deserved someone more loyal than Peter. She flourished the papers in her hand, saying, 'Come on, dry your eyes, I think we might have tracked him down.'

'But where is he now?' Rosie's question hung in the air like a dark rain cloud.

Grace continued reading aloud. 'He was returned to his regiment and...' she skimmed her eyes down the page '...and from Amiens he was transferred back...' She paused dramatically to give Rosie a triumphant look. 'He's come home, Rosie,' she hollered. 'He's back in England.'

Rosie felt as though her heart was about to explode. 'But where?' she cried, dashing tears away with the back of her hand.

Grace began to giggle. 'He's at Haddon Hall. He transferred there on the third of October. It's a house just outside Knaresborough, one of those the War Office commissioned as a convalescent home for the walking wounded. He's right on your doorstep,' she cried, her cheeks flushed with success at having so clearly pleased her friend, for by now Rosie was up on her feet and hugging Grace and gabbling, 'Thank you, thank you, Grace. What would I have done without you?'

'Think nothing of it; it's my job, and it plainly means a lot to you,' said Grace, releasing herself from Rosie's arms. She looked sympathetically into Rosie's glowing face. 'So you won't be marrying Peter?'

Rosie shook her head. 'I'll explain everything to Peter and all of you after I've found Milo,' she said, and then in a voice wobbly with emotion she added, 'I'm sorry, Grace, so dreadfully sorry. I never meant to hurt Peter.'

Grace gave a sad, little smile. 'He'll most likely be devastated but...' her smile widened '...knowing Peter he'll soon get over it.' She thought of Peter's last leave and the girl who was his commanding officer's daughter. Peter hadn't been true to

Rosie and she could hardly blame Rosie if her affections now lay elsewhere. She was in love herself, and she knew what it felt like. She gave a little shrug. 'Still, I would have liked you for a sister-in-law.'

Rosie heard the disappointment in Grace's voice. 'We can still be friends, can't we?' she said, guilt niggling again, but inside her chest her heart was thudding fit to burst. Milo was alive and well and close by in Knaresborough. She could barely contain her excitement. She wanted to grow wings and go as the crow flies, straight into Milo's arms.

However, she felt honour-bound to make true part of the lie she had told Helen, and after treating Grace to a hasty lunch, Rosie bade her a grateful farewell and rushed back to the station to catch the next train to Knaresborough. *I'm coming, Milo,* her heart sang as the train rattled out of the station.

THIRTY-TWO

Milo was in his dormitory, lying on his bed bored and restless. He was to be released in two days' time, and as far as he was concerned they couldn't pass quick enough. He'd tried reading Jack London's *White Fang* – Celia had recommended it – but for all it was a stirring tale, he couldn't concentrate. He wanted to get back to Wakefield and find Rosie.

The door opened. 'Someone to see you, Simmonite,' said the chap who worked in reception at the front door of Haddon House. He walked away whistling and thinking he wouldn't have minded if the red-haired girl had come to see him; she was a cracker.

Milo got to his feet and straightened his clothes. He wondered who his visitor was. It couldn't be the doctor; he'd seen him yesterday. It must be someone from his regiment, he thought, as he made his way to the front of the house.

* * *

Rosie waited nervously in the foyer, glancing round at the fine architecture and the paintings on the walls. It was certainly a splendid place, and although there was a faint odour of antiseptic mingled with manly sweat, Milo must be comfortable here. She flicked at her hair and straightened her little cloche hat, all the while wondering if Milo was well enough for her to see him. Had he been injured again, or gassed when they returned him to the battlefield? She shuddered at the thought.

She thought of all the bloodstained, broken young men she had nursed in the Clayton and later at Beaulencourt and Étaples; the limbless, the blind and those driven crazy by phosgene gas or the constant bombardment of shells, bombs and bullets. She thought of the terrible wound in Milo's back, sharply reminding herself that it had almost healed when last she saw him. Then there were the letters, or the absence of letters, and the nights she had spent comforting dying men. She had seen it all; and before the war, and during the war, it had always been about Milo.

Now she was here, and no matter what had happened to him she was here for him. She had found him.

She moved restlessly from foot to foot, too hot in her heavy camel coat.

Then, through the glass doors, down the long corridor she saw him loping towards her with his long, easy stride. He walked tall and straight. His black hair, grown long again, falling over his forehead and curling about his ears. For all the heat in the overly warm foyer, a trickle of cold sweat ran down Rosie's back.

* * *

Milo saw Rosie. He halted suddenly, flicked back his forelock and stood with his arms hanging by his sides, his dark eyes staring. A familiar sweetness clogged his throat. *Oh, my God, look at her, look at her,* his mind cried. *She's found me.*

Then he was running.

Rosie's heart pounded in her chest as she yanked at the glass doors, running full pelt into Milo's open arms. He folded them round her, and she buried her face into the curve of his neck, breathing in the smell that was his alone. She felt the old familiar strength in his arms as they embraced, and as she lifted her face to be kissed all the sweetness in the world flooded through her body.

Slowly, they released each other and gazed in wonderment at one another. Dark eyes meeting pure grey-green eyes that sparkled with love and yearning.

* * *

They walked in the garden clinging to each other, almost afraid to let go, and as they sauntered they shared all that had happened since Beaulencourt.

'I nearly went crazy when I came back from Calais and found you had gone,' Rosie said, her voice wobbling at the memory.

'When you didn't answer my letters I thought you'd stopped loving me, that you'd felt only pity for me because I was wounded.'

'How could you think such a thing? I've always loved you, and I always will now that I know what love means,' she cried, her breath billowing in the cold air.

'I suppose it's because I never really believed you could

love me as much as I love you.' Milo sounded almost afraid. Nervously, he lit a cigarette.

Rosie drew a sharp breath and stopped walking. She leaned towards him earnestly. 'Now you're just being silly. I know it took me some time to realize what love really meant, but once I'd fathomed it out I knew it was you I loved. A proper, grown-up love that a woman feels for the man she wants to spend the rest of her life with.'

Satisfied that she had convinced him, Rosie went and sat on a nearby bench. She leaned back against it, her eyes challenging Milo to doubt her as he came and sat beside her.

Milo ground his cigarette butt under his heel and then took both her hands in his. 'And that's what we have. A proper, grown-up love that a man feels for the most wonderful woman in the world. I know it too, and now that we've found each other we'll never let go. Then, whatever else, we'll be safe together.'

They turned to face each other and kissed, revelling in the touch and taste and the passion that for too long had lain dormant. When Milo told Rosie that he was due to leave Haddon Hall the next day, she could barely contain her joy.

They stayed seated on the bench under the bare branches of a chestnut tree, sometimes in silence or talking animatedly, simply content to be together. Rosie was glad to be wearing her camel coat, for the afternoon was chilly. Yet with Milo's arm around her she thought she never need feel cold again. After a while, the light began to fade, the afternoon drawing to a close and both of them aware that Rosie would soon have to return to Wakefield. Reluctant to be parted yet again, if only for a day, they walked back to the house.

'Before you go there's someone I'd like you to meet,' Milo said, leading her to the library. Rosie blinked her surprise, and then she thought it could be a fellow soldier who Milo had fought with; maybe it was Charlie.

They entered the large room lined with bookshelves. At a table close by the door, a red-haired woman was handing over a book to a lad with one arm. She glanced sideways as Milo and Rosie came into view. The book in her hand thudded onto the table. She stared. Using his good hand the lad picked it up, thanked Celia, and after nodding at Milo and Rosie, he left.

Celia continued to stare at Rosie. The colour had leached from her cheeks and her eyes, like tourmalines, gleamed grey-green. She appeared to be gazing into another time and another place.

'This is the girl I told you about,' said Milo, steering Rosie closer to the table.

Rosie allowed him to do so. She was too busy doing her own staring. *Is this what I'll look like in twenty years' time?* she was asking herself.

Celia dropped her gaze and gave a quick shake of her head before looking up at Rosie and Milo. 'Ah, yes, I remember. This must be Rosie Nobody.' She gave a wan smile.

Rosie gave Milo an enquiring look. He grinned. 'I told Mrs Asquith all about you, and how we kept being torn apart,' he said sheepishly, then went on to say, 'Mrs Asquith's been helping me to choose good books. I've been doing a lot of reading lately.'

Rosie looked from Milo to Celia. She was still struggling to come to terms with how like herself this woman was. When she looked into Celia's eyes she saw her own. Even her mouth and nose were the same shape as Rosie knew her own to be. *They say everybody has a double,* she thought, *and this Mrs Asquith must be mine.* She struggled to find something to say.

'That's very kind of you, Mrs Asquith. I'd almost lost the battle trying to get Milo to read.'

Celia gave a half smile. 'It was my pleasure. He's an interesting young man.' The smile faded, her brow creasing and her mouth drooping at the corners. She swallowed audibly, her lips pressed together as she fought to find her words.

'He told me the story of how you came to be connected… how… how you were left behind… for his grandfather to raise… and how you had no idea who… the woman… the woman who gave birth to you was.' By now, Celia was labouring over every word and tears brimmed her lashes.

Rosie's insides trembled. She felt utterly confused and embarrassed by Celia's distress. She looked at Milo, seeking his help as to what they should do. He looked back at her, equally at a loss.

A soldier entered the library, books in his hands. Celia stood quickly, her hand palm outwards to stop him in his tracks. 'Not now,' she said abruptly, stepping from behind the table and ushering him back out of the room. She locked the door behind him and then sought refuge behind the table again, but she did not sit down. Rosie turned wary eyes in Milo's direction. *What's going on?* they asked. Milo raised his shoulders a fraction and shook his head.

Celia drew a deep breath as if to pad her insides for what might come next. Her facial muscles seemed strung too tight as her eyes flicked from Milo to Rosie, and when she spoke her voice was almost a whisper. 'Do either of you recall a dark blue cloak with a velvet lining and an embroidered collar?' The words floated on the air.

Rosie gasped. Through huge eyes she looked from Celia to Milo, only to see that he was equally amazed. 'I… I have a blue cloak like that,' Rosie said, her voice high and breathless and her face masked with curiosity.

She stared hard at Celia, willing her to explain.

Celia seemed to shrivel. Her head dropped to her chest and she crossed her arms, her hands gripping her shoulders as if to give protection from some dreaded force. 'The blue cloak was mine,' she said. 'I am the woman who abandoned you, Rosie.'

No one spoke. The silence deepened around them. Rosie felt confusion and anger lurching inside her. 'You? You're my mother?' she gasped.

The strength went out of her legs and she reached for Milo's arm, afraid she might fall to the floor. He grasped hold of her and she could feel his body trembling along with her own.

'That's why I thought I knew you,' Milo cried. 'At first I thought it was because you look like Rosie, but something in the back of my mind told me I'd met you before.' He paused thoughtfully, rubbing his chin with his hand. 'That's why you were so distressed when I told you my father had been killed. I should have guessed you knew more than you were letting on.'

Celia gazed at him, her eyes begging forgiveness. 'I am so sorry, Milo. I never knew that they had stooped to such wickedness. I was fearful for my own life, but I never knew they had taken your father's.'

Rosie's mind was whirling. 'Who were *they*?' she cried.

Wearily, Celia wiped her hand across her forehead. 'It's late,' she said heavily. 'Come back tomorrow. Bring the cloak and I'll tell you everything.'

'Why not now?' Rosie's impatience flared.

'Tomorrow. Just bring the cloak. There is something I

must show you.' All the life had drained from Celia's face and Rosie reluctantly allowed Milo to take her arm and lead her to the door. He turned the key.

'Until tomorrow,' Rosie said, her world turned upside down and she not knowing whether to feel overjoyed at finding her mother or angered by the woman who had abandoned her.

* * *

'I should have known it,' said Milo, as soon as they were outside the library and walking to the foyer. 'All those questions she asked, like where on the road were we when you got left with us, and then the way she broke down when I told her Dadda had been killed.' He shook his head angrily. 'She wasn't just interested in my story – she was fishing. I could kick myself for being so stupid.'

'You're not stupid, Milo. Celia Asquith is one devious woman, and I'm not sure I like her one bit,' Rosie said hotly.

'But she's your mother! You've found her at last.'

'I wasn't looking for her,' Rosie replied disconsolately, and then viciously adding, 'and she certainly never came looking for me.' She was hurrying along the corridor now, Milo keeping pace with her as they walked out of the house and on to the driveway.

'Oh, Rosie, darling,' Milo said, as he folded his arms about her, desperate to make sense of what they had just learned and to ease Rosie's confusion. 'I know you must be shocked, but aren't you even a little glad to learn that you're no longer Rosie Nobody?'

Rosie's eyes were as dark as pools of deep water when she raised her gaze to meet Milo's. 'I've been without a mother for so long it doesn't seem to matter anymore. I don't know *her* and *she* doesn't know me, and I'm not sure I want to know her after all this time. As long as I have you, I don't need anybody else.'

'Oh, Rosie,' Milo groaned, holding her all the tighter and tenderly kissing her. When he released her he asked, 'What will you do now?'

'I'll come back tomorrow with the cloak, just as she asked – but only out of curiosity,' she sneered. She tossed her hair and shrugged. 'I'd have been coming back anyway to bring you home.'

THIRTY-THREE

The next morning Rosie got up early, and in a flurry of excited apprehension she dressed carefully. This time she chose a soft, blue woollen dress to wear under her best navy blue coat. A bright red hat and scarf completed her outfit, a cheery note for today was special: Milo was coming home.

She deliberately did not dwell on the thought of meeting Celia again. The woman might be her mother but she meant little or nothing to her, she firmly told herself as she descended the stairs. Mothers who abandoned their children so easily didn't deserve thinking about.

But, she would fetch the blue cloak from Sophie's mother's house, and she would listen to Celia make her excuses and then leave, putting her back into the past where she had always belonged. She had managed without her thus far, and she would continue to do so; after all, she had Milo. What more could she want?

She had telephoned Mrs Forsythe late the previous evening on her return from Haddon Hall, all the while thanking her lucky stars that she had kept in touch with Sophie. Mrs Forsythe had told her that Sophie was at home, and preparing for her forthcoming marriage to her fiancé, Toby.

Rosie had smiled down the telephone, thrilled to learn that Sophie's officer, the man she'd met whilst working as a VAD at the Clayton Hospital, had turned out to be the one; their love for one another had also held fast through the writing of letters, she mused, just as hers and Milo's had done.

* * *

Sophie greeted Rosie warmly, and although Rosie was eager to be on her way to Haddon Hall, over a cup of tea she politely, and equally warmly, listened to Sophie rattling on about her wedding plans. She hoped to soon be making her own. Giving Sophie and Mrs Forsythe her grateful thanks, and carrying the blue woollen cloak wrapped in a brown paper parcel, Rosie hurried back to Wakefield for the next stage of her journey.

She hadn't felt so exhilarated for some time, but the thought of meeting her mother again did not lie easily with her. She didn't know what to make of Celia. Maybe, after she had heard what she had to say, she would find it in her heart to look more kindly on the woman, but right now as the train trundled towards Knaresborough, Rosie felt no affection for her. In fact, she thought Celia was cruel and heartless to have abandoned her. However, she consoled herself, she would never have met Milo if things had been different.

When she arrived at Haddon Hall, it was to find Milo waiting for her in the foyer, a bag holding his few possessions at his feet. He took her in his arms and held her close, fully aware that meeting Celia again was putting a great strain on her. Rosie clung to him as though he were the only solid thing in her life at that moment. She felt his heart beating against her own and knew that, come what may, she was capable of hearing what Celia had to say and then getting on with the rest of her life.

The man in reception led them to a room on the upper floor. 'Mrs Asquith will see you in here,' he said, opening the door into a large, airy drawing room. Celia was waiting for them, looking very calm and composed as she bid Rosie and Milo to sit on a sofa on the opposite side of the fireplace to the chair she was seated in. Rosie breathed a sigh of relief as she sat down. She didn't want to have to deal with any overt demonstrations of affection, or tears. She placed the parcel with the blue cloak inside at her feet.

Celia noted this. 'You brought it then. I was afraid you might change your mind,' she said.

'I brought it because I want to hear the story behind it,' Rosie replied coolly. 'It's been one of my most precious possessions for my entire life although I really don't know why. Eli wrapped me in it when I was very young and when he gave me away to the Threppletons I couldn't sleep unless it was tucked under my chin. Then sometimes I'd dream of Milo and Eli, and the vardo and the horses. I never dreamt of you – but then...' Rosie looked directly into Celia's eyes and gave a little shrug '...I didn't know you, did I?'

Celia flushed. 'I'm so sorry, Rosie,' she murmured.

'So you should be,' Rosie retorted. 'Eli gave me away because I was a constant reminder of how his son met his death. I didn't understand that then but I do now, so I no longer blame Eli.' She let the words hang in the air, wanting them to find their mark. 'I also can't really blame Celeste Threppleton. She was insane. But I can tell you this,' Rosie continued, warming to her theme, 'until Godfrey took me under his wing I had a pretty miserable childhood. Now, who do you suppose was to blame for that?'

Milo reached for Rosie's hand, encasing it lovingly in both of his own. In a low voice he said, 'Just hear Mrs Asquith out and then we'll go.'

'Oh, I'll hear her out all right,' Rosie cried, pulling her hand free. 'I have a right to know, and when I've listened to her excuses I'll forget all about them, just like she forgot all about me.'

Celia leapt from her chair, and taking a few short steps she went down on her knees in front of Rosie. 'Please, Rosie, please, let me explain how it was,' she begged, her voice cracking. She reached for the parcel, tearing at the paper until the cloak spilled out into her hands. Feverishly, she ripped at the stitching under the collar. It split apart, the gold locket sliding from its hiding place into her hands. With trembling fingers she flicked it open.

'This is your father,' she said brokenly, 'the man I loved with all my heart, just as you do Milo. Like you, we were torn apart, not by war but by the wickedness of the man I'd married.'

Rosie took the locket, and holding it in the palm of her hand she gazed at a handsome young man with kind eyes. 'Who is he? Where is he now?'

'I don't know,' Celia said, the despair in her voice and the pain and longing in her eyes letting Rosie know that she must have loved him deeply.

'Tell me about him,' Rosie said gently.

Celia sat back on her heels and sighed, a sigh so deep that Rosie imagined it came from the very depths of her soul. Then, her eyes and voice adopting a dreamlike quality she said, 'Callum was so beautiful it made me think that that was what a guardian angel must look like. He was adventurous, interested in nature and culture. He liked to travel, to discover new places, and he laughed a lot, taking pleasure in the world around him. Best of all, he was kind, gentle and loving – everything that my husband was not.' Spent, she closed her eyes, her chin drooping to her chest.

'You must have loved him very much,' Rosie said softly, 'but if your husband was so unkind, why did you marry him?'

In the next half hour, Rosie and Milo learned that Celia's mother had died when Celia was seven and her father, an inveterate gambler, was all she had. At just seventeen she had married Joseph Asquith, a middle-aged wealthy banker, to save her father's business and his reputation. Only after they were married did she discover that Joseph was a violent and unfaithful husband and she, Celia, no more than a trophy wife. The marriage was never consummated.

Shortly after her father died, Celia had fallen deeply in love with Callum, an itinerant Irishman who worked in the gardens at the Hall. They had planned to run away together. Sadly, Joseph learned of their love affair and ordered his henchmen to deal with the gardener. Celia never saw him again. She had hidden her pregnancy from Joseph but when it became impossible to conceal it any longer he threatened to kill her. Fearing for her life, she ran away.

'Some of the rest you already know,' Celia said heartbrokenly. 'Milo's father saved me that night and the next day you were born. I was caught and brought back to Haddon Hall where I lived as a prisoner for the next two years.' She paused, a strange noise gurgling deep in her throat. It sounded like a grim chuckle. 'Two years to the day you were born, Joseph died of heart attack in the arms of one of his mistresses, and I have lived here, alone, until war broke out.' She gazed imploringly into Rosie's eyes. 'I had no hope of finding you,' she said, these last few words spoken very gently and full of regret. 'I did search for you, Rosie. I roamed the fairs and the markets but the gypsies I spoke to couldn't, or wouldn't, tell me anything. For years I lived with the hope of finding you.'

Rosie, stunned into silence, felt a strange movement inside her chest as though her heart was softening. She gazed into Celia's eyes and saw the yearning and suffering she had endured. *You've loved and lost,* she thought, *but I haven't. I've found Milo, and now I'll find it in my heart to accept that you had no control over what happened after you gave birth to me.*

Rosie stood, and taking Celia's hands in her own she gently raised her to her feet. 'Mother,' she said softly, 'I'm glad we've found each other.' The pure joy on Celia's face made Rosie's heart lurch as they fell into each other's arms.

Milo, who all this time had been sitting watching and listening, got to his feet and enveloped the two women in a huge embrace. Tears turned to smiles, and as they broke apart Rosie asked, 'What was Callum's last name?'

Celia looked startled. 'O'Leary,' she said.

Rosie giggled joyfully. 'From never having had a surname, I've now got three. Threppleton, Asquith, O'Leary,' she said, ticking them off on her fingers. 'I'm no longer Rosie Nobody.'

Milo grinned. 'And once we are married you'll be Simmonite, but in my heart you'll always be my little red-haired Rosie Nobody.'

ACKNOWLEDGMENTS

First and foremost I thank my agent, Judith Murdoch. Her sound advice and encouragement keeps me going. I am also extremely grateful to the team at HoZ/Aria for their friendly guidance, particularly the fantastic Hannah Todd, Martina Arzu, Hannah Newton and Lizz Burrell; as usual, their sharp eyes and broad vocabularies improve any story.

As always, my sincere thanks to my son, Charles, and his wife, Martina, and my nephew Paul Downey and his wife Anne Marie, whose daily love and support make it all worthwhile. They patiently listen to me as I tell the tale. Many thanks to my nephew Andrew Downey and his wife Sharon for jogging my geographical memory of West Yorkshire, and to the Tolson Museum, Dalton, Huddersfield for its wealth of WW1 information. Special thanks to Helen Oldroyd for her loyal friendship and the interest she takes in my writing, and a huge thanks to all who buy, read and review my books. Their support is invaluable. Thank you Thomas Duffy for locally promoting my books in your shops. Finally, thanks to my grandson Harry Walsh and the Downey boys, Jack, Matthew, Lewis and Alex for making me a proud and happy grandmother.

ABOUT THE AUTHOR

Chrissie Walsh, born and raised in West Yorkshire, was trained to be a singer and cellist before becoming a teacher. When she married her trawler skipper husband, they moved to a little fishing village in Northern Ireland. Chrissie is passionate about history and that shines through in her writing.